KINDRED

www.charlottebedgoodauthor.com

Kindred: Fate is Ever Weaving

Print Edition ISBN: 978-1-3999-4706-0
E-book Edition ISBN: 978-1-4478-6862-0

First Edition: March 2023

This is a work of fiction. All of the characters, organisations, and events portrayed in this novel are either products of the author's imagination or are used fictitiously.

To My Thirteen Year Old Self

You Did It

Charlotte Bedgood

REALMS

Earth
The Protected Realm

Zika
The Zikan's Home Realm

The Cre-este
Realm of Ivan The Great

Ryazark
The Realm of The Gods

Mysc
Nightmare Realm

Hamiean
Realm of Knowledge

Porton
Zika's Sister Realm

PROLOGUE

Fate. A divine thing that to most beings can only be explained when miracles and mysteries occur but, for some, fate is more than that. It is an intricately crafted web of events that binds the very fabric of the universe together and affects every living thing across it. Fate is untouchable, it is profoundly ingrained into the souls of our beings and the lives that we live, developed by something very much unknown but so much greater than us. It is what keeps our souls experiencing different lifetimes repeatedly, interacting with other beings in a constant and never-ending cycle.

It explains why every so often when the universe seeks to shift and change some, to expand or contract, a fracture in the seams of its very structure begins to arise and two conjoined ethereal souls split from each other, floating away through time and space, longing to merge back together as one. These two souls call for each other, lost in the depths of the universe, and long to be together - whole once again. As the universe erupts and the two beings split from one another, catastrophic events begin to take place, rippling as the serenity is shaken and all is thrown out of balance causing mayhem and chaos.

This chaos is felt as the web of fate designs a new journey, the journey of two lost souls who must find each other again to end the hostility that the universe feels. Like a mother seeking her children, the universe screams to have the souls back in its arms once again in order to restore its peaceful state. These two souls, as one, are the embodiment of true and undeniable love; love that is represented within the mind mentally and the body physically but apart they are destructive and dangerous.

Continuing their journey to find one another, they scour for a web of destiny to entangle themselves into in hope, and almost knowing that the fates will bring them together someday somewhere in the universe. Finding a home in a new life, as a living being, the two of them begin a new adventure, unaware of who they were and who they are fated to become. One empty beating heart, longing for the other.

These are known as The Kindred Spirits.

ONE

Thunder rocketed and flaxen streaks of lightning rumbled across dark ashen skies, syncing with screams of human voices crying for help; eaten by waves of distressing rumbles as they blurred into one. Below, desolate streets were decorated with rotten leaves pushed by flurried winds, whilst wilted bodies were laid heavily upon them. The stench of death lingered in the air.

My body stumbled, bringing me towards my knees, but the hard concrete didn't rocket against the skin of them. Instead, two hands held me, and I shakily looked up at a cloaked man, whose face couldn't be seen in the blur. He shouted something but the words never made it to my ear as the sounds around crescendoed and died within an instant. A clatter above and my head jolted passed him, as I looked up towards the skies once more, seeing as they began to fracture at its core. The fissure grew larger and, inside, I saw nothing except pure, mind-consuming darkness.

Chills caused hairs on my body to rise, and a cold shiver tingled down the back of my spine until it wrapped around into the pit of my stomach. My anxiety and fear bubbled like never before as the sky rumbled once more.

The reptilian arm of a winged black demon appeared, before the creature crawled its way out of the sky, bigger than anything to have ever existed before, looking around for its prey. Its heavy yellow eyes stopped, landing in my direction, before it stretched its three long necks as it dropped out, landing perfectly with a waft of its wings in the air.

It was ready to eat, and I was the feast.

With a loud whoosh, my perception of the creature pulled back and I was suddenly miles away, watching it at a distance as it began to soar in my direction. I tumbled backward, breath catching in my mouth, panting in fear of it. Pushing back on my hands, I had just enough strength to lift myself up but, as I turned to run, I was halted.

There, in front of me, I stared at a version of a frail woman so familiar to me. Myself. Except my naturally blue eyes were mystified in darkness and black blood was pouring down cheeks that were unnaturally pale, a contrast to my normal golden skin. As though staring in a mirror, I lifted my hands to my own cheeks to feel for the blood, but I quickly understood that this figure wasn't a reflection of myself.

It was another impression.

Arraetta. The voice echoed from her, without once opening her mouth.

Stepping back, I planted against a brick wall, that had somehow appeared behind, and shook as she moved forward. I was trapped. I watched as the blood poured onto the floor, slithered across it, and crawled up my static legs like a tsunami. It stuck to my skin as it began to consume me, but no matter how much I attempted to flee, to break free, I couldn't move.

The sludge burnt my flesh as it reached my throat, tight enough for me to be unable to catch my breath.

"H-elp… me-e!" I managed to scream, shutting my eyes tight, but no sensation ever came. Instead, a familiar voice pulled me from the

darkness.

"Arri, Arri, wake up!"

My eyes bolted open, and I jolted as I looked in the face of my best friend, Genie. My heart was pounding heavily in my chest, it hurt so much that I thought I might be going into cardiac arrest. A wet, cold, unwanted cloth swept my forehead and I winced, closing my eyes, "you're okay… you're okay."

But no matter how much Genie tried to calm the situation, she knew that it wasn't going to be alright - that this was just the beginning.

Ever since I could remember, strange things have happened to me. Unusual, otherworldly things.

For most of my life, I have slept without dreaming, without my imagination wildly creating stories. I don't think it was for any reason other than, I would guess, my body would never truly enter a state of REM, I would just linger on the edge. But, every four years, my dreams would trickle in. At first, little flashes that would jolt me from my slumber, over a period of weeks, getting deeper and deeper until I was trapped in hallucinatory nightmares.

These nightmares would worsen over more weeks until the finale would occur. The blackout. There would come a point where I would be so delirious, from the nightmares, that my body would shut down and my mind would suck me into another world, which I could only describe as purgatory. It felt like forever whilst I was trapped, as weeks passed by as my body lay comatose in the real world.

Yet, it was neither the nightmares or my comatose state that were wild and otherworldly, nor was it the blackout. It was what occurred just beforehand.

"What time is it?" I murmured, wincing at the pain in my skull as I tried to find my watch.

"About five," she replied, bringing the cloth down, "don't think I'll be letting you go out today."

"And, who do you think is going to deliver Jafar's finest pizzas?" I joked, cringing again as my head throbbed gently.

"Arri, what if-"

"It's too early," I told her, beginning to make my way out of the sweat-soaked bed and balanced myself on my feet, "this happens, we know it does."

"Please, I don't want you to be out," she begged, fingering the damp sheet with a look of disgust on her face, "you can do without that job."

"You know that isn't true," I told her, stumbling across the stained carpet on my way to the door, "I have rent to pay."

"Which my parents can support you with!" Genie half-bellowed, and I winced again, as the sound rattled around my head, before she whispered, "sorry."

I remember my first occurrence was when I was eight years old. At the time, I had come to reside with foster parents in a town, just outside of London, and I was a pleasant, unassuming little girl, with not much of an interest in anything, except for drawing and the stars. John and Sue took me in when I was seven and had treated me just like their own child, but they were only there until someone would come forward to take me for good.

In the summer, things were normal. I excelled in school, had a few friends, and enjoyed ice cream in the park. But, at night, my nightmares were becoming more frequent, and I would scream in fear of them. I don't remember the vividness of them, at that time, nor did they come to imprint themselves in my memory, but I remember the feeling of terror. John and Sue did everything they could to help me, they even sent me to see a councillor, but it was no help.

That's when the day came. Standing in my bedroom, my body began to uncontrollably shake, whilst the feelings in my fibres began to disappear one by one, like excessive pins and needles. The room suddenly lit up in a flaxen colour and I looked down at my fingertips, seeing that my veins had become more prominent - glowing. At that time, I was so fearful of it that I'd screamed, and that seemed to push something else - a sharp pain in my head. I don't remember anything else.

Sue had found me, and I had been taken straight to the hospital, stuck in a coma for four weeks. I never saw John and Sue again. I wasn't sure what had happened, but I moved into a foster home where I resided for a number more years; no one ever speaking to me about the event.

The one thing that the incident had caused me to do was become silent. I stopped talking to everybody, and I went through a period where I had to be examined. Everything was ruled out and, eventually, it was diagnosed that I had post-traumatic stress disorder, leading to speech loss, and that I'd have to go to speech therapy. Even that wasn't beneficial because I wouldn't say a word.

Until the day I met Genie. The foster home had taken the children to a large playground when I was eleven. It was one of those fancy parks on the grounds of a large manor with lots of children of all ages laughing and playing. As per usual, I sat at the table being ignored by the adults and other children, left to my own devices to draw away.

What are you drawing?

My head tilted up and eyes connected immediately with ten-year-old Genie, who was leaning over the other side of the green metal picnic bench, looking down at my drawing.

That looks like somewhere in a fairy tale.

Her voice then was sweet and soft, it still was, and I liked the fact that she was so interested in what I'd created.

I see it sometimes. I replied.

My voice was softer than hers, almost a whisper and low enough that no one else could hear. Genie laughed and sat down properly. She proceeded to tell me about a fairy tale that she had read, and it turned out that she was just telling me the story of Rapunzel. But her way of telling it had intrigued me so much that we went to play together and that's when the adults noticed how different I was.

Six months later, her parents fostered me, and the rest was history.

The rest not including the blackout that then occurred when I was twelve, once again when I was sixteen, twenty and, in my twenty-fourth year, I awaited the inevitable. Prepared as much as I could.

Over the years since then, I could understand more about why I didn't speak to anyone for a long time. I could see that, absolutely, any child facing haunting nightmares would go into shock. It was just unexplainable; it was all unexplainable.

Yet, when I had the blackout when I was twelve, Genie was mesmerised by it. I remember the same feelings occurred as I stood in the lounge of our house, my body began to glow and my veins stuttered to life, but numbness settled and, once again, I succumbed to darkness.

Unlike John and Sue, who had witnessed a thing they could not mentally comprehend, Genie leant down and held me closely, soothing me into a peaceful slumber – a place that felt like home. She told me that I was the most enchanting thing she had ever seen, she had seen what these blackouts made me become. Ethereal.

"Please take your phone with you today." I looked at Genie as she waved it at me and placed it down on the side, "I've charged it."

"I'll be fine without it."

Phones. Technology. I disliked it for the most part. It made me feel overwhelmed, there was so much energy emanating from the tiny thing that was held in everyone's hands, and the waves of radiation from it made me feel like I had a constant dull headache. I couldn't explain why I reacted the way I did, but it caused me to be one of the very few people who rarely used a phone. I even used a map for work.

"It's only for a few weeks," Genie pointed out. "I love you."

"Love you too," I smiled gently.

Being a few inches taller than me, she kissed my forehead and waltzed away, ready for her day ahead. Genie was a dancer; she was training at the top school in London and had her entire life cut out for her, except Genie's dream was different to what most would've expected. I knew that her mum wished to see her in the west end, in sold-out ballet shows, but Genie just wanted to fall in love with a good man, who could give her everything she ever wanted, have children, and teach babies how to dance.

I truly admired Genie's capability to strive for whatever she wanted and, when she set her mind to something, she never failed at getting it; not her school or whichever man she desired at the time. But there was one thing that she would never triumph with and that was me. I was the most stubborn person she had ever had to contend with, although this was much more to my own detriment than hers. Yet, I'd softened quite a lot over the years under her influence and allowed some of her ways to become my own.

Genie enjoyed the finer things in life and allowed her parents to pay for everything she desired, but she was never stuck up about it and her calming and caring temperament was praised by everyone who knew her. I did enjoy those things too, but I would never admit it and I only allowed myself to live for what I felt I was worth.

Genie constantly joked about me falling in love with someone, but I felt like I wouldn't deserve that kind of love. It wasn't because I wasn't a physically attractive person but more so because of the four-yearly unexplainable phenomena. Genie was the only person that understood who I was; there was nobody else who knew what I went through - even we had managed to keep it secret from her parents, who witnessed some sort of aftermath of it; usually me being rushed to hospital, but they'd never truly seen me like she had. I felt that there was no one that I could confide in about it because I would've imagined telling people that, when I blacked out, I caused unearthly things to occur and that would cause them to cast me aside, locking me up in an institute for mentally unwell beings.

Just before lunchtime, still ridden with a headache, I grabbed my phone, threw it into my pocket and hauled my bike out of the front door, groaning when I saw the bin bag perched outside of it. The one thing I didn't enjoy about living with Genie was how she hated taking the bins out, as she feared that she might be bitten by a gigantic rat. I suppose it wasn't a surprise seeing where we lived: a large council estate.

We'd lived here since we were eighteen-year-old university students, on the tenth floor of the twenty-storey block of flats that peered out across the distant skyline of central London. At first, Genie was very against any idea of moving into such a rundown place, after being brought up in such a posh end of the city, but I managed to convince her that it would be good for the soul, and the pocket, and it massively helped for my twentieth-year blackout as a power outage across this estate was normal.

I trudged down the concrete stairs, bike flung over one shoulder, whilst the bin bag, in my other hand, burnt at my fingertips, fighting to break free. I had to push past the usual chavs dominating the stairway, neither of them moving out the way or acknowledging my presence, before I placed the bike down at the bottom, tutting at the two-year-old sign on the lift that said, 'out of order'. It wasn't going to ever get fixed after hooligans decided to start a fire in it one night and the other lift was at the other end of the building and half-broken. I pushed my bike to the mould-slathered bins, hauled the bag in and then very quickly peddled away.

I longed to be away from this city, away from the overpowering electrical currents, dreaming of pastures new. Somewhere I could hide away in a cabin, without all the hustle and bustle of everyday life, but I knew that was something too far down the road; a dream that wasn't going to come true anytime soon.

Flicking past buses and cars, jumping into pedestrian-filled cycle lanes, I rode my bike as though nothing could stop me, until I reached the dire place known as Jafar's Pizza Palace. A place that was far from a palace and more like what it was: a poxy old kebab shop that had more rats than the Pied Piper could handle. But it was work and it paid my bills, especially as they constantly churned through staff, making shifts easier to come by.

The main reason for the high turnover was because my boss, Sam, was an arsehole and only cared about his greasy pizzas and dog meat kebabs. I often wondered how a place, with a two-star score, could have so many people ordering from them, but I knew his cheap prices could not be beaten in these parts. Really, my dislike for Sam came from the way he spoke to me, as though I was a piece of filth under his shoe, but still, without fail, he would hand me, with disdain, an envelope full of cash every shift and that's what kept me coming back.

Little delivery cap on, I picked up my first bag of hot pizzas, chained them to the back of my bike and cycled off.

Flying through the streets of London, I delivered pizza after kebab after box of chips and so on, sometimes dropping off one item, sometimes many, but I was never late, and I never went anywhere except the customer's address. I was quick and that was what made me good at my job, that's why Sam could hardly complain about my customer service, he would only complain that I was too sweaty and that his customers would not like that. Truly, no one cared with the dire heat the summer had to bring, and it could be forgiven. I hardly stopped for breaks, much to my own detriment, but, on occasion, a kinder customer would offer me a glass of water and we'd make small talk about how hot it was.

The world was getting hotter but still, it was better than having to cycle in the cold pissing down rain or through windy snow blizzards that came in the late winter. Even if scientists complained about global warming, my only care was surviving day after day so that one day I could make that cabin dream a reality.

"Done, Sam," I told him as I placed the pizza bag on the counter with a huff, my stomach growling from the lack of food and excessive exercise. He placed a pizza and a box of chips down on top of the bag.

"One last order," he told me, "Sherice hasn't shown."

I groaned, "come on, I've been on for eight hours."

"You want the money," Sam raised his eyebrows, stating the fact clearly before he placed a miniature pizza box next to the chips and the usual white envelope, "the small pizza is yours, pocket the envelope, deliver my pizza and go home. It's on your way."

"You don't know where I live," I said, amused. This little win of being given a pizza meant that Sam must like me at least a little bit.

"See you tomorrow," he grunted, before beginning to shout commands at the chefs in the kitchen. I placed the three boxes into the bag, secured the cash into the inside pocket of my jacket, and left.

Sam was wrong, the delivery was ten minutes in the other direction and in my least favourite place of our delivery radius. I only hoped that he had paid me enough to cover the extra time I was doing for him.

Down a dreary and littered street, I pulled up outside one of the overgrown lawned houses and jumped off my bike, bringing the bag off it and walked to the front door. I wasn't scared of the place, in fact, the only thing that I truly feared was the nightmares I had and even they, sometimes, provided a strange comfort, when others could not. I knocked on the door, hearing bass music pulsating from inside. I sighed. It felt like the delivery was going to take much longer than I'd hoped.

I knocked louder, tapping my foot in aggravation, before I saw the figure of a large, burly shirtless man, through the stained-glass window.

He swung the door open, almost off its hinges, and looked down at my tiny form with a glare in his eyes, then turned his gaze to the bag and then back at me, "you're late."

"Late?" I squeaked and then spoke up, "I only left the pizza shop ten minutes ago."

"I ordered two hours ago!" he barked, trying to act tough, though I had been through this so many times that it was almost second nature for me to just smile and wave. I removed the pizza and chip box from the bag, balancing my own little pizza on top as I tried to organise myself, "what's that?"

I went to grab my food, but he picked it up first and opened it, rolling his eyes at me. He tutted, "I didn't order this, and I know that you've only included it as a sorry for being so late."

To my utter astonishment, he threw my mini pizza at my face, and I winced from the heat of it as it seeped down the front of my clothes, covering me in grease and tomato sauce. In shock, I watched as he grabbed the bigger pizza box and chips and went back inside, slamming the door behind him. I'd had abuse hurled at me by customers in the past, but I'd never been treated so lowly. I had to swallow my tears and I shook from the shock of it. I looked down at the pizza, that was splattered across the floor, feeling my stomach churn from hunger, once again.

"Fuck this," I murmured, coughed to clear the tears and then stormed to my bike. As I cycled home, I let the tears fall. I wanted to get home, take a shower, and climb into bed but I also wanted to go and shout at Sam and ask why he would send me to a place that was in the other direction. However, I wasn't weak, and I wasn't going to act like a child in front of him. I was just his worker.

I cycled up the streets, almost causing several accidents as I dove around speeding cars and cut through lanes. And then, I rounded a corner and skidded. Not able to keep control of the bike, I ended up flinging it over and caught my body underneath it. I gasped in pain as little grazes spiderwebbed, over the palms of my hands, and I could feel more through my jeans. I wanted someone to shout, 'are you alright?' but I was alone on the street. I murmured in pain as I hobbled up, picking up my still-intact bike, blinking away newly falling tears.

My eyes came to a stop on a wire of a telegraph pole above where I could see the static dancing colours of green, blue, red, and pink. I frowned, wiping my eyes to see clearer, leaning further forward until a car horn blasted behind. I squeaked, turning to watch as the sparks of currents sang from the headlights. My breathing quickened and I quickly shuffled to the side, turning as the main street, ahead of me, began to disco similar colours – the telling sign that an episode was coming.

It was too early but I felt the trigger sound in my head and the noises contrasted with one another; people, cars, buzzing, electricity.

With a burst of some sudden strength, I jumped onto my bike and allowed my subconscious to guide me home, hoping and praying that I wouldn't blackout until I got there. I heaved air into my lungs, allowing it to push me faster and to keep me conscious, and soon I found the bottom of the staircase. Not caring for how much worse it would make me carry the only tool I needed to stay employed, I hauled the bike up the ten flights of stairs, stumbling a little as sweat, tears and fragments of kaleidoscopic fractures clouded my vision. I unlocked my front door, threw the bike against the wall, and slammed the door before I dove into my bed and under my duvet.

Darkness.

TWO

The fissure above tore and darned mercilessly - glitching. The roars of creature's broke sound barriers, in the skies, whilst bodies of humans ran back and forth on glass-strewn pavements, pushing into one another without mercy. In the centre, I stood watching them all, unable to comprehend what was happening - helpless.

The whisper of a hand, on my shoulder, turned me in its direction but all I saw were the same figures, running. Another tickle of a touch behind and I turned once again but, this time, a figure slammed into my shoulder, followed by another, and another, until I was hit so hard that my body fell backward onto the concrete ground below. Blinking, no one surrounded me anymore and my eyes fixed on the ashen skies once more, watching them whirl tumultuously, cracking with flaxen lightning.

Then, the ground below began to move upwards but I couldn't see the force behind it, my back cemented to it. I hovered rapidly closer to the clouds, watching as they ripped apart, like a mouth waiting to eat, until the spine-tingling darkness above swallowed the Earth below. I flinched, shutting my eyes tightly to stop what was to come.

A clatter and my eyes sprung open, heart beating rapidly in my chest as my eyes tried to focus on the dimly lit ceiling above. I grunted and shakily put my hand to my head, rubbing the pulse that sat in the centre of my eyebrows.

"Arri!" Genie screamed from the other side of the door, "do you have to keep your damn bike here?"

Although I didn't want to be yelled at by Genie, I was thankful that the blackout hadn't come and, instead, I'd just had an episode. An episode was like the blackout, except it was quicker, usually less than a couple of hours, and always began with things going out of control - like the electricity dancing in front of my eyes. Then, my panic would irrationally build until I'd pass out. The main difference being that I didn't suddenly spark to life, like a neon light bulb.

Throwing myself out of bed, I balanced myself against the bedside table, pausing for a moment before I stumbled to the splintered door, opening it to look at Genie, as she attempted to balance my bike in its usual place.

She huffed, looking at me before her slightly angered temperament changed to an expression of worry, "oh, Arri."

"I'm fine," I murmured as she came over, wiping my face a little, with a disgusted look on her own, as she fingered the dry sauce, "it's just pizza."

"You look like hell," she told me, "you should've called."

"I haven't been back long," I replied, not sure whether that was the truth or not. I peeked my eyes up to look through the mini glass window at the top of the door, to see the night sky outside. I looked back at her, "where have you been?"

Genie blushed and walked through to the bathroom, before she pulled her pants down, without a care, and started to pee in front of me, "I have just met the most beautiful man."

"Just?" I laughed gently, walking into the bathroom myself and looking in the cracked mirror at my grubby face, seeing that my messy curly bun was all over the place whilst my nose had a stain underneath it from the sauce.

"This morning," she informed me, "on the tube. I was just sitting there, minding my own business, when I smelt the most incredible aroma, and I looked up into his dashing green eyes as he looked straight into mine and..." she sighed dreamily at the memory. "He is just so handsome, the most gorgeous man I have ever seen. We went up and down the Northern Line for like three hours."

"Who wants to go up and down the Northern Line for three hours?"

"His name is Freddie," she said, "he's a bodyguard, of sorts, and we both chatted, as though we'd known each other forever. We talked about so much and then, when we realised we'd been in our own world for so long, he invited me for coffee, which led to lunch and then, later, to dinner."

I was mesmerised at her tale as she shoved me over a little to wash her hands, soaping every inch of them. I stood back and leaned against the door, "Genie, you meet so many men."

"I'm not joking, Arri," she breathed in this strange, and overwhelming, way that I'd never seen her do before, then she turned around to me, "I love him."

I burst into laughter then, much to her disdain, "Genie, you cannot fall in love with a man you have known for five minutes."

"I have known him for twelve hours actually," she replied, disappointedly, "look, just because no one is knocking at your crusty old front door, doesn't mean you have to stop someone tapping on mine!"

"I had sex two weeks ago!" I announced.

"I meant *love*," she stated and stomped her foot a little, "not sex, I mean pure and unimaginable love, and that is what I felt for him."

I only believed her for a short moment because I'd seen this before. Maybe not to this extent, but Genie would fall in love with any man that treated her well, and most of her exes had treated her like a queen.

I wanted to say to her that she was just crazy, that this love would not last or at least I wanted to witness it if it did, but I didn't want to spoil her adoration for this Freddie.

"So, are you seeing him again?" I sighed and she squealed, taking my grubby hands in her clean ones.

"Yes, tomorrow," she nodded, "we are having lunch, and maybe dinner."

"What about your school?"

"What about it?" she said, her eyes twinkling, "shall we have a takeaway?"

* * *

Over the next few days, I was on edge. The flare-up from the near-blackout didn't come to fruition again, and I was silently hoping that I would be able to enjoy the comfort of my own bed without being coddled to death by Genie, but she insisted I slept with her, *just in case*. As each day went on, I went to work, praying that there would be no angry men that I'd have to deliver to, whilst Genie continued to date her new beau. She'd tell me of the flowers that he bought her, the overpriced dinners that he treated her to and how he'd open every door, so that she could walk through first. Four days in and I was already curious to meet him because he sounded too good to be true. Were men really that chivalrous these days? Or was he out to flirt with her before bedding her and breaking her heart?

At the end of Thursday, I was lingering in the peacefulness of the flat, enjoying the calm of a hot shower, the water pouring over my sweaty body as I soaped every inch of it. The peacefulness, however, was soon destroyed as I heard the front door slamming open, and closed, before the bathroom door was pushed wide open. I turned to look at Genie, as she grinned from ear to ear, a new bouquet of flowers in her hands.

"Where are you going to put that?" I asked her.

"I'll find a vase," she squealed and hugged the bouquet, as though they were him, "what are you doing on Saturday?"

"Working," I answered, leaning down to pick up my bottle of conditioner, "I have to work an extra shift."

"No, you don't," she tutted, "we are going out."

I answered as I looked back at her, "why? Has he broken your heart already?"

"Broken it?" she squeaked, waving the flowers again, "would he really buy me flowers if he was going to break my heart? Arri, I will marry this man if it's the last thing I do."

"Then, why do you want to go out with *me*?"

"We have been invited to... a ball." She giggled, running off into the kitchen and I frowned at her declaration of attending a ball, as though we were living in the nineteenth century. I suddenly squealed as the hot water turned cold, from her putting the tap on in there.

"Genevieve!" I yelled at her, and she apologised as the water, immediately, went back to its standard temperature.

"It's Freddie's friend's birthday," she said, "and he is having a real-life ball."

"I'm sure you'll fit right in."

"You are invited too!" she shouted happily, "both of us are going."

"I can't go," I said, rinsing the rest of the soap off.

"Yes, you can," she answered, "you can get one poxy shift off to come and enjoy a night with me. And you can meet Freddie."

I tutted, "and, what do you expect me to wear?"

"I've already thought of that," she said, clapping her hands, "we will go and buy you a dress tomorrow. And, don't you say no! I told Freddie that tomorrow I couldn't see him as I would take us dress shopping."

"You're lucky I'm not working until tomorrow night."

"And, you're not working Saturday," she stated and then ran out, slamming the door behind her, shaking the unsteady mirror cabinet.

A ball in the twenty-first century sounded out of fashion, but it could be one of those high-end charity balls. I could wear a little black dress and blend in. Genie's parents, who were incredibly well off, had hosted one when we were both thirteen and it was quite a splendid event, though we were only allowed to attend until nine o'clock before a babysitter took us home. If it was going to be anything like that, it would be a breeze, but if it was something more like a traditional ball, like the kind they had in the eighteenth-century with choreographed dances then that would be something else. That would be the kind of event that Genie would fit graciously into, and she'd pick up every dance in a heartbeat, without fail, mesmerising everyone who saw her. I had my two left feet and no natural rhythm, although I had learnt a basic version of the waltz to help Genie whilst she was at dance school.

The next day, I had planned to take a day of rest, but that wasn't something that Genie allowed, and we were out by ten o'clock, sitting on the busy tourist-filled tube on our way to Notting Hill. She was adamant that we went to one of the finer dress shops and I knew that meant she would splurge on a jaw-dropping dress.

It was busy, as expected, with Portobello Market singing brightly as we passed, but Genie pulled us on further to a smaller borough full of shops.

"There!" she squeaked and pointed to a dress shop that held a gorgeous wedding dress in the window, "isn't it perfect?"

"Are we here to buy you a wedding dress?" I asked and she tutted, pulling me over so that she could stare dreamily at the window. The dress was indeed beautiful; it would curve exquisitely with her tall and slender body, and it fished out into a mermaid's tail at the bottom. I allowed her to ogle at it as I scanned across the street, to see what else was around. I saw a beautiful, paint splattered portrait in the window of an art gallery across the road.

Art, the one thing that could truly provide me respite from this mad world I lived in. Once I had a brush in my hand, hours would pass by as I brought images to life, feeling as though the worlds I painted were alive right in front of me. As Genie's passion was dancing, mine was painting and, in the beginning, I had been one of the best artists at my university. I used to draw streets with passers-by, creating finer details intricate enough that anyone could look through a magnifying glass and think that person was truly real.

But after my blackout in my twentieth year, my art changed.

Rather than painting with such detail, I began to create the same images as though they were like fast electricity currents, and only I could see truly what was underneath them. It felt as though I'd painted the first ever pictures that could dance. I'd place my hand onto them in front of my teacher as I told her to watch as it came alive before her. But it didn't. Instead, she referred me for counselling and, within a couple of months, unable to comprehend that only I could see the true nature of my work, I quit art school. And I suppose it came with the territory of being a human being, with strange ethereal powers, that only Genie knew about, but even Genie could not see what I had painted.

"Arri," Genie tugged my arm and as I turned around she pulled me into the shop. I was worried she really was going to buy the wedding dress, but she smiled brightly as the pink haired shop worker, whose badge named her Paula, walked over to greet us.

"We are here for that," Genie pointed down into the shop. I followed as she was gesturing to where, in the back centre of the shop on a mannequin, there was the most eye-catching dress – a glittery golden princess gown that even I could not contain my look of awe towards. Paula turned to the dress, for a moment, before looking at Genie with a smile.

"I'm afraid that is reserved," she said, looking over at it, "for a prom."

"Please, don't waste it on a prom!" Genie begged before she, literally, threw me forward towards Paula, "look at her, she would look perfect in it, wouldn't she?"

I gasped and turned to her, "no, Genie, I can't-"

"-Please, at least let her try it," she beseeched, ignoring me and holding her hands up, as if she was praying. Paula didn't know what to do. I was about to stop her, tell her not to be so over dramatic but then Paula turned and looked me up and down, though not as if to judge me but to fit me into the dress.

"You are right," Paula gave in, nodding, "it would look perfect on you."

"You don't have to," I answered, half begging.

"She does," Genie squeaked, grabbed my hands and then pulled me over. Paula locked the front door, swivelled the 'open' sign to 'closed' and then walked us over to the flaxen gown. It glittered under a central spotlight and had an underbody of gold muslin and an overcoat of fleece-coloured tarlatan, "how could you let anyone wear *that* to a prom?"

"Are you going to tell me what the occasion is?" Paula chuckled as she moved around to the back of it to release it from the headless mannequin it graced itself upon.

"A ball," Genie answered, with glee, "a real life ball."

"I hope there's a prince," Paula chortled, pulling the mannequin's body up so that she could easily lift the dress out, "this dress is fit for a princess."

"Have you got something black?" I whispered, though I was mesmerised by how amazing the fabric was and how I felt like I would look incredible in it. It would be most extravagant piece I would have ever worn in my life, and I knew I had to wear it.

"Are you ready?" Paula waved her hand towards the dressing room.

* * *

It was late evening, by the time I was on the cycle back home from a shift, and I enjoyed watching the sun caress the edges of the sky as it dipped to welcome in another night. Ripples of reds and oranges cloaked the lightly clouded sky.

Once I reached the block of flats, I wandered over to the bench in the middle of the small, desiccated park, next to the concrete structure, leant my bike onto the floor and lay down on the seat to look up as the stars began to reveal themselves one by one. On top of my passion for art, I also took ecstasy in watching the gems that decorated space, keen to find a centred understanding of why we were here and who we were destined to truly become. Although science had been one of my weaker subjects in school, I had a minor obsession with astronomy and astrology, feeling deep in my soul that maybe I was not meant to be on this planet. Maybe I had come here by accident by a force unknown, a secretly housed being that's life force didn't depend on the oxygen humans breathed but, instead, the frequency of currents. Yet, like human beings, I breathed the same air, and my body was no different to every other that passed me by.

After a few quiet inhales, I allowed myself to shut my eyes, listening to the sound of soft winds against the leaves of the lone tree. The sound soothed me, muting out the loud barks of a dog just streets away. As I dipped further, I felt as if I was almost falling into a meditative state. The wind provided a soft whisper, howling louder with every note, and soon I felt drawn to blink open my eyes, staring up at the black starry night sky above.

A crunch to my right and I looked over, no longer on the bench in the park, but in a field of tall green grass, lit by a humongous halogen moon that hung over the rising hill ahead. There, on top, a black figure looked down at something over the peak and I watched curiously, for a moment, before they turned to look at me, their face obscured in darkness. I rose to my feet and began to tread through the slightly damp grass. I could feel the squelch as they would gently sink and rise, with every step, but at the same time, flowers began to grow in my wake, in mesmerizing bright colours.

I gazed back up to the figure on the hill, understanding it to be a man by the way his muscular body was shaped, but still his face could not be seen. He raised his hand up to me, shaking his head for me to stop, and seemed to shout something, but the sound of it sank before it reached my ears. I tried to shout for him, to ask him who he was, but his reply came in a strange archaic language, that I'd never heard before. His gaze landed back down over the peak before he looked at me again. He screamed *Arraetta!* Waving his hand for me to stop again. And, then, something rose from the ground below, consuming his being before it pulled him away.

I paced forward quickly, the peak of the hill getting further away, the closer I got, whilst I tried to shout for him; whoever he was. I fell over then, crying some, closing my eyes tightly to stop the tears from falling, not wanting to be weak. I pulled my hands away from my face, struggling from the friction of the black sludge that stuck to them, looking confused for just a second, before a sharp pain injected itself into my wrists. I squealed in agony, feeling as the black sludge sucked sharply against every fibre of my arms, taking over my body inch by inch. I tried to pull it off as much as I could, my breathing becoming more ragged and hectic as I begged for someone to help. I opened my mouth to yell, but the black sludge peeled itself away from me, like a serpent, and waved around in the air in front of me, teasing the deep, ingrained fear that niggled in my stomach.

Then, it shrieked. An echo of my own scream.

I gasped in terror, my mouth opening as my eyes widened and I watched as the black serpent dove into my mouth, immediately trickling down the insides of my throat. It burnt, like a hot pan against the skin, but the pain would not go as it devoured my insides. My heart thudded, like sticks against a drum, and I prayed that death would overcome me quickly.

Arraetta, you must set yourself free, called a booming male voice, as I suffocated from it. The voice knocked some sense into me, but the black slime wasn't allowing me to break free, which rose the panic even more. The sound of a loud screech to my right and my eyes moved in its direction, seeing as strange crow-like figures ran towards me, grabbing and tearing away at my skin. It felt, at first, as though they were trying to attack me, but I soon realised they were freeing me from the embrace of this dark matter.

Arraetta, you must awake! The same voice commanded.

I jolted up right, choking for air and attempted to get my breathing back to normal. My ears wailed with a piercing note, and I shut my eyes tight, breathing in and out as everything began to go back to its normal state. I was back to reality, my hair clinging to my forehead drenched in sweat as I sat on the bench.

It was a nightmare, that was all it was, but it felt so real. I feared for these nightmares, I longed for the blackout to come so that I may regain some sort of peace again. I wanted to sleep in the serenity of dreamless slumber and wake up feeling free once more.

My vision was woozy as I stumbled to my feet, pulling up the bike to provide me with a little support, and balance, and took in the space around. The gentle buzzing of the tires allowed me some solace, clicking away as they spun on my way to the stairs.

The journey up them took me a while; sweat beaded my forehead and heat kissed my cheeks as I scaled to the tenth floor. I just about managed to get my bike onto the landing before I, breathlessly, fell to my arse, leaning carelessly against the piss-stained wall. I needed to get my vision back to normal.

I heard a door open down the way and then a loud gasp.

"Arri!" Genie squeaked as she pelted it down to me, sock-footed, diving immediately down to my height, "Arri, oh, come on, let's get you in."

"I'm okay," I grunted, holding my head shakily, "I just need five minutes."

Another figure joined us, and they hoisted my bike up to the side. My eyes rolled up to peek at an indescribably charming and handsome man. After placing the bike to the side, he knelt into my blurry vision, and I could see slight worry on his face. This was Freddie.

He tried to make light of the situation, speaking in an outlandish English accent, "I hoped we would have met on a better occasion."

"I need to get her into the bath," Genie said.

Without exerting too much effort, Freddie scooped me straight up into his strong arms and carried me to the flat. Through hazed eyes, I looked at his smartly-trimmed beard overshadowing his dark golden skin, not seeing a single hair out of place before gazing further up to his emerald eyes. He looked as though he held the world in them. He didn't look down at me once as he gently placed me down, on the broken lid of the toilet, and he then swapped with Genie, who half-balanced me upright as she turned on the taps. She grabbed one of the tattered blue towels from the side, dipped it into water before she started to clean my nose. This meant that I was having a nosebleed.

I heard a clattering from the hallway, and it jolted me, but Genie placed her soft hands onto me to help me relax, "it's just Freddie."

"Freddie," I murmured, leaning my head against the wall and stared down to the floor by the door. Freddie's feet appeared and I listened as the two conversed with each other, as if they were a couple that had been together forever, though I could only hear the beginnings and endings of their sentences. My ears throbbed.

Freddie disappeared then, the front door gently closing behind him as Genie continued to clean me.

I was unsure how long had passed before I finally came around, more present. I was in warm soothing bath water. I could hear gentle voices in the room next door and the light smell of cooking tickled my nose. I sat up slowly, grumbling before getting up and climbing out of the bath, flinging a towel around myself.

The bathroom door, which was ajar, opened and Genie's eyes widened at me before she worriedly stepped forward with another towel, "let me help you."

"I'm fine," I murmured, allowing her to throw a second towel around my shoulders.

"Yeah, absolutely fine," she tutted in anger, though she didn't pitch her voice any higher as she knew it would make my head throb even more, "it was eleven thirty when you showed up, I've been thinking the worst all night. You said your shift finished at eight and I called Freddie because I was so worried."

"You shouldn't have called him," I answered, stumbling past her into the hallway, "I was downstairs. I just had an episode."

"An episode!" she squealed in annoyance, "you are supposed to call me."

"How could I call you?" I asked as I leant against my door frame, "I was in a dream."

"Why were you falling asleep outside?" Genie asked, baffled, and I couldn't really give her an answer, other than I had found comfort in it. I looked over as Freddie peeked around the corner and I could really see why Genie found him very attractive.

"Hey." He waved, a tad awkwardly, "I have made food."

"I should sleep," I said, hoping that my tone was grateful.

"No, Freddie went to the shop and bought food for you to eat," Genie huffed and pointed in the direction of the kitchen, "now, you go and eat."

"I don't think Freddie would appreciate me sitting around in a towel," I pointed out but Genie's continuously cute aggression made me decide to just go along with it.

Freddie had made some pasta and I sat down at the table slowly as he served it. He looked at me curiously as though he saw something that no one else could see.

"It was wonderful to meet you," he cleared his throat and bowed his head in a strange fashion, "I hope to see you tomorrow."

"I don't think we'll be there," Genie answered him, saddened by the fact.

I forked pasta into my mouth, "no, we'll be there, I'll be fine tomorrow."

"Arri-"

"-We have to go," I smiled at her, seeing that her face was lighting up again, "I have an enormous dress to wear."

"Well then, I will endeavour to see you at the ball," Freddie said, before Genie walked him out. I could hear them kiss and mutter things to each other, and I allowed the sound to bring me some peace, from the evening that I had had, knowing that other things were normal in this world.

THREE

That night, after the nightmare that had shook me on the bench, I hardly slept a wink, but was soothed by the gentle sound of Genie's breath as she dozed next to me. I often wondered whether her dreams were made up of fluffy bunnies and rainbows because, even for someone as sprightly as her, she would be exhausted with dreams like mine. Sometimes, in the worst of times, I used to watch her sleep and I allowed that to gently rock me to sleep. But, the days of being a child were over and I could no longer use that tactic to switch off.

I rose early and snuck back to my own room, staring at the dress that was hung up on my broken wardrobe. It looked too perfect to be in such a damp ridden, paint-chipped room, but it helped balance the grimness of my surroundings. When Genie and I moved in, we both agreed to paint our rooms and I spent hours helping Genie paint it to look perfectly pink, but I could never decide on what colour I wanted, so, instead, I painted stars onto the ceiling in glow-in-the-dark paint, which eventually faded, leaving one of two here and there. Most of the furniture in my room was salvaged from what we'd found in the stairwells, items others in the building had thrown away, most of it still functioning properly, even despite the slight damages.

I decided to tidy my room for the next few hours, washing my clothes, putting new sheets on my bed, tidying up books and neatening up all my paints. The weather outside was gorgeous and the room benefited from a bit of fresh air. I picked up my last blank canvas and placed it onto the easel, urging myself to paint something new after a long hiatus. I picked up the dark blue, squeezing just a little onto the edge of my hand, like a moisturiser, and stared in wonder of what to create. My eyes peeked out to the sunny day outside, the world awakening fully once again, and watched as two birds fluttered together. I smiled, wondering which one was going to win their race as they flew off the balcony, out of sight.

A reflection in the window and I turned gently, looking at the ball gown that glimmered slightly from the sun. I gazed down to the paint on my hand, then up to the gown and then back to the paint before I had a sudden, and slightly childish, thought. I picked up a soft brush and hopped over, imagining the ways I could just enhance it a little bit. A sash, maybe? I could paint my shoulder to add the effect to it. I dabbed the paint into the paintbrush, reached up to a section and then-

"Don't you fucking dare!" Genie bellowed behind me, and I turned, splodging the paint brush as it dropped, out of my hand, and onto the carpet below from shock, "that dress cost me two grand, you are not ruining it."

"I wasn't ruining it," I answered, picking up the paint brush before walking past her to the easel again, "I was thinking about ways I could draw it on here."

"You are the worst liar known to man," she replied, seeing through my lie before she changed her tone, "how are you feeling?"

"Better," I answered and it was true, except for the anxious bubbling feeling, that sat in the pit of my stomach, as I continued my daily preparations for the upcoming blackout.

"Well, you'll be glad to know," she told me, coming over to hug me over the shoulders from behind, "I have booked us into a spa morning at a salon, where they'll do our hair and makeup plus a really amazing massage too."

"Do we have time?" I asked.

"Lots," she nodded profusely in her excitement, "it's only nine now and we need to be there by ten thirty, then we'll be back by one o'clock and the car is picking us up at two."

"The car?"

"Yep, Freddie has one of his drivers coming to pick us up," Genie replied, "right, I'm going for a shower. Don't you dare paint on that dress!"

* * *

By one o'clock, we were in a taxi in a mad rush to get back and into our dresses in time for the pickup.

Genie brought snacks and a bottle of prosecco into her room whilst we changed together, making little comments about how we were going to make our entrances, before we acted them out like little children. We both looked incredible; Genie had a long silk green dress and her hair into a smart up-do, whilst I had my hair down in ringlets over my shoulders.

"You look like a princess," she commented as she stared at me in the mirror, "and, the princess shall go to the ball!"

"I look like I've stepped out of Cinderella," I joked, "you look like you're going to one of your mum's charity balls."

"I'll take that as a compliment," she replied sweetly, poking her face into the mirror as she checked to see if she was still perfect, "being Cinderella has its pluses. You might get asked to dance."

"By a prince?" I joked.

"You never know," she shrugged, "Freddie's family are aristocrats."

I squeaked, "what?"

"That's why it's a ball," Genie replied and knocked me gently with her hips. She picked up my hands then and started to sway around the small area of her room, humming a rendition of a classical song for effect. After a few circles, her phone pinged and she picked it up, gasping a little, "the car is here!"

"Don't panic," I laughed gently as she rushed about to get a bag together.

"I'm so excited."

"I can tell," I answered as she continued her mad dash to make sure everything was perfect before we left.

As we exited the flat, and after Genie checked that the door was locked several times, we headed across the concrete balcony towards the staircase. Our wonderful eighty-five-year-old neighbour, Mrs Jenkins, peered out of the open window of her kitchen as we passed by her.

"Oh, you girls look lovely!"

"We're going to a ball, Mrs Jenkins," Genie shrieked and spun on the spot.

"How exciting!" she replied with joy, "I went to a ball once, it was a wonderful time. Make sure to take a lot of pics, do you have your camera?"

"We'll take some on our phone," Genie replied, waving it around.

"Ooo, lovely," Mrs Jenkins said, "it's nice to see you dressed up, Annie."

I laughed, "it's Arri, Mrs J, but thank you."

"We have to get going or else our car might leave!" Genie pulled me away from Mrs Jenkins' window and we headed down to the ground floor. There was a group of teenagers in the park, who wolf whistled at us, and my face lit up red, whilst Genie, jokingly, blew kisses at them to make them blush.

Parked up in the middle of the street, besides the parked cars, was a very shiny and modern black stretch limousine with a 40-something year old male driver, who stood by the side waiting for our arrival. He was kind enough to let us know that we could help ourselves to anything in the back and put on whatever music we'd like.

Our journey took around an hour but that flew by, as we sang at the top of our lungs to a variety of random pop songs and went through the mini bar very quickly. I was so deep into enjoying myself that it wasn't until Genie said *whoa!* that I looked out of the blackened window, to see we were driving through a large gate and up a very smooth road, surrounded by trees.

"Where does Freddie live again?" I asked.

"He said they live in a community, whatever that means," Genie replied, "but, maybe we aren't going there, maybe the party is..."

She cut herself short, with a loud gasp, as we emerged from the trees and pulled to a slow stop at a crossroads, that split off into different sections of a colossal estate of houses. The car continued to drive forward, once the driver was satisfied no cars were coming. I couldn't see ahead, only the substantially sized houses one after the other, split by fences, as we continued onwards. In the middle of the road, which separated us from any vehicles driving the other way, was paving with beds of colourful flowers, in the centre, whilst the middle of each section was split with towering oak trees.

The car pulled to a stop at several intersections; my eyes seeing as more houses were further away. It was the strangest place I'd ever set foot in, but I'd heard that gated communities were becoming a common thing as they were secure. There were at least fifty houses we passed by, with ten in each intersection, before the car tilted uphill just a little and the houses were no longer surrounding us, just vast gardens.

The car straightened again as we slowed down. I was desperate to see where exactly we'd arrived, straining my neck as much as I could against the window, but I could only see a pillar and an open iron gate. I heard voices by the driver's car window, followed by laughter before he drove onwards.

It was on the right-hand side of the car, where Genie sat, where I could finally catch a glimpse of the biggest house - *no, manor* - that I had ever seen in person, save that of a stately home. Genie and I were blown away by it as the driver drove across a gravel driveway and went clockwise around a large fountain in the middle of it until we pulled up just behind a procession of other black vehicles.

I turned around in my seat and looked up at the house, instantly wishing that I could be so lucky to live in such a big house. Genie and I, still quiet, watched as a valet dressed in blue robes came to the door nearest to me and opened it.

Although I was closest, Genie shuffled out first and I slowly scooted out afterwards, unsure where to look. Given what I could see, from standing in front of it, the house was at least as big, at the front, as Buckingham Palace, but was made up of, what looked like, two deep storeys. It was built out of chalk stone, with window after window looking out onto the promenade below, whilst the only way in, from the front, was the double front doors which were almost the size of the two floors.

Surrounding the front of the house were ornate green gardens that spanned and disappeared around the side of the manor, whilst the driveway was paved with soft orange gravel that glinted a little under the harsh summer sun. The place was paradise. And, what made it even better was that I didn't feel overwhelmed by a clamour of electricity - as if it didn't exist at all in the place.

But it did, of course. Radios were on well-dressed security personnel, some people on their phones and cameras surrounded the area.

"You made it!"

I turned as Freddie stalked down the steps, at the front of the house, and towards us. He was dressed in the finest white garments, threaded with the same blue that I'd seen the valet wear. He was a gorgeous man, and I could tell why Genie was instantly smitten by him. Even more so, I felt a peculiar, warming aura around him.

As I wandered a little after Genie, I watched as Freddie leant down and whispered something into her ear, causing her to giggle. His eyes flickered up to me as he loosened his hold on her and he bowed gently, causing me to stumble a little, "I am glad to see you have recovered."

"Thanks for your help."

"The birthday boy is eager to meet you," Freddie said and Genie laughed. I knew that laugh; it was the laugh she would give when she was planning to play matchmaker and I really wasn't going to play that game.

"This place is huge," I pointed out.

"Quite," he nodded, then looked at Genie, "so, ladies, are you ready to have some fun?"

"We already drank a bit on the way here," Genie admitted with a giggle.

"Well, I guess you shall be bringing the party to us," he laughed, eyes on her for a moment longer before he put his arm on her lower back and pushed her towards the house.

As I followed behind them, I couldn't help but feel like everyone was watching us - most likely Genie - but I wished I'd opted for a more subtle dress. But, once we were inside the grand hallway, all those nerves evaporated as I looked around at its captivating beauty.

The first thing that took my attention was a painted mural which would capture anyone's attention, depicting a world that one would only imagine in fairy tales. It was familiar yet very distant, and one section of it seemed to tell the story of majestic warriors, on white horses, whilst another section told of the stars. The mural was lit by a golden glass chandelier that hung from the centre in all its magnificence.

But it wasn't the chandelier that really drew my attention; it was a large portrait that spanned from floor to ceiling, at the top of the stairs, of three very regal people, gazing down on all of those who entered.

On the left was a strikingly beautiful woman with glimmering brown eyes and auburn hair, which was delicately woven with silver strands, pulled back into a slick bun. She must've been in her late fifties, as was told by the gentle wrinkles, which were slightly masked by a soft layer of makeup. Her thin lips had a layer of rouge lipstick painted on them, matching the main colour of her floor-length gown, which had golden flowers sewn into it, whilst a blue sash sat from her shoulder to waist. This dress was complemented by two-inch heels giving her a little bit more height to elevate her more against the man that I presumed to be her husband, on the right-hand side.

This man was a tall, slightly pot-bellied sixty something year old gentleman, with a thick grey and ginger beard and a moustache that lined his round nose. His face was prominent with wrinkles and the painting made him look like a very kind man with many stories to tell, especially through his humbling brown eyes. This gentleman looked as if he'd stepped out of a mediaeval aristocracy, wearing long white suit trousers and a shirt, a white and gold embroidered waistcoat and a military jacket with buttons from top to bottom, which had a unique symbol engraved into each one. To top his outfit off, he had a navy sash from his right shoulder to his left waist, that same symbol, or even coat of arms, decorated into the centre of it.

And, though this man sounded as if he would be the most striking person in the painting, it was the man that sat in front of them, on whose shoulders they both gently rested a hand each, that really stood out. He was the most handsome man I'd ever seen a painting of and, looking at him, made me feel like I'd seen him before. If it really was a regal family home, most likely I would have seen them on the news, at some point, but the pace of my heart said otherwise.

In this portrait, the man in the middle must've been around my age but his brown eyes told me that he was much older. He had luscious golden locks that swept down to just below his pointed ears and his face was well-groomed with not a wisp of a beard or moustache on it. His own tender hands rested on the lap of his navy-blue trousers and, in the same fashion as the other gentleman, I presumed to be his father, his military-like jacket was blue, matching his trousers, which were embroidered heavily with gold flowers. He also had the same sash his father and mother wore with the emblem prominent too.

The sound of a clock chiming and I looked to the wall to see an enormous clock with two faces, with one having a different time and pattern to the other. I didn't think much more of it, guessing it to just be some sort of astrological ornament.

"Arri!" Genie was walking ahead in the hallway to the left of the staircase, to the entrance of a room I presumed was the ballroom. She waved frantically, as though she was suddenly going to lose track of me, and I moved quickly to catch up to her. The pressure in my bladder was suddenly evident to me, all the alcohol that I'd consumed over the last few hours just waiting to break free.

"I'm going to use the bathroom," I told her, taking hold of her hands. She hopped up and down as though having a tantrum and pouted.

"Too early to break the seal," she whispered.

"Yeah, not for me though," I reassured her, eyes flicking up to

Freddie who was watching our interaction. I, then, looked back to Genie, "you go ahead, I'll come and find you."

Freddie instantly gave me instructions of where to go and I sauntered off, leaving them to enter the ballroom. Although I was a stranger in this place, as I walked up the maroon-carpeted staircase, that was held down by thin gold metal bars, I strangely felt right at home. Ten large steps in, the stairs opened to a landing of carpet, where beautiful fresh flowers stood on each side of the oil-stained oak banister, before the stairs continued upwards again for another ten until I was on the second-floor landing. To the left side, a long velvet rope cut off stairs to a wing of the house, much like they did to prohibit entry at a stately home, and a man in a long blue kaftan robe stood guard, not making any eye contact with anyone. Although I was slightly tempted, in my tipsy state, to sneak a look at that section of the house, I was becoming more desperate for the bathroom, so I went up the final set of five-stairs, on the right, that led up to the east wing of the house.

The hallway went straight ahead for a few moments before it split around to the left and led into a long, wide corridor that went right to the back of the house. Strangely, this part of the home was very empty, apart from a few guards that were plotted at strategic points, but there must've easily been twenty doors to different rooms. I managed to find the golden lectern sign post that Freddie had told me about, and briefly stopped to inspect it. There was a language printed on it that I'd never seen before. My fingers caressed the words as though I knew what they said but I concluded it just said 'bathroom' with the way the arrow was facing, and I was right. I opened the white door and walked into the biggest bathroom I had ever seen.

In the centre of the room was a large, free-standing ceramic bath, with golden taps, whilst a toilet and sink were in other parts of it too. Windows gave visitors the view of the right side of the house, looking out to the tops of a garden and, beyond that, past the trees that surrounded the property, shimmering in the sunlight, was the 'real world'. Even I looked like I'd fit in as an ornament in the room.

When I was finished, I began the task of putting my dress back on again, having to pinch sections of the zip together to fasten it all the way up.

The corridor was still empty when I left, and I couldn't help but take a bit of a wander down it out of curiosity. This one extended right through to the back of the house, where a large window overlooked the rest of the garden. Down both sides were many doors and, at first many were closer together, indicating smaller rooms, but the distance soon grew larger as I travelled onwards.

A woman, wearing a long green gown, sauntered out of one of the rooms, in a hurry, and she greeted me in her native tongue before shuffling away towards the entrance of the house. I was very curious about the language as I'd never heard it before. Not that I'd heard every language in the world, but it just didn't seem like it was real.

I noticed one of the doors on the right-hand side of the corridor, a little further down, was slightly ajar and my curiosity got the better of me. I couldn't pinpoint whether this was a hotel or somebody's house. If it belonged to those in the picture, I wondered how much money they had to own to live in, what essentially was, a palace.

I listened for any noise but there was no sound from within, so I gently opened the door and was hit with the soft smell of sandalwood, lingering from a bottle of aftershave that must've been sprayed. It looked like a large hotel suite.

Against the navy-painted right wall was a queen-sized four-poster bed, whilst a door, to its left, led through to another room. In the centre of the room, there was a glass coffee table and grey sofa, facing an electric fireplace with a television on a split wall above, whilst, on the other side, I presumed to be a closet cut off by gold and navy curtains.

I hadn't realised that I'd stepped inside the room until I heard the gracious sweeping of a shoe against the floor and the presence of someone in the doorway behind me. Their breathing gave it away that he was a man, and he cleared his throat, clearly amused by my presence.

Slowly, like a child caught before they were to get in trouble, I turned around expecting to see someone standing there waiting to drag me out. Instead, I came face to face with the very man that I'd seen in the portrait, at the entrance of the house. Just like I had felt by looking at this portrait, there was the same strange tug as I stared up into his mesmerising chestnut eyes. As our eyes met, the amusement on his own face fell, his lips open in awe and dismay.

At that moment I knew. This man was the love of my life.

FOUR

I'm unsure how long we lingered there, entranced in each other's gaze, but it was voices down the hallway that jolted us, from our frozen postures, causing both of us to laugh gently. I felt my hand rubbing my wrist, eyes unable to meet his again, whilst I tried to come up with an excuse of why I was standing there.

"Seraiah," he suddenly whispered and his hand came down into my view in an offering, for me to shake it. I tilted my head up at him, eyes locking once more, and I swallowed, softly pressing my teeth onto my bottom lip. It was usually a sign of nervousness, but I felt something in the pit of my stomach. A strange and uncontrollable desire for him.

His eyes mirrored the same look as he looked down at my lips, throat swallowing before he looked back up at me again. As though he was slightly off balance, from the captivating meeting, he steadied himself just a fraction and, in return, I placed my hand into his. As we touched, it felt as though my hand had never touched warmth before and goosebumps rose up my arm and vibrated right to the centre of my core.

He didn't shake my hand, instead, he raised it to his velvety lips and kissed it tenderly, lingering for a moment too long, as though the taste of my skin was something he wanted to memorise forever. Something deep inside my soul burnt for more, a mild pulse beating between my thighs and my thoughts whizzed through, what I imagined would be like, a lifetime of us together.

He coughed a little, straightening himself up and began to speak in the same language that the woman had greeted me with earlier.

"I am sorry," he said, humoured by my confusion, switching to English, "you must be Arri."

"Yes," I blew out in a hushed, still slightly tranced voice.

"You are Genevieve's friend," he chuckled.

There was an interesting twang to his voice; on the one hand, he sounded like he could be an Oxford scholar, but, on the other, he had this odd swing in the way some of his words were pronounced, just like how Freddie spoke.

Straighten up, Arri.

My whole body seemed to finally find its balance as I attempted to talk, without sounding like I was a little intoxicated, "you know… you know Genie?"

"Yes, she is betrothed to Freddie."

"Betrothed?" I squeaked, shocked by the sudden news, "they have only known each other for five minutes… she can't marry him."

"You are quite hilarious," Seraiah whispered, his eyes twinkling, "she is not getting married, I should have said that they are courting each other."

"*Courting*?" I raised my eyebrows, "do you know what year this is?"

"You are mocking me," he glared at me jokingly, "because of my accent and way of words."

"It is a little outlandish," I said and then laughed a little when he feigned shock. Then he tutted, searching for a remark to sprout back at me. I continued, "I've not heard someone talk about *courting* before."

"I think it should return," he said humorously, "it is a little nicer than *dating,* is it not?"

"I don't know," I shrugged, enjoying this, "I don't date."

At first, he looked a little shocked and then there was something else - relief, maybe. As though me dating someone was something he really didn't want and, on meeting him, I didn't want him to be with anyone else but me. But, why? Was it the same feeling that Genie had felt about Freddie?

"A beautiful woman like you would surely have many men lining up at your door."

"Oh, how many times have you used that one?" I laughed and he smiled, shaking his head in mocking disapproval.

"How much have you drank today, Miss…?"

"Kinsley," I added, "do I seem drunk?"

"No," he said with a smile, "before I left Freddie and Genevieve, she informed us that she would need to go and find her friend because, as she put it, 'she was no doubt drunkenly spewing up in the toilet.'"

I gasped, "I was not, I was just… I was admiring the view."

I reminded myself to speak with Genie afterwards and tell her to stop telling lies to beautiful strangers. Then again, maybe I wouldn't have bumped into the gorgeous man standing in front of me.

"The view?" He raised his eyebrows.

"From the bathroom."

"Of yourself?" he jested.

"Myself?"

"Yes, you were in the bathroom down the hallway?" he countered and raised his hand in the direction, "it has quite a large mirror."

The realisation of what he was implying hit me and I gasped again at him as he tutted and inwardly laughed.

I stepped past him into the hallway. What he'd said made me think about how he was *just* like other men, clearly just after something rather than being interested in me, but despite that, I strangely wanted to stay with him.

"Allow me to escort you back to the ballroom," Seraiah chuckled, but, instead of stepping back into the hallway, he went further into the room, seemingly looking for something. Of course, it just so happened that I was looking into *his* room. The sound of a drawer opening, and some mumbling, as he engaged in a conversation with himself, before he walked out of his room, closing the door behind him, "My speech."

He waved a docket around, rolling his eyes and I frowned, "what for?"

"My birthday."

"Oh," I answered, wide-eyed - it was *his* birthday, "oh!"

"My mother insists I make one now that I am old and decrepit," he smirked proudly, folding it into his pocket and I laughed lightly. He most certainly was not old, he was perfect and, from the looks of his outfit, it was as if both of us had been sent the same dress code. Like the outfit he wore in the portrait, his suit was midnight blue with golden embroidered edges, yet this one was only in the style of a simple business suit rather than the aristocratic mediaeval type clothing and he didn't have a sash on either.

Seraiah coughed and I peered up at him, watching as he gestured towards the back end of the house, rather than the way I'd come from. I blushed, knowing that I'd basically eyed him from head to toe, and he'd watched. "What is with the blue and gold colour scheme?"

He chuckled and we began to walk together, "they are our family colours, do you not like them?"

"I do," I laughed gently, "it's just everywhere; even on you now… and on your painting in the entrance."

He cringed, "I hate that portrait."

"Why?"

"What better way to tell everyone we are royalty?" He said and I stopped, turning to him in shock. He, a little caught out by what he'd said too, returned the look before he cracked up some and continued to walk onwards, "I am surprised you have yet to guess, Miss Kinsley."

"Are you related to The King?"

Seraiah barked with laughter, "the British king? No, no... let me just say that we are aristocratic nobles, and we shall leave it at that." He turned to me. "Are you coming?"

"Should I curtsey?" I squeaked and he laughed again, clearly enjoying my shock at it all, "are you... what are you then?"

He stopped, still waiting for me to continue walking. He cleared his throat, as if answering the question was disdainful for him, "a prince."

I suddenly began to laugh. This was beginning to be the weirdest week of my life. First, Genie met Freddie, then we were invited to a ball, we bought a dress for me where the shop owner said she hoped I'd meet a prince, because the dress was *fit enough for a princess* and, suddenly, I was staring into a real life - or maybe hoax - prince. A prince.

"Well, Your Highness, I'm sorry for being so crude."

"Crude?" he countered, "that is not a word I would use to describe you, how are you crude?"

We walked on together, "well, I'm not royalty."

"It does not make you crude," Seraiah pointed out as our hands brushed against each other, from walking a little too close. I moved mine so that it was holding my other, stopping it from swinging against him, though I would've liked to touch his once again, "what is Arri short for?"

"Arraetta," I answered, the feeling of it foreign on my tongue. I didn't ever use my full name apart from when I had to make important phone calls. *Ar-ray-et-ah,* it was the strangest way of spelling a name. I once did some research into what it meant, but the only spelling that ever came up with a similar sound with Arrietta, but the 'rae' gave it a slight twang.

"Arraetta," Seraiah repeated not once but twice, like he was tasting the words on his tongue, and my heart skipped when he did, "that is beautiful."

"Is it?" I laughed, the sound echoing around. I threw my hand over my mouth, in slight embarrassment, and met his eyes once more, seeing how humoured he was. I lightly giggled and turned away continuing onwards, "so… how long have you lived here?"

"Over fifty years," he answered and then he backtracked, laughing lightly as a smile rose on my face, "the family, of course, not me personally."

"Well today could be your fiftieth birthday," I chimed flirtatiously.

"I am old and decrepit after all," he said, referring to our earlier conversation, and we both laughed like old friends.

As the laughter died down, I looked more closely at the hallway we were walking through, noticing a variety of different paintings of the countryside and animals, and even a few more portraits of the aristocratic family. One made me smile, it was of Seraiah when he was much younger, and I could see that he would've been a nuisance.

He didn't say anything as I looked at them, just waited for me until I was ready to move on. As we approached the end of the hallway, I could finally see out of the huge windows properly, seeing that there was a lake at the bottom of the garden, a fountain sitting in its centre.

"You are very lucky," I said breathtakingly.

"Sometimes," he shrugged, "it does get a little too much."

If only I could agree with him. I could understand the life of a prince could get claustrophobic with all the protocols, presuming there was a lot, but he had everything at his beck and call. He didn't have to want for anything.

"I know what you mean," I nodded mockingly, "I sometimes think 'my God, what would I do if I was poor right now?'."

He tutted, chuckling, "you are something, Arraetta."

"Arri," I corrected but he passed it by.

"If I were not in the position I am in," he continued openly, "I would have enjoyed a quiet life in a cabin somewhere, waking up to views of a forest, enjoying the freedom of life."

"I always wanted that too," I replied and we connected eyes, for a short moment, before we both looked away again, "but, you know, *money*."

"And, *status*," he added, both of us taking a few moments to look outside at the beautiful summer's day, "Freddie could easily get away from this if he wanted."

"Genie said he's a bodyguard?"

Seraiah looked at me and burst into laughter, "a bodyguard?"

"Is he not?"

"Freddie is in charge of many things," he informed me, still amused, "but he definitely is not a bodyguard. Are you sure that your friend, Genevieve, has not told you something incorrectly, Arraetta?"

Genie did lie sometimes but it wouldn't make sense for her to lie about that. Spending this short amount of time with Seraiah, however, had me hoping that Genie and Freddie would see each other more often, so both Seraiah and I could too. Prince or not.

"Do you like wine?"

"Sometimes," I answered.

"Well, please be sure to try some of our wine," he smiled politely.

"Is it poisoned?" I joked.

Seraiah smirked, "Miss Kinsley, you truly hurt my pride. The wine is from our winery, I am sure you have had some before, no doubt, but it shall be flowing all evening."

We walked down a set of stairs, that descended to another hallway, and were met by two static men, who stood guard by a set of large double doors, the sound of music and chatter muffled from inside. To the right, there were two other double glass doors, which led out to the gardens – closed, but there was a smattering of people crowded out there, not noticing us inside. At the end of the hallway, the corridor tunnelled back to the front entrance of the house, whilst to the left another hallway followed a similar pattern, to the one we'd crossed above it. This place was like a strange maze.

"Arraetta, I must ask you," Seraiah said as we came to stop, in front of the entrance to the ballroom, "do you dance?"

I laughed, "I've had to dance with Genie in the past, whenever she needed a partner."

"It is a tradition here that there is a dance on special occasions," he said, "and, I would very much like to have that dance with you."

I blushed, "I'm... I'm not that good."

"I shall lead," he insisted, "all you have to do is follow me."

"I... okay," I agreed and was surprised that I wasn't even reluctant about it.

"Wonderful," he smiled, "now, I would be honoured to enter the room with you but, due to a variety of circumstances, I shall have to take a different entrance."

Seraiah took me aback by bowing courteously before walking away down the corridor. I watched for a moment, partially taking in his beautiful physique whilst also playing the interaction back in my head. Regardless of whether Seraiah was truly a prince or was just trying to jest with me, he was a man that I wanted to get to know a lot more.

As I turned towards the doors, the two guards didn't hesitate to open them for me, and, suddenly, the quietness of the corridor was engulfed by a very busy room, of at least one hundred glamorous people. I almost felt at ease as I took them all in, glad that it wasn't just myself and Genie dressed up, but, as I entered, I felt the gazes of many on me. I did everything to dodge people, avoiding making eye contact as I made my way into the ballroom, until I looked to the back of the room and saw the older gentleman from the portrait, looking straight in my direction.

This time, however, I didn't exactly think his eyes were so kind. Instead, he seemed to be watching me as though I had just become the bane of his existence. A heavy, unruly expression on his face. He moved his eyes to Seraiah, who had come to stand next to him, and I wondered if I'd seen tension between them as Seraiah spoke to him. The older man turned away from me and nodded, gruffly, before he moved away.

I felt like the eye contact lasted longer than it did, but really it was mere seconds as time seemed to speed up again as I accidentally knocked into someone, almost spilling their drink. I apologised very quickly, moving onwards to try and find Genie.

I finally saw her, standing on a chair, waving profusely at me. Smiling, I pushed through the people until I came to a table nearest to the door. Genie dived down onto a chair and patted the empty one next to her.

"Where have you been?" She raised her brows at me, and I smiled, wondering whether I should reveal that I had just been swept off my feet by a prince. As I sat down, I finally let myself take in the grandeur of the ballroom. It had a similar feel to the hallway, with long red and gold curtains decorating the windows, draped from high ceilings. A small orchestra was on a stage on the right-hand side and, nearby, many people were dancing in formation, whilst others sat and stood around the many tables. If anything, it was a bit like a wedding the way the room was decorated, with little cards labelling the seats. Men were dressed in smart tuxedos, whilst women wore dresses of all shapes and colours.

"Earth to Arri," Genie whispered and I looked over at her to see she was holding a glass of wine, in her hands, for me to take, "drink?"

I swivelled around, seeing the half empty bottle of white wine and I laughed lightly, picking it up and reading the label, recognising the name immediately. 'Zikan Winery,' it boasted. Although Seraiah had yet to reveal the name, it made sense that someone from an aristocratic family would own one of the top wineries in the world.

I usually wouldn't choose to drink it because the wine was very expensive. Not only was I hard on cash, but I also couldn't bear to pay a large amount of money for something that would be gone in an hour.

"Where's your boyfriend?" I asked as I placed the bottle down on the table and picked up the glass she'd poured for me.

"He has just gone to speak with Seraiah," she said with a smile, "you must meet him, now he and you are destined to bed one another tonight."

I gasped and smacked her arm lightly, "Genie, where are your manners?"

In a way I was secretly thanking her for making me wear nicer underwear because, from our short meet, I knew I would happily share his bed. It wasn't just because I liked him for how he looked but also because his flirtatious nature mirrored my own and we seemed to have a similar sense of humour. But I didn't want to tell Genie that I'd already met the prince, at the ball, just yet.

"I am only speaking the truth." She grinned, stifling a cheeky laugh as she cast her eyes over the ballroom, most likely searching for the prince, or even her beloved.

"So, Freddie…"

She took hold of my hands and tapped her feet a little against the floor, "oh, he is so wonderful, isn't he? I knew you'd like him."

"I've hardly met him," I smiled, feeling like the meeting with Seraiah had rubbed off on me, "but, as long as he treats you well, then that's all that matters to me."

"Who are you and what did you do with Arraetta Kinsley?" she joked and we both laughed together, the sound echoing out into the crowd, causing a few heads to turn as the music suddenly fell quiet.

The room grew silent, in a matter of moments, and we both saw Seraiah walk up onto the dais, just before the orchestra. Even if he was joking about being a prince, I could feel his regal ways seeping off him as he gently scanned the crowd.

Seraiah began to speak in that beautiful archaic language once again, addressing the room, drawing a few barks of laughter before he cleared his throat.

"...So, to accommodate our guests, who only speak the English tongue," Seraiah said, switching languages, looking towards me and Genie. He waved gently and both of us returned it, blushing some as a few people looked, "thank you all for coming to this celebration in these dark and uncertain times."

"That's Seraiah," Genie whispered.

I know.

"We hope that one day we shall return home and claim our rightful place," he continued, his voice full of hope. There were several cheers, "but, for now, we must continue living as we have, until that time is right. And that is why we are here celebrating what... feels... like my one hundredth birthday."

Laughter ensued and Genie moved to whisper in my ear, "so, apparently, Seraiah is an heir to a throne." *I know that too.* I looked at her as she spoke, still trying to keep half an ear on the speech. "Kind of sexy, right?"

"And, Freddie's his bodyguard?" I asked her, waiting for her to confirm what she had said a few days before.

She shrugged a little, "kind of, he's also Seraiah's best mate."

I would've questioned it further, but both of us jumped when Seraiah spoke a final phrase into the microphone, followed by everyone echoing it, "Shrang-e-la!"

We both laughed a little at our reactions and sat back down on the chairs, sipping our wine.

"So, I probably should tell you something," I told Genie, ready to spill the gossip about meeting Seraiah in the hallway.

Distracted, her head tilted up to look at someone, a beaming smile appearing on her face, "hi!"

Genie hopped up and I turned my head, as she moved to share a soft kiss with Freddie. He was standing next to Seraiah, whose caring eyes caught mine, making me feel powerless with need for him. He bowed gracefully and stepped forward passed the two, "are you ready for that dance?"

That question seemed to jolt Genie out of her canoodling, and she looked at me wide eyed, a smile growing on her face, "no way."

Although my eyes flicked to her, I didn't pay too much attention to her reaction, feeling an unknown force tugging me to my feet. I took hold of Seraiah's offered hand, gentle tingles rising in my fingertips as we touched, sending a wave of exhilarating energy through my body. Neither of us lost eye contact, for a moment, as he took a couple of steps back, until he turned to lead us both through the crowd.

Chatter had risen since the speech, but as the both of us made our way through to the centre of the empty dance floor, everyone fell quiet to watch us. When we came to stand opposite each other, our eyes connected once more, and I felt a fire burn in my heart - I'd never felt more full of hope and adoration in my life. I felt truly alive.

"First, we bow," he whispered, moving to do so. I thought my curtseying would be awkward, but it felt natural as I copied what I had seen in movies, deeply lowering my body, until I rose once more, our eyes not leaving one another.

"I may not be the greatest," I murmured to him as he stepped towards me.

Gently, without removing his eyes from mine, he placed his left hand onto my waist, which sent a delicate sensation up my side, whilst his other hand intertwined with mine, pointing it outwards. For what seemed like a long while, since I had last done so, I flickered my eyes to the crowd that had gathered in a circle around us and I quivered, suddenly nervous.

"Arraetta," Seraiah whispered and I was suddenly looking straight back at him as he commanded, "trust me."

The strings of a violin began to play, melodically starting up the song, and, within a few seconds, Seraiah was waltzing us around the room in the most natural, perfect way possible. I felt like I had not only danced forever but that I had danced that forever with him. The murmurs of the crowd, as we sauntered around the room perfectly, began to disappear and it was just the both of us staring deeply into each other's eyes. It was as though we were telling each other our stories, the music enhancing the peaks and troughs of them. I had never, in my life, felt like I fit more perfectly in one place. It was as though all my life's worries and fears would disappear because of Seraiah.

And then, as the music came to an end, the echoes of the voices in the room began to rise, like a cacophony and I was back in the real world, both of us finishing how we started – with a bow.

Pulling me out of my semi-stunned state, Seraiah complimented, "a natural."

After a round of applause for the both of us, the music began to play again and couples once more began to flood the dance floor, leaving us little room to continue the conversation. There was nothing more I wanted than to grab Genie and pull her to the bathrooms to shout about it all, but my eyes scanned across to see that Freddie and Genie were enjoying themselves, dancing together. The perfect place for her.

Seraiah put his arm out to me, and I took it. "Would you like to take a walk in the garden?" he queried as he led me in the direction.

I looked out of the window at the beautiful garden and smiled, "sure."

FIVE

I was glad for the fresh air away from the claustrophobic space of the ballroom. The sunlight kissed my face and the gardens seemed even more beautiful, as we walked through them. Pavements lined with gravel and beds of colourful flowers; nothing rotting in sight. I heard a slight murmur and scuff of feet behind us and turned to see that we were being chaperoned by two forty-something-year-old men, both of whom looked like they could easily pick me up and swing me around, without any issues. I suppose they thought to follow Seraiah in case I posed any danger to him. I laughed at the thought.

"Do you find something funny, Arraetta?" Seraiah asked amusedly.

"I just find it funny that you have two bodyguards following you," I answered.

Seraiah turned to look over his shoulder.

"They are only with me because you are here," he confirmed, "I am usually capable of strolling around the house without them."

He turned and called out something and I watched as they both bowed, before slowing down and leaving more distance between us.

"That's a beautiful language," I said.

"Yes, it is our native tongue," he informed me, "we tend to use it around the house."

"What is it?" I asked.

"Maybe I will show you someday."

I blushed and turned my head away from him.

"I'm sure that you find yourself in the company of many women..."

"Oh, and how many times have you used that line?" He mimicked what I'd said earlier, and I chortled a little, shaking my head, as he continued, "you are quite incorrect in that manner, I do not find myself in the company of many others. Other than my mother and my friends."

No mention of his father, I wondered why.

"What of your parents?" Seraiah asked and I shrugged, gazing up to the sunny skies above, the topic not always the best to bring up on a first meeting with someone. He cleared his throat, "I am sorry, I did not mean to upset you."

"You didn't," I smiled at him politely, "it's a whole complicated tale and maybe not one for right now."

"Another time then?" he asked and I laughed gently, shaking my head.

"I don't mean to sound rude," I replied, not wanting to go down the avenue I was going to take because, really, I wanted to be the opposite, self-assured kind of person, "but, I am fairly sure you can find someone better than a pizza delivery girl."

Seraiah paused for a moment before saying, "maybe I should have the pizzas delivered to me?"

I reddened, turning my head away to hide my smile before I looked back at him, "I'm afraid that you are outside the radius of Jafar's Pizza Palace."

"Oh, it is a palace?" he joked, "I should make sure to visit."

"Do enjoy your visit, I'm sure you'll enjoy your rat infested pizza," I laughed and curtsied to him for extra effect.

"Maybe I can open a position in the kitchen here just for you," Seraiah said, flirting, "I shall order pizzas every day so that you can come and visit."

"I suppose I should just be one of your maids then."

"As long as you only take part in making my bed," Seraiah answered a little seductively and the back of my neck burnt from it, a picture of us both in his bed later that evening crossing my mind. I cleared my throat and turned to look up to the sky, pushing the thought away. I knew that his comment had slightly stunned him too.

"I did not mean to make this something more than it is," Seraiah said, the path taking us down to the beautiful lake that radiated in the sunlight, "I had only meant that-"

"-Don't worry, Your Highness," I interjected, looking at him, "I wouldn't expect to be your wife, I'm not quite cut out for princess duties."

"You could learn," he answered truthfully and I bit my lip, thinking about the idea of it all and how strange this evening had become, "my mother is an excellent teacher."

"I thought you weren't making this out to be more than it is," I answered nonchalantly and spared him another glance. He pouted slightly as he figured out his next comeback. Then, I laughed lightly, "if you want me to sleep with you, you can just ask."

Seraiah choked at my suggestion, "I did not think you human women were like that."

"Human?" I raised my eyebrows at him, a little taken aback by his wording.

"You are quite... human," he answered, thinking about his way of phrasing it, "in a case to some... women, who like to sleep with many others."

"Oh, so because I'm a *human* woman I can't sleep with other men?"

"No, that is not what I meant," he charged back, seemingly fearful he had upset me but I decided to find the funnier side of it. I concluded that it was possibly because English wasn't his first language. What he truly was trying to say to me was that he found me somewhat attractive and didn't expect me to be the *type of girl* who flung herself off to other men.

"Do not worry, Your Grace," I joked and spun around in a fluttery circle, saying sarcastically, "you can see I am *obviously* the embodiment of a perfect *human* woman but deep down inside there's something strangely... ethereal about me."

Seraiah stepped forward, pulling me into him and I swallowed hard, "I *can* feel something different about you."

"Oh?" I squeaked, my heart pounding in my chest. He inclined his head, his mouth lingered just a breath away from my own, both of us standing by the lake, whilst the rest of his party gave no interest in it. But, as he was about to dip in to kiss me, I heard an overwhelming sound, like a loud frequency and I winced, pulling backward before looking up.

Seraiah, caught out by my sudden movement, at first was about to apologise but then he also looked up. His questioning words rebounded as I saw a strange shimmer in the sky.

"Are you okay?" he asked as I halted.

I was unsure exactly what I could see, but it seemed like a large dome of electricity, which spanned the entirety of the estate, or town, that we were in. It was naturally too high to truly see but I could see the splinters of electricity, that spat from it. And, as though the horn of an episode had just sounded; my heart began to race. I blinked and the sky above cracked and began to turn into a dark, ashen colour with cords of golden currents, ricocheting through the clouds like a dark omen. I felt my hands begin to tingle and I shook as echoes of horrific screaming sounded all around, combining with the crescendo of unmelodious music in my ears. The usual panic attack rose in my body, and I could feel Seraiah briefly touch me before he jumped back, eyes wide as he watched.

"Arraetta?"

Without another word, I began to run back towards the house, trying not to trip over the edges of my ridiculous dress. The only thing I knew was that I had to find Genie. We had to get home. I couldn't have this episode, or the after effects of it, in this house no matter what.

I heard Seraiah calling after me, but the sound soon disappeared as I ran back into the ballroom, pushing and shoving through the crowd until I caught sight of Genie. She was meeting with Seraiah's father and, presumably, his mother. I couldn't stop to talk as I grabbed her from Freddie's loose grip and pulled her towards the entrance, startling a few people in the process.

"Genie, we need to go," I begged and her eyes widened in realisation, nodding emphatically before she echoed a goodbye to Freddie, taking the lead for me as we ran out of the room.

In the grand hallway, two guards moved to shut the front door with quite a thud, and another thirty-something year old man stepped forward from them. I had no time to really care for who he was, I just needed to leave.

"I cannot let you leave," he said, aiming the dialogue to Genie as I gripped onto her.

"She needs to get home," Genie begged him and the man's eyes briefly came down towards me before he looked up, shaking his head.

"I am sorry," he apologised, repeating, "I cannot let you leave."

"Is everything okay?" Freddie's concerned voice echoed behind us, and I heard Genie exchange some sort of words with him, but they instantly became incomprehensible. I was doing my best to keep myself upright, but I knew my weight was becoming heavier against Genie's arm. If I didn't get away soon, I would collapse right in the middle of the hallway.

"Arri," Genie whispered, coming to stand in front of my blurred vision, as she took my face in her hands, "we'll go in here, come on."

"H-Home," I squeaked hoarsely, yet not trying to tug away as she pulled me into a side room, to the right of the main door. It was a formal lounge and she gently shut its door behind us, guiding me to sit down on a hard chair, "G-Genie."

"You're okay," she whispered, nodding, but I could hear the worry in her tone. "You're okay, I promise, you're okay. Just breathe, one... two..."

She quickly grabbed some tissue, from a pot on a side table, before she came to hold it over my nose, mopping up the blood that had begun to spurt from my nose. I felt my breath slow down, but I had the same feeling that I was going to pass out.

"Breathe, Arri," she whispered and I blinked to try to keep myself conscious.

That's when I heard the most soothing sound – the sound of her voice disappeared, blending with the gentle tweets of birds and the flow of a river above my head. I tilted my head up to the noise and saw a portrait on the wall opposite – a place that I'd seen so often in distant dreams. I felt my body calm a little, some strength rattling my bones. Much to the disdain of Genie, I pushed past her and made my way over to it, shakily placing my hand onto the picture.

A river ran deeply into the heart of a forest and forked off into two different directions. There, on the riverbank, sat a windmill and a small house where children giggled and ran around in circles with each other. Up the river, which forked left, and disappeared around the back of some of the trees that lined it, in the very distance, climbed a mountain so high it was cut off by the edge of the canvas. But, to me, I could see it so clearly. I could feel myself standing in the river, with the water gently moving around me, and I looked up at the bright blue sky. The sun gazed down on me and the warmth I felt was invigorating, making me feel freer and more alive than I had ever been.

"Arraetta." A hand was placed on my shoulder and the world before me returned to its state of stillness, my breath returning to its struggle. I slowly turned to look at Seraiah, whose gentle and calming eyes soothed me, for a short moment, before I felt a 'ping' of sorts in my head.

I shrieked in pain, grabbing my head as I keeled over.

"Please, we need to go home," Genie begged as I fell to my knees, the throb in my head only getting more intense.

"We are going to help," Freddie soothed her as she cried and I winced as I heard Seraiah shout out to someone. I screeched again as another sharp pounding rocketed through my skull and I cried, the tears from my eyes and the blood from my nose leaking onto the floor.

"Genie, you must tell me what is happening," Seraiah begged her, kneeling down before me wanting to help.

"The blackout," she whispered, tearing up, "we shouldn't have come, we shouldn't have come."

"Arraetta, I can help you," Seraiah whispered and I leant up, needing to stand to my feet all of a sudden.

He tried to stop me but allowed his arm to be my resting post. I could feel a tingle in my arms, and he yanked himself away gently, jolted by it, as a gentle glow began to radiate around my body.

"That is impossible," he said.

I stumbled back until I was leaning heavily against the wall, the entire room beginning to spin slowly, as I blinked to try and stay conscious. Seraiah stepped forward and I winced as the pulses of light from all around danced before me, needlessly bright.

"Where is Marie?" he yelled and immediately cringed as he knew he'd shouted too loud. As though I was on a gravitational ride at a theme park, the room tilted backward as my body sat down next to the wall and my hand found itself holding a plug socket, whilst I still struggled to catch my breath. Freddie was holding Genie back from helping me.

"Arraetta, we are going to help you," Seraiah whispered as he came to kneel close – but not too close.

"What do you want with me?" I shouted and then winced as the pain hit my head. I panicked as the room around started to crumble, pieces of the ceiling dropping down one after another, before a hole in the ceiling appeared. Above, the clouds whirled in darkness, whilst silhouetted bodies hovered not too far below them. I shook, needing to escape, choking for breath until the word 'no!' was yelled by Seraiah as he jolted forward.

I felt the electricity from the socket pull at my skin and my body was flown back as the room around me sped up to the speed of light and disappeared before my eyes. Red, blue, and yellow sparks washed away all normality as I was suddenly lost in the tranquillity of a pulsating space of colour. I blinked, floating gently free from dismay, as if I had become one with energy myself.

The peacefulness ended all too quickly as I blipped away from the space and stared up at the wires of a telegraph pole, the skies above it shrouded by light pollution. Just for a split moment, everything was calm as I floated there before it was ripped out from underneath me, and gravity pulled me to the ground. The noises crescendoed louder and my head turned as I saw the overpowering headlights of a car come to collide with me as I fell on top of it with a thud.

Sudden darkness.

Then, there was uncompromising pain. Vessels burst inside my skin, causing large bruises to form instantly, whilst deep cuts aggravated the surface, pouring dark red liquid onto the concrete ground below. I coughed heavily, trying to clutch at sections of the road, so that I could find a way to pull myself to my feet and run away from it all. I'm unsure whether my vision was blurred because I was crying or from the knock to the head, but I felt dripping from my forehead, hinting at blood. Several people had run over to offer support for the mess that I had come to create.

I couldn't hear for a short while, trying to make sense of the shoes that crowded around and trying to read the lips of a woman, who was speaking directly to me. But soon the piercing sound of deafening sirens split through the crack of silence and the mutters of those, in the vicinity, rose higher like a tuneless choir, echoed by a blaring car alarm and hissing steam just behind where my body was spread.

I blinked to clear my vision, attempting to allow my eyesight to look further than those surrounding me, to try and identify where I was, eventually hooking onto a light which streaked in and out with every blink. The street was semi shrouded in darkness but the blue lights of an ambulance, which soon pulled up, provided reflection on everything around me. Like a finger running around the rim of a glass, the noise began to warp once more, booming rapidly until I shrieked in unimaginable pain, the pitch so loud that it caused glass from the building's windows and car mirrors to smash. Several people screamed as the street was plunged into darkness but not one person knew it had been me that had done it. Instead, as I screamed, the skies thundered above, electrical currents of gold rocketing through ashen clouds.

A strange sensation overcame me, and I found my body pulsating, mimicking the sky's gentle rhythm. Somehow, with some miracle force, I managed to stumble to my feet.

There were three women, whose eyes widened on seeing my ability to stand, echoing each other's words, telling me to take it easy, but I knew I couldn't stay. I had to get home; it was the only place I was going to be safe.

I pushed my way past them, shaking from subdued pain, and found myself on my way, keeping to the darkened streets; the lights of which would continue to power on and off as I walked past. Sometimes I would stumble drunkenly, swaying from one side to another, grabbing on to fences for support but it was that unknown force that drove me onwards.

As I rounded a corner, I could see the two familiar large concrete buildings a couple of streets away towering over the estate, and I thanked the Gods that I was nearly home. Safe where I could crawl into bed, away from the world, and let the shadows of deep slumber overcome me.

But then the skies above suddenly halted its tumultuous bellowing and, in that moment, that same wave of pain crashed through my body. It was as if the lightning was the only thing keeping me alive. I'd always known that I needed electricity to keep my body moving but I'd never struggled after the currents had dissolved into the sky.

My stomach burnt and the heat was seeping its way up my spine, tickling the back of my skull as the throbbing pain returned, without grace.

I fell, my head striking a lamp post, and I struggled to allow air to fill my lungs. My sight faded in and out, like a kaleidoscope in segments. I was screaming for help, hearing the words *please, someone help me* repeat in my head, silenced on my tongue as my body wouldn't allow me to cry to waste any more breaths. Instead, it was fighting mercilessly to keep me alive.

I succumbed to darkness for split seconds at a time, each time jolted awake by the static that would power me back up again, continually repeating the process until my body let my mortal physique die.

* * *

Gasping and spluttering, I woke, catching the end of a loud bang that ricocheted around the estate. Car alarms blared horrendously loudly, dogs barked, and residents came to gather around to see why the glass on their homes, vehicles and streetlamps were destroyed. But none of them saw what was truly happening.

Energised by a new current of energy, I could feel that the strength in my body had returned, lifting my dirt covered hands in front of my face to see that my veins were alive with the flaxen light, which provided a strange hue in the little space that I sat in. I could see in the decimated car opposite what Genie had told me about all those years ago.

You were so beautiful. She squealed at age twelve and then explained exactly what I had looked like. She had said that my body had lines of gold light throughout it, and I had strange designs on my face, which were so beautiful. She talked about how my irises were no longer their natural shade of blue but, instead, had turned to the same golden colour.

And she was right. I had never, in all the years I had been through this process, been able to witness its true nature. Genie had always been too worried to film it, even when I'd asked, which was admirable of her.

I could see how I was like some sort of ethereal golden torch but the visual only lasted a few moments as it pulsated in and out until I felt very alive.

Back to my feet, I continued my journey back to the flat, not feeling at any point like I would blackout, instead waltzing through the crowds of citizens, whose attention was never on me but on the issues at hand; the broken lights, the smashed windows, how they were going to be able to afford to repair it. Whatever was happening to me was what had caused the chaos; it was as though I had needed to suck up all the energy, from everything electrical, to breathe life into my body again.

I made it back to the street close by my building and stopped just down the road when I looked up to the tenth floor. There he was. The tip of Seraiah's head at the edge of the balcony, alongside, who I presumed to be, Freddie. I found myself hiding. Why would he show up at my flat? He had witnessed something chaotic and otherworldly that only Genie understood, yet he had acted as though he had seen it before. I could hear his words whisper in my ear – *that's impossible.* Of course, that could indicate that he was just mesmerised by it but when he yelled *no!,* as my body somehow transported me to near home, it was like he knew something.

"Why are you hiding?"

I jumped and spun to look at my troublesome neighbour's eight-year-old son, Tom, staring at me curiously.

"Ew, you have blood all over you."

"It's just a costume," I said hoarsely and he raised his eyebrows, comically placing his hands onto his hips.

"It's not Halloween yet," he answered, "and, why are you hiding?"

"Why are you up so late?" I asked, wondering how late it was since it was dark, "what time is it?"

"I think about eleven," he shrugged and he pulled a phone out of his pocket, "yeah, eleven."

I'd left the ball most likely around five, after causing a dramatic accident, so I must have been stumbling around for hours. Time always worked strangely in my world of blackouts but, even for me, six hours passing was a long time.

"Aren't you a bit young to be out this late?"

"Aren't you a bit old for wearing fancy dress?" Tom retorted and then stuck his tongue out at me, "mam kicked me out because she has my Uncle John over."

"Your dad's brother, I hope."

"I'm going back now," he shrugged and then peeked to the building as if eyeing something, "it's pretty dark out, all the lights went off."

"I saw that," I answered, then a great idea popped into my head, "hey, Tom, how do you feel about doing something for me?"

"What's it worth?"

"Five pounds?"

"Five pounds!" he squealed and stomped his foot dramatically, "have you seen the price of inflation these days?"

I was highly amused by his attitude but was willing to barter with him. A kid like Tom would have had great knowledge since he had to look after himself most of the time, like a lot of kids on the estate did. From time to time, he'd knock on our door and ask if we could lend him a couple of quid and I'd pull out my bare tin of cash, and give him some, because he needed it more than I did.

"Okay, ten," I answered and put my stained hand out to him. He was about to shake it when he made a sound of disgust and jumped away as if I was covered in rabies.

"Ten pounds," he answered firmly, "now, what is it?"

"On our floor," I replied to him, "there are two men, I need you to tell them that you saw me leave in the opposite direction."

"You *are* hiding!" he exclaimed with a cheeky grin, "did you not pay your rent?"

"I've paid my rent without fail every month, thank you," I scowled, still humoured by his temperament.

"Okay, I'll tell them," he answered, "I'll tell them I saw you on Billy Street."

"Great, thank you."

He lingered for a moment, arms folded, and stared at me before he held his hand out in a give-me-the-money way, "cough up."

"Knock tomorrow," I told him, "I don't have anything on me right now."

"Fine." And with that, he waved and then ran to the building. As he went to complete his task, I decided to take the back entrance, up to the flat, by walking down the alley behind me. It was strangely nice to be in a darkened neighbourhood as it offered my head some rest from the pain that had taken over me. I silently hoped that my body had healed itself miraculously and that all I would need was a cooling shower. Then I could just tell Genie that I had overcome the blackout. However, it was still too early. My blackout usually came around the end of June, which meant it wasn't the correct date for me to have an attack so either I'd been blessed, and it had come early, or worse was yet to come.

My feeling of strength was soon overridden as I felt nausea suddenly rise, in my throat, and I tumbled over, splintering my fingers as I tried to grasp the fence for support. In the ground underneath, pulses of something started to throb and murmur. I frowned, leaning my ear down to it to listen further, resting my palm against the concrete. A low vibrational hum danced under my fingertips, pulsing until I squealed, feeling an uncomfortable sensation. Trickles of electrons seemed to be seeping down my back, and into the ground below, and it felt as if someone was trying to rip the skin from my back. Then, out of nowhere, those remaining lights that hadn't smashed from my earlier shriek, and quietly painful death, indicated on one after the other including the one light that lit up the alley.

Like sunlight caressing the tip of the houses, the hidden towers behind them breathed back into life, and the lights switched back on.

It felt like I was being pounced on by a million scratching ants as the static kissed my fibres until my body slowly released each particle of energy it had consumed.

I flung myself back in pain and hit my head against the fence, wincing as the throb rose adding to my earlier collision. All the pain that had subsided hit me again, with no remorse, and I gasped out for help, once again silenced with no hope. I brought my arm over my body shakily, scooting gently back as I prayed for someone to come and save me.

The light in the alley danced a little as shadows overtook its hue and I blinked to try to stop my own darkness overcoming me.

"No, no, no, no!" I heard a panicked voice to my left and looked up at the man, who I had flirted with at his birthday ball. He skidded down to my side, "Arraetta, stay with me."

I attempted to speak but nothing left my mouth, leaving me gasping for air like a goldfish.

Seraiah looked up to his right and my own eyes followed to see that Freddie was also there but there was no sign of Genie. Suddenly panicked that they may have done something to her, my inner stubbornness grew stronger, and I grabbed hold of Seraiah.

"G-e-enie, Genie," I murmured, my newfound strength dropping immediately as I murmured in pain, woozily swaying.

Seraiah gently pulled my head up, "Arraetta, we are going to get you help."

"There is a ring in thirty seconds," Freddie said.

My eyes fluttered open, and I looked back at Seraiah, adamantly.

"Genie," I murmured.

"She is safe," Freddie answered in a matter of fact manner, looking down at his watch. He started to count down from fifteen and I watched Seraiah close his eyes, taking a deep breath, before his body strangely came alive in the same way my own had, except with midnight blue patterns across his face.

He leant forward and whispered, "*you* are *safe*, Arraetta."

In a calming way, he lifted his hands onto the side of my head and cupped it before he began to whisper something in a different and strange language. My head tingled gently, though the sensation was not painful, as I lost myself in the depths of Seraiah's eyes, blinking slower and slower until I succumbed to the realm of deep slumber.

SIX

I clawed for air as my eyes fluttered open and I stared down at a flowing river, trickling away peacefully downstream. The sound of sweet birds, the river and a gentle breeze created a beautiful atmosphere and, as I sat up, I noticed the fork in the river, through the tree line, and the windmill on the bank, that led to the mountain ahead. The tranquil and calming nature of it made it feel like home, but where had I seen this place before?

Feeling the flowing water around me, I saw that I was in the river itself and began to swim towards the windmill. On the bank, I spotted a young man, maybe in his mid-teens, sitting reading a book. He then turned his head towards me, and I couldn't help but feel like I knew him from somewhere, but where?

"Are you real?" he suddenly asked, coming to kneel down on the edge and waving his hands around in the water, to coax me over. I went to answer but as I got to the edge of the embankment nothing came out of my mouth, "are you truly the Spirit Nymph?"

I tried to answer again but I couldn't say anything, like my mouth was zipped shut. He stared at me curiously, "my grandma used to read me stories about you all the time, saying that you can get whatever your heart desires if you meet a Spirit Nymph. Is that true?"

"Seraiah!"

He looked over to the direction of the voice. Seraiah? Where had I heard that before?

"Look, I have to go but can I ask for something?" I looked at the boy – Seraiah, "I mean, if this truly is real." He laughed. "Can I request that you do everything you can for me to find her?" He laughed again awkwardly. "My Kindred Spirit, even if it means turning my life upside down in order to find her, will you do that for me?"

"Seraiah!" It was the voice of an older man but, before I could see who it was, I was floating away downstream. Suddenly, a huge wave of water engulfed me, and I was thrown underwater, struggling to breathe as the tide sucked me in, without remorse.

Uncontrollable panic streamed its way into my body, devouring the sense of calmness that had been and as I tried to swim towards the shimmering sunlight above, a cloud of darkness fogged my eyes. I was once again reaching death's door. But, before the knock sounded, the gloom faded back into sunlight and I spluttered, my eyes flickering open again. With no control over my body, I climbed to my feet, not one drop of me drenched, and found myself on the riverbed surrounded by masses of forest.

Before me everything seemed peaceful, but it was the creak of an old door, behind, which pulled me to turn in its direction. A log cabin stood there. Its exterior looked enticing but through its open door I could see the pure blackness, which only gave me another feeling of despair.

One foot after another, controlled by something unknown, my body walked in the direction of the cabin, whilst, in my mind, I was screaming for it to stop as I feared what was beyond. Nothing stopped me as I was pulled into the darkness and the door slammed shut. I lingered there in deafening silence and, when the strings that had held me disappeared, I dropped to my knees shakily and curled into a ball, tucking my head into my arms as I shivered in terror.

Arraetta, you are safe, a soothing voice echoed into the depths of my ears, as though it was lulling me to sleep.

My eyes closed and my body began to fall backward but, instead of hitting the ground, I was once again somewhere else, floating gently down a long dark passage; a crevice of light underneath me glowing vividly as I approached it. Gently my back sank to the floor and was cushioned by a fleecy woollen carpet. Particles of noise began to caress my ears and I could hear several voices. Blinking, I looked up at the underneath of a large oak table. A long tablecloth covered the top of it, its edges hanging just above the carpeted floor. I pulled myself into a sitting position, everything seeming much bigger than it should.

"My main concern is the safety of my wife and daughter," a boisterous male voice stated and I blinked, automatically peering out slowly from underneath the cloth, looking up into a much more expansive space. It was a large dining room that looked like that of a mediaeval room, yet it had a strange modern element to it, with a large glass roof that rose high above. Pictures lined the wall but the body, in which I was trapped, wouldn't allow me any sight of who was depicted within them, instead turning their head towards a group of around five men that sat at another table not too far away.

"We can look to move them," another younger fellow replied, "but not until the second sun has risen, it would be unsafe."

"It is unsafe to keep them here at such risk," the first man spoke, frustrated, "we must make plans for them to go to Earth."

The younger man, with interesting facial features that had strangely gifted him with a third eye, in his forehead, was about to speak but then his eyes flickered past the table of men, and he did a double take. Whoever I was impersonating hid quickly, knowing they were in trouble.

"We shall leave this," the first man spoke again, after a short moment, "and resume tomorrow."

"Of course, Your Majesty," another replied.

I placed an idle hand over my mouth to quiet myself, hiding from whoever was out there. Everyone made their leave, apart from one heavy footed man. I peeked through the slit, in the rim of the cloth, and watched as the black boots began to wander around.

"Hm, I wonder who may be hiding in my dining room," he chuckled before I pushed back, stifling a giggle. I saw him come to kneel in front of the cloth, pause and then rapidly pull the material over the table, looking at me as he shouted, "bwah!"

A squeal of laughter reverberated, around the space, as I shuffled back, no chance of escaping the big arms, which came to take me into him. He picked me up and lifted me higher, turning me like a game of aeroplane as laughter rocketed from my vocal cords and then he pulled me down to face height, "were you sleeping?"

"Pa," I giggled as he nuzzled my nose with his own, looking into similar brown eyes. In the reflection, I could see a young girl, not much older than five, "Pa, why are you sad?"

My hands stroked his beard-covered face, fingers caressing the bags underneath his solemn eyes. Pa smiled gently, "do not concern yourself with such matters as sadness, little one."

"I am sorry, my lord…" came an apologetic voice.

Pa's head tilted at the intrusion, and I followed his line of sight to a thin woman who curtsied.

"I have been looking everywhere for Her Royal Highness."

"Do not worry," Pa chuckled lightly, "I believe she has taken to sleeping under my table… have you not?"

I giggled again as I looked at him, running my finger across his rounded nose, "Pa, you have a big nose."

"How you offend me so, Arraetta," he answered with a chuckle and, as though being forced back from the front of a viewing screen, I dissociated from the scene just enough to create a barrier between my adult self and the child that 'Pa' held in his arms. He murmured something else, but I could not understand as it translated, immediately, into another dialect, and I watched whilst making no interaction as he placed me back down. Except, instead of returning to the height of a child, I began to shrink into the ground below, becoming smaller and smaller.

Snapping back into the forefront of my mind, a bubbling sound rebounded, and I, immediately, looked down at the familiar strange black sludge, that was crawling its way up my legs and arms. I yanked at it, tugging as hard as I could to free myself, but it was to no avail. I looked back up to scream at my 'Pa' to help but he wasn't anywhere to be seen.

I was in the field that had rocked my nightmares, a few nights prior, but this time I could see the dark figure on the hill, silhouetted by the large moon. I managed to shout *help me* and his head snapped in my direction, and, soon, he was running to rescue me. That's when I saw the shroud disappear with the physique of Seraiah appearing in its stead. The ability to shout once again tickled my throat and as the thick sludge drowned my body, I just about managed to call his name.

Arraetta, he yelled, *I'm here, hold-* But his calls were too late, and I succumbed once again to the void of nothingness.

Five, four, three, two, one, ready or not here I come! The rhyme filled the space and the tension on my face softened as I removed my hands and sprang up to my feet. Once again, I embodied that same young child as earlier but, with the understanding, that it was me. This feeling was joyful and freeing and the little giggles that tickled me were exhilarating.

I felt the full force of being this child as she ran down a busy cobbled street of people, dodging them in glee as various people shouted things in varying degrees of happiness and frustration. I was hunting for someone.

The streets around were just like a large town as if I had stepped out of a fairy tale, but with a modern twist with the varied type of glass used to decorate them. As a small child the world seemed vast, including the bellowing signs that labelled shops, gently rocking with the soft breeze, and the market stalls laced with fruits and flowers of all colours, shapes, and sizes.

As I ran further, still on the hunt for my prey, I came to notice an almost end-of-a-city and could see that humongous cascading waterfalls lined the rim of the world I was within. I made it down to the end of the road, which led into some Oriental-like gardens with rocks, a stream and interestingly shaped trees and flowers.

Stopping, without needing to catch my breath, I triumphantly placed my hands onto my hips and scoured the edges of the rocks in search of someone.

Finally, a gentle giggle sounded, from behind one of the large ones, and I smirked, tiptoeing in the direction until I leaped forward, "got you!"

Behind the rock, there was a young girl, who had the same third eye as the man from the room I had slept in. She squealed as I revealed myself, gracing her with my presence, and she stood as we embraced each other in a friendly hug.

"Okay, your turn," she said.

"Princess!"

At the call, the two of us knelt into a hiding position, my hand covering my mouth to stop the laughter as she peeked over to lookout.

"It is Yarma."

"It is because we are not supposed to be here, Freyda," I squeaked to her, giggling lightly again and the girl – Freyda – gasped a little, darting into a hiding place.

"She has spotted me," she whispered, peering over and gesturing with her eyes to tell me that the woman was about to come around to us, "should we run?"

Agreeing immediately, I darted for it, running with Freyda away from the woman, Yarma. We took a different road and could hear her annoyed groans behind us. It seemed that Yarma wasn't fit enough to be chasing little girls around the place and we were able to create a lot of distance.

At the top of the street, we closed in on a beautiful glass palace, that stood behind tall walls. Both of us managed to get close to it but we came to a sharp halt when we saw the third-eyed man, a little bit older this time, standing with a few others, his arms folded, tutting at us both.

"Oh no," Freyda murmured and we both exchanged guilty looks before shuffling towards him as he walked to meet us.

"Now, girls," he spoke disappointedly, "what have we said about leaving the palace grounds?"

"Sorry," Freyda and I echoed, my squeaky voice sounding much more childish than Freyda's.

"It is for your own safety," he replied before looking directly at me, "Your Highness, we cannot have you wandering around here without an adult."

"I do not want to be kept in there, Dayfid!" I stomped, crossing my arms and I felt the pout on my face. Dayfid raised his eyebrows at me, before he placed his hand onto my shoulder.

"We were only at the gardens too, Papa," Freyda added and fluttered her eyelashes for effect. I could see that he was the type of man to cave easily but he was also clearly a professional.

"You are supposed to set a good example, Freyda," he said, placing his other hand onto her shoulder, "you are older."

"But, I am the princess," I stomped again, folding my arms.

"And you know that it is important that the princess stays inside the palace grounds," Dayfid replied, turning his attention to me, "no one is stopping you from having fun, girls, but this place is too big to wander by yourselves, alone."

"B-But-" Freyda answered.

"-Is everything alright?" The addition of a female voice had us looking at the most elegant woman I had ever seen. She had a golden aura surrounding her, that I wasn't even sure was able to be seen by the naked eye, with luscious brown hair and deep blue eyes - I knew, in an instant, that this was my mother.

Dayfid stood and bowed deeply to her, as did Freyda, as he spoke, "Your Majesty, I was just asking the girls to play within castle grounds."

"I do believe that they know those rules," my mother replied, her eyes twinkling in humour as she looked at me, "Arraetta, let us go for a nap."

"I am too old for a nap!" I whined, pouting as she held her hand out to me, waiting patiently for me to go with her. I soon gave in, turning and waving to Freyda, who smiled and returned the gesture, "please do not be angry, Ma."

"I am not angry," she laughed lightly as we joined a few other women and were followed by guards to a large gate that led into the palace grounds. Easily, and without giving me any choice, she lifted and carried me. I wasn't sure exactly how old I was, but I believed myself to be much smaller than an average child, almost the size of a three-year-old with the temperament of a seven-year-old, "but, you are so small and fragile, Arraetta, you must stay in the palace in case you get lost."

"I am not fragile," I moaned, stumbling over the word a little as I pouted, "I want to play with Freyda."

"You can play with her again tomorrow," she answered, pushing my head so I was leaning into her shoulder, murmuring soft words into my ear as sleep overcame my child self.

Peacefulness. Freedom.

A sharp rumble awoke me, and I blinked my tired eyes awake, sitting my little body up on a large bed, in a vast room. I grumbled and rubbed my eyes, looking around as a sharp gust of wind blew the soft curtains inwards before they were still once again. Another sharp rumble, this time screams of terror sounded, from the other side of the window coverings, followed by inhuman wails. I slowly slid off the bed, tumbling to my hands and knees as a longer earthquake sounded and I shook in fear.

"Ma?" I shouted and stood up, looking around, "ma?"

Another rumble.

The curtains blew furiously as I moved towards them, turning up my nose as smoke burnt my nostrils and eyes. I heard more screams and monstrous wails as I peeked around the curtains, and I could see how the once-beautiful skies above were covered in ashen clouds. I tiptoed forward, wincing as the palace I was in shook. Above me, there was a shattering and I looked up as a sharp piece of glass fell from the ceiling, coming directly past me, and disappeared directly down to the ground below.

I moved to look through the gaps of the balcony, "ma-ma? Pa-pa?"

I jumped as a large black winged creature, flew over the top of the building, and headed down towards the city below. I watched as it landed on a building, moving its head down to swallow something - a person - with one mouthful before it looked up and belted a wail, releasing black matter into the ether. My eyes cast up as a silhouetted body began to appear in the sky, floating there.

"Arraetta!" the panicked voice of my mother shouted from inside the room but I didn't turn to look at her as I watched small, inhuman, demonic creatures taking pleasure in killing their prey. I felt my body be picked up from behind and the familiar scent of my ma overtook me as she turned me into her.

"Ma, what is happening?" I murmured into her, not able to see where we were going. Ma's arms were tight around me as her footsteps hurried back inside but then she yelped in pain, freezing on the spot as she came to drop me.

"Arraetta, run."

"Ma?" I was scared.

Click, click, click.

I slowly stood up and peered around her, seeing as the winged creature, seemingly blind, heavily moved through the curtains.

"Arraetta," Ma murmured, looking at me, urging me to leave, "run, please."

I gasped as the creature stepped forward again. Hunting.

As though I was trying to be the hero, I immediately ran in front of Ma's back and put my hands out in a protective stance, "leave us alone!"

Ma, who was jolted by my sudden heroism, spun around, immediately, as the creature darted its way towards me. She grabbed and threw me, without remorse, across the room, towards the door, "run, Arraetta, now!"

I watched as she gave me a look. A look of fear, of worry, of guilt.

Then, the creature opened its mouth and swallowed her in one before it lifted its head and released the ethereal air from its mouth.

"Ma-ma!" I screamed in anguish. An explosion of flaxen lightning rocketed above, smashing through the ceiling glass, and pierced straight down through the mouth of the creature. It wailed in pain as the lightning burnt its insides until it disappeared into ash. Through the slit of the torn curtains, I watched as the silhouetted bodies above began to fall heavy like rocks from the sky.

Before I could see anything further, I was picked up by anonymous arms and carried through a variety of corridors. All the while I cried for my ma. Soon, I was placed down in a glass room where, in the centre, there was a dome arch with shimmering matter amid it.

"Princess, you are safe." It was Dayfid. He had been the one to rescue me from the balcony. He had such deep sadness in his eyes as he attempted to wipe the falling tears from my own.

The huge doors to the room opened with a thud and Pa rushed in, on edge with panic and worry, not giving anyone his focus except for me. Dayfid stood back and bowed as Pa turned me to him.

"Pa," I wept, "ma-ma!"

"I know, I know," he said, calming me and stroking my face, "Arraetta, you must stop crying and listen to me."

I couldn't stop.

"This is very important… please."

I allowed my tears to dry a little, still releasing pockets of sob-filled breaths.

"Arraetta, you must go now. You are going to Earth-"

"-But-"

"Arraetta, my lavrae," he whispered to soothe me, "you are going to Earth, it is safe for you there. This life will be forgotten but one day you will come to find these memories once again, I promise you."

The room shook and I wept in fear, looking around. Pa placed his hands on my shoulders so that my attention would come back to him,

"You must always remember your name, it is important that you do. You are Arraetta, Princess of The Cre-este." His next words disappeared as I whimpered from another quake in the room. "Arraetta, look at me. Lavrae."

"Pa," I whimpered as he kissed me on my forehead. I went to go after him as he walked away, screaming for him but it was to no avail.

Dayfid held me back. Then, a soft chemical cloth was placed over my mouth, my vision blurring rapidly as I was picked up and moved away from my father, who disappeared away from me. His body lit up with something I couldn't truly see as I finally succumbed to sleep.

* * *

"Pa!" I shouted and bolted up.

"Take it easy, take it easy," a woman's voice spoke softly as I was pushed back down against the damp sheets of a bed. I blinked, feeling woozy and hot and my head throbbed. I murmured something, moving my hand up to my forehead, which was gently caught by another.

"You need to rest, Arraetta."

"S-Seraiah?" I muttered, blinking to look over at the blur of Seraiah and a woman's figure, who came to lean over me, "whe-" I winced. "Where am I?"

"You are safe," he answered, but his words reverberated in my head as nausea rose in my stomach.

"I don't feel good," I breathed, but neither he nor the woman answered, engaging in their own conversation instead, overshadowing my silent plea for help.

I blinked, closing my eyes again, wondering whether I was truly back in the real world or whether another nightmare was about to seize me in its grasp.

My voice croaked as I whispered as a few tears fell, "Ma and Pa are dead."

I lifted my arm again and covered my eyes as my sobs left me. Much to my surprise and relief, I felt the part of the bed next to me dip gently and Seraiah's mixture of aftershave and sweat engulfed my senses. He held me and caressed the top of my head. I felt my right arm getting lifted tenderly by another hand. The sensation of a sharp prick caused my arm to tense, for a short second, but the weakness that I felt throughout my body allowed me to give in to the serum's sensation as I continued to sob. Slowly, I fell back into another bout of slumber, this time dreamless and peaceful.

A thumb stroking against the skin of my hands woke me from my sleep and I knew instantly it was Genie's. I felt groggy, as if I'd be living in the land between life and death for a long while, and my head was pounding. The fever I'd awoken to, however long before, wasn't quite gone but I knew that I was out of the hallucination phase.

I blinked my eyes open and tilted my head, seeing Genie sitting on a chair, her head laying on top of the duvet with closed eyes.

"Genie," I murmured, my voice hoarse. She bolted upright and looked at me, a big tearful smile growing on her tired face.

"Arri," she whispered, coming to pull herself to her knees, on the bed next to me. She stroked damp strands of hair out of my face, "how are you?"

"I feel like shit," I laughed weakly. She grabbed a bowl from behind her and drew out a damp cloth, ringing it out before coming to dab my head with it.

"I've been so worried," she said, tearing up a little, "you just... you..."

"Hey, it's okay," I replied, bringing up my arm to take hold of hers, seeing how there was a cannula in it, attached to an IV bag. "I'm here now."

Genie nodded, gulping back her tears, and tried to stop them from dripping onto me as she continued to wipe my face, "Freddie said I had to be brave and I've been so brave, but it's been so difficult and

I… I just don't want to lose you, Arri."

"Tomorrow, I'll be fit enough to get ice cream with you." It was a long running joke we had, and she laughed.

This laughter sparked the entrance of a forty-something year old woman, who came in and smiled sweetly at me.

"It's wonderful to see you awake," she said, coming around the right side of the bed and, immediately, placed her hand on my cheek, "My name's Marie, I'm the family doctor. You still need to have lots of rest, your fever hasn't quite gone yet."

"Family doctor?" I murmured.

"Seraiah's family," Genie answered for her and I looked at her, in surprise. Genie wiped her face a little. "You've been here since the incident, you're lucky to be alive."

"Very lucky," Marie added, messing about with some medical equipment, "it's been a very tense time in this house."

"Sorry for causing so much trouble," I said, trying to keep things light.

"No trouble," I looked over to see a dishevelled Seraiah enter, "you have caused no trouble."

If my face wasn't already flaring from my fever, the redness would give away how much his presence made me blush. Genie stood up and both her and Marie curtsied a little, it seemed like so much had changed since the last time I'd seen them together.

"How long have I been out for?" I mumbled, moving to sit myself up. Marie immediately stopped me, pushing me to keep me in my lying position.

"Over four weeks," Genie answered, sitting back down next to me, "it's not like the last time, Arri. You… you…"

It was hurting her to say it aloud, but having lived through it, prior to my hallucinations, I knew exactly what she was going to say.

It was Seraiah who said it for her, "you died."

"Several times," Genie interjected with a bit more confidence, clearing her throat, "your wounds were… they were so bad, Arri. But your body has healed because of your power."

"*Almost* healed," Marie corrected matter-of-factly.

"Does everyone know about me?" I asked Genie, my eyes flicking to Seraiah as the memory of his blue-veined skin popped into my head.

"Genevieve told us about you, Arraetta," Seraiah replied and I looked at him as he came to stand at the foot of the bed, "you are not alone in this world, even if you have been for a long time. We are very similar."

"You are the same as me," I stated, not quite a question.

"No, not quite," He gently shook his head, "however, we are both foreign beings in this world, as are my people. And you are welcome here with us."

I nodded, though I was unsure what *here* even meant. And how were we very similar but not the same? Had the things I had seen in my dream been real? Memories? Or were they simply a dream. Deep in the pit of my stomach, I felt incredibly sad to watch my ma die. She had died because of me, because I had been stupid enough to run in front of her to try and save her, yet she was just trying to save me.

Click, click, click. I shivered at the sound that echoed in my mind and looked over at Genie, wondering what I could tell her that didn't sound crazy, especially since I couldn't even comprehend what I'd seen.

"You okay?" Genie asked worriedly, stroking my head.

"Yes," I swallowed and offered her a soft smile, "I… I'm just tired."

"I think we should let Arraetta rest," Marie piped up and I watched as Seraiah spoke to her in his language, looked at us and then left.

I didn't need telling twice about rest, I could feel the fog of sleep overcoming me, instantly, and I fell back into dreamless slumber.

SEVEN

They said I died five times, each time resuscitating me was more difficult, but they worked hard to make sure I would come back; the car incident, amongst everything else, had caused one of my ribs to puncture a lung, whilst other bones in my body were broken and shattered. I was only lucky because I wasn't human.

Over the next week, I rested and slept – dreamlessly – and my body miraculously healed itself. Seraiah would come in once or twice a day to see how I was doing, though it could've been more – I had an inkling he also came whilst I slept sometimes. Genie was beside me a lot of the time, working closely with Marie to quicken the healing process, but it was mainly the power, that seeped in my veins, that had helped me to overcome the pain. By the end of the sixth week, Marie allowed me some respite from the bed on the basis that she would check up on me twice a day, and if I felt ill I had to return.

It was when I was allowed to roam more any sight of Seraiah became scarce. I'd been wanting to have a full conversation with him to find out more about what he'd said: how we were similar and who he truly was. It was strange how I'd felt so at home when I walked in on the day at the ball, yet spending more time alone there made me feel the opposite, especially when Genie would be out. I hardly ever saw Freddie, though I'd often hear his voice here and there and, sometimes, he would swing by my room to pick Genie up before taking her into London.

I wondered whether Seraiah and his family knew anything about who I was; I hadn't told anyone about my wild dreams, not even Genie. I felt like telling Genie would mean that Freddie wouldn't be too far behind knowing and, in turn, Seraiah would know, and I didn't trust that. I trusted her, but I felt on edge about everyone else knowing my personal business when I'd hardly had a conversation with any of them.

"Excuse me, ma'am..."

I looked over from where I lay in the bed. I was resting again from slight dizziness, due to the phantom pain that still was in my ribs.

"Hi, Kadey," I smiled at her, "please just call me Arri."

It was during the sixth week that I was introduced to Kadey, who was one of their maids. Kadey had specifically been assigned to me and was there to help me with everything I required, from bathing to dressing to doing my hair. I found her presence a little bit too much to handle because I hadn't ever been used to services like that. I still didn't know if my dreams were very much just that or whether they were memories, but if it were all true then I, no doubt, would've had someone like Kadey in my life. Maybe Yamma. According to those dreams, I was a princess. My pa had even said it to me *Princess of The Cre-este,* but what did it mean?

"As much as I would love to," she replied, "I cannot, it is against protocol."

I slowly nodded.

"I'm sorry to interrupt you," she continued, "but, Her Majesty The Queen would like to have tea with you."

"The Queen?" I choked, sitting up straight, "with me?"

"Yes, ma'am," she nodded with a smile.

I hadn't seen any of Seraiah's family since that brief glance across the ballroom that fateful night. I believe they had visited me during my period of being unwell, but, just like how Seraiah was now never anywhere to be found, neither were they. I wondered whether there was some magical portal that they disappeared through, but really it was probably just because they resided in the west wing of the house, far from my sick bed. Still, Seraiah's room was only down the hall, so it was strange that he was never around.

After making myself look presentable, I followed Kadey through to the west wing of the house; the first time I had been there. It was a very similar corridor to the east wing, and it went straight down in a line to a large door at the end with a variety of others along it. It was decorated with beautiful paintings of landscapes no human could ever have dreamt of, making a change from the regal portraits that were in the other corridor.

Further down, a large, tall door to the right opened and I watched as Seraiah stepped out, looking at me, surprised, as he closed the door behind him. Then, he offered a soft smile, bowing gently. I blushed, moving my eyes away.

"I am glad to see you are well," he said and stepped a little closer to me, "I hoped to catch you today, to talk about things."

I nodded slowly and then realised I was just staring at him, so I cleared my throat and curtsied a little, "I'm going to see your mum."

"My... *mum*," he chuckled, which made me redden even more, "well, I shall not keep you."

He bowed a little and then we lingered in each other's presence a while longer, both of us equally captivated by the other. I felt something tug at me; the want to have so much more with him, as though both of us were made to be on this planet together though I couldn't put my finger on why.

My legs finally moved, and I stepped towards him, wrapping my arms around him in an embrace. Although taken aback at first, Seraiah returned the hug and I lingered in the overwhelming scent of his aftershave and, strangely, paint. I felt whole in his arms.

"I wondered what was taking so long."

I jumped away from Seraiah and turned to look at the source of the voice: a living, breathing version of the woman in the portrait - Seraiah's mother, The Queen. She looked amused by what she had seen, and I itched my wrist, peeking over at Seraiah, who looked just as caught out as me.

"Mother," Seraiah bowed and turned to me, doing the same, "Arraetta."

The way he spoke my name; it was like a soft kiss tickling my skin, it felt warm and captivating and I only wanted to hear *him* say it repeatedly. It felt as though the only person who should ever call me by my full name was Seraiah, like it had been created for him to whisper, sing, *moan*. It made me ache for him in ways I had never ached before, and I knew that, with each murmur of it he might make, it would make me powerless against him.

I watched as he walked away, down the corridor, towards the main section of the house and then I turned to Her Majesty, blushing profusely as she still had that same humoured look on her face. Kadey, who had waited patiently by the door, also had a similar look.

"Thank you, Kadey," The Queen spoke to her and Kadey curtseyed before leaving. The Queen looked at me, "come, Arraetta."

And, as though she had summoned a dog, I walked after her, without question or comment, entering the room she had been in.

It was one of the more contemporary rooms, of the house, with the windowed back wall adorned with grey and black patterned wallpaper. Over the windows, which looked down onto the large side garden, were beautiful dark red curtains, intricately adorned with a gold leaf pattern. By one window, sat a beautiful oak grand piano and the other a red chaise. One wall was decorated with bookshelves full of well-placed ornaments and books and, on another, a large flat screen television. In the centre, beside a classic fireplace were two plush dark grey sofas and a matching armchair. From what I could guess, they didn't watch TV too often because the sofas were placed with more of a view of the fireplace.

In the room, another maid skilfully, and quietly, began to serve some tea as The Queen gestured to me to take a seat on one of the sofas, taking her own on another.

"How are you feeling?" she asked.

"Um, good thanks, Your Majesty."

"Oh, please, do not call me that, just call me Tara," she half-blushed, waving her hands at me, "you are part of the family now. I am sorry we did not get the opportunity to meet at the ball, as soon as my son informed us of your arrival, I could not wait to meet you."

I flustered, "well, I suppose I wasn't there too long."

"There are plenty more times for balls," she replied enthusiastically, "now, Arraetta, why not tell me a little bit about you."

I was slightly taken aback by the question, what on Earth would she want to know that would be so interesting to her? Would she want to know about my blackout? But, surely, she would already know about it because she was one of the people who witnessed the beginning of it. Or, maybe she wanted to know what I did for a living but I was sure that telling her that I delivered pizza, to make money, wasn't going to be appealing to someone of such high regard.

"What do you want to know?" I stumbled.

"What do you like to do?"

"Um," I replied, a little taken aback by the question, "I like to paint."

"And, would you like to do that here?"

"All my art stuff is at my flat."

"We can pick you up some new things," she answered, then paused after seeing my face that I'd subconsciously changed to being almost a look of horror. She laughed. "But, if you are like Seraiah, I am sure you have your own painting utensils that are more preferable."

"Like Seraiah?" I wondered aloud.

"Yes, he paints too," she beamed proudly. That explained the scent that had lingered on him, "the paintings in the corridor, he did those. In fact, we have quite a lot around the house, he is very good." She suddenly laughed. "But I am sure he will not mind a little competition."

She winked at me, and my face flushed.

"Did he... did he paint the one of the windmill?" the painting that I'd seen on the night of the incident had come to mind instantly.

"The Wicker Windmill?" Tara nodded, "yes, he used to go there a lot when he was a young boy. A place of freedom, I suppose."

"It's a real place?"

"Yes," Tara nodded, "very much so. Maybe you shall visit someday, I am sure Seraiah would love to show you."

I blushed at the thought of being with Seraiah alone, but, apart from our flirting at the ball, I couldn't understand why he would be so interested in showing me places he loved to go to.

"Your... Tara," I said, "Seraiah said we're similar."

"In many ways," Tara smiled, "you are both gifted with Rapidfire."

"Rapid... fire?"

"Yes, it is the power that runs through your veins," she replied, "much like that of my own, and my husbands, but yours is very different."

"Different?"

"There is only one other whose body houses flaxen Rapidfire," she answered, coming to stand up, "or, what is truly known as Divine Rapidfire. It is the most powerful Rapidfire to ever be in existence and it can destroy the cruellest of things."

I remembered the thunderous bolt of lightning, that split the monster in two, from my dreams and turned it to ash, shivering a little as my ma's scream echoed. Was it real?

Tara walked over to her desk, pulled out a draw and then took out a thick book, which looked ancient. She walked back over to hand it to me.

The front cover was engraved with genuine gold lettering and, in the middle, was a gilded medallion. In the centre of the medallion was, what looked to be, a door in the middle of a waterfall. It reminded me of the waterfall I had seen in my hallucination, and I wondered if it had any connection. The title I could not understand, written in a language that resembled that of the Greek alphabet, though these letters had no hard edges and looked to have been crafted with softer lettering.

I opened the first few pages, each one containing an image centred in the middle as though this was a storybook, with paragraphs of writing surrounding each one. The pages were like old sheets of parchment, making the book look much older than it was. I stopped when I came to an image of a mammoth God-like man which covered the entire page. His gaze was fixed down at a child in his arms, this child had enchantingly curious eyes and she stared out at me. An image flashed in my head of the younger version of myself, that I'd seen in the reflection of his eyes, and I knew instantly that the man was my father, *my pa*, and the little girl was me.

It was in that instant that I understood that they were not dreams but memories. I understood it because my mind had been telling me through fractured nightmares and hallucinations things that I could never accept, until this moment, as I stared at the drawing of myself and my father. Although I was older, I could see myself in her and I remembered how Pa looked from those small moments I spent with him, whilst I was asleep. He told me that one day I would remember again and that I should never forget who I was.

"Arraetta," I jumped as I looked up at her. She smiled softly, "this is the only copy of this book; it was created when we arrived on Earth so that we could preserve our faiths and the myths that we had journeyed with."

"So, so it's just a myth?" I stumbled, swallowing.

"No," Tara shook her head, "we know it to be real."

"How?" I asked her, intrigued.

"Let me tell you the story that we know," she answered, "the man in this book was known as Ivan the Great, and this is his daughter, who has never been named, who was born in his realm."

I looked back down at the book, wanting him to do nothing more than to raise his head and look at me. Nothing more than for him to just confirm the truth about everything; that what I had seen in my dreams was indeed the truth.

"Ivan the Great was a king born in the peace before The Great War of the Realms," she told me, "he is believed to have defeated the great tyrant, Roxecluf, a mammoth beast that unleashed what we would come to call The Dark. Ivan locked Roxecluf in a great vault in one of the realms and thus ended the first era of The Dark."

"That sounds like the Greek myth."

Tara beamed, "yes, similar, I suppose. However, he was not a God, he was merely a man, who convinced the realms to unite to defeat Roxecluf. Ivan prayed to the great goddess, Keatra, the Goddess of Divine Rapidfire, and asked her to gift him with her power. Keatra agreed but made Ivan promise that, on the day of his death, his soul would go to serve the Highest Gods for eternity."

"Isn't that a little unfair?" I frowned, feeling like a little child hearing a fairy tale for the first time, "I mean, she owed it to him to help him defeat Roxecluf."

"The Highest Gods rarely intervene with the affairs of the living," The Queen countered, "offering Ivan the power, of Divine Rapidfire, in exchange for his soul, was a worthy sacrifice, for Ivan could offer as much in death as he could in life. You see, the Highest Gods are almost like a celestial council, they give true balance to the universe, and, in their eyes, one must give something to receive something greater."

"But, surely that wouldn't balance out?" I asked, a little too enthusiastically, "he basically gave them his soul in exchange for not only this Rapidfire but he, also, saved realms from everlasting war. I mean, surely, he deserves more than just 'oh, hey, give me your soul when you die, and we'll make you a slave to us'."

Tara burst out laughing at this, "you have a good eye for detail, Arraetta, so let me finish the story and you can tell me if you think it worthy."

I sat back like a child, holding the book in my hands, my hand resting on top of the drawing. The entire story was clear as day in my head and I could see silent interactions between all the beings she spoke about.

"When the war was over and the realms began to rebuild, Ivan had a choice to keep his gift or to share that gift with others," she continued, "if he chose to keep it, he would continue living a normal life alone, with the burden of great power, but if he chose to share the power between the realms, at the detriment of the possibility of a future war, he would be gifted marriage to the deity, Reona. Reona was Keatra's only daughter, the Goddess of the Divine First Passing, and she was believed to be the most beautiful goddess to have ever been created."

"I'm guessing he chose the goddess," a feeling of love and happiness passed through me, knowing that this woman was my ma.

"Ivan fell in love with Reona instantly," she nodded, "he would rather have suffered another war, than to be alone for the rest of his life. On top of this, Reona was guaranteed a place with him, whilst he served the Highest Gods, because she was a goddess herself. Both made the decision to live a relatively mortal existence by creating a blessed realm known as The Cre-este."

I jolted slightly, the words ticking around my head '*You are Arraetta, Princess of The Cre-este.*'

"The realm of The Cre-este was divinely protected, but there was someone within, whose soul grew dark and cold," Tara's tone turned and I could see that she was coming to the part of the story that she wished she didn't have to tell, "it was rumoured that Ivan's brother, Eric, had become infected with The Dark from the war but had kept it hidden. When Ivan married Reona, Eric grew sour because not only had Ivan managed to gain divine protection, but he had also gained marriage to the most beautiful goddess to have ever lived.

"Eric disappeared for many years and Ivan came to forget about his brother, concentrating on continuing to create the haven that he and Reona wanted to build. And, on the first day of the Divine Spring, it was rumoured that Reona birthed a little girl, who had come to be known as the Goddess of Divine Rapidfire. The rumours were not confirmed until many years later, when a child of the realm of The Cre-este became parts of whispers across others.

"Do you know why I'm telling you this story, Arraetta? If you are Ivan's lost daughter, you are a confirmation of thousands of years of myths."

I looked up from the picture that I'd idly been fingering the outline of, whilst I'd listened.

Goddess of Divine Rapidfire? Thousands of years? The air suddenly became more claustrophobic. I had come to somewhat comprehend that maybe, just maybe, those hallucinations were memories, and I knew that I had some strange power in my veins, but how could I be a goddess? And how could it have been hundreds of thousands of years before? That would mean that somehow, I had travelled through time.

I placed the book down next to me, before rushing from the room, ignoring Tara's worrying calls after me. I needed some fresh air as quickly as possible.

My mind was racing with thoughts of the story, mixed with the images from my dreams and an overwhelming feeling of something, I'd never truly felt before, hit me in my chest. Grief and incomprehensible sorrow. Tears tickled my eyes, threatening to spill out, but I did my best to keep them at bay as I made my way outside.

I turned my mind to the other things Tara had spoken of. The Dark. But what was that? Was it the creatures that attacked The Cre-este that night? Or the black matter that constantly haunted my dreams? Yet, from the tale, it sounded like the most chilling thing in existence, a destroyer of life, with the only thing capable of destroying it being Rapidfire. Maybe it was what described the darkness of death, all-consuming and fateful. I shivered at the thought, swallowing the ingrained fear of my sudden demise. Whatever The Dark was, I had so many questions I needed answering.

Outside in the peaceful gardens at the back of the house, I took a breath of fresh air. The birds tweeting and the gentle hum of a hedge cutter provided me solace, for a short moment, as I leaned heavily against a wall, eyes pinned shut to allow the tears to dry.

Do you know why I'm telling you this, Arraetta?

I shook my head to clear Tara's voice from it and opened my eyes again, taking in the beautiful summer's day, eyes peering up above. Tilting my head to the side, I saw the gentle pulsating energy that domed above. Curiosity overcame me as I wondered what exactly it did, although I guessed it had something to do with energy because I felt more energised than ever being underneath it.

Still, the curiosity didn't last long as my thoughts moved back to the discussion with Her Majesty. I wondered how they had come to gain such knowledge, even if it had been a myth to them for a long time, until I had appeared. I felt frustrated because I knew but a minor detail about my own past and they seemed to know everything. I wanted to know everything.

And still, how could somebody travel through time? I didn't think that concept would even be possible. Then again, everything that had happened to me was essentially *impossible.*

I groaned in annoyance.

Had they only kept me on their estate so that they could find everything they wanted to about me? Prod and poke me until I'd confirm that their legends were true. But, to what avail? Only someone would do that if it was an advantage to them. Was my power that advantage? Or was there a wider game at play? They were here, on Earth, just like I was. Yet, it seemed like they had been there forever.

Suddenly, I thought about Genie and how she was part of it all as well. Except, I wasn't sure whether she was being held against her own will because she knew about me, and about Seraiah. I knew that people could be threatened into submission for having knowledge of things that could pose a threat to them. Shit.

I had to find Genie.

Immediately, I went to head back inside, but a giggle echoed across the gardens, and I knew it was her laugh. I began to walk down in the direction of the lake, seeing Freddie and Genie lovingly looking at each other, like they were the happiest couple in the world.

Seeing them together made me pause for a short moment. Maybe I was wrong, maybe Genie and Freddie were deeply in love, and she was only there because she wanted to be with him, and me, to some extent. No, how would she be able to resist a man who was giving her everything she ever wanted in, what had been, a matter of weeks? Had she no thought about the consequences - would she, with me, be trapped forever?

Freddie nervously moved down to one knee, a tiny box opening in his hand, and Genie, joyous, flew her hands to her face. My thoughts spiralled and moved back to thinking how she would be trapped further if she went through with it. I rushed down in an instant and, before Freddie could roll the final question off his tongue, I forcefully shoved him into the lake. The ring disappeared somewhere in it as well.

Genie screamed in shock as Freddie spluttered in the shallow end. I was sure that the guards had stepped out of their hiding spots as I could feel the eyes of others on us all.

She turned to me and, without remorse, slapped me. Even the birds fell silent from its echo.

"What the hell?" she shouted at me as Freddie climbed out of the lake, coughing. Genie continued, "what are you doing?"

Although the slap was hard, and painful, I came back at her with the same amount of anger, "what am I doing? What the hell are you doing? You've known him for five fucking minutes and you're just going to let him ask you to marry him?"

"Yes, I am!" she answered, tears forming in her eyes, "and, you've just ruined it."

"I didn't ruin anything," I spat back, glaring at her, "I've saved you."

Genie started to cry, and I could tell Freddie wanted to hold her, but he stood back, dripping, watching the interaction carefully. I could see Genie wanted to slap me again, her fist clenched a couple of times, as she took jagged breaths then she stepped back, "you're a selfish bitch, Arri."

I nearly winced at the insult, but I also felt my pride stopping me from doing so and I tucked my shoulders back, holding my head high. "We need to go."

"No," Freddie said, stepping forward finally, "do not be ridiculous."

"This has nothing to do with you," I glowered at him.

"It has everything to do with him!" Genie answered, "you just… you can't help yourself, Arri. I'm twenty-four years old, I can make my own decisions. Why can't you just be happy for me?" She didn't let me answer. "I know why, Arri, because you can't just let things happen - you have to always be in control of every little thing, including me. My happiness. If you are unhappy, then I must be unhappy."

"That's not true," my shoulders sagged as I murmured the words.

"It is true!" she screamed and took hold of my shoulders, shaking me like a child, "everything is about you, it always is."

Genie lightly shoved me, causing me to step back a little, before she stormed off. As I turned, I flinched as I saw Seraiah's cool gaze staring at me, from but twenty feet away from us, and he didn't stop Genie from walking past him.

Freddie grumbled in his language and rushed after her and I wondered if he'd called me a name of some sorts. I'd deserve it I suppose.

Everything is about you, it always is.

Seraiah walked down towards me, and my body hardened as I braced for another brutal confrontation but, instead, he came to stand by me, facing out to the lake.

I looked around, seeing a few guards watching us - no, *me* - intently from across the gardens. I turned in the direction Seraiah was standing, with his hands in his pockets. His sleeves were rolled up on his white shirt, leaving his golden forearms out for the summer sun to kiss.

"Circumstances," Seraiah commented and I frowned as his head tilted towards me, eyes meeting mine, "that is what has caused us to be where we are today. It is the circumstance of Genie and Freddie meeting that brought you to us."

Was that really all he could say? It's the circumstance of Genie and Freddie meeting that brought me to them. Of course, it was circumstance - it couldn't be anything else. Here he was trying to be trivial, in his pursuit of enlightening me, but what was he really saying? That I was in the wrong for barging in on both? Of course, I was wrong, but I couldn't help myself. I needed Genie to see, but I supposed I did the opposite.

"What do you want with me?" I asked, moving my gaze to the spout of water in the centre.

"I do not want anything but your happiness, Arraetta."

"Then, how can I be happy when I am trapped here?"

"We are all trapped here," he answered back, "do you truly believe I wish to be stuck here, on this planet, when I had a perfectly good home to live in? Everything is fated, Arraetta, your being here on this planet, in this realm, being one of them."

"What does that mean?" I shouted at him, "you all just go around speaking in fucking riddles. One minute I'm just living a semi-normal life, then I go to a ball, meet you and find out you've got magic powers, like I do, and now I'm being forced to come to terms with all this and-and amongst that, figure out how some loony tale is related to me."

Seraiah turned to me as I took a breath from my ranting, not an ounce of anger in his face, it was softened in some sort of understanding, or maybe curiosity. "It is not *loony*, it is the truth, why are you so fearful of that?"

"Because I showed up here and..." I paused, trying to come up with some sort of answer, "and, you are all creeping around me, not letting me know anything about you yet you seem to know everything about me somehow."

"That is where you are wrong, Arraetta," he said to me, "do you truly believe we know everything about you? How can we when you turned up on our doorstep six weeks ago? If we knew everything about you, surely, we would have known about you since our arrival." He sighed. "But, you are right that things have been kept from you. What is it you truly wish to know?"

What didn't I want to know? I wanted - needed - to know everything that he did. I wanted to know what our power was, how we were similar but different, what he knew about my father and what he knew about me. I wanted to know why his people were here and whether the reason was because of The Dark, or something else.

"Why are you here?"

Seraiah looked thoughtful for a moment, and I could see clearly that he was coming up with a way to give me a non-answer. Something that would tell me a little but not enough to paint the entire picture, as though it was taboo to tell me more.

"I-"

"Forget about it," I spat and started to storm up towards the house.

"Let me show you," he shouted and I stopped. I didn't turn as he walked towards me, his footsteps prominent on the grass, "allow me to help you understand. It is not the answer you are looking for, but it will allow you some respite at least."

I turned to him as Seraiah pulled his shirt over his head and I almost turned away just to subdue the blush of seeing his magnificent physique, but my stubbornness made me watch. I was selfish, I was intrigued about what he was going to show me, and it obviously wasn't to show me how much of a God he really was.

His eyes tilted up and I frowned, wondering what he was looking at, but his eyes connected back with mine before he stepped back a few paces. My face was contorted in confusion as he closed his eyes, took a deep breath, and concentrated on something.

That's when his body began to come alive with the power that seeped in his veins. It began in his left arm, first in pure blackness until it met his elbow and turned to the midnight blue, that I'd seen the day he rescued me from my demise. The rest of his body began to glow, and strange symbols appeared like tattoos across him. Truly, he was divine.

"Seraiah!" a concerned male voice yelled from the top end of the garden but Seraiah ignored them as he opened his eyes, causing me to gasp. They were glowing the same colour as his veins.

"Arraetta, we are similar you and I," he grunted, clenching the fist that was black as though it caused him pain, "we both possess Rapidfire except yours is… it is much more powerful. Divine Rapidfire."

"Seraiah, stop this," my head moved to turn to look at the owner of the voice but I paused as Seraiah maintained eye contact with me.

Seraiah walked forward and I didn't move as he came to stop in front of me. He put his good hand out for me to take and I placed my hand in his, mesmerised and without fear.

"I can control my Rapidfire, as you will too soon. We… we were made to work together as one… be together as one."

He closed his eyes, gripping my hand and, soon, I could feel him pushing his energy through his body and into mine. My body reacted without hesitation, lighting up brightly in the same golden glow that I'd seen in the car reflection.

Seraiah opened his eyes and that same feeling of wholeness, of longing, of needing nothing but him once again rocketed through my bones, sending a shiver down my spine. And, in the mirror of his eyes, I could see how beautiful I really was.

"You see now, Arraetta?" he whispered. Then, he took a step back and the golden colour disappeared, with Seraiah still glowing. An explosion of sorts sounded above, and Seraiah sank to his hands and knees immediately, as though he had been electrocuted and his power disappeared. I winced in reaction also, feeling my head throb but I had the feeling the little bit of energy, that Seraiah had pushed into me, had somehow protected me.

I watched as the same guy, who had told us we couldn't leave on the night of the ball, stepped in immediately to help him. He was dressed in a dark blue suit, an earpiece in his ear. His thick black hair wafted in the wind as he turned, looking past me and he barked a couple of orders, in their language, before his eyes fell on me.

"Ma'am, I think it is wise you step inside," he said and I understood it to be more of an order than a suggestion. Seraiah was breathing heavily, clenching his left fist and I could see that the black Rapidfire still remained, pulsing. The air suddenly began to grow colder too; a shiver running up my spine.

"Jonah," Seraiah bit quietly, head tilted towards the floor but something was different in his voice.

Jonah shifted a little, his eyes back on me but, this time, they were almost *begging* me to go. I felt a hand on my shoulder, and I looked up at another guard that I didn't recognise before three others moved past us to Seraiah.

"What's happening?" I asked.

"Dixon, take her away!" Jonah shouted. I felt the air change from the warmth of the summer day to an icy winter one. Dixon, the guy next to me, placed his arm across the front of my shoulders and pulled me back a few steps, coaxing me to turn.

And though he tried, I couldn't help being transfixed at Seraiah's changed temperament until his eyes shot up to look straight into mine. No longer were there the remnants of human eyes, instead the only thing that remained in his sockets were pure black voids whilst little veins ran onto his paling cheeks.

His body pushed to come forward but Jonah, and the two other men, grabbed him and held him back. Dixon, with no other choice, lifted me up as if I was nothing and carried me up the garden to the house whilst Seraiah, at the bottom, did his best to break free from the men.

At the top of the garden, Dixon placed me down and turned me to face the house. I jolted as a large, stout man walked out of the house in a hurry. Seraiah's father. His heavy, unkind eyes landed briefly on mine before he walked past. Dixon didn't allow me to see what was happening, just pushed me onwards into the house and straight through the front entrance.

I swear, for a moment, I heard Seraiah cry in pain, and I winced at it. Those void-filled eyes imprinted in my mind, causing my heart to fire in fear. What was wrong with him? Is that what happened to me when my power was alive too? Or did the forearm that looked infected, that seemed to have caused him pain, cause that to happen? Questions swirled around my head, overpowering any sense I had and all I knew was that no matter what, I wouldn't leave until they had been answered.

EIGHT

Genie and Freddie were already gone, and I was left to pace the large space of my room, waiting for someone to come and tell me that it was okay to leave. I wanted to find Seraiah, mainly to see if he was okay, but also to find out about what exactly it was that had taken over him. Infected him.

Dixon had posted himself outside my room and I guessed he was still there because I'd not heard much movement in the hallway. After a while, I lay down on the floor, in the middle of the room, and closed my eyes, falling into an uncomfortable nap that was dreamless.

It was the coolness of the room that awoke me, and I grimaced from the feel of it, moving to close the window that was open. I couldn't see the back gardens at this side of the house, only onto the lower ground rooftop that was decorated with beds of flowers like a secondary, unreachable space. I wasn't sure what time it was, but I guessed it was late afternoon.

Moving to the door, I slowly opened it and peeked out, seeing that the corridor was empty of any guards. I was quite hungry, but I also wanted to find Seraiah.

Closing my door, I started to walk down the corridor, towards the front of the house, slowing down when I came to Seraiah's doorway.

It was slightly ajar, but it didn't sound like there was anyone inside. Knocking gently, I stepped back and waited for a few moments. Then, I pushed the door open and noticed that the room was barely lived in from the tidiness and lack of smell, a change from the night of the ball.

Hearing voices at the entrance of the corridor, I wondered whether I would be confronted about why I was outside Seraiah's room, so I did the only thing I could think of - hide. I moved quickly into the room and shut the door, standing by it, and listened to them speak.

My heart pounded as I came to recognise that there were three of them - Seraiah, Jonah, and Dixon.

Fuck.

They were closing in on Seraiah's room and I was hiding in there from them. I looked around swiftly, eyes landing on the bed, but I couldn't see a way of me fitting under there, unless I somehow crushed my bones to make myself flat enough. I grumbled, looked at the window and decided that it was my only way out.

I opened it outwards and climbed quickly, scrambling to hang on to the frame, whilst attempting to close the window behind me, as the height from the window to the roof below was a little further than I'd hoped. I was fortunate enough that my strength was enough to close it before I landed on my feet just below.

The window was still slightly ajar so I could hear them, when the door of the bedroom opened, and they continued to talk but I was unsure what they were saying, as it was in their native language. I wished I was able to magically understand.

I scanned around the rooftop and saw a ladder hidden in the corner, that led up to the roof above, which meant that was the only way to escape. To my own luck, the ladder was on this side, of the rooftop garden, so I could move swiftly along without being spotted.

Up and over, I went, not taking any chances, and I found myself looking out towards the skyline of London. It looked so close yet it was so far away. We were somewhere north of the city, but I couldn't have guessed where we were, seeing as the journey, I took to get there, was made up of myself and Genie drinking, and I'd not since left.

Walking a little further across towards the front of the house, I saw how majestic the house truly was in the little village that it topped. The houses looked tiny in comparison, even though they were relatively big. The place wasn't symmetrical, most of the houses were to the right, of the view, in an estate of, what I guessed to be, at least five hundred houses, a little shop, a school, of some sorts, and another larger building.

To the left, however, there was one street of houses, whilst a path cut directly through the middle, leading up to a small farm-like house which was surrounded by numerous fields. It must've been one of the first buildings, on the land, as it was older than the rest. A little further down was a park that a few people milled around in with their children.

They must have been successful in keeping themselves hidden away, from outsiders, as the main thing keeping trespassers out were woodlands, that spanned the surroundings of the entire property, that went a good couple of miles back, excluding towards the entrance gate which wasn't so deeply hidden at the other end from the house.

I decided it was time to get down from the roof, if anything, to get out of the blasting heat. I managed to find the ladders, that took ground staff down to the gardens, and descended as quickly and carefully as possible. There were quite a few workers around, but no one noticed me, which I was thankful for.

I walked around to the back of the house, intending to go and get some food, as I hadn't eaten for hours, and the events of the day were finally taking its toll.

Going around the corner, I walked straight into someone, who jogged into me, and we fell to the ground immediately.

Typical.

Seraiah looked down to me as though entranced and his gaze fell to my lips, then back to my eyes and I did the same, feeling that familiar tug. Until a radio crackled from next to my ear and I watched as he sat back, bringing the radio to his mouth and he spoke into it, chuckling.

I frowned as he stood up, holding his hand out to me. I took it and allowed him to bring me to my feet, both of us dusting off.

"Hiding," he said.

"Who?" I frowned.

"You," he answered and I rolled my eyes.

"Absolutely not," I said to him.

Seraiah laughed, "I felt your energy in my room and my window was wide open."

"Partially open."

"So, snooping then?" he challenged and I tutted, not doing a lot to hide the blush on my face, from the embarrassment of it.

"No, I was looking for you," I said truthfully, "I was going to see if you were alright."

"Explain to me then, Arraetta," he said, folding his arms with a cocky look, "how you were looking for me."

I grumbled and moved to push past him, but he grabbed my upper arm and turned in my direction. I looked at him, "am I in trouble?"

"I am sorry if I scared you," he said sincerely.

"You-"

I was cut off when the loud, slightly angered temperament of another came to join us and I looked to see that it was Jonah. He came from the direction of the back door, followed by Dixon and another. Jonah and Seraiah spoke for a long moment, Jonah's eyes swung to me every now and again but neither acknowledged me.

The conversation wasn't full of anger, it was just a discussion, but I felt left out.

"Can you speak in English, please?" I interjected and everyone looked at me. I sighed, "I know I'm not-"

"-Climbing is reckless, ma'am," Jonah interrupted, "I am aware you do not know the rules here but you should come to understand that the more you break, the harsher the consequences are."

I winced, wondering exactly how many *rules* I had broken since I'd arrived. I'd barely done anything, except maybe I was a little rude to Tara, when I stormed out, caused Seraiah to do something strange and climbed a roof to hide the fact that I was trying to hide from them.

"Then, why don't you tell me the rules?" I crossed my arms and looked at him and, if the air wasn't so serious, I'm sure everyone would've laughed. "And, who you are, that might help too."

Jonah didn't seem to be the kind of guy who enjoyed being angry. In fact, I could see some kindness in his eyes. For a man that wouldn't have been much taller than five foot six, he possessed great authority. He nodded to me. "Jonah. I am the head of security here."

"Ah," I whispered. It all made sense.

"This is Alex," Seraiah said, "but we call him Dixon. And, behind you, is Travis."

"Nice to meet you, ma'am," Dixon said to me, whilst Travis just nodded, lingering in the background.

"Okay, well," I said, flicking my eyes between them all and then to Jonah, "I won't climb again."

"If you do, I will have to assign a personal guard," Jonah said.

That was a threat and that would mean no personal freedom.

"I swear," I held my hands up as if to surrender to him and it caused Seraiah to laugh.

"Now that I have found you," Seraiah said, "let us go and talk."

"No more power, Seraiah."

Seraiah bit back jokingly to Jonah before he guided me towards the house. I turned around to look at the three guards, who were already walking away in the opposite direction.

"Can we eat first?" I asked, slightly begging whilst placing a hand on my stomach. On the way into the house, Seraiah spoke to a maid, and I knew he was telling her to bring me some food.

As we went through to the grand hallway, I flagged a door next to the ballroom, that was closed off, and had a guard standing outside it, not paying anyone attention.

"My father's wing," Seraiah told me, tugging me around and up the staircase, "best to keep away."

"Don't you like your father?"

He murmured something in his language, coming to finally answer once we'd reached the upper floor west wing, "there are many things I will fill you in on over time but for now just know that it is best to stay out of that area of the house, even if you are feeling *curious*."

He was right. I was feeling curious, but I could see that even talking about it wasn't something that he wanted to do, and I was able to let that curiosity die easily. On top of that, from the brief moments I'd seen his father, I knew that I didn't want to encounter him anymore than I had to. So, I changed the subject.

"Is Jonah always that much of an arsehole?"

Seraiah chuckled, "sometimes."

Seraiah and I arrived at the room, that we'd exchanged a small hug outside of, before he opened the door. I was pleasantly surprised when we walked into a huge traditional library.

Hundreds of dark oak shelves were filled with thousands of books over two storeys. It was like walking into a whole different world. There were windows that graced some of the mezzanine level, but the one thing that provided most light was a strange fake sun, directly above in the ceiling, which sent down a soft tungsten light. The most mystical thing about it were the incredible floating butterflies that surrounded it in the drifting dust; I knew, instantly, they were not real, but I couldn't figure out how they were projected.

I found myself wandering in deeper, stroking the tips of my fingers against the leather spines of the books before walking around the corner. There, in the centre of the bookshelves, was a small seating area with a couple of brown leather sofas and, to my surprise, a painter's easel, stool, and table of paints.

A squeak above startled me, and I saw the sunlight suddenly turn into a fluorescent moonlight, the butterflies, immediately, shredding their wings and turning into glowing fireflies. The dust settled and disappeared too, leaving just the swarm to gently fly together in rhythm. It was truly breath-taking.

"I do need to get that fixed."

I hadn't realised Seraiah had wandered off into a different direction until he walked back over, balancing a bottle of white wine and two glasses in one hand, whilst he had something small in his other.

"The squeak," he continued, pointing a free finger back up at the moon-light and I looked back up at it.

"It's beautiful."

"Yes, it is something," he placed down the bottle and glasses on a small coffee table, that sat in the middle of the two sofas, "the one back home was much nicer, it would naturally change with the hours but this one I have to do by the power of technology."

He waved around a small device in his hand to indicate what he was talking about, and I laughed a little. He smiled, "wine?"

"Sure." I asked him, "Are you angry at me?"

"No," he answered honestly, "never. I would not be angry with you ever, though I find you pleasantly surprising."

"Because I climbed on the roof?"

"Because of many things," he smiled softly, pouring the wine, but he didn't elaborate and I wondered what he meant. Instead, he handed me a glass and poured the other for himself.

"I don't think anyone likes me here," I said to him, moving to look at his painting.

"I do not think they have a reason to dislike you," he answered, sipping his wine before joining me at the painting, "my mother says you paint."

I looked at his painting with a fondness, almost as though his art was mine, "yes."

"This one I started a while ago," he said. It was as if we were both viewing art in a gallery, "I have only just placed it back up again, maybe to continue it."

"Is it based on a place you know?"

"A place I imagine often but have never been to."

"Why are you trying to paint a place you have never been to?" I asked him curiously, "I find it hard to paint without a reference."

"Well, it was supposed to be Ryazark," he answered, turning to look at me. I gave him a slightly confused look. He chuckled, "ah, Ryazark is the land of the Gods, or at least one of them. I do believe that I have been there in a previous life, but the image is faint in my mind.... do you not paint places you have never been to?"

"Most of mine come in dreams."

"Dreams can carry significant messages," he replied, softly stroking his finger across the canvas, "sometimes the Gods are trying to tell us things."

"Well, mine are pretty messed up," I said, shrugging, "so they're probably just reaffirming that I'm a nutcase."

He looked at me, a mixed expression of curiosity and humour on his face, "or, maybe it is something much deeper. I, for one, have suffered from some of the most surreal dreams but I believe I can see a message within them."

"Like what?" I teased, "did you get a message that I was going to be appearing in your life?"

I connected eyes with him again and that deep sense of longing lingered between us once more. He didn't even have to say anything, his answer was going to be *yes,* I could see that in his expression. I swallowed a little and then turned swiftly, going over to sit down on one of the sofas to give us some space. I knew he was watching me and there was, no doubt, that he felt the same way about me as I did him, but I didn't want to be the one to admit it first.

Seraiah chuckled, "I have had many dreams... about you... in a sense."

"Do I really want to know?" I raised my eyebrows at him as I sipped on the wine to hide my smile.

"The Gods came to me in a dream and told me about my Kindred Spirit."

My Kindred Spirit, even if it means turning my life upside down to find her, will you do that for me? Seraiah's teenage voice whispered in my ears, and I remembered how he'd spoken to the Spirit Nymph. This was the first time I'd heard anyone mention that phrase outside of my hallucinations, which only made me more curious to know what it meant.

"What's a Kindred Spirit?"

Seraiah watched me intrigued. I couldn't get my head around why he often gave me that look, as though he were trying to come up with a way to tiptoe around the subject. His expression changed as he thought for a second more before finally answering, "in essence, it is a connection that is created, through extraordinary circumstances, that cannot be explained except for God."

"Sounds mystical," I joked and his lip twitched, giving me a short look of disapproval. I blushed a little, "so, is it like a... soulmate?"

"In the human sense?" he chuckled, eyeing me, "I suppose so, except a Kindred Spirit is more than just connecting eyes across the room and feeling a spark. It is a heavily fated thing that is incredibly rare."

"Why would you want to be heavily fated to something?"

Seraiah beamed, "I thought it sounded quite romantic."

"What?" I joked, continuing, "*Here's your life, just to let you know, your fate is controlled completely, and this person is the one you have to marry.*"

"I like that idea," he added and our eyes connected again. He sipped his wine, "I, for one, am happy with being a Kindred Spirit."

"How do you know *you're* a Kindred Spirit?" I frowned, extremely confused by the whole thing.

"Apart from the message from the Gods?" he answered, "it is because there are two Kindred Spirit's, in existence, and I am one half of another who is *my* Kindred Spirit, we form, as a whole, what is known as Kindred."

I looked around a little as I tried to take in what he was telling me; it kind of made sense but strangely made none at the same time. If it was like a soulmate, but also nothing like it, then how could it be that there were only two in existence? I understood he said it was rare, but I couldn't wrap my head around what the actual meaning behind it was. What did it mean when he said that he was a Kindred Spirit and that his other *half* was also one?

"I can see you are trying to understand," he smirked, still watching me with that same curiously humoured expression.

"Well, if you are one Kindred Spirit," I said, placing my empty wine glass down on the floor, next to the sofa, "then, who is the second?"

Seraiah raised his eyebrows at me and then chuckled, shaking his head. He turned to the painting behind him, picked up a flat brush, out of the pot of murky water, and dabbed it into some of paint, tutting, "oh, Arraetta, how I would have loved to live as a human."

"What does that mean?" I gasped.

"To be ignorant to one's own fate."

He began to paint, and I thought about his words. I didn't understand whether he was saying that humans ignored their fate or whether he was saying that, because I lived as a human, I was ignoring my own. Was Seraiah saying that *I* was the other Kindred Spirit? That this insane feeling that I had towards him was because of my being one?

Before I could ask my next question, a knock sounded on the door and Seraiah called for the person to enter. It was a maid carrying some food and, instantly, my stomach grumbled at the smell of it. She came and placed it down on the coffee table, that was in front of me, and left without saying another word.

Crispy potatoes, cheese filled filo, hummus, and carrot sticks. I dug in almost immediately, looking like I'd never eaten in my life, and I knew that Seraiah found it amusing. He didn't interrupt, or speak any further, seeming to be painting over the original image on the canvas.

"But, what does a Kindred Spirit mean exactly?" I asked, standing after rapidly shovelling the food down. No doubt I'd have terrible heartburn.

"Divinely connected and divinely powerful," he answered after a short pause.

I almost wanted to shake him into being more coherent because every answer, he gave me, was like something he'd read from an ancient text. Divinely connected and divinely powerful, what did *that* even mean?

"Like... friends?" I coaxed, though I knew that wasn't what it was at all. I blushed. Seraiah burst into laughter, the sound of which echoed around the corners of the library, reddening my face even further. He murmured something under his breath, in his own language, still chuckling, before he cleared his throat and finished whatever he was doing on the canvas. Then, he stepped away and turned to me.

"Come here."

He held his hand out for me to take and I took a moment before moving forward, to accept it, aware my fingers were probably a little greasy. As my hand grasped his, my fingers tingled, as they had done every other time we had touched, and I looked up into his enchanting chestnut eyes, time slowing just a fraction. It felt like my soul was on fire, with the need for him, and I swallowed to attempt to stay in the present, rather than disappear into the deep carnal thoughts in my mind. Naturally, he tugged me forward, to pull me in front of him, until I was looking directly at the canvas. It had dark green, ancient symbols in the centre.

"You ruined a perfectly good painting," I whispered, before gasping a little as he placed his free hand onto my hip. He twisted his other to guide my palm towards the image, bringing my fingers to touch the cool, wet paint. My heartbeat rapidly, in the centre of my chest, as his soft fingertips stroked the back of my hand, placing themselves into the crevices between my own fingers. My small hand was covered by his and his other hand slithered under the hem of my top, so he could squeeze my hip softly. In a normal situation this may have felt rushed, but I wanted nothing more than for him to throw me over the side of the sofa and have his way with me; I burnt for it.

Seraiah's mouth came down to linger next to my left ear, his breath tickling my skin and I knew that he was teasing me. "You smell good, Arraetta."

"That's the food."

"Hm," he replied, still so close to my ear, "close your eyes."

I slowly allowed my lids to close, wondering what was about to take place until I heard more whispering, from Seraiah, but, this time, in that strange archaic language I'd heard in the alley, before I blacked out, somewhat similar but also different to his day-to-day one. At first, things felt surreal and uncomfortable, as though the air in the room was taking a new form, before Seraiah's whispers grew quieter and quieter and everything settled into serene peace.

NINE

I heard an elevated moan of pleasure. A woman's pleasure. My own.

I immediately opened my eyes, the feeling of my own damp skin against another's, whilst my sight was covered by a curtain of delicate golden locks. Heightened breaths left my mouth as my hands grasped onto the back, of the person I was lying with, whilst his own groans entwined themselves with my own. The senses of my body were gradually flourishing fibre by fibre as the soft aches of my hamstrings captured my awareness. My legs were being pushed up and back around the hips of the man. I could feel something deep inside me, moving back and forth in an incredibly magical rhythm, each thrust drawing me closer to pure elation. I felt the man lift himself out of my arms and I looked him directly in the face. I was staring into the enchanting eyes of Seraiah, both of us, once again, speaking without saying a word to one another.

Seraiah leant back down again, driving himself deeper and harder, each pulse as blissful as the next. But it was what I saw, above Seraiah, that took my breath away the most; Seraiah and I were one with each other in an expanse of twinkling stars, somewhere out in the universe. Divinely connected. Colours of blues and pinks and purples and golds painted in waves around glistening galaxies and planets that distantly watched us. Applauding us.

Seraiah's hands tickled my hips as they moved around to hold and hoist me back to a sitting position; my eyes once again connected to his, the universe forgotten. He bounced me against him, as though I was weightless, an exhilarating rebounding sensation echoing each movement, below my waistline. Both of us entwined as though nothing else was ever meant to be.

Seraiah leant in to kiss me and I instinctively reciprocated, the two of us tasting everything - and nothing - through our tongues. The kissing came to a stop as both of us neared a climax and, as we opened our eyes, our gazes connecting, both of us were glowing neon blue and gold as one. His hand gripped my waist, and he rocked me up and down. Harder, faster. My back arched, the orgasm peaking until the warmth suddenly disappeared and only a tingling cold lingered; the facade of the experience falling back to the normality of a tranquil cool library, my hand still lingering on the easel before me.

Seraiah moved his hand from mine, and I pulled my own paint-stained one away. My eyes flickered to the painting, seeing how our hands had formed a strangely entwined print on the canvas. Seraiah cleared his throat, walked over to a back section of the room, and returned with an old rag. His eyes did not leave mine as he came to stand before me, picked up my hand and started to clean it.

"Do you now understand?" he asked, the damp cloth tingling the creases of my palm.

"I…" I murmured, clearing my throat, "what was that?"

"That is Kindred," he answered, eyes drifting down to my hand, "it is the divine connection between Kindred Spirits, or so I believe."

"It felt…" I trailed off.

"Real?" he humoured, lifting one of his hands up to stroke my cheek, "I am sure that the reality of it is much better than a fantastical dream, wouldn't you agree?"

"But, we were..." I gulped, not even able to say out loud *we were having sex*, "what does that mean for us?"

"If you have not figured that out yet, then I would suggest you take some time to do so," he laughed, still massaging my hand, then he removed the cloth, leaving a clean palm. He threw the rag down, next to his paints, before returning to where he had left his glass of wine and necked the final drop.

"It didn't feel like..." I looked over at him, "it didn't feel like we were, you know... having sex."

"Then, what did you think it felt like?" he asked indulgently, seemingly enjoying how much this was making me squirm. "I can tell you that it felt as though our souls were meant for nothing more and nothing less. Having met you now, Arraetta, I can tell you that it is becoming harder to fight the urge."

My face reddened, but in a way that I knew exactly what he meant because my own urges grew stronger with every day I spent in his presence. It wasn't just the feeling of wanting to be with him sexually, but it was a need to be with him all the time, as though being apart from him was painful.

"I guess for me," I replied, looking at him, "it felt... it felt ethereal for want of a better word. It didn't feel like... sex, well, it was like it, kind of, but it was..."

I stopped to think of a better conclusion, of my sentence, which made him smirk. He watched me through darkened eyes, "go on."

"I suppose I was going to say," I answered, connecting eyes with him, "it felt like the most satisfying feeling, yet now I feel as though I never felt anything at all."

"I like to see it like a fragmented memory," Seraiah said, stepping towards me once again, "as though when we are not mortal beings, we are free to be with each other in that way, entwined as one."

I flushed even more, moving away from him, towards the sofa, but I stopped as he caught my hand in his, "some souls are destined to die and be reborn over and over as part of cataclysmic events."

"Cataclysmic?" I turned to look at him and watched as he moved his smooth hand to cup my chin. He stroked my cheek tenderly with his thumb.

"Us meeting again is one."

I was sure the astonishment was clear on my face as he said this and he quietly laughed to himself as he removed his hand, watching my reaction. I wanted to know more; first, how did he really know this? Second, why would we not have just remained in that state, for eternity, if we were fated to be one like that?

"Arraetta, what happens now will simply be fated," he said, "and, I know that this fate has been worth the great sacrifices we have made to be here."

"Sacri..." I trailed off, remembering what the young Seraiah had said to the Spirit Nymph. I wondered whether that had anything to do with the sacrifices he was talking about, "Seraiah, I... I saw you when you were a little boy, by a windmill."

"If you are talking of the Wicker Windmill," he said, "I have been there a great many times."

"There was a nymph," I added and then he raised his eyebrows, nodding as the memory must've come to him.

"That was you?"

"I... I don't think it was me," I shook my head, "I think I was in her eyes."

"I forgot about that," Seraiah smiled, "I suppose I may have caused a bit too much destruction to find you then."

"Seraiah, I don't know why you're here, or what happened," I answered honestly, "but, I don't think that you asking a water creature to help you find me caused whatever to happen."

"Let us hope you're right," he answered, "whenever we go home, I'll be sure to go by the river to speak with her… or maybe I should just thank you."

"I wasn't the nymph!" I tutted mockingly and he laughed.

"I don't know, the nymph was cute," he wiggled his eyebrows and I smacked the back of my hand against his arm. He feigned pain, rubbing himself, to add melodrama to the situation, and we both burst into laughter. It was nice for us to both laugh so wholesomely. We hadn't really done so since the ball.

"Seraiah," I said and he looked at me to urge me to continue, "why are you here?"

"In this room?" he joked and I tutted at him. His lip twitched but I could see there was sadness in his eyes, "it is not a tale for tonight."

"Some other time maybe?" I asked, full of hope, but there was still a slight hesitancy in Seraiah as he slowly nodded in agreement. I couldn't understand the apprehension; what was so bad that he couldn't tell me about it? Or was the subject so hurtful to talk about that he couldn't bear the thought of it.

He checked his watch and whistled, "wow, it is late."

"What time is it?"

"Gone eleven."

"What?" I gasped, "but, how?"

"That experience, we probably would have been in there for a while," he answered and then stood back, "a bit like when we paint and just zone out, time just flies."

"I should probably get some sleep."

"Let me walk you to your room," he offered and I agreed without hesitation.

As we walked down the corridor together, there was a rising feeling of giddiness in my chest, alongside a curious revelation that was overcoming me; the feeling of being alone in this world beginning to disappear. I was finally able to fit in with people who understood the things I had to go through, and I had just found out that I was, essentially, in a fated relationship with the most handsome and caring man.

The journey back to the east wing was far too short, both of us walking, peacefully, in each other's company, hands lingering close. Soon, we were standing outside the door to my room. It felt as though he was dropping me off on a first date.

I placed my hand on the cool brass door handle, not moving to open the door and turned my face to look at him. Seraiah leaned over me, in all his glorious splendour, placing his arm on the frame of the double door, eyes connected with my own. He was at least ten inches taller than I was and it made me feel so protected, as though nothing could move through him to get to me.

"Traspea, Arraetta," Seraiah murmured softly, a charming smile curling at the corner of his delicate lips.

"What does that mean?" I whispered

He chuckled, "it means good night."

"Traspea," I repeated, my voice still hushed.

"You need to roll your 'r'," he said and repeated the word, emphasising the sound, "traspea."

"Traspea," I repeated and he nodded, my pronunciation correct.

I kind of hoped, at that moment, he'd kiss me; I believed that there was a mutual feeling of something growing and that, with a kiss, we'd have confirmed that. But, instead, as though saying goodnight to a child, he leaned down and pecked my forehead before stepping away. Then he bowed his head and walked down the corridor.

"Traspea," I whispered, watching him near his room, at the other end of the hallway.

"Traspea!" he bellowed back, slightly jolting a guard with the force, and turned to throw me a wink before he walked into his room. I stifled a laugh as I hung around in the quiet hallway, for a few seconds longer, in the hope that, maybe, Seraiah would come out of his room just to speak with me again. The memory of what had taken place in the library echoed in the corners of my mind as I walked into my quiet and lonely room, but it gave me comfort as I prepared myself to go to bed.

Following our encounter in the library, spending time with Seraiah was all I wanted and the thought of it had kept me awake, for a fair few hours, before my body forced my brain to shut off to allow me to rest. I wanted to know everything that Seraiah knew about Kindred Spirits, *about us*, and to experience our entwining for real, not just in our heads. And, maybe he knew more about my parents, about how my pa had died and what had come of my home realm. Maybe if Seraiah could spare the time to teach me his native language, I could read the book word-for-word and truly immerse myself to try and understand.

As I left the bedroom, Kadey was swiftly moving down the hallway towards me. From the look on her face, she wasn't expecting that I'd be ready before she arrived.

She swiftly curtsied, "Your Grace, I-"

"-I'm going to have breakfast," I informed her, curtseying a little back, "and, then I'm going to find Seraiah and-"

"-I'm afraid His Royal Highness has left," she interjected and the bright, gleeful nature in me dropped. For the entirety of the morning as I'd got ready, I'd been so excited about seeing him and, suddenly, Kadey had ripped that enthusiasm out from beneath me.

"Left?" I squeaked.

"Yes, ma'am," she nodded, offering me a look of understanding, "he flew to Italy today with His Majesty, they have gone on business to the vineyard."

"He didn't say," I whispered. It also meant that, without Seraiah there, I was alone as Genie had left, and wasn't speaking to me any longer, and I hadn't seen Freddie since earlier the day before.

"I apologise I was not here last night to dress you," Kadey moved the conversation on to distract me from my woes, "I finished my shift around ten o'clock, but tonight I shall happily work later-"

"-Don't be silly," I smiled, "you know I'm not in need of someone to dress me."

The way she looked me up and down told me otherwise. I suppose I had hastily dressed in the hopes of Seraiah being there to talk to; I had so many more questions for him.

"There shall be another maid starting soon," she said, "it is usual for you to have at least two, at any time, but currently it is only I who is tending to you."

"Do you ever get a day off?" I laughed.

"Ma'am, if you don't mind me speaking out of turn," Kadey said, "I am hoping that you may choose me as your First Lady once you become queen."

I choked on air as she said the word *queen*, not even having had a single thought about that being a possibility. But with the connection between Seraiah and I - the Kindred Spirit connection - it would mean that we would marry, that I would be his wife and thus his queen. At least that was the gist I got from the day before. The thought of it gave me all sorts of strange new feelings; uncontrollable desire, excitement, nervousness and being completely overwhelmed by the prospect. In another way, I also wanted to fight the feelings because I didn't believe I was made just to be a housewife. Yet, I wouldn't just be a housewife - I'd been a queen, a ruler.

"You seem surprised," she laughed.

"A little."

"It would be the greatest honour for me," Kadey offered me a smile, which I returned as we walked around the corner into the grand hallway.

I had half forgotten that Kadey was even talking to me about her want to be my First Lady as I was caught up in the thoughts of being queen.

"What would it mean?" I asked her, bringing myself back to the conversation.

"In our realm," Kadey continued, "the First Lady is the highest maid of honour to work for the queen; it would mean being your closest companion, apart from Lady Genevieve, of course, and you would be able to confide in me for anything you would require."

"That sounds like what you do now." We came to the door of the dining room where I usually ate breakfast.

"It is with much more responsibility," she answered and I could see that she was very passionate about this.

"Why do you want to do this?" I asked her, "don't you want to go out and make a career for yourself elsewhere?"

"No, ma'am," she shook her head, "working for the royal family is something I have wanted to do since I was a little girl... Well, I was obsessed with becoming a princess first, but after that."

I laughed, "well, we can swap if you'd like, I'm quite good at cleaning."

"Maybe not so much at dressing," Kadey answered jokingly and then gasped, throwing her hand to her mouth as though she'd offended me. I burst into laughter as she continued, "I'm sorry, Your Grace."

"Kadey, come on," I shook my head at her, glad she'd lightened my mood again after finding out that Seraiah had abandoned me, "if you are going to be my First Lady, you'll have to make sure you keep your sense of humour."

"Kadey!"

Both of us looked over towards the corridor, on our right, to see

Mrs Finch, the head of house, standing at the top of the staircase that led down to the kitchens. Mrs Finch, who I assumed hadn't noticed me when she'd called out, curtsied immediately, "apologies, ma'am. Kadey, could you please help Jeramiah in the kitchen?"

"Yes," Kadey nodded, curtsied to me and then rushed to the kitchens. I turned to the dining room and pushed the door open, being greeted by one of the male servants, Cedric, who bowed gently as I entered.

"Morning, Cedric."

"Good morning, ma'am," he replied politely, "the usual?"

"Yes, thank you," I replied as I sat on a chair he'd pulled out for me. The usual for me was a cup of coffee and porridge, though I knew I had the option to have whatever I liked. Genie often would have fruit and yoghurt, whilst Freddie would have a mixture of things throughout the week, most often opting for a good hearty full English breakfast. I hadn't had the pleasure of dining with Seraiah at breakfast yet, but I'd guessed his choice would be like Freddie's, what with them being so close to one another.

This was the first morning I'd dined alone, and it felt strange being in such a large room, sitting alone at a table big enough for ten people.

It wasn't so much the pressures of dining alone, but more the fact that my whirling thoughts still took over my mind. First to be addressed was that Seraiah had left for Italy without telling me he was going somewhere. It stung that he hadn't wanted to mention it or invite me along with him. It wasn't as though that was something you would forget.

Second, if I was going to be with Seraiah, as we were intended, then, as Kadey said, it was likely I *would* be the next queen and that frightened me even more. Yes, I suppose if I had grown up in my home realm, I would understand that it was in essence my duty to govern, but I had only known the life of being a human, and a semi-normal one at that. I didn't have a clue about how to rule, nor did I understand how I could suddenly be a wife.

And to top it off, the only person I could confide in about my troubles was Genie, and she wasn't around.

I just wanted to shout out to her about everything that I had learned, thus far, that I was somewhat growing madly in love with a man, I'd hardly spoken to, and that I finally understood how she felt about Freddie. I was just weeks behind her. I wanted to tell her that maybe if it came to it, as I believe our fates told us, I would marry Seraiah in a heartbeat.

Consumed in the depths of my thoughts, I spent most of the morning wandering the hallways of the house wondering what I could do. The one time I wanted to have my phone, I didn't have it because it was still tucked away in a drawer at my flat and all I wanted to do was call Genie and ask her to come back. Maybe they had a house phone, but I was too wary to ask in case they listened into my pleading calls from another line.

Maybe Genie and Freddie had gone with Seraiah to Italy also and they were all together sipping wine in straw hats and white outfits, basking in the glow of the summer sun. It sounded nice but envy wasn't my colour, so I brushed the thoughts aside in the hopes it wasn't the case.

Sometime mid-morning, I found myself in the library, staring at the somewhat spoiled canvas that still stood in the easel, dried with my handprint and the faint fingertips of Seraiah. I caressed the stains as I imagined what had taken place the night before, careful not to fragment the images. I allowed myself to dip into the memory deeper, hearing those echoes of moans, my mouth watering at the feeling that pulsated between my legs.

"Seraiah," I murmured and then cleared my throat, jolting myself out of it. I bit my lip and then giggled, looking around as though someone was in the room with me, watching my solo frolicking. I ran my finger over the canvas, over the cotton humps of the faint rolling hills Seraiah had created, thinking about what I could paint on the canvas. On the table next to me there were a couple of pencils, and I chose a light one, beginning to get to work.

I first began to craft the hands into something more realistic, doing my best to imagine Seraiah's skin without dipping into the desire I felt, sketching every little detail before adding in my nails. I drew the symbols Seraiah had painted, leaving the slightly broken one as a tattoo on top of Seraiah's hand before moving onto the rolling hills, doing my best to depict a place I'd never been to. Then, I decided to get some more paint brushes, from the back of the room, where I'd seen Seraiah go off to get the cloth, before returning. I'm unsure how long I worked on the hands for, followed by the hills, but I guessed hours had begun to pass as they always did when I painted.

I wondered whether there were any books in the library on Ryazark, maybe like the book that Tara had shown me. Surely, they would have had something to remember and honour the place in the vast space I stood in. I took the time to skim my fingers over the spines, feeling at the little indented symbols on them that represented the language they spoke.

Most books on the lower level, at first, seemed to be adaptations of our own as a few of them stated the authors name in a standard spelling but inside, however, those books were purely written in their own language. I noticed that they had a book by Jane Austen and the similarities in the layout of the name told me that it was 'Pride and Prejudice'. I wondered whether I would be able to translate it, so I threw the book to the floor and continued onwards in a hunt for more works.

I scaled the ladder that led up to the mezzanine level, doing the same technique of looking at the books. All of these were much different in shape and size; many were handmade books and a lot of them looked to be around hundreds of years old. One book was falling apart at its seams, and I scattered a few pages out of it as I peered in. Immediately, I threw the pages back in as neatly as possible and hoped that I hadn't destroyed something important.

Onwards I went until I came across a gold-laced glass case that encased a handcrafted A3 sized book, which was carved from wood and ingrained in the most beautiful ancient symbols. On the cabinet was a small knob with a keyhole underneath and not much to my own surprise, it was locked. My interest in finding a book on Ryazark left immediately and I was on a mission to find the key in no time.

My first port of call was to check underneath and on top of the cabinet, which was top and tailed with gold, but it wasn't there. I wandered around the mezzanine to see whether it would be anywhere in a little pocket but there was no luck. Beginning to climb down the ladder, I scoured the tops of shelves until I saw at the back of the room, a wooden door.

The door was well hidden by bookshelves, and I had a slight inkling that maybe the key was kept in there. I wandered around the cases and stood at the door, placing my hand onto the brass handle and twisted it. Expecting it to be little more than a little study nook, I was surprised to find that it was a dimly lit concrete staircase that led down somewhere.

TEN

Creeping down step-by-step, my heart raced in my chest, as though I was about to sneak in on someone or find something terrible. Maybe there was a dungeon full of skeletons, or maybe it led to the servants' quarters, if there were any in the house at all. At the bottom of the staircase, there was a slightly ajar wooden door, like the one in the library, with sunlight creeping through it.

I gently pushed it open, and my eyes widened as I took in another space - a large suite that looked much more lived in than any of the other spaces in the house. I knew, immediately, it was Seraiah's just from the way it smelt. It was a modern space with soft curtains that covered large windows, ahead from the door.

To the left of the room was a wooden desk with a lot of paperwork thrown all over it. To the right, in an alcove, there were two leather sofas, with clothes on top of one, and to the left-hand side of that alcove was a table full of all sorts of strange things, including a crystal ball, that mimicked the same colour as the moon. Other things were on the table, beakers with strange liquids in them, ink and feather, paints and paintbrushes and rags. Stepping forward, I could see that there was also a book that had lots of writing in it, in a mixture of languages - presumably Seraiah's language, English and even Latin, from what I could tell.

On the back wall, behind the table, was a beautiful painting of the stars that mirrored that of what I had seen the evening before, when I'd shared a moment, with Seraiah in the library. I wondered whether I was able to bring it alive there and then, so I leant up on my tiptoes, over the desk, and placed my hand on it, closing my eyes. A few moments later, I peeked open one eye to see that nothing had changed, and I sighed, stepping back.

I fingered at the book for a few moments, gently folding the fragile paper to try and make some sort of understanding about what was written by him. From the English words he used, he was experimenting with something and, sometimes, he drew things - odd shapes and circles that I didn't understand. I opened it towards the front of the book, seeing a large golden orb, that was on the front, with large rings that surrounded it.

It was as though a painter; a scientist and an astrologist had come together to create something.

My eyes immediately landed on the orb, that sat next to it on the table, wondering whether that was what Seraiah had been drawing. Before my curiosity could get the better of me, I felt a very strange wave of energy push through me and I squeaked, jumping backward as the curtains lit up. I was confused at how the sunlight was so close, causing my body to tingle from an unnatural vibration.

I stepped up to the curtain and gently pulled it open, shocked at what was on the other side of the glass. There, through the floor to ceiling window, was no sunlight or exterior but, instead, it was a large orb, almost the height of the ballroom I'd been in on the first day of my visit. And, just like the picture I had seen in Seraiah's depiction, gentle rings surrounded it, pulsating slowly. Unlike Seraiah's picture, it wasn't as vivacious and was more like a very dull colour of gold.

Although I had no idea what it was, I could feel how my body felt truly alive by just being around it - as though I was feeding off its energy. I wandered back to the book and flicked to see if there were any more drawings and stopped when I came to something more distinctive.

It was the dome of electricity that surrounding the entire community. I just didn't understand what it was there for and the entire segment, of that part of the book, was in Seraiah's own language, so I couldn't decipher anything from it.

Maybe I would find a way to bring it into conversation, the next time I spoke to Seraiah, so that I could ask him about it.

I placed the book back to the page it was originally on and wandered over to the desk, smiling as I took in the bookshelves, at the back, that had a variety of ornaments and pictures on.

One of Seraiah's jackets was lazily hung on the edge of his worn leather office chair. I looked at the paperwork, most of it looked boring from receipts to a diary to newspapers. It was obvious he'd been there recently and must've worked there a lot. I fingered at the papers, stopping when I came across another drawing underneath one of the small piles.

Sketched with absolute precision was a drawing of me.

I hadn't spent enough time with Seraiah for him to have drawn an image so intricately of me, but it was as though I had sat for him whilst he had done it. I was lying down, clothes messy with a smile on my reddened face, looking straight up out of the picture.

I didn't know how I felt about it; it was beautiful but also very *intimate*. I had barely any time to get to know Seraiah; he hadn't really told me a thing about him. Save that of a few things at the ball, the showcase of his power in the garden, and who we were to each other. Yet, he was drawing pictures of me as though he had known me forever.

I had one part of me - the part that was falling madly for him - that wanted me to scream *I love you even though I've just met you* at him whilst the other part of me, the stubborn and on guard part, wanted me to stay reserved and cautious.

I slid the picture back underneath and took a deep breath, remembering my original task was to find the key. I pulled open a drawer full of paperwork and pens, shuffled around but didn't find a thing. Then, the same with the next drawer - nothing.

Then, finally, as if my prayers had been answered, I found a little box and, curiously, opened it to see a very small key that would perfectly fit inside the cabinet. I hoped that my curiosity over the book would be worth all the hassle.

I headed back over to the curtain and peered through one last time, frowning at the shiny object, in front of me, and began to rack my brain about what exactly it was for. From the feeling I got in the room, it felt like it was a ball of energy. The only thing I could think, out of everything that I had somewhat learnt about Seraiah, is that it would be used to power his Rapidfire. I only guessed that because, if it was like what powered through my own veins, I had already come to learn, through the battles over the years, that I thrive off and needed energy, especially electricity.

In a way, the other thing, that the orb could have some connection to, is the dome as electricity in that greater form would need something big to power it, or so I would presume. It would make it some form of generator, or conductor.

Back up to the mezzanine, of the library, I wandered over to the cabinet and prayed for the key to fit in. It did. *Click.* The key turned, to the right, and I twisted the little knob at the same time; the glass door opened.

Gently, I removed the book from its enclosure, closed the glass door and sat down on the floor against the wooden balustrade.

Leaning the book on my thighs, I stroked the cover before opening it to reveal a black and white sketch on the first page of someone, with their eyes closed, that I did not know. Across their face were similarly ingrained patterns, to that of Seraiah, in a strange archaic language that I couldn't comprehend.

I opened to the next page and was pleasantly surprised when I came across an almost instruction manual, of sorts. Although I could not understand what the text said, I could guess from the pictures what it was trying to say. It was a book on how to use Rapidfire. Each page gave it away as there were more intricate images, including ways to hold your hands, with different drawings of them to showcase a different meaning. Another part seemed to show how to use different ingredients, almost like a witch's handbook, whilst other pages seemed to be spells - although I couldn't say for sure because they were all in the same language.

I sighed, wishing that I could understand what it said. I had to find a way to learn.

The door to the library opened and I sank against the balcony to hide myself.

"Arraetta?"

My eyes widened as I slowly placed the book down and peered over the top, looking down at Tara, who was looking up towards me. She smiled, "my dear, we have been invited to tea with Sheika."

"Sheika?" I frowned.

"Yes, our shaman," she informed me, "come."

Did queen's get invited? I thought they normally just went wherever they wished. Either way, I didn't have much choice in the matter, so I told her I'd be a minute and she went to wait for me in the corridor.

I threw the book into the casing, hid the key behind the curtain on the window shelf above, and went to join her.

Tara didn't speak to me as we went up to meet Sheika the Shaman.

I didn't sense that she was angry, from what had happened the day before, but I wouldn't have been surprised if she was. Instead, she said hello to some people every now and again but remained in her own thoughts.

We were guarded by two nameless guards, who followed behind at a close distance, ready to take me out, if they needed to.

Tara led me up a long path towards the old farmhouse, that I'd seen from the roof, of which was surrounded by fields, with a large forest to the back. It was the epitome of a witch's hut. Wind-brushed trinkets that hung from the veranda, at the front, and a table of incense that let off a pungent, earthy smell. Although not necessarily unpleasant, the stench stung my eyes.

As though expecting us, a short older podgy woman, with white hair and an abundance of wrinkles, appeared at the door in gypsy robes. The one thing that stood out the most was the prominent lines on her face, like how my own Rapidfire would show, except hers were almost like scars. She beamed from ear to ear, curtseying ever so gently to Tara, before the two exchanged a hug.

"Good afternoon, Sheika," Tara greeted.

"Your Majesty, I am glad you came," Sheika smiled at Tara before she turned to me, flinging her arms out as if to engulf me in a hug. Instead, she studied me at arm's length, "well, you are just beautiful."

"Oh," I blushed, taken aback, "thank you. I'm Arraetta."

"I know who you are," she smiled brightly, pinching my cheek a little, "it wouldn't be just anyone who could bring a smile to our prince's face."

I reddened further as she turned to look at Tara and asked us both to follow her inside.

Much like the outside of the house, the inside was like a spiritual shrine, with many crystals, antiques, dream catchers, more incense and even a witch's altar. It seemed like Sheika was a hoarder and I wondered whether many of her things were from her home. In the corner of the hallway, a cat was lazily purring, but it was the yapping of a little dog that took me by surprise; a cute little Jack Russell, who jumped at my legs for attention as I entered. I knelt to and stroked him as he whined at me. I loved dogs, so I was easily distracted.

"Arraetta?" I was called from another room and saw they had already moved on. I petted the dog, one last time, before going through, seeing them both waiting in the lounge. At the table, Sheika sat with a crystal ball resting on top of it, to its right side, and an empty chair opposite, whilst Tara perfectly perched on the edge of the sofa.

"Come, my dear," Sheika said, encouragingly, pointing to the chair. I walked over cautiously and took the seat opposite her, "do not worry, I do not bite. Do not let a little magic scare you."

"What are you going to do?" I asked, nodding at the crystal ball.

Sheika barked with laughter, "no, my child, we are not using that. Unfortunately, I do not have a place for it, so it lives on the table. Now, give me your hand."

She offered her soft old hands and I gently placed mine into them, wondering what was going to happen. Sheika closed her eyes, for a short moment, before opening them and looking at me.

"You must relax, Your Highness," she said and I nodded, allowing the tension, that had unconsciously built, to leave my body.

"I'm sorry, I just don't know what you are doing."

"Well, I suppose that would make sense," she smiled and then spoke to Tara for a short moment before standing up and leaving the room. Tara was reading a book; she looked up to offer me a smile before returning to it.

The room fell into a gentle silence apart from the odd turn of a page and the ticking clock, whilst in the distance there was a clattering of cups and a hum of a whistle kettle. I had a lot of questions I wanted to ask Tara, but the atmosphere made me feel like this wasn't the right place.

My thoughts turned to Seraiah, and I wondered what he was up to, whether he was thinking about me and whether Italy was somewhere he loved to go to. I wanted to make sure that when the opportunity arose that I would be able to go there with him. I could imagine us both sipping on Negroni's, with our already golden skin even more sun kissed. I'd be wearing a short floral summer dress and a white hat, and he'd be wearing a white shorts and t-shirt two-piece. I could even feel the warmth of the summer sun on my face as I imagined us walking barefoot down the beach together.

But the warmth of the imaginary trip disappeared as the shuffling of Sheika's feet brought me back into the room and I looked to see her carrying over a tray of tea. She placed it down on a coffee table, giving a cup to Tara before she picked up the other two and sat back down. She placed a cup in front of me – something green and murky – and I winced at the strong smell of it.

"What's that?" I asked, apprehensive.

"My dear, please just drink the tea," she half-demanded and her stubbornness really was almost unable to be argued against. I picked up the cup, my eyes shifting between it and Sheika and lifted it to my nose, inhaling the putrid smell and grimaced.

"What's in it?" I whispered.

"It does not matter," she replied, tutting, "you are as stubborn as Seraiah, this will help us get the answers we seek. It is not poisonous. Now, drink."

I nodded, slowly, before sipping it, trying not to heave at the disgusting taste, allowing it to trickle down my throat. A few more gulps and Sheika lifted her hand, removing the cup from my grasp. She placed my hands back in hers before closing her eyes and taking a deep breath. I had wondered why Sheika didn't drink the tea also, if it allowed her to see what she needed to, but I came to notice that she was trying to calm me. That's when the effects of the tea engulfed me, and my body began to attempt to fight the comatose state it was falling into. My vision fractured.

"I- I need some fresh air," I immediately stood up and stumbled, dashing out of the room until I made it out to the front of the house. Outside, although the air was fresh, the sudden hit of it turned my stomach and I vomited to the side of the veranda. The constant motion of the bile flowing from my mouth tore at my insides. After a bit, feeling the flow stop, I grumbled, wiping my mouth with the back of my wrist, and breathing deeply in the hopes that I'd never have to go through drinking that tea again. The world resettled around me, eerily quiet.

I looked up to the trees, noticing that there was no breeze or chirping birds; something didn't feel right. Stepping backward, I saw that none of the trinkets were twinkling, and the incense smoke was darting up towards the sky. A crackle of crumbling thunder distantly echoed above, and I jolted in its direction, seeing that the once-blue sky had turned ashen grey, with a whirling of clouds forming in one portion. I stepped forward, lifting my head to see more of it, but stopped as I could hear a tuneless piercing note. The horror of it rose, trickling a shiver up my spine. Another rupture above, the unmelodious tone reverberating with it, followed by a strange glitch that seemed to jump time. A woman screamed and the sound rebounded around my ears. I ran towards the end of the path, the wind dramatically rising and becoming unbearable, but stopped before I reached the end of it. A man ran around the corner, green eyes piercing through my soul. I watched as a claw of darkness pierced his flesh and he yelled out in pain. The trickles of that same black sludge, from my dream, was clawing its way through the sockets of his eyes, consuming him from the inside out and back again. I couldn't move, but I felt as if my body was trembling in fear.

A flash of flaxen lightning above, and my eyes darted up. The clouds seemed to whine and then scream horrendously in pain; the ground shook beneath me as another ripple of thunder rang out above and the sound of a whipping crackle blasted.

"Arraetta!" roared a panicked voice; it was Seraiah. My heart bounded against my chest as I managed to find my feet again, searching for him, but the path kept getting longer and longer, swallowing my calls for him. Ahead, a tunnel of darkness began to form and, though I tried to move from it, it was no use. I screeched, shutting my eyes to prevent the void from consuming me.

Silence.

All except for my breath, which was ricocheting out of control, reverberating in the hollow space that surrounded me. The thud of my heart rose, in my chest, as I braced myself to be pounced on by something unimaginably fearful. My body shivered as I felt the presence of another, their body just in front of my own and no matter how brave I encouraged myself to be, nothing would make me look at what it was.

"Hey," my eyes bolted open at the soothing sound of Seraiah's voice, as his hand was caressing my forearm. I was in a room of pure white light with nothing there, except for an altar covered in beautiful flowers of all colours, shapes, and sizes. Seraiah stood in a cleanly pressed white suit, with a blue and gold flower pinned to the chest pocket.

"Are you both ready?"

I turned my head to see another older man, dressed in white robes, standing by us, a large archaic black book in his hands. It was as though this man had appeared by magic.

I realised that he was the celebrant, and this was our wedding.

"Wait, I-" I gasped, immediately turning to Seraiah as though to say *I'm not ready yet* but cut myself short as a shudder tickled my spine. The ravishing gent that was Seraiah was no longer in existence, it was just the shell of him, his eyes were the same as I'd seen by the lake - pure darkness - whilst his Rapidfire shone through, but only in pure black streaks. Seraiah stumbled forward. It was as though he was possessed by a demonic being. Black blood trickled over the shoulders of his suit, drenching it as it poured down onto the floor. I stepped back in fear, breathing heavily, seeing the white walls of the space begin to turn to that same ashen grey. Like a sandstorm, the black liquid started to consume the space and I screamed, moving backward faster as Seraiah's being was devoured by it.

"Arraetta, save me!" he begged, though his voice was shrouded by something hellish. Then he jumped towards me, a loud hollow roar reverberating, from his chest, causing a cacophony of deafening sounds to rebound against the corners of the indistinguishable room. I attempted to scream, edging backward to stop him from tackling me and covered my eyes.

Just as though a bag of dust had been thrown on top of me, a sharp breeze hit my body. All began to settle again.

I trembled, once again trying not to look in case something more ungodly was awaiting me. The wind died down and the cold lifted as warmth began to tickle my arms. Light pierced through the skin of my hands, and I gently peeked through the gaps of my fingers to see where I'd landed. I moved my hands in awe and found myself sitting by a building in the same mystical place I had seen in my dreams only weeks before. I grasped the wall and pulled myself to my feet, noticing that even as a human adult I was still quite small in comparison to the scale of the place. It was not necessarily made for giants, but it easily felt as if even the smallest person here would be at least seven feet tall.

Except there was no one around, not a soul, just the quiet and calm cobbled streets of The Cre-este.

I sneaked around the corner and found my eyes gazing up to the large palace, that peaked at the top of a hill. By the looks of it, it would take at least ten minutes to get there; it was a humongous place. No wonder they didn't like me running around on my own as a little girl.

As I was about to step forward to head towards the building, I could hear a giggle resounding nearby and I looked around for the culprit, my eyes soon landing on the back of a little girl. She was heading to the oriental garden. It was me.

"Wait!" I called and picked up my feet, running after her as fast as I could, but she didn't notice me and I watched as she hunted for her friend, speaking in a language not too dissimilar from Seraiah's. Once she disappeared around the rocks, I looked up to see, not more than two miles ahead, the cascading waterfalls that surrounded the entire city. Almost like a fortress protected by monstrous walls, except these were incredibly serene and only faintly made a splattering sound.

"Beautiful, isn't it?"

If I hadn't been so on edge, I might've screamed but my body didn't allow anything to leave my vocal cords. I spun around to see a tall, Viking-like man, with a chunky grey beard and soft loving eyes. This was Ivan - my pa.

"You… you're…" I stumbled, eyes prickling with tears as I was so overwhelmed by seeing him, needing him to confirm it to me there and then.

"Your father," my pa nodded with proud watery eyes, "oh, how you have grown to be so beautiful, my little Arraetta."

He held his arms out to me and I immediately moved into his grasp, my head resting mid-belly, my arms barely stretching around his waist. He felt how I guessed he would, squishy but firm, and his slightly musty smell overpowered my senses. I cried into him for a long moment.

The sound of pattering feet jolted us away, from each other, and we watched as little me ran back up the hill.

Pa barked with laughter, “you were always a troublesome one.”

“I wish I could remember,” I whispered, saddened that I couldn’t share in his amusement.

“You will in time,” he placed his large hand on the back of my shoulders, before wafting his other hand gently in the air, the realm coming to life with the faint spirits of people, who once graced the realm, as he did. I knew that no one knew we were there, watching them. “Come.”

ELEVEN

We began to walk the way that *little me* had run off, towards the palace. Pa didn't take a step away from me as he pushed through the spirits that walked the streets, though I felt the need to dodge them in the hopes they wouldn't feel us there.

"Pa," I coughed, "I… are you real?"

He laughed, "in some sense, yes."

"I mean, is this all a dream again?" I asked him, "like the last time."

"Arraetta, the answers to all your questions shall come in time," he replied, "but I can assure you that I am very much your father and this place was once your home."

I nodded, still a little uncertain but I think it was because so much had been thrown at me in such a short period of time. Not just learning about myself but the nightmare, that I had seen of Seraiah coming to attack me just moments before, had me on edge thinking something was going to come at me again.

"You are safe here."

I looked at him as he offered me a kind smile.

"Was this the day of the attack?"

"No," he shook his head, "the attack took place many months later."

"But, I saw it happen," I answered, "in a dream, I went to sleep and woke up."

"Your memories will often merge together," he replied, "sometimes you may see things that look like the same day, but it is, in fact, a different space of time. I believe you will find that, with this particular memory you see before you, your mother took you to bed as I remember she was very keen to make sure you got enough sleep."

"Why?" I asked. We could see the interaction with Freyda's father at the top of the hill, though still a little distant from them.

"Your life is a long one," he said, "your mother believed that adequate sleep would help keep you youthful, which it did, of course. If you were still here, I cannot imagine she would have you at the age you are."

"What do you mean?"

"You are much older than you think you may be, my child," he answered, "you were a baby for a very long time, then I remember she made a decision that she wished you to age."

"Wished me to age?" I coughed.

"There are many ways to prevent ageing," he informed me, which left me even more confused.

"Then, how old am I here?"

"In Earth years?" he chuckled to move on with the conversation as we reached my younger self, who was stomping in front of Dayfid, "this is Dayfid; he was my greatest friend and swore an oath to protect you at all costs. This is his daughter, Freyda, who was your greatest friend."

"What happened to them?" I gulped.

"I believe that they are still alive," Pa answered and I felt the hidden tension leave my body, "I am unsure where, however, I am, unfortunately, not in contact with the mortal world any longer."

"Mortal world?"

"My, my you ask many questions," he smiled, "I am sure you have come to understand that I am no longer alive."

It saddened me to hear those words come from his lips, so I didn't question it further, deciding that I'd felt enough emotion for one day. However, the one question I did want to ask him was how, if he was no longer alive, were we communicating, if it was not a dream.

We were, however, both interrupted by the dominating and radiant presence of my ma, who was even more beautiful than how I'd seen her in my dream… or memory. I looked just like her, in a way, with the same curly hair and dashing blue eyes, yet I didn't have her small nose and the radiance around her felt different too - gentle, loving, powerful.

My eyes tickled with tears as I watched her join the memory, but it was the sound of my pa's gentle sobbing that stopped them from falling. I looked at him as he watched his wife greet everyone and I could see the pain and anguish, that it caused him to see her, as though she was there in real life. I could tell that all he wanted was for her to look at him, to acknowledge him, but we were but ghosts observing the moment.

I grasped his hand and squeezed it to offer support.

"Sorry," he cleared his throat as we both watched Ma carry my younger self away and he turned his back, looking down to the city below, "I have not seen my wife for a long time."

"I saw what happened to her," I replied, "I was a child."

"And, something you should never have witnessed," he said. "No child should ever have to witness their mother being…slaughtered by such a dark creature."

"What was it?"

"It is known universally as The Dark," he breathed, some anger and resentment in his voice as he spoke, "though I am sure you already know something of it."

"Only a little," I nodded, "although Seraiah hasn't really told me much."

Pa smiled, looking down at me once again, "tell me about Seraiah."

I reddened at the thought of Seraiah, whilst Pa sat down on the cobblestone floor. Even sitting, he was around my height. I laughed a little, "you are so big."

"You are just small, Arraetta," he answered, "just as your mother created you; she wished for a daughter that she could dote on, one that would grow into a beautiful and smart young woman and she always liked the idea of you being small enough to carry around. She was also very adamant that you would marry one day, so *please* tell me about the Zikan prince."

Pa knew exactly what he was doing, bringing the conversation back around to Seraiah. It showed how smart he was. I squirmed a little, unsure how to handle the conversation, "he is... he is very nice, and he treats me well."

"Arraetta, do not think that I do not know what you are," he answered, raising his eyebrows and I knew exactly what he was talking about.

"A Kindred Spirit."

"Yes," he answered, "now, tell me about Seraiah, your Kindred Spirit."

"He's... he's away in Italy right now," I said and allowed the details all to flow out, as though I was a young girl in love for the first time, "he didn't even tell me he was leaving, he just showed me things about being a Kindred Spirit and then was gone the next morning. I honestly don't know how I feel about everything, Pa, I like him, but I'm overwhelmed by it all. I know that I was a princess here, but, all my life on Earth, I've just been a normal person and now I've been thrown back into it all."

"As you should," he replied.

"But, why?" I asked, "why is it now that I'm beginning to remember?"

"Because now is the right time," he replied, clearly humoured by the situation, "you must not question the will of the Gods and you also must not question The Universe."

"I'll have to get married though, Pa!" I blasted, my hands flailing in the air as though it was the most shocking idea, "I don't know how to look after myself, let alone be in a relationship with… with a prince. Prince's are for fairy tales."

"Arraetta," he laughed, standing back up again, "you fret over small details; you are a Kindred Spirit, no matter whether Seraiah came with a title or not, you would always end up marrying him because it is what you are destined for. And I believe that you are more than deserving of the greatest destiny there has ever been created."

"Is it really the greatest destiny?"

"To be loved for eternity," he smiled softly, "that, my dear, is the only thing ever worth living for. Now, you must go."

"Why?" I gasped, not ready.

"You cannot have everything at once," Pa repeated, "we will meet again soon, I promise. Lavrae, Arraetta."

"Wait, what does that mean?"

"It is a word for many things, but it encompasses all things to do with love. Until we next see each other, my lavrae."

I watched as the realm began to be filled with soft white light, the fabric of it disappearing around us as Pa nodded, overcome with happiness. Before he disappeared, I shouted, "Lavrae, Pa!"

I inhaled deeply, eyes blinking open as I stared at the dry log fireplace in Sheika's front room, allowing the cacophony of noise, surrounding me, to softly fill my ears. I grunted a little, sitting up and cricked my neck, seeing that the sun was beginning to set outside the window, the room dimly lit by a couple of side lamps. The clock was still ticking, in the background, and the soft clattering of cutlery against a plate could be heard in the other room.

Slowly, I stood and walked through the hallway, the sound of the person eating becoming more prominent as I arrived at a slightly open wooden door.

I was about to go in, but I felt nervous about seeing Sheika again, guessing it was her, so I decided that I'd head back to the house. I guessed that Tara had left, no doubt bored with how long I was unconscious. I stroked the cat, that was still sleeping, before opening the front door and going outside.

I peered at the dull sky, worried that I was going to see the same thing I had earlier, but nothing was out of the ordinary and I stepped down from the veranda, heading back towards the house.

It was nice to be alone, with no guards, so I took the opportunity to take a walk through the main street. A few people milled about, some greeted me kindly, but I didn't expect any of them to truly know who I was. I was glad for it.

As I came to the end of the street, where the road turned down the long driveway to the front gates of the complex, I took a deep breath of the cool air and looked back at the grandeur of the palace that stood at the top of the road. It reminded me of how the palace peaked in The Cre-este.

"Ma'am."

I looked to see Dixon walking towards me, and I stiffened, "hi."

"I am to escort you back," he informed me, waving his hand in the direction of the house, and I swallowed, wondering whether he genuinely thought I was about to make a dash for it.

"Where did you come from?" I asked.

"It is my job to make sure you are safe," he replied honestly, which meant that he'd been watching me since Jonah threatened to assign me a personal guard.

"I don't need a bodyguard," I said to him.

"I do not make the rules, ma'am," he said, "it is a little late for you to be wandering around the grounds on your own."

"I used to do it in London."

"Yes, but things have changed."

I was about to say something else, but I bit my tongue and nodded, beginning the journey back up towards the house, Dixon in tow. After a few minutes, I was a little annoyed by the new presence of a guard.

"Don't you have something better to do, Dixon?" I turned to him.

"You may call me Alex, ma'am," he replied stiffly, "Dixon is a little..." Informal, was the word. "I do not have anything better to do because this is my job."

"Well, you're wasted here," I answered, "I'm sure there are better positions to find yourself in than watching over me."

"Keeping you safe."

I wanted to say something else, but I felt like I was talking to a robot or something. I could tell by the way he stood with his shoulders tucked back and the way he spoke that he was well-trained, but it made him seem less like a person. He was a good-looking man too, not that anyone seemed relatively unattractive in the house anyway. He was taller than six feet with soft porcelain skin. Everything seemed neat on his body, except for his shoulder-length brown wavy hair, that looked hard to maintain.

"How long have you been following me?"

I saw the tug of his lips then and I couldn't help but smile as he stepped forward in a way to make us continue walking.

"It is not your job to know where I am," Alex replied.

"But, Jonah only threatened it."

"I have been watching you before The Commander spoke with you," he told me, "he was just trying to implement his authority, as usual."

"The Commander, hey?" I laughed, "the title suits."

"Very much so," he agreed, "he is not such a bad guy but do not tell him I said that, I am sure he would punish me for it."

I noticed that Alex's accent was a lot stronger than the others, which made me wonder when he'd started to learn English as he seemed to be just a little younger than Seraiah. We made it to the iron gates of the house before I spoke again, "do you prefer excitement in your job?"

"Excitement?"

"Yes, do you want me to act up or do you want me to be boring?" I asked him.

Alex chuckled, "ma'am, it is not up to me how you wish to be. I will surely adapt to you as I already have." He paused for a second as we walked. "Be mindful there are cameras in the house, ma'am, we will find you no matter where you go."

I winced at the thought of it, were there cameras in the library? And, what about Seraiah's study nook? Even worse, what about in my room and bathroom? Were they watching my every move like a rat in a cage?

"Do not worry," he grinned, "your personal space is yours. I am just making you aware that you are always being watched, even when I am not around."

"Great," I grimaced, "anything else you wish to tell me, Alex?"

Alex was thoughtful for a moment before he moved his hand to a little button. inside his blue jacket, and spoke into a small microphone. I saw the less serious side of Alex as he communicated naturally to the person on the other end before it cut off.

"I wish I knew what you said."

"I am sure you do," he replied with a smile, "I shall walk you back to your room."

"Is there somewhere to get a light evening snack around here?" I joked, feeling the hunger pangs from the day's lack of food.

Alex nodded, "I am sure you are aware you have the ability to have anything you wish, ma'am."

Once I was in bed, after eating, I tossed and turned for a long while until I succumbed to nightmarish sleep, haunted by the images of what I'd seen during my hallucinations, fragmenting constantly, yet I was seeing other things too - death, destruction, friend turn on friend, the end of the world. It all felt so real yet, when I woke up, the fear of it all had disappeared, leaving only a hollow numbness. It wasn't necessarily that I felt alone anymore, especially knowing my father was somewhere in the infinite universe, but the consistency of these dreams made me wonder about what was going to come. Would I ever be free of the torment?

TWELVE

After an awful night's sleep, I wanted nothing more than to stay in bed. In fact, after finding out that my every step was being watched, hiding in my room sounded like the perfect way to spend the day but I wasn't lazy, and I surely just had to find a way to get used to it, as quickly as possible.

After grabbing a quick shower, I threw on some clothes and walked out of the door, seeing Alex stood across, in a fairly relaxed position, that soon turned to being his usual regimented way, bowing in greeting.

"Have you been standing there all night?" I asked.

"No, ma'am," he replied, "you shall be glad to know that I have since slept."

"So, now you're on personal guard duty?" I replied, a little gruffly, "you weren't with me all day yesterday."

Before Alex could reply, I heard loud feminine laughter, from the bottom of the hallway, and I turned to see, none other than, Genie walk around the corner, looking behind her before her head snapped in my direction.

"Missed me?" she asked, after a pause, and I frowned, confused by her sudden niceness as I didn't exactly deserve it.

I started to walk down, Alex following at a distance, "I thought you had left."

"I thought yesterday was long enough," Genie grinned, enveloping me into a big hug once we met, "plus, I missed you."

"I missed you too," I murmured into her hair, "I'm sorry about what happened."

"I forgive you," she whispered and then pulled back, beaming, "we are going out."

"Out?" I raised my eyebrows.

Genie looked at Alex, "oh, hey, Alex."

"Lady Genevieve," Alex greeted, and I laughed at his sincere salutation. I wondered whether Genie being in a relationship with Freddie meant she had a more formal title, yet I hadn't heard anyone call Freddie anything like Sir or Lord or similar, so maybe it was just a polite gesture.

"Anyway, *Lady Genevieve,* where are we going?"

"To pack the flat," she replied, "I've told Julie that we're moving out, so she knows to start looking for a new tenant."

"Are you moving here too?"

"Yes, I'm going to be living here with Freddie," she told me, pointing to a room back up the hallway, "they're moving us to that room."

It was as though a weight had been lifted from my shoulders, when she told me, as it meant that I wasn't going to have to put up with being alone. If I'd learnt anything from my rashness, it was that nothing was worth losing Genie over.

"Come on," she said, pulling me towards the entrance of the hallway, "I'm glad you're dressed, I thought I'd have to come and drag you out of bed."

"Truthfully, Kadey dressing me every day is becoming claustrophobic," I said to her.

"You have to get used to it, Arri," she said matter-of-factly and I wanted to agree with her, but how can anyone just get used to someone dressing you all of a sudden? It was surely unnatural past the age of ten.

We rounded the corner, towards the steps of the grand hallway, and I stopped, looking at Genie, "how are we going to pack that whole flat in a day?"

"With help," she told me. I eyed Alex, whose eyes were a little glazed over as he listened to something in his headpiece before he lifted the mic and spoke into it gently, then I raised my eyebrows at her. She smiled, "come on, you'll see."

I followed her to the stairs and stopped at the top, immediately making eye contact with Seraiah; the air became warm as a strange sense of euphoria and relief overcame me. I whispered, "Seraiah."

He gazed up at me, longingly, and my heart pattered in my chest, happiness hitting me immediately. Genie descended quickly and I followed. She curtsied politely to Seraiah before embracing Freddie.

When I reached the last step, Seraiah and Freddie both bowed to me and I blushed, about to return it back, when Seraiah held his hand up.

"You need never curtsey."

"But, Genie did," I pointed out.

Genie chortled whilst the two men smiled knowingly. I took it that it was because Genie, in terms of rank, was *lower* than Seraiah and myself, but I still didn't enjoy being treated differently just because of status.

"Then, why do you bow?" I asked.

"That is because we are men of the house," Seraiah replied and then looked at Freddie, "shall we go?"

"Yes," Freddie answered, placing his hand into Genie's and pulling her out of the door, which was opened by one of the doormen. Seraiah waved his hand in the same direction, and I started to walk ahead of him.

"I thought you were in Italy?" I asked as we were hit by the sun's warmth.

"I was," he answered, our hands brushing against one another's, "I arrived in the morning but caught a flight back late evening as the distance was a little... difficult."

He didn't need to explain more, I understood that he meant the distance between *us* was difficult. It had been difficult, although I suppose I'd been so wrapped up in my own thoughts that, until I'd walked into the grand hallway, I hadn't realised the amount of tension I was holding in my shoulders. That, and the hallucination I'd faced was terrifying.

Outside, Jonah, Travis and two other men were waiting by the first of three large black SUVs. I wondered whether Jonah had gone to Italy too because I hadn't seen him the day before and he looked a little exhausted. Whilst Seraiah and Freddie went to chat to the security members, I followed Genie over to the middle car.

Alex made it to the car in time to open the back door for me, whilst Genie was climbing into the front. The door closed.

"It's so exhausting," I sighed exasperatedly, lying down on the back seat.

Genie was busy typing away on her phone and I tried to zone my eyes in to see who she was texting, probably someone from her school, but I was still tired from my terrible sleep so I couldn't see who. I closed my eyes, for a moment, turning to relax onto my back, and almost - *almost* - fell asleep but Genie finally quit texting, "how long are they going to be?"

I opened my eyes and saw her lean over to the driver's side and fiddle with something that caused the car to power up. I sat up and saw that all of the men had turned to the vehicle as she did, but Genie innocently sat back and rolled down the window, sighing in a breath of fresh air.

"How are we going to fit all our stuff in these three cars?" I asked her, realising that, although they were big, there was no way we'd be able to get everything in without doing several trips.

"They've hired a van," she answered, leaning her head on the rim of the window, as she watched the men interact.

"What do you think they're talking about?" I asked her.

"Wish I knew," she shrugged, "the language is so complicated, I have hardly learnt a thing."

"You're learning?" I gasped. Maybe I was slightly flabbergasted that she was taking the time to learn a new language since she'd never had an interest in learning them before, but I supposed if she had a future with Freddie, it made sense that she would do everything she could to secure it.

"Obviously," she laughed, "I have to learn, you know they're only speaking English for you and me? They hardly ever do otherwise."

"I want to learn," I told her, a little jealous, "I want to be able to understand them more."

"Then, you should talk to Seraiah," she answered, tutting dramatically, "honestly, they are taking ages."

As though they heard her, the men broke off their conversation and walked over to their respective vehicles. Freddie opened and shut Seraiah's car door as though he was Seraiah's personal chauffeur and then got into the driver's seat, leaning over to kiss Genie gently.

"That looked like a mind numbing conversation," I joked as the parade started to move.

"Protocols," Seraiah answered, mimicking, "stay with the pack, do not think about making any moves that may cause harm to our future queen."

He was jesting but I couldn't help but blush, once again, when he called me the queen.

"Jonah isn't all that bad," Genie said.

"He doesn't like me," I answered, folding my arms with a fake pout.

"I do not know why you believe such a thing," Seraiah answered, "he has never said a bad word about you."

"I just get the vibe."

"Jonah has a hard job," Freddie piped up, "especially when he has to keep someone like Seraiah in check."

I grinned as Seraiah rolled his eyes, "you should watch yourself, Freddie."

"You will find the protocols easy soon enough," Freddie continued, looking at me, through his mirror, as we came down to the front gate of the community, slowing as the first car pulled through them as they opened. Freddie followed on.

"Rules, protocols," I rolled my eyes, "God, you guys are boring."

"Boring," Seraiah tasted the words in his mouth, as though he'd heard the words for the first time, before he piped up immediately in his language. Freddie chuckled and shook his head.

As we passed through the gates, the car in front turned left whilst Freddie immediately darted to the right, bolting it down the road as fast as he could. I looked out of the back window to see the vehicle in front had halted, whilst the one behind was doing its best to keep up with us.

Freddie commented something else which made Seraiah laugh and I heard the name Travis in there. The car behind caught us in no time but was unable to overtake because we were on a country road.

It was the first time I noticed an earpiece in Freddie's ear, and he spoke back through it; his facial expressions turning a little sour before he ripped out the piece and let it hang off his jacket.

"Are they mad?"

"You have no idea," Freddie said, slowing the car down as he relaxed in the chair. I looked at Seraiah who had a greatly amused facial expression, staring out of his own window.

Genie fiddled with the radio for a little while before she groaned in annoyance, sitting back and looking at her phone.

"Babe, we connected your phone yesterday," Freddie said a little sharply. My mouth twitched into a smile at the word *babe*. It wasn't like the term was unusual, of course, but their interactions made the surrealness of my life feel more real.

"But, it won't work," she grumbled, playing music out loud on her phone, "look."

"It will," he groaned, reaching for it but she pulled it out of the way.

"Concentrate on driving," she said, but he pulled to a stop in the middle of the road, "Freddie, you can't stop here."

"No one comes down this road."

The parade halting gave enough time for Jonah to fly out, of the rear vehicle, and walk up to the driver's side, fixing his suit, but Freddie didn't even notice.

Freddie took Genie's phone out of her hand and fiddled with it, "you haven't even got it connected... here."

The music started to play out and Genie smiled, leaning over to kiss him gently before she started to scroll through her phone.

It was then that Jonah knocked, and Freddie wound down the window. A heated conversation began to take place between Freddie and Jonah, whilst Seraiah wound his own window down so that he could join in as well. Jonah's eyes would scan to me every now and again and I knew that I was involved.

Genie turned in her seat to me before she moved her phone in my direction. The message on the screen read *It looks like the boys are in trouble.* I laughed and covered my mouth, as I realised it echoed, but it was enough to cut off the conversation between the men as Jonah stepped back, frustrated.

"Ladies, please refrain from encouraging these two," Jonah said to

Genie and myself, mainly his eyes on me.

"I didn't encourage anything!" I said exasperatedly.

"You did say they were boring."

"I said-" I cut myself short as I decided it wasn't worth bringing up my exact conversation to the guy who obviously implements the rules. I also couldn't believe they'd ratted me out.

"Either way, any more reckless behaviour will result in a return to the palace."

Jonah didn't stop to say anything more, he moved back down to his vehicle, whilst Seraiah and Freddie put their windows back up.

"Arsehole," I glowered, which made everyone laugh as Freddie pulled the car away. I glared playfully at the two boys, "thanks for throwing me in it."

"There was no mention of your want to break the rules," Seraiah defended, holding his hands up, "although, there are many ways to break them without being caught."

"I shall pretend I did not hear that," Freddie piped up. Seraiah and I shared a look and I smiled, realising that Seraiah was much more reckless than I could have imagined. I could've guessed that, of course, from how he'd hurt himself, just to show me his true self, and the anger it had caused between everyone, including his father.

Once we hit a bigger road, Jonah's vehicle swung around to the front, but I noticed he was in the passenger seat and, next to him, it looked like Alex was there. I wondered what the relationship between Jonah and him was because, from knowing Alex for little over twelve hours, I could see he took his job seriously but maybe he feared stepping one foot out of line.

I didn't realise how far out of London we were until we drove into the north end of the city, around thirty minutes later. Conversation had been light between Genie and Freddie, sometimes even Seraiah for some of it, but most of it had been in comfortable silence. Even

Genie's random selection of pop music and her humming along to it was soothing.

I peered at Seraiah, who had his eyes closed and his breathing was steady but a little jagged. I could see that he looked a little unwell by the paleness of his golden cheeks. Naturally, I lifted my hand gently to his cheek, but Freddie's soft voice cut me off.

"He is unwell."

I looked at him and sat back, gazing at Seraiah with some sort of protectiveness I didn't know I should really possess. It was a feeling - a need - to make him better somehow, even if he was just a little under the weather. "What happened?"

"He, uh," Freddie said, "he collapsed last night."

I gasped, whispering, "what is he doing here now?"

"He insisted," he replied, "it is the reason why he is back here in London, well, one of the reasons."

"Shouldn't he have had a doctor look over him?" I asked.

"He did," he said, "he, apparently, said that he had to get back because he was worried."

"About?"

"You," Seraiah interjected and I looked as he sat up to make himself more comfortable, eyes still closed, "I had the strangest nightmare, and an overwhelming feeling that I must return as soon as possible."

"That's reckless," I breathed in annoyance, "you collapsed."

"I'm fine."

"Yeah, you look fine," I bit, folding my arms for effect. I knew Freddie was listening in, but he didn't interject with the conversation; I wasn't sure what Genie was doing.

Seraiah's hand gently moved its way up to my arms, prying them loose as he came to take hold of my right hand. He leant back again, closing his eyes as his thumb stroked against my skin soothingly. I guessed the motion of it quelled any sick feeling he had.

I had yet to learn what exactly Seraiah's *love language* was, but I could come to guess that it was touch. And this was Seraiah being affectionate, in a way that would soothe any anger, and it worked. I wasn't angry at him; I just couldn't believe he would fly back from Italy just to check up on me.

"Alex says there's cameras everywhere," I murmured, "so, why didn't you just check those?"

"There may be cameras but they are not always watching," Seraiah answered, "there specifically are no cameras at Sheika's and, when they went to find you, you had gone."

"Which explains Alex."

"Which explains Alex," he agreed and we both looked at each other. He smiled, "by the time we were in the air, I received news that you had been wandering the complex."

"I wasn't running away."

"I never said you were," he chuckled, "although, I would not blame you if you were to try, I suppose, it can be a little difficult to get used to all the *rules* and *protocols*."

"Which is boring," I repeated humorously. Seraiah laughed and I did too.

"Because you wandered, you will have noticed that Alex is now following you," he said and I nodded because he'd been outside my door that morning. He continued, "Jonah made the call that you're to have a guard with you, just in case something happens to you as it did to me. Jonah, although he can be a cock, is only doing what is best for us."

"Jonah said he will need that in writing," Freddie piped up and we looked as he held his microphone up. I laughed as Seraiah was gobsmacked that Freddie would do that, but I could see that he found it hilarious.

"Do that again and I may have to fire you," Seraiah said, which

Freddie replied to in their language and both of them laughed, like old pals, about something I wished I understood.

"So, what is your language?" I asked, catching Freddie's eye in the mirror.

"You have not guessed already?" Freddie asked amused, "Zikan, of course. We are Zikan's from Zika who speak Zikan."

"Well, we don't just speak 'Earth' here," I tutted and then let out a short laugh at Seraiah's bemused look.

"Zika is not the size of Earth," Seraiah replied, "it is a realm, about the size of Australia, so we only have one language. Unless you count the ancient language, that is used for purposes of spells, which, these days, is just Ancient Zikan."

I wondered how realms worked in the stead of planets; I imagined they were places with magical portals going in and out of them, or maybe a piece of land that floated in never ending space. Or maybe it was but a kingdom, in a world of many kingdoms. I was intrigued to find out more, I just had to find the right time to not sound like an idiot.

"Arri is great at learning languages," Genie said as she placed her feet onto the dashboard, to which Freddie retorted that it was dangerous, though she passed it by as if it was nothing, "I reckon she'd learn yours fairly quickly."

"Is that so?" Seraiah mused, "I suppose Zikan is not far from your own native language, Arraetta."

"It doesn't sound anything like English," I answered, not a thought about what he actually meant.

Seraiah and Freddie burst into laughter, "Cre-estian."

"Oh," I nodded, realising that made more sense, though I hadn't really thought about it before now. In all those dreams I'd had, even the meeting with Pa, I'd understood everyone completely, but then again, I probably hadn't been speaking in English but in fact Cre-estian. But how could that truly be possible? If our languages were so close, it would surely mean I'd be able to understand Seraiah and Freddie, yet their words were so foreign. Was it a trick of the mind? Or was my mind compensating for the lack of understanding?

THIRTEEN

I was glad when we pulled up outside our flat as fresh air, from the claustrophobic conversations, was what I needed. My door was opened from the outside by Travis, and I slipped out, seeing a group of kids eyeing the cars, as though we were celebrities visiting the area. It felt as if it had been years since I'd stepped foot there, even though it had only been around six weeks, but there was a slight numbness I felt. Maybe I had breathed in the fresh air from the house, outside of the city, for so long, that I felt flat, or maybe I just no longer felt attached to the place anymore. Nothing, as expected, had changed. I walked around the side of the vehicle with Genie, both of us stopping to look up at the rundown building.

"Well, I definitely won't miss this," she whispered and I nodded.

"You know the lift doesn't work," I pointed out, my arms aching at the idea of having to carry all of our stuff down ten flights of stairs, over and over again.

"I hadn't forgotten," she grumbled, taking Freddie's limp arm as if he was offering it to her to hold.

"How do people get up there?" Seraiah asked.

"There's an elevator at the back but it's a ball ache to get to," Genie told him, "and it's so slow. What time is the van coming?"

"I think in about three hours," Freddie placed his arm around her waist, "should be enough time to get started."

I watched them both walk on together and then saw Seraiah come into my peripheral vision. I looked up at him, "are you ready for all these stairs?"

"I have been here before, remember," he chuckled and I did remember. I'd asked Tom to tell him I was elsewhere. I wondered whether the kid ever did get around to telling him, or whether Seraiah just knew exactly where to find me.

I started to walk towards the staircase and looked over my shoulder, seeing Alex and Travis following, whilst Jonah and the other two men remained chatting.

Alex and Travis were contrasts of each other. Travis was the kind of guy you'd see on security outside a nightclub; a big, brutish sort of fellow that you wouldn't mess with, although he was quite attractive, in his own way. I knew I didn't want to get on the wrong side of him.

Neither of the men chatted, they just followed us all at a distance. I guessed that they were going to be on duty to help haul everything down the stairs with us, unless there were others who were about to turn up. I knew that there was a high number of staff at the house - or *palace* as Jonah put it.

I grimaced as we climbed the stairs. I had no clue how I used to throw my bike onto my shoulders and carry it up them without any issue. My calves were burning by the fourth floor, and I stopped to take a few deep breaths, whereas Seraiah was perfectly fine.

"Do you want me to carry you?" he joked, though I could see that a part of him hoped I would say yes.

"It's not that high," I said, wiping my forehead, "it's just very hot weather and I've been used to your so-called grand staircase."

"It is grand," he chuckled.

"Not like this."

"Well, my staircase definitely does not smell like piss," he pointed out and we laughed, receiving a strange look from a nearby lad, who was bouncing down the steps, blasting out grime music from his phone. I started to walk onwards again, making deliberately heavy footsteps.

"You are a child," Seraiah joked and I gasped, turning to him.

"I suppose in comparison to you, I am." He grinned.

"You are older than me," he replied.

"I'm twenty four," I told him matter-of-factly.

"In Cre-estian years?" he raised his eyebrows and I tutted, rolling my eyes at him, but he continued before I could, "I could make it that you are over six millennia years old."

"I am not over six million years old," I stomped, gentle echoes of laughter coming from the men behind us.

Seraiah barked with laughter, "I said millennia, not a million... it means one thousand."

"Oh," I mumbled and then joked it off, "at least I look good for someone who is six thousand years old."

I wondered how Seraiah came to learn such knowledge, although no doubt, in the library, there were books on the myths of times gone by and it probably read something like *six thousand years ago...* I, for one, didn't want to think about how old I was and still was quite happy to pretend that I merely was twenty-four years old.

"That I cannot argue with," he replied and I looked away, trying to hide the blush.

"Seraiah, will you tell me why you are here now?" I asked him.

"Well, it is my plan to help you pack."

I tutted at his attempt at changing the subject, "Se-rai-ah."

"Ar-rae-et-ta," he repeated in the same tone and I stared him down for a moment until he gave in, "it is a long story, it is not one for a staircase in the middle of a block of flats."

"Is it really that deep?"

"Yes," he nodded, "but, I shall tell you that it is not our plan to stay. We have a war to win."

"A war?" I squeaked, thinking about how war, to me, was far off in another country away from me and I was safe where I was, "a war with who?"

"Arraetta, do not feign naivety," Seraiah raised his eyebrows at me, though his humour had fallen flat and I could see that it wasn't quite a conversation he was hoping to have with me at that moment, "The Dark, of course."

The Dark was the thing that Tara had told me about, but no one had really told me anything since, apart from a small mention from my pa. It was part of the Zikan's myths about him, the myth about *me*. It was what I had seen devour my ma, or at least something.

"Your mum told me a little bit about The Dark," I said to him, and I could see there was a little bit of humour in his face from my casual use of *mum*, "but I thought it was destroyed."

"Not quite," he answered, his expression serious. I noticed Seraiah clench the hand, that had turned black into a fist, and I swallowed, a strange thought overcoming me. Had what I had seen from Seraiah in the dream, and by the lake, been a replication of The Dark?

"Then, how…?" I said, wondering what exactly my question was. I could stand there and ask him a million questions about everything, but I guessed Seraiah wouldn't give in so easily.

"Arraetta, you are pushing me into a much deeper conversation than I wish to have right now," he answered, though the lightness was back in his tone, "I wish my mother had not teased you with information just yet, I do not think you are ready for all of this."

I gasped, "I am ready."

"Are you?" he raised his eyebrows, "you barely knew of this life apart from your odd run ins with your power, every few years, and now, that it has all been thrown at you, you need to slow down."

"How can I slow down when I don't know anything?" I echoed around the hallway. I winced as I realised it was quite loud, so I continued quieter, "you're keeping it from me on purpose."

"I am not, Arraetta," he offered gently, "I promise you I shall show you all you wish to know but we must approach these things slowly."

"Well, tell me one thing," I said to him, "what is the difference between Rapidfire and Divine Rapidfire?"

He sighed, nodding some, whilst he figured out how to describe it.

"Well, you could describe Divine Rapidfire as a tree," he said, "a tree that was planted from a single seed, a source of energy, that helps many beings survive. From that tree, each branch sprouts a flower and that flower, with some of the energy from its mother, is the Rapidfire. Does that make sense?"

Divine Rapidfire was the original source of energy and Rapidfire is what sprouts from it, taking its energy from the source. But did that mean that, if I housed Divine Rapidfire, that everyone was feeding off my own energy? Was that the true cause of my blackouts? So many questions were swirling around my head, and I just wanted to ask him more. I could tell by the look on Seraiah's frustrated expression that no more serious questions were going to be allowed.

"Now, Arraetta, may we continue?"

"Well, speaking of Rapidfire," I said to him, beginning to walk backward up the stairs, "I do have a bone to pick with you about your arm."

As I was about to pick that bone with him, but before I could continue, my foot slipped on the step, and I fell. Seraiah magically managed to catch me as I bumped my back on the stair edge. Alex and Travis were also on standby, but let Seraiah be my hero.

"These stairs aren't designed for you to walk backward on, Arraetta," he pointed out, tutting in worry.

"I'm fine," I replied, mimicking his tutting, "anyway, as I was saying-"

"-I do not need your scolding," he interrupted as I stood to my feet, "I have had enough scolding from everyone else."

"Did it hurt?" I asked him.

He grimaced at the thought, most likely at the pain, and I knew the answer was yes, it did hurt him. "It does not matter whether showing that part of myself caused me pain, Arraetta, all that matters is that I showed you the truth."

Or some of it at least. It looked like he wasn't about to admit to me that he was, in fact, infected by something - The Dark, or some darker power, at least.

I was about to continue, but Genie's voice echoed from above, "Are you two coming?"

"Yes," we both chimed. Our echo of each other made us laugh, which broke the tension and I decided to go back to being light hearted again.

"Race you up there!" I screamed.

With a head start, I managed to get a bit ahead of him, but Seraiah was so quick that he dashed up in front very easily. I had to stop, the exertion nearly killing me, but I soon made it to our floor, seeing Seraiah leaning against the wall, silently laughing at me. Immediately after, the two guards flawlessly appeared behind.

"Do not start a challenge you know you cannot win." He laughed.

I scoffed, bemused by the situation, "whatever, at least I'm not choosing to lean against a piss-stained wall."

He cringed as he moved away, looking at the wall, before turning to me as I smirked at him. Seraiah was about to make a comment, but we were interrupted by Genie.

"Come on, you two," she shouted from our door before she disappeared inside. I looked at Seraiah and he looked back before he waved his arm for me to lead. He came to walk beside me, and our fingers brushed against each other, as they usually did, both of us internally coaxing the other to hold hands but neither of us taking the bait to do so.

At the door, both of us grimaced at the sight of Genie and Freddie kissing each other passionately.

"I thought you wanted us to hurry," I commented, shoving through the middle of them into my mess of a room. It hadn't been touched since the ball and there was a damp and musty smell that lingered which made it very unpleasant. We would have to do a lot of work if we were to pack up the entire place.

"Me and Freddie will start in my room," Genie told us.

Without even looking, I mumbled, "sure you will."

"Do not be jealous of them," Seraiah whispered as he came to stand behind me. It sent a shiver down my spine as his breath tickled my neck, but it didn't last long as he walked into the room and over to my sheet-covered paintings, "so, this is where the magic is made, huh?"

"Did you not see this when you came to find me?"

"No, we did not make it inside your flat," he informed me, "I could not detect your energy in the building, we merely arrived here."

"Arrived here?"

"Yes, much like how you disappeared," he answered.

"I don't understand."

"I shall show you soon," he smiled, pulling off the sheet from one of the canvases. The painting had blurred electric-like lines across it, but it created a place that flashed in my mind - the exact place I had seen on the painting, at the ball, and the same place I had seen in my dream - the windmill and the river.

"It's..."

"Beautiful," Seraiah whispered as he knelt down, gently stroking the texture with his hands, "not at all like the one in the library."

"Sorry?"

He looked over at me and stood up, "I went to the library this morning, I saw that you had painted over the other parts on the canvas."

I blushed, "oh, sorry, I-"

"No, it's okay," he smiled, "but this is a whole different piece altogether. This is the Wicker Windmill."

"How... how do you know?"

"I am unsure," he answered, stroking the canvas gently, "I suppose I can see the intricacies of it."

"But, no one has ever been able to see my work."

"You are saying this to me," he chuckled, looking at me, "we are the most in sync people in the universe, are we not?"

"I guess so," I murmured.

"I remember how you brought my version of this painting alive," he said, "the one in the downstairs sitting room, do you remember?"

"I... yes, I do a little, you saw that too?"

"Yes," he nodded, "but only a fraction, I felt like a spectator watching a moving image."

"I can... sometimes I can see the image moving," I told him, "but only when it is truly finished, if an artist's work ever can be."

"Is this finished?"

"This was my first piece, following my blackout at twenty," I informed him, coming to kneel next to it, "it was the first time I had created art like this, with the electrical lines. It was as though it was all I could see but, as I pressed my hand to the drawing..." I did so. "...it would somewhat come to life, and sometimes I would just go there. Into the painting."

"Can you show me?"

I connected eyes with Seraiah, both of us so close that we could kiss, but it wasn't the right moment. He was looking at me with curious hope, as though being there - at the windmill - was everything he could ever ask for.

"I can try," I answered, although truthfully I wasn't entirely sure how I had done it before.

"You could try using Rakatan," Seraiah said and I frowned at him. He continued, "it is a form of breathing, it allows you to hone your power into something. You breathe in and out several times, feel like you wish to be there - in the painting, or in the place - and allow your body to take you there. Your power, naturally, should work."

"Does that work for you?"

"Not always," he shook his head, "truthfully, I have not had the blessing of being able to revisit a place like this for a long time, no matter how hard I come to try. I suppose the incident - the attack on our realm - locked away some of my more treasured memories."

The attack on his realm. More questions sprouted - I needed to know more but it was hard to ask when he was unknowingly being so open. It was as though my questions shut him down immediately, so I gently coaxed him instead.

"In the library the other day," I said to him, "you took me to a place, is that not a memory?"

"It is something," he replied, "although I cannot say what exactly, a memory, a vision but you are wondering how I managed to get there? I did not use Rakatan, I have mastered the art of using ancient writing. That is a story for another time, however. For now, let us try Rakatan."

Seraiah placed his left hand on the painting, whilst he urged me to place my left hand into his right. As I did, he moved it to be placed on top of his.

"Close your eyes."

I did as he said, my eyes gently closing.

"Breathe in… breathe out," Seraiah instructed softly and I did so, copying the rhythms as he repeated that several times, "now, imagine you are in this painting, in the place and feel it. Feel it within your body. Allow your power to push through from yours to mine."

At first, it was difficult and strange. I was unable to feel my power, as though there was a band of resistance stopping me from going forward, but I allowed myself to relax and push through as much as I could. This was the first time I was being taught how to use my power and I wasn't going to waste it.

Moments later, I felt tingles within my arm - almost like the feeling of a spider running down the fibres. I breathed again, feeling the touch of a soft wind, listening intently to the breeze as it tickled the trees. But it was the soft flow of water that jolted me to open my eyes and I saw that I was no longer in the flat.

I was there on the riverbank, looking directly at the Wicker Windmill. The peacefulness of the place energised my body, feeling like nowhere was better than this place right there. I listened as the windmill creaked gently as it was powered by the river. I smelt the scent of fresh air, the purest I had ever breathed in, and felt truly alive.

But where was Seraiah?

I jolted, just a little, as my body seemed to remember it was not physically in that place and I listened as the skies above rumbled. I looked up, seeing as the blue skies faded to grey and drops of water were beginning to fall, one after the other. I felt as one heavily landed on my cheek and I jumped, blinking. Within that moment, I was back in the room, seeing that Seraiah's hand was still on the painting.

He was still staring into the picture, tears filling his eyes. It was as if the longing to be there had hit him as well. I was about to ask him if he was alright but felt a chill crawl up my spine, my head snapping in the direction of the window. My ears became attuned to strange whisperings, and I stood to my feet, listening as the whispers became louder - unpleasant, demonic sounds. As though being controlled by someone, I dazedly left my bedroom, walking towards the front door.

Genie skipped out of her room just as I was about leave but I didn't acknowledge her as I went onwards to the outside.

"Arri?" echoed her distant voice.

The demonic whisperings began to mix with a symphony of helpless cries and a dark, foreboding choir-like tone as I left the flat. My eyes cast up to the once-blue skies, seeing the ashen grey clouds painted above for miles. A ripple of thunder cracked, and I watched as the sky began to break, ripping at its seams as a fissure began to open far above.

I winced for a moment, my mind seeming to glitch, pulsing a terrible throb in my head and, within a blink, I saw as time had somewhat leapt forward but, equally, slowed down to a fraction of its speed. The skies were swirling in a circle, whilst numerous silhouetted souls hung from nothingness like decorations. A loud, unnerving roar echoed through the skies and there was a loud thud as the Earth quaked. I saw a dark creature, much like the one that had swallowed Ma in the vision, crawl out of the fissure, dark matter surrounding it like a cloud.

I winced again, the same pulse throbbing in my head and time leapt once again. The skies thundered and a flash of flaxen lightning rippled through the clouds.

"Arraetta?!" the same panicked screech of Seraiah screamed in the distance. I moved to go forward, immediately needing to find him, but I felt a hand take hold of my own.

"Hey!"

In a flash, what had been presented, before me, disappeared and I found myself back in the present. No more ashen grey sky, no more harrowing echoes, or monsters, just the loud hum of London and a gentle piercing noise that remained in my ears.

My eyes immediately darted to the culprit who had brought me, thankfully, back to reality and I saw Tom standing there, with his arms folded. I felt the tickle of the warmth of the day return to my skin as I dazedly looked down at him. Tom was the only person in focus, though I could feel the presence of the others to my right.

"Tom, this isn't the best time," Genie said worriedly, placing her hands on the back of my shoulders. I felt a liquid trickle out of my nose and placed a hand over it, kneeling heavily. It was as though I was incredibly drunk and could only understand patches of what was happening.

"Hey… you," I whispered.

"You owe me ten pounds!" Tom said, stomping his foot. He was holding his hand out to me in his usual comical way, and I might have laughed if I was not feeling so incredibly lethargic.

"T-Ten… yes, yes, I do," I agreed, feeling Seraiah move my hand away from my mouth as he knelt beside me. He placed a tissue over my nose. I murmured, "ten pounds."

"Why do you always have blood on you?" Tom asked, perplexed.

"Here you go, how about I give you twenty instead?" Seraiah pulled his wallet out, but his kind gesture went straight over my head. I was already standing up. Seraiah and Genie were trying to stop me, but it was as though they didn't exist. Fragments of images of the gloomy sky kept fracturing in my mind as, one foot in front of the other, I walked into the flat. I had to find money for Tom, and as I walked, I whispered to myself *ten pounds* repeatedly, so that I wouldn't forget whilst my thoughts were clouded by the distorted imagery.

"Arri," Genie squealed at the same time Seraiah said, "Arraetta."

Freddie was in the hallway on the phone and tried to speak to me as I passed, but I couldn't understand what he was saying and just kept moving, trying to keep myself from seeing those images. I began to pull out drawer after drawer, looking for my box of money, soon falling to my knees beside my bed, to try to find it under there. Drops of blood fell from my face and I lifted my hands to it, reality slowly kicking back in as I saw how shaky they were.

"Ten pounds," I murmured, two knees falling into my vision. I could feel my face being cupped by the soft hands of Seraiah as he pulled me up to look at him.

"You are okay, Arraetta," he said calmly, "breathe."

Breathe. I gasped for air, feeling my throat constrict and I gulped, needing to keep on concentrating, "I... ten pounds."

"I have sorted it," he whispered, attempting to keep his eyes in my eye line as I went to look down for the box once again. The only thing that Seraiah knew to do, in that moment, was to hold me tightly to help calm my breathing.

"Marie is on her way," the sound of Freddie's voice echoed and I grumbled, feeling my head pound from its reverberation. I murmured something, blinking as I tried to keep my breathing in rhythm with Seraiah's, but I struggled, suddenly drifting into nothingness.

A strange whiff of mould and my eyes blinked open, hazily taking in the half-broken door of my scuffed wardrobe, before they shut again. Like a glitch, I stood and watched as the sky fell, the horror of the voices echoing through my mind, then silence as I once again blinked my eyes open to see I was still lying on the bed.

I groaned and curled into a ball, feeling a shiver trickle down my spine and soon, slumber overtook me once more.

I stood on the balcony, the cacophony of noises rising, watching as all the silhouettes of bodies appeared up in the frozen skies, the clouds rumbling with a ripple of golden lightning.

A deafening sound of thunder and I opened my eyes, slowly and cautiously rolling over to look up at the ceiling of my bedroom.

I placed my hand on my head, wincing at the ache that was throbbing in my forehead and shut my eyes to stop the dim sunlight from outside making it worse. The door opened. It was Genie walking in, noticing I was awake.

"Oh my God, you had us so worried, Arri!"

"How long was I out for?" I murmured, not making a move to sit up.

"About an hour or so," she said softly, sitting down next to me, "does your head hurt?"

"How did you guess?" I joked and then grimaced, covering my eyes with my arm.

I heard the floor by my door creak and footsteps as the person walked over to us both; it was Seraiah, "here."

I could hear a box being unsealed and the sound of a paracetamol wrapper squeaking as Genie pierced it open. "Arri, sit up and take these."

I removed my arm from my face, catching eyes with an extremely worried Seraiah before looking at Genie and slowly sat up. I took the glass of water she held out to me and the two paracetamol and slowly took them, feeling horrendous. Genie squeezed my arm and excused herself to go and find Freddie, whilst Seraiah softly sat in her spot, stroking my forehead, and looking at me with intense eyes.

"I was very worried," he said, taking the glass from me and placing it on the side table, "you do not deserve this, I should not have done that to you."

"It's not your fault," I smiled gently, cringing at the pain in my head, "it's what happens in the build-up to my blackout."

"So, that was not your blackout weeks ago?" he asked and I looked away from him, "you must be open with us, Arraetta, I cannot help you if you do not let me."

"I don't need your help," I whispered and lay back down, "it's not been so bad since what happened."

"I do not wish for you to go through this alone," he said, "your burden is as much mine-"

I shook my head, "no, Seraiah-"

"Yes, Arraetta," he whispered, stroking my hand, "you and I… we must go through these things as one now, I cannot see you like this again. Do you know how hard it was for me to see you the way you were after the incident? It has scarred my mind, I cannot… I cannot see this happen to you again, there must be a way for it to stop."

I lifted my hand and stroked his face, smiling softly, "it's only every four years."

Seraiah frowned, another thought conjuring in his head as if he was calculating something but he didn't get to expand on it as Marie hurriedly walked in, bag on her arm. She gently placed it down on the floor and placed her cool hand against my forehead.

"I think you're becoming my favourite patient," Marie joked. I smiled at her attempt at a bit of light humour and Seraiah spoke with her, for a few moments, in Zikan before he left the room, leaving me with her.

"I honestly feel fine now," I lied.

"I'm surprised considering how damp ridden this room is," she said, nodding to the mould that layered the wall, "do you get ill often?"

"I didn't faint because of the dampness."

"I'm making light conversation." She smiled and I relaxed a little as I let her ask me all the questions she needed as she checked everything over. Her evaluation was simple; if I was to remain and help the others with the packing, I'd need to take it easy and not do anything strenuous. Seraiah, Freddie, and Genie, as well as Alex and Travis, were to keep a close eye on me in case of any changes. And, with that, she packed up her stuff, said she would come back, if needed, and left.

Several hours later, the entire flat was packed with a pile of things, outside the front door, to be thrown away. Genie had recruited everyone to help lift stuff up and down the stairs and to my surprise, Seraiah wasn't afraid to get his hands dirty, helping to lift a lot of the heavier stuff. All the while, I remained inside, being mindful of how fragile I was feeling post-collapse. Really, it had knocked me sideways and, in the moments, I was left alone, I concentrated on taking deep breaths to recoup my energy. I knew Seraiah knew that I wasn't feeling too well, I could hardly lift a thing, unsurprisingly, and when we all sat in the lounge to eat chips from the chippy, my appetite had gone.

We had nearly finalised all the packing, when Seraiah commented on the half-finished paintings that were leant against the wall. "You should take them," he said.

"And, store them where?" I joked, "one of your lavish rooms?"

He chuckled, "you… you can store them, with my paintings, in the basement."

"How come I've not seen this secret basement?"

"Secret?" he raised his eyebrows, "what do you think we keep down there?"

"Who knows," I grinned at him and he shouldered me softly before reaching down to take hold of two of the paintings.

"The baths are down there, I suppose," he said, heading out.

"Baths?"

"Yes, we have Roman baths underneath the house," he nodded and I picked up the final two canvases, before following him out of the room.

"You built your house on Roman baths?"

Seraiah laughed as we went outside into the fresh air, "no, we had similar ones in the palace, but they were much bigger. When we arrived here, my father commissioned them after hearing about Roman history."

"Is that why you always disappear?" I joked.

"Are you always looking for me, Arraetta?" he answered seductively, making me snort.

"You wish," I murmured, though it was absolutely a lie.

"The baths are rarely used by anyone but myself," he answered as he leant over and looked down at the park below. I followed his eyeline, seeing Genie chatting happily with Freddie and Jonah, "you may use them, if you wish."

"Is it… clean?" I asked and he blew out an air of laughter, looking at me flabbergasted.

"Arraetta," he shook his head. "I cannot come to comprehend where you get your thoughts from sometimes."

"Why do you not shorten your sentences?" I replied to him, blushing.

"Once again, you are mocking me," he tutted, then immediately corrected himself, "*you're* mocking me."

"I like it that you are posh," I mimicked his tone, leaning against the balcony, facing the door to my flat, "it makes me feel as though I have stepped into a different century."

"I suppose it is a different time," he added, coming to stand over me as if we were a loving couple. I blushed, looking away from him, "why do you shy away from me, Arraetta?"

"I'm not shying away from you," I stuck my tongue out and then pushed him away as I heard Genie's voice, echoing closer in the stairwell, "so, when are we going to see these baths?"

"Whenever you would like," he replied, watching me as I stretched dramatically like a cat against the balcony, "you are such a child."

"I'm older than you, remember," I replied mockingly, "six millennia, was it?"

"Six million, more like." He chuckled.

I gasped jokingly, trying to come up with something else to say but Seraiah got in there first.

"Do you remember at the ball when you said that if I wanted you to sleep with me, I should just ask?"

I remembered just as he reminded me and I felt a touch of embarrassment hit, but I was able to retort quickly back as I remembered something he had said.

"Do you remember how you told me that I was a perfect example of a *human* woman?"

Seraiah winced at the memory, shaking his head at the thought of it, "I did not mean it as it appeared."

"I have slept with other men," I told him.

"I have no doubt you have," he said, "I actually was trying to tell you that-"

"-I'm so indescribably beautiful that I cannot compare to the heights of *human* women," I interjected with a grin on my face.

"I do not think it would be wise for you to lower your standards to that of a *human*," he replied honestly, "I do believe you are indescribably beautiful."

"Genie's human," I pointed out, moving past his reddening comment, "she's beautiful."

"Although I can agree in some parts," he replied, walking over and pulling me to face him, "she is but a drop on your perfection."

He brought his hand to my face and stroked my bottom lip. My breath caught, heart pounding in my chest, and I hoped that he would lean down to kiss me, but he broke away as Genie's voice echoed once more from the final set of steps. Seraiah had a twitch of a smile in the corner of his mouth, and he picked up the canvases. Meanwhile, I gripped the railing of the balcony, trying to subconsciously calm myself.

Genie, followed by Freddie, finally made it up to where we stood, and she blew out a big breath of air.

"Thank god for that," she whistled and smiled at me, "let's double check we have everything and then we can go to our new home."

I nodded, surprisingly thankful that she'd appeared and interrupted us. Of course, I'd wanted nothing more than for him to kiss me but, in truth, I was nervous about it. I knew he knew that too, which was why he had pointed it out earlier and why I guessed he constantly teased me, thinking that I would soon throw myself at him. I just hoped the teasing would soon be over and the real thing would commence.

FOURTEEN

I felt a feeling of overwhelming joy when the concrete block, of my former home, was out of sight, never to be stepped into again. Surprisingly, Genie cried as we journeyed back – she was an emotional woman, so maybe it wasn't so astonishing. I, on the other hand, didn't care for the place any longer and was excited to be able to call Seraiah's home my own. For the first time in a long time, I felt like I belonged somewhere, even if the last few weeks had been strange and overwhelming. I knew that I could start something exciting and fresh there, and it was even greater that Genie was going to be living there with me.

Her plan, as she revealed in the car, was to continue at dance school, as she had been doing, until she graduated and then she was going to become a dance teacher for the Zikan's. She was also boasting how she was already learning the language and couldn't wait to be challenged in a full conversation. But I wondered whether she thought about the future with Freddie. If they were truly going to return home, and we were going to go with them, how was she going to see her parents? What if she and Freddie had children? How did they manage to get from Zika to Earth in the first place? Was it going to be easy to visit both places? Or would they reside on Earth together?

And, what of me? I would surely go back with Seraiah or maybe, after the pending war that Seraiah spoke about was truly over, we would create our own realm as my parents had done.

When we reached the house, the car door was opened for me and I climbed out, looking up at the beautiful house I would come to call my home. On this early summer evening, I had a renewed love for the place, breathing in the smell of freshly cut grass.

The Zikan guards were already working to get everything into the house and to the correct places. Genie had taken the time to label the boxes accordingly, so they would have no trouble knowing what belonged to whom, though Genie had a lot more than I did and there was a passing comment, made earlier in the day, that maybe she should have a second room for it all.

Inside the house, from the top of the stairs, Tara was watching Genie amusedly as she charmingly bossed around the staff, asking them to drop whatever it was they were doing and make sure she had everything in order. Tara moved her eyes over to us and Seraiah bowed gently; she nodded for us to follow her to the west wing, and we did.

"Mother, are you well?"

"Yes, I'm soon to go to bed," she answered, smiling, then looked at me, "Arraetta, I am very excited that we have moved you in so quickly."

"I haven't brought much," I admitted.

"That is because she does not own much," Seraiah told Tara and I slapped him on the shoulder lightly before blushing, realising the interaction may be too early in our relationship, especially in front of his mother. It caused them both to smile though.

Seraiah spoke to Tara in Zikan, for a short moment, and whatever it was he had said, she seemed to agree with it.

"Charles will be back tomorrow," she told us both, a strange shift in her tone and Seraiah's stance as she highlighted it, "it is high time we start to make plans."

"Plans?" I squeaked nervously.

"For Iontine and the bonding ceremony," she replied. I couldn't help but flush red at the thought of both, they sounded like intimate celebrations, of sorts, and I wondered how I would be involved. I didn't have a clue what Iontine was, but the bonding ceremony sounded very close to marriage; was that the marriage of Freddie and Genie? Or Seraiah and me? If it was for us, I was suddenly very aware of how quickly things had moved and I hadn't even kissed Seraiah yet.

Seraiah noticed my tension and he placed his hand around my waist and squeezed it for comfort. He switched the conversation back to Zikan, telling something to her, which Tara seemed a little taken aback by then she nodded, "I shall bid you both good night."

"Good night," I murmured, curtseying a little, even though Seraiah immediately grabbed me, a sign that I should stop. Tara smiled at us both before leaving for her chambers. She walked with such grace and decorum, that it radiated off her like an aura, and I couldn't help but admire her, wondering whether they were about to give me some form of etiquette lessons so I could mirror that of Her Majesty.

Seraiah and I were suddenly both alone, no guards in sight, and I felt nervous again. I guessed there was some sort of camera watching us from the corner together, but it felt incredibly intimate to be without a guard after what had taken place on the balcony of the flats. I looked up at him, for a short moment, before moving out of his grasp and rubbing my wrist.

"Are you well, Arraetta?" Seraiah asked, a little concerned.

"Uh, yes," I squeaked.

"Come, let us go to the library," he suggested, waving his hand in that direction. I reddened at the thought of us being alone there again. Seraiah chuckled, "you do go awfully quiet when you are nervous."

"I'm not nervous."

"Do you expect something to happen in the library?" he joked, although I could see he was also doing it to see how much teasing he could get away with.

I cleared my throat, "I was merely wondering why the company of books excited you so much."

He laughed and shook his head, "also, the company of wine, painting and maybe a reading of Pride and Prejudice."

I felt my cheeks flush as I remembered that I'd left the library a little messy the day before and, carelessly, had thrown the Zikan novel onto the floor, guessing it to be Jane Austen's most famous novel just by the way the words sat alongside her name. The fact that Seraiah knew I'd been snooping made me nervous that he might have known I'd be down to his little hideaway too, so I quickly changed the subject.

"Maybe I'm more inclined to see your so-called Roman baths."

He clicked his tongue, attempting to stop a smile from rising to his face, and stood back and folded his arms, "okay, we shall read Pride and Prejudice, drink wine and enjoy a bath."

"I... I don't have a swimming costume," I replied, biting my lip.

He smirked, staring at me with his dark brooding eyes.

"Oh, Arraetta," he murmured and then flicked his head up to someone behind me. He suddenly spoke in Zikan, and I turned my head to see one of the servants bowing their head, before they moved down the corridor quickly. Seraiah continued to me, "you do not need anything but your birthday suit."

Naked. With him.

Our gazes settled on one another again, both of us lustful. At that moment, I just wanted to pounce on him. I swallowed, trying to stop the overwhelming feelings from rising within but the thud of my heart, and the dampening in my knickers, was giving it all away. A clearing of a throat and we turned to see one of the maids, whom

I hadn't had the pleasure of meeting; she curtsied as she spoke to Seraiah and he nodded, waving me to follow her.

The walk to the baths seemed to take a lifetime, partially because I was battling with the nerves of being fully alone with him, in what sounded like, such an intimate setting. Most likely without cameras, or guards. Just us, *naked.*

Around the house, the boxes were still being lugged to their respective rooms, but neither Genie nor Freddie were to be seen, so I couldn't have invited them to join us. Something told me that, if we did, they wouldn't have said yes anyway; Genie knew I needed to be alone with Seraiah. I needed to get to know him. Even in those moments of being with him in the flat, I still felt like I didn't know a thing about him.

Down the grand staircase, we walked to the left towards where the stairs down to the kitchens were and down the corridor that led to the back end of the house. The maid opened a door on the left and stepped aside, allowing me to lead us down a dimly lit yet well-decorated staircase. I'd expected it to be cold, but it was pleasantly warm and felt like a unique entrance to a spa.

I was instantly captivated by the room; there were large lamps of fire that were lit on the walls, surrounding a huge rectangular pool of water. The dimming daylight outside pierced through a stained-glass window on the right of the room, whilst the biggest source of light was a wooden chandelier that hung from the ceiling above. The baths were surrounded by stone paving and the water was clouded by steam and some sort of floral fragranced bath formula. At the back of the room, there were two rain showers behind a glass wall, but the feature that stood out the most was the ever-flowing miniature waterfall that cascaded gently into the water.

"This is beautiful," I whispered in awe.

"Quite," Seraiah agreed. I looked over to see he was by one of the loungers, removing his shirt. I immediately turned my head, flushing, and he chuckled having seen my reaction, "you should not look away, Arraetta, this is all yours."

I was red as a tomato as I thought of something to say but couldn't come up with anything that wouldn't make me stumble like a fool. A few moments later, I heard a subtle splash and I turned to see that he was already in, swimming backward, journeying to the other end of the bath.

"Are you coming in?" he smirked.

"I… I thought we were reading Pride and Prejudice," I stumbled, fingering the edge of my t-shirt as thoughts of being naked in there with him were making me feel all sorts of things.

His lip twitched, "it is nice and warm in here, Arraetta."

I wandered close to the edge of the water and peered down into it, then looked up at him. His gaze didn't move from me. I bit my lip, and he scanned my body in a way that meant to coax me to take my clothes off; I wondered whether he was taking physical pleasure from all of this.

"I will come in," I told him, clearing my throat, "but you'll need to close your eyes."

He grinned cheekily and closed them, placing his hands over them before turning away from me, "how is this?"

Seraiah had the most beautifully chiselled shoulders, and I had the urge to jump onto his back and allow him to glide us around the bath together. I swallowed, walked over to the lounger, and nervously began to remove my clothes. I continuously peeked over to him to make sure he wasn't watching. Strangely though, I wanted him to spin around, to see the want in his face, but he respected my boundaries.

I sat down on the edge of the bath and placed my feet into the warm water, before slipping in.

"May I turn around?" he chimed. I dipped low enough to cover myself completely before making a noise of agreement. Seraiah spun towards me, cocking his head to the side as he looked in my direction, "it is deeper over here."

"I'm sure it is," I replied.

"Do you not like it deep?" he asked seductively and I blushed, tutting at him. I was about to retort back but the door opened and the maid, that had led us in entered, carrying a tray on which was a bottle of champagne, in a metal ice bucket, and two champagne glasses, held on a stand to prevent them from falling. And, on the side, was a copy of Zikan 'Pride and Prejudice'.

Without saying another word, she placed the tray down, near to me, at the side of the bath, bowed and left the room, closing the door behind her. I had been so distracted by her arrival that I didn't notice Seraiah swimming up to me until, under the water, his hand touched my lower back. I squeaked and turned to him as he stood tall, the water just above his waist.

"She brought the good stuff," Seraiah eyed the bottle, before looking over at me, "although, I am sure Marie would disapprove if she saw you were drinking after today."

"I'm sure one glass won't hurt," I said, doing my best to keep my eyes on his face and not scan the rest of his glorious physique, which was dripping with water that caressed his skin.

Pop.

Like a skilled bartender, Seraiah picked up the glasses and poured a decent amount, first handing me a glass and then taking his own. I leant back against the bath wall, attempting to stop my body from floating up to reveal itself whilst Seraiah picked up the book and turned it over.

"Why this book?"

"I felt that maybe I could translate it," I shrugged.

"That would be a guessing game," he pointed out and then placed it back down, picked up his glass and swam over to the other end of the pool, "come, join me here."

He sat down at the end, where I guessed there was some sort of built-in seated area. As much as I would have loved to sit next to him, naked, I was nervous because I wasn't the most confident and I suppose I worried he would turn up his nose if I revealed myself.

Though, I knew that it was only a little gremlin, in my ear, telling me that.

"I'm comfortable here," I replied nonchalantly.

"Okay, but do not blame me when your legs begin to hurt," he raised his eyebrows in amusement, sipping his champagne. He leant his head against the ledge, of the pool, and the water gently dampened the edges of his golden locks, as he looked up to the ceiling.

"But, why would it be a guessing game?" I asked, bringing the subject back to the book.

His eyes cast down to me. "The structure is very different," he said, "you should just allow me to teach you some things."

"Like what?" I asked and took a sip of my champagne.

"Now is not the time for that," he said, licking his lower lip gently and staring at me broodingly, "you should really come here, Arraetta."

"And, to whose need is that?" I quipped, that same deep throb pulsing between my legs.

He studied me, for a moment, clicking his tongue before his lip twitched and he said darkly, "oh, Arraetta."

I swallowed, then mimicked, "oh, Seraiah."

A smile grew on his face as he shook his head, "do not tease me so."

"I am not teasing you," I replied, biting the edge of the glass.

Seraiah said something in Zikan to himself before he placed the glass down, on the side, and swam towards me as if he were a creature seeking its prey.

"We barely know each other," I said nervously, scooting backward.

I was expecting him to come and take hold of me straight away, but, instead, he turned around to lean against the wall next to me, that same cheeky look on his face.

"What would you like to know?"

Any sort of normal question went straight out of my head, and I kept thinking about how both of us were two very naked people together in a bath full of clouded water. I wanted him to spin me around, pin me to the edge and make love to me. I swallowed at the thought of the ecstasy of it.

"Arraetta?" he said amusedly and we looked at each other before I turned my head.

"What is... what is your favourite colour?"

"Is this a date between children?"

"Surely, you have one."

Seraiah was right, the question was childish, but it kept the seductive thoughts from bouncing around my head. He cleared his throat and then swam around to the front of me, keeping a little distance, an intense look of admiration on his face, "I do not think I really saw colour until I saw you on the night of the ball. It was as though all love and light had faded away from me, for so long, and, yet, when I saw you the vividness of life returned. I do not believe I have a favourite colour, but I do have a favoured feeling and that is the warmth and beauty that shines from you every time you walk into a room. I have known you only a short while, but it feels like I have known you for a lifetime."

If my face wasn't already a wild shade of pink, it was, in that moment, as he told me those things. The way this man spoke to me, I wondered whether I was trapped in some sort of incredible fairy tale dream; I'd never been told anything as romantic in my life.

"But, I do know *your* favourite colour," he smiled and I swallowed, before taking a sip of my champagne, coaxing him to tell me with a gentle noise of approval. He swam forward so that he was close to me, then lifted his damp hand to stroke my cheek, "it is blue, a little darker than your eyes but lighter than the colour of my Rapidfire."

I gulped at the proximity and, trying to calm myself down from an overwhelming and *stimulating* experience, I joked, "actually, my favourite colour is red."

Seraiah chuckled before swimming back over to the other side to get his drink, turning to me, "anything else?"

"What... what will happen when you defeat... The Dark?" I asked suddenly and he half-choked on his drink.

"I thought we were doing children's questions."

"I was just wondering..."

"What will happen to *us*?" Seraiah replied, moving back over to the bucket of champagne, his glass in his hand. He reached over for mine and I handed it to him, watching as he poured, "I hope that we can rebuild our home, live similarly to now, without the fear of war on our shoulders."

"You don't think everything will change?" I asked, taking the glass from him.

"I think much will change," he answered, somewhat solemnly, "but I cannot say what, nor would I wish to guess. I have adapted to every obstacle thrown my way; things we have learnt being here on Earth will benefit our people back home."

I suddenly felt sad about it all and chewed a little on the edge of my glass. I thought about how much things probably had changed for him and his family and, now, he was expecting to win a war against something deadly. The Dark.

I shuddered thinking about it and then noticed he was looking at me curiously.

"I wish I could get inside of your head, Arraetta," he said honestly.

I smiled. "It's a maze in there," I tapped on my head with my knuckles comically, making him chuckle.

"It is only a maze if you do not share it," he replied, "but, I shall not press you, Arraetta, I am only glad that you are here in my company."

Another gazing match between us began, my breath catching in my throat as I stared into his beautiful brooding chestnut eyes. I reached over for my glass, which I had set down, but ended up knocking it over, the glass itself rolling into the water. Seraiah immediately darted his hand forward, picking the glass up as though it was a prize trophy. The move brought him much closer to me, both of us standing opposite one another.

His hand moved up to my cheek and gently stroked it, soon moving to caress my lips and not once did we lose our gaze. I could feel my legs quivering slightly, in the water, and the want for him grew deeper with every second that went by. His soft touch moved down my neck, tracing it and his eyes followed. I gently bit down on my lip, overpowered by feelings of desire. Not once did I stop him as his finger tickled my shoulder bone; I just felt as his hand rose over the skin of my breast until he was cupping it softly, his finger stroking the tip of my nipple, producing a quiet gasp of air from my mouth.

As though that gasp granted him all the permission he needed, he moved forward, pinning me back against the edges of the bath. And it was all I wanted, just allowing the moment to take place naturally. Seraiah's sweet warm breath blew on my face as he lowered his head towards my own, slightly trembling as though he was just as nervous about this. The hand that cupped my breast rose back to take the same position on my face, hovering over my lips, teasing, and luring me to lean in and take the bait. Automatically, I licked my lips and swallowed my nerves, neither of us making the move to close the impending gap.

"God, I am burning for you, Arraetta," Seraiah whispered, his eyes moving upwards to gaze into mine then back down to my lips, lingering, until he swallowed and looked away in frustrated disappointment; the heated moment between us becoming cold instantly.

"Seraiah?" I murmured, hurt and confused.

"I am sorry, I cannot-"

"-Don't," I whispered sharply, swallowing back the tears that were battling to break free. I nodded a few times, trying to make the situation better, "I… it's okay, I should… I should go to bed."

As I went to turn, he grabbed my arm, "Arraetta-"

"-Let me go," I gulped, using the moment to pull myself out of the water and rush over to the lounger, without a care that he would see me naked.

"Please, Arraetta," he begged as I threw on one of the robes, turned away from him as the tears began to fall. I grabbed my clothes, from the pile on the floor, and heard Seraiah shuffling himself out of the water, "please, know it is not you."

"Then, what is it?" I shouted at him in frustration, seeing him, standing in all his naked glory, upset that I was crying. I rubbed my eyes to stop the tears, "because you can't just go around playing with people's hearts."

"Please do not cry," he murmured, stepping forward as I turned towards the exit of the room. He rushed after me, coming to stand in front of me, "Arraetta, please let me explain."

I growled in anger, "let me leave."

"We cannot do this, not until the bonding is complete," he said, trying to reason, but it only made me feel more frustrated, "I have so much desire to be with you, it is deeply frustrating, I know, but we cannot risk binding our souls together too soon."

"Bonding?" I shouted at him, "bonding! What the hell is this bond, Seraiah?"

"It is-"

"-Because you obviously know far more than I do about it," I interjected, breath flaring, "and, what, because of this so-called bonding we can't kiss, huh? And, on top of that, is it not for us to decide when we want to do things?"

He swallowed and slowly nodded, "you are right."

"You know, it's not fair," I whispered, swallowing my tears and standing up straight, "it's not fair for you to just... do these things to me... not if you know there are consequences. Good night, Seraiah."

I shoved past him and exited the baths, jogging up the steps to the main section of the house, where I attempted to not slip on the parquet flooring as I dripped all over it. Tears spilt down my cheeks and I did everything not to make eye contact with any of the staff, who may have enquired as to my well-being. There were no guards either, not even Alex who was supposed to be my personal guard. Guarding me from everything but heartbreak.

Back in my room, I let myself sob. I wished it wasn't Seraiah that had caused this pain as it was him who I wanted to come and hold me and tell me it was okay.

But it was Seraiah who had caused it. I felt abused. He had teased me since the moment we had met, he cared about me and was the last person who would break my heart, yet he still had done it. He'd taken pleasure from every moment of it; first, the meeting at the ball, then his reveal to me, of who we were to each other, and the images of us both together. Following that, he had teased me all day, whilst packing the flat, asking me why I was nervous and, when those nerves were finally swallowed, in the bath, he pulled away incredibly quickly. And why would he touch my breast like that? Watching me quiver under his touch like I was his little toy to play with.

Not until the bonding is complete.

We cannot risk binding our souls together too soon.

I wanted to shout 'fuck you' in his face, to be free of the torment of it all, to tell him that, if it was going to be this painful, that it wasn't worth it, but I couldn't. I couldn't because I knew, no matter what, I couldn't escape from the feelings I had for him. That every time I saw him, I fell for him more and that I was, somehow, undeniably, and indescribably, in love with him.

FIFTEEN

I restlessly tossed and turned for hours, thoughts of the whole situation, between Seraiah and I, mixed with the events from the day, whirling around my head. Seraiah wanted to protect me, I could see that, but that protection was coming at a greater cost to our relationship. He didn't want to tell me anything because he didn't think I was ready but, when he did, the realisation, he was being more open, would hit him and he would abruptly move on from it.

I climbed out of bed, around four o'clock, and wandered the empty corridors of the house, hiding from some of the night guards, that wandered the hallway, when I heard them shuffling about. It wasn't the first time I'd roamed the halls at that time; the week after I'd woken up, I spent a few early mornings wandering as I couldn't sleep, and I liked the peacefulness of the house then. One morning, I had come to learn that the baker would arrive around four thirty, as the smell of freshly baked bread would rise, from the kitchen downstairs, and it made my stomach rumble.

I found myself outside the large doors of the library, drawn to sneaking a peek at the book, once again, but I was a little apprehensive that Seraiah would be in there also. Not because I felt like I was invading his personal space, I just didn't think a four-in-the-morning confrontation, following the night before, was a good idea.

I decided to be brave and headed in, gently closing the door behind me. The room was very dark with only the soft moonlight peeking through the windows. I wished I had my phone, or even just a torch, so that I could have seen better. I found my way to the ladder and climbed up onto the mezzanine level, wandering over to the bookcase to see the book exactly how it was left.

Reaching up behind it, I found the key, that I'd secretly left, and thanked the Gods that Seraiah hadn't been trying to find it to look at the book too. I opened the shelf and pulled the book out, looking around for a spot to sit in and opted to sit nearer to the window where the light would be somewhat better.

Sitting against the balustrade, in a relatively hidden position, I opened the book and began to study it again. I struggled to understand some parts of it, not just because of it being in a different language but because it was hard to read in a relatively dark room.

I wondered if there was a way that I could hone into my power and bring some light to the space I sat in, without putting on the lights of the library. I had done it the day before with Seraiah, although that was for a different purpose. I also wasn't sure whether Rakatan was just for going to another place, or whether it could be used for other purposes, but I decided that I would try and give it some sort of go.

Closing my eyes, I placed my hand onto the book and breathed in and out several times, listening to the words in my head, that Seraiah had said to me, and imagined what it would be like to feel the light around me. I felt the tingle crawl up my arm again and a feeling of hope washed over me so quickly that I, immediately, opened my eyes to take in the space around.

No changes anywhere, not even a hint of change on my body with the soft prickle under my skin that I'd felt. I was disappointed that my attempt at using my power didn't work, although it was most likely not the right way to use it.

I lifted my hand up in front of my face, palm facing away, before I turned it around to face me.

"Come on, Arri," I murmured, "you can do it. Breathe in… breathe out."

I closed my eyes once again, to see if it would work for a second time, and jumped when a sharper tingle resonated up my arm. I saw the light through my lids and flicked them open, looking as my arm brightly lit up, with strange symbols, in a prominent golden colour. It was the first time I'd managed to see my power come to life, without feeling an opposite effect.

I saw as my arm was not only glowing but giving off a light clouded hue, just above it, like a gentle haze from a sun ray. However, the power wasn't much further up my arm and had come to a halt, just before my elbow, and, before I could use it for the purposes of seeing the book, it began to pulse gently, fading with it until I was in the dark again.

I grumbled in annoyance, wanting to give it another go, but felt a strange rumble, below, followed by a sharp flash of pain that rocketed in my head. I winced as my energy dissipated for a moment, a similar feeling to how I felt after any of my episodes. Then, as though it kicked back in immediately, I felt a soar of energy, in my body, that felt like I was being super charged.

I grimaced as the overpowering shock of it overwhelmed my body and heard a loud crackle sound below the floors of the library. I jolted, weakness spreading through my fibres, and I grunted as I tried to catch my breath, doing everything to stop an episode from happening. I dropped the book on the floor, with a thud, not intending to return it to its original place, and moved as quickly back across the mezzanine and down the ladder.

At the bottom, I held myself against the ladder, for a few moments, before rushing out of the room. I wasn't sure if I passed by anyone, even though I already heard several concerned voices, throughout the house, before I headed into my bedroom. I darted under the covers, breathing heavily until I eventually fell asleep.

The next morning, I awoke with a throbbing headache, but I decided that I'd face the day, in hopes that I hadn't done anything detrimental during my attempt at using my own power.

Alex greeted me kindly, outside my door, and I just hoped that he hadn't been watching the cameras because I wasn't ready for any sort of confrontation.

The door was already open to the breakfast room, when I went down for breakfast, and I could hear the voices of Genie, Freddie and, to my surprise, Seraiah in there. I had yet to dine with him, at that time, as he usually ate elsewhere. As I entered, Seraiah and Freddie stood up and bowed. Seraiah stood for a little longer, trying apologetically to catch my gaze, as Cedric pulled out a chair, next to Genie, for me to sit.

"How are you this morning?" Genie asked.

"A little tired."

"As am I," she answered, "Freddie was up this morning, the generator blew."

"The generator?" I questioned.

"It is our energy source," Freddie explained, "a big ball of energy, beneath the house, that helps us survive here."

It must be the same ball of energy that I'd seen, in Seraiah's study nook, as that looked like the only thing remotely powerful enough to do such a thing.

"It also powers the shield," Seraiah added and I looked at him briefly, hoping that he wasn't about to say, *'you destroyed it this morning'.* Instead, he offered me a soft smile, "I do apologise, I believe it was me that may have caused the outage as I was testing a few things this morning, so some of us will be feeling worse for wear because of it."

"Do not worry, Seraiah," Freddie chuckled, "I do not mind feeling shit for the sake of your magic tricks."

Freddie's lightness was welcomed, and we all laughed, and Seraiah reacted by smacking him over the back of his head.

"I had picked up on a unique energy," Seraiah explained, "you know that I am always looking for a way to make it stronger."

I had a feeling that the foreign energy, that Seraiah picked up on was my own. How he managed to use it, I was unsure, but something in me knew that I was part of the whole charade. I was just glad he didn't know it was me. Or I hoped he didn't.

"I hoped you would not mind accompanying me to Sheika's," Seraiah said and I looked at him, seeing his gaze on me.

I grimaced at the thought of seeing that woman again after she had made me drink the strange tea last time. I wondered if Seraiah knew about the tea, maybe he was asking because he didn't.

"We will talk to her about Iontine and the bonding ceremony," Seraiah continued, as if answering the question that was about to come spilling out of my mouth. Those two things, once again, had cropped up from the evening before.

"Okay," I nodded.

Freddie spoke to Seraiah in Zikan, and Seraiah agreed. From the sounds of it, Freddie was asking Seraiah to do something, and I guessed that it was to do with Genie as Seraiah's eyes shifted to Genie, back to Freddie and then over to me.

Seraiah offered me a soft smile, the same apologetic look on his face and I felt my lips rise subconsciously. Really, I cursed myself for it because he would, immediately, guess that meant the night before was forgotten but I was just trapped in the feeling of desire I had for him.

Following breakfast, Seraiah and I left together to see Sheika. I just hoped she wasn't going to do some strange voodoo magic again because I didn't want to have another episode, especially in front of Seraiah. All I wanted to do was get in, find out any information I could and get out as quickly as possible. I had the sneaky suspicion that Seraiah wanted to do the same thing.

As per usual, Alex followed us at a distance, accompanied by Travis.

"Which one is your personal guard?" I asked Seraiah.

"All of them," he chuckled, "most work on a rota, although I tend to confine myself to the library, and my study so that I can have a little bit of time alone."

I smiled as we descended the small hill from the manor, towards the first row of houses. It was a breath-taking sight every time I left because the entire road was beautiful, from top to bottom, with the colourful beds of flowers and majestic gardens.

"Is Zika like this?" I asked him as I looked at the village.

"A little," Seraiah replied, "Zika was quite old fashioned; a little bit like how you may imagine a place in a fairy tale. Our buildings were made from stone and were painted in so many different colours."

"Sounds magical."

"Yes, it was," Seraiah smiled a little solemnly, "to get to our palace, you would go up through the winding roads of the town, that pushed past the busiest of markets, and homes, and, eventually, you would make it to the top of a slight hill where large gates sat. Through those gates, around a mile or so again, you would get to the palace… which was five times as big as this place."

"Wow," I smiled, imagining how breath-taking it was.

"Yes, and, at the bottom of the town, was the sea that would cascade over the edge of the world, like a magnificent waterfall," he informed me.

"So… does your realm sit on top of The Cre-este?" I felt a little strange saying the place for the first time, as though I was saying it incorrectly.

"No," he smiled, "although I could see the resemblance."

"You seem to know a lot about it," I said to him.

"Some," he answered truthfully, "although I do not feel I am the best person to speak to you about The Cre-este. I am unsure who it would be; we have only documented through stories we have been told."

I nodded, wondering whether to push further. I decided against it as we continued onwards. I went back to what he spoke about earlier, "how do you know that your home is no longer there?"

"What do you mean?"

"You spoke in the past tense like it no longer exists," I told him.

"I do not think the Zika we knew exists," he answered, "although our land will be there, who knows what terrible things The Dark has infested in our world."

"The Dark," I said to him, "you said you would tell me of it."

"Yes, I shall," he replied. Another non-answer. "However, there are more *important* things to talk about today and you do not need to be overloaded with information."

I subconsciously rolled my eyes, which Seraiah smiled gently at, moving to try and take hold of my hand as if that would make the situation better. I moved my hand away too quickly, "don't."

Seraiah sighed, both of us moving into uncomfortable silence as we continued walking together. A couple from a house greeted us both and Seraiah returned the greeting, whilst I faked a polite smile.

"We were attacked," Seraiah spoke, after a few minutes, "there was a teller who told us that our world would succumb to darkness and would only be saved by the light. We were never informed of the date, but our armies prepared for the worst and something worse than that appeared. I cannot tell you exactly how many of our people died but I can tell you that little over three hundred of us made it to

Earth. Women, children, slaughtered mindlessly by them. They have no remorse because they can do nothing more than feed on fear and pain."

The thought of it made my heart pump rapidly. It was terrifying to think that so many were dead because of such a monstrosity. But what was it? A collective of dark souls out for vengeance? A plague that spreads with fear and pain? But, the most important thing, how had it changed Seraiah? Was what I saw by the lake, and in my hallucination, a form of it or just an image that my own mind had manifested?

"What happened to your arm?" I asked him.

Seraiah cringed away from the subject. I could see as his whole body stiffened and something flashed in his eyes - the memory, maybe. He looked thoughtful, coming up with another way to divert the subject, and he got his way as we came to the path that led up to Sheika's house.

To be honest, even if he had decided to continue speaking, I wouldn't have listened as the haunting of the hallucination struck in my head and I halted for a moment. I felt Seraiah about to ask me if I was alright, so I started up the hill at a pace, ignoring the worry that I felt in my core.

We came to Sheika's doorstep, the pungent smell of incense overpowering my senses, once again. Seraiah paused for a moment before he stepped up to knock on the door.

We listened to the little dog yip from inside. It took a few moments, but Sheika eventually shuffled through, both of us listening, as she told Russell to be quiet before opening the door to reveal that she was wearing pyjamas.

"Apologies, Sheika."

"Do not apologise." She smiled brightly, "I was hoping you would swing by, at some point, it is wonderful to see you both together."

I couldn't tell if she was being sincere, by saying that, but I could certainly tell that Sheika was a good person just from meeting her. I didn't sense anything bad about her, although my intuition could be all over the place for how on edge I was, just in case she brought something out like the tea once again.

She coaxed us into her home, and through to the kitchen, where Seraiah and I took a seat at the table, whilst she placed the kettle onto the stove.

"Now, to what do I owe to this pleasure?" she asked, turning to us both.

"I think it is about time that Arraetta understands what the bonding ceremony is," Seraiah said. Sheika looked at me with her old eyes, for a moment, before she nodded.

"It was a conversation we are due to have," Sheika said and sauntered off into the other room. The room settled, the clock ticking away and the kettle humming. Seraiah and I sat in the silence of it all, waiting for her. A minute later, the kettle was screaming, and she came back through with a large, heavy book in her hand. She turned the kettle off, before walking over to us and placed the book down on the table with a thud, "let me make some tea."

"Ah, no I'm alright," I rushed out and she raised her eyebrows, ignoring me, and walked over to the stove.

"Scared of the tea?" Seraiah joked under his breath.

"I'm happy not to have another hallucination," I said in the same jesting tone. I watched Seraiah take in what I said, and a strange realisation came over him.

"When I collapsed," he whispered; loud enough for us just to be the ones to hear. I nodded, but the conversation couldn't continue as Sheika interjected.

"It is wonderful to have you both here," Sheika remarked, "and what a joyous occasion it will be when you come together in matrimony."

If I had a drink, I would've surely spluttered it up as I looked at

Seraiah, then to Sheika and back to Seraiah, whispering, "married."

Seraiah looked amused as though it had been obvious. I mean, of course, it had been obvious - I was to get married eventually but I didn't think it would be so soon.

"You are two fated souls, Arraetta," Sheika said, placing a cup of black tea in front of me, "and, in order for you to come together as a whole, you must bond."

"And, what does that incur?"

"It is very similar to a marriage," she continued, "however, the vows are different and you shall, in a sense, hand-fast. Except, it is without a ribbon." She flipped open the book to show us two hands, with numerous tattoos on it. "Legends tell that these tattoos appear on the forearms of the two Kindred Spirits as their bond solidifies."

"Are they permanent?" I found myself asking, although they were beautiful so I wouldn't care if they were.

"I believe so," she answered, "anyone who comes to be in the presence of either Kindred Spirit, following the bonding, would know immediately who they were. But we must make sure the energy is at its strongest prior to the ceremony, that is why it shall follow Iontine."

Iontine - there was the mention of it again.

"Seraiah, you must surely have informed your wife of something," Sheika raised her eyebrows and I blushed as she named me his *wife*. I looked at Seraiah as he eyed me before he sat up straight.

"I thought it best we speak of these things here," Seraiah replied, "Iontine is the festival of the Gods. It is where we celebrate, and worship, the divine beings of the universe in hopes they will provide us more sustenance."

"Sustenance?"

"Power," he answered, "in a form. Rapidfire being one of them; the rest is enough energy for our people to survive on this planet."

"And the... Gods just give that to you?"

"So far," Sheika interjected, "but much has changed this year and I would not be surprised if our festival comes with some... *hiccups*."

I must have been one of the biggest *hiccups* that had happened, there was no doubt about that.

"Iontine will take place in August," she told me, "and, your bonding shall take place the week following. It will be a wondrous occasion."

"That's so close," I breathed. I felt Seraiah's gaze on me, but I couldn't bring myself to look up at him.

Part of me was ecstatic about the idea of Seraiah and I marrying each other, but another part of me was saying that I still had my whole life ahead of me. Then again, what kind of life would I live without him? I couldn't even imagine it. I didn't *want* to imagine it.

"Before we continue," Seraiah said to Sheika, then turned the conversation to Zikan quickly, mentioning both the names of Freddie and Genie in the sentence. Sheika nodded to him before she stood and moved out of the room. Before I could inquire, Seraiah leant forward on the table, "Arraetta, please do not fear these things, I know it is overwhelming."

"Aren't you scared?" I asked him.

"Yes," he said honestly, "but not of marrying you, Arraetta, you are exactly the person I always dreamt of being fated to."

I blushed, "then what are you scared of?"

"Losing you in the process," he answered. I was taken aback by the answer, but I could get that he could sense my apprehension - the rabbit, constantly on edge, waiting to run from the wolf.

Sheika interrupted by coming back in, a small plastic bag, with herbs, in her hands, and she placed it down in front of Seraiah.

"What's that?" I asked.

"It is for Genie," Seraiah replied, "for her headaches."

"Headaches?" I gasped. It was the first time I'd heard of her having them; were they that severe that she had to take herbs over paracetamol? I needed to ask her about them the next time I saw her.

"Now, it reads here," Sheika said, flipping the book open as she sipped her tea, "that the meeting of the two Kindred Spirits is, by no means, an occurrence that will commonly take place, for it actually is the rarest occurrence to happen in the universe. When the universe deems it worthy to bring these two together, following a longevity of distance and time, it means that the universe is seeking to bring peace in a time of chaos. The two shall entwine their souls, in a bonding, that will create serenity for thousands of years across the plains of existence, even after the departing of the souls from their mortal bodies."

Sheika looked up to us both, seeing that, for once, we were listening intently, and then she turned to the next page of the book. I couldn't bear to look at Seraiah as I didn't know what he was thinking: did he think it sounded romantic? Because it kind of did… Or would this be a little bit too much for him to take in? Or maybe he already knew all this…

"Now, the era of serenity will not come easily," she said, reading further, "in this book, it tells of a time of turmoil, and mayhem, and a great war that soon shall follow the binding of the souls. For, as we all know, for one exchange another must be made in order to keep the balance across the universe."

"What war?" I asked curiously, "surely we could just… not… bond, right?"

Seraiah gave me a *you're not serious* look. The idea of postponing matrimony was obviously not on the agenda for him. Then again, if he'd met the nymph back in Zika, that meant that he'd been waiting for a very, very long time for me.

"There is a great reason, child," Sheika smiled kindly, "for there carries more greatness, in your connection, than there does without. Firstly, I have seen how you are together, the pain of no unity carries clear and has already begun to affect those around you. Secondly, the further we push the bond, the more destruction will be caused in the worlds that are currently shrouded in chaos. A much greater war, that takes less time, is much more acceptable than a war that continues to grow slowly, eventually creating more destruction. I am sure you understand."

"Is there another way?" I asked naively and I received a humoured look from Seraiah. I continued, "no, I mean, I get the concept but, surely, we could find another way around the whole war thing."

Seraiah had already mentioned the war with The Dark on the stairwell, so surely a second war wasn't going to be wanted if there was already one impending. Unless the war with The Dark was the chaos that they truly spoke about. The thought of it sent a shiver down my spine; it wasn't a war I wanted to be fighting.

"I do not think there is another way," Sheika opened and I looked at her for a moment, seeing a slightly solemn look on her face.

"The universe is all about balance, right?" I said with my newfound knowledge, from Tara's lecture, "so, maybe we could sacrifice something."

"Like?" Seraiah raised his eyebrows.

"What about... I don't know... what about our Rapidfire?"

"No," Seraiah told me sharply, "amongst all things, I could not ask anyone to sacrifice their power and, even if we could, I know it is needed to fight The Dark."

"Well, maybe just mine then?"

"You would have to sacrifice the entirety of Rapidfire," Sheika interrupted, "you will be asking to give in the greatest power to ever be given to mortals in return for no war."

"I think it's reasonable," I shrugged, looking at them both as they returned perplexed looks as if it was a stupid idea, "don't you think it's caused enough destruction already?"

"And what of those whose life depends on Rapidfire?" Seraiah asked.

"What do you mean?"

"How do you think we survive, Arraetta?" he stated and I looked at him, for a moment, as the realisation of it washed over me. Without Rapidfire, we would all die.

"But, not everyone has Rapidfire," I said to him.

"No, but those of us who do cannot survive without it," he answered, "It is our life force. You speak of sacrificing when you do not fully understand how Rapidfire came to pass."

"How can I understand when no one will tell me anything?" I asked him frustratedly. I could feel the tension in the air; I could tell that Seraiah could tell me more, but I knew he was always apprehensive about doing so.

"Rapidfire was gifted to many in power," Sheika informed me, "in return, they had to sacrifice their vitality. There are some of us who have greater knowledge than others; it will take time to explain the full story, but I do not think it will harm you to know a little more."

"We are here to talk about the bond," Seraiah said.

"It won't harm me," I repeated, glaring at him.

Seraiah sighed dramatically and sat back, folding his arms, "go ahead."

"Although the legends say that Ivan the Great defeated Roxecluf, and The Dark, in a tremendous battle of power," Sheika told me, "his efforts were only enough to lock The Dark in the realm known as Nowhere. It was rumoured that The Dark would be locked there, for all of eternity, should nobody ever enter that realm again. However, someone also was in the realm, Ivan's brother Eric and he is believed to be the reason that The Dark has come to be released from its chamber.

"After the war, Ivan the Great met with the highest Gods for a final time. He had fallen in love with the goddess Reona, on his original visit to the Gods, and he wanted to marry her. They offered him Reona's hand but in exchange for his Rapidfire to be shared with other realms. Ivan agreed but only on the premise that his gift would no longer be housed with him but another."

I had a feeling she was going to say it was me. They had talked about me housing the Divine Rapidfire.

"Who that person was became a decision of the Gods," Sheika said, telling us both the story rather than aiming at me, "and no one knew who that person was. However, you are the bearer of flaxen Rapidfire. It is only known that the bearer of Divine Rapidfire has the gold lightning power, this is because it is in its purest form which makes it the most powerful."

I felt like I was being dragged back and forth with the knowledge of who I was. But everything they had told me so far, deep down, felt true. The biggest evidence came from the colour my veins turned and my meeting with Pa... who was in a completely different realm.

Sheika continued, "the person who houses Divine Rapidfire holds the power of one thousand suns within them. They can create, and destroy, havoc within an instant. Its son, the Rapidfire, has similar abilities but it requires many, to work together, to power as a whole. Almost like pieces of a puzzle."

It all made sense, but I had so many more questions about it. Yes, she told me of its origins, and I understood that we couldn't sacrifice the life force, within us, without dying, but, the biggest thing, I wanted to know was how I could control it. If I embodied a power so great that it could destroy things, within an instant, wouldn't I be the person to fight against The Dark.

The thought did make me shiver, because the last thing I wanted to do was run head first, into battle, against something that scared me, but if I could destroy it in an instant, it would mean that it would be over quickly and there would be no need to fight.

"Now, let us get back to the bond," she finished.

"But, you didn't tell me how the Rapidfire works."

Seraiah dramatically groaned like a child, "Arraetta, can we not talk about what is here at hand?"

"Why do you always move the conversation?" I asked him in annoyance.

"You are constantly asking questions," he continued, "I told you we must slow down."

"Slow down, slow down," I mocked before snapping, "what's so secret about it all?"

"There is no secret," Seraiah huffed whilst Sheika watched us both bicker, with a bit of amusement on her face, "you have barely been here for five minutes and you want to know everything."

"I deserve to know everything!" I stood up and placed my hands, heavily, on the table.

"Not yet!" Seraiah matched my stance but was louder in his booming tone, "you are not ready to know everything, you are still a child."

"Fuck you, Seraiah!" I shouted at him, tipping the mug of tea over, "you're more of a child than I am, sitting there sulking because I ask fucking grown up questions. Argh."

Before he could come back at me, I stormed out, without saying another word, and rushed back to the house in anger. I couldn't believe how he was, once again, blocking me from information that I wanted to know - needed to know. What was such a big secret that was so hard for him to tell me? I was going to be his wife, his queen and he couldn't tell me anything I should know.

No matter what, I would find out everything.

SIXTEEN

Back at the house, I slowed down my pace and wandered up the stairs, attempting not to allow my angered thoughts to continue to cloud my mind. I commanded, without remorse, that Alex leave me alone, when I'd arrived at the house, and, surprisingly, he did just that.

Arraetta, a soft whisper, from the east wing, called and I frowned, freezing on the spot as I came to the beginning of it.

"Genie?" I called gently, stepping forward to look down the corridor. No one was there. I frowned and walked onwards, looking around a little, before continuing to my room.

Arraetta, the same soft whisper called back down the corridor, towards the entrance of the house. I frowned and turned around in its direction, once again seeing no one.

"Hello?" I called, my voice echoing as though it was never ending.

"Hello!" a voice boomed, behind my ear, and I squealed, as I spun around to face it.

Nothing.

My heart pounded in my chest, as I scoured the empty space, ahead of me, until I heard a scuffling of feet behind. Slowly, I turned in its direction, fear overpowering my senses as I prayed there was nobody there.

Hope was dissolved when I saw a woman, standing in the centre of the corridor, with her back towards me. She was tall and slender with long curly brown hair whilst a dark cloak covered her body, her head convulsing a little as she stared down at something.

"Ma?" I squeaked, stepping gently forward.

I halted as the space began to quake and I jumped, watching as the corridor began to crumble, preventing my escape. I heard an ear-piercing wail from the woman, and I flicked my head back towards her, seeing both of us seemingly floating on a long piece of flooring. Surrounding us was the dark ashen sky that I'd seen so prominently in my dreams. This time we were just below it and I shook, feeling coldness trickle down my spine as it began to fracture.

"Help me!" She screamed.

The woman mechanically turned towards me.

I froze on the spot, eyes wide in fear. This woman wasn't my mother, it was *me* – except my eyes were black, with veins sprouting from them. I could feel my heart rapidly beating, within my chest, as she began to trudge towards me, black sludge trickling down her cheeks from her eyes and dripping like blood onto the floor. The clouds began to whirl around us, like a high-speed tornado, as she wailed again.

"Help me!"

She tripped; the sludge beginning to drip down her arms, onto the floor, before it wormed its way towards me. I wanted to run, but my whole body was frozen. My breath was out of control, needing nothing more than to scream for help, but I was unable to make a sound. Something tugged at me, and I wobbled backward, out of the trance, before turning and running. But the floor of the corridor was only getting longer the more I ran. That's when the space froze, fear trickling up my spine as I stopped again, breathing in and out.

Click. Click. Click.

Like that of a rattlesnake, the noise sounded just behind my being. Shivers prickled my body, and my hands shook as I slowly turned again.

In front of my face, were the void-filled eyes of my doppelganger, who seemed to struggle for breath as she watched me curiously for a long, slow moment. Then, she screamed again. A sound that resonated through my body as I swallowed the bile in my mouth, falling backward onto the floor. I attempted to crawl away but came up against another wall.

I didn't have a chance to get my bearings as she jumped at me, causing me to wince, but there was only sudden silence. I trembled, trying to catch my breath, but I was struggling intensely. I felt two large hands cradle my upper arms and I thrashed back and forth, trying to stop this person from taking me.

"Arraetta, you are safe," came a familiar whisper and I blinked my eyes open, looking up into the face of my pa, "you are safe."

"Pa?" I barely squeaked, looking into his kind eyes.

"You are safe here." He whispered, helping raise me to my feet as I attempted to catch my breath. He brought me into a much-needed hug, and I felt the tears rise.

I whispered, "why does this keep happening?"

"That is not a question for me to answer," he said and then gestured that I take a deep breath. As I concentrated on my breathing, I was able to take in the place we were standing in, it was some form of long fairy tale-like bridge floating on pure white clouds.

"Where am I?"

"You are on the bridge of Ryazark," he said, "someday you shall cross this bridge, daughter, and join me."

Still attempting to regain my composure, I walked to the bridge wall.

"I heard your cry for help," he continued, walking over to stand by me.

"I... I don't know what happened," I panicked, the image of my darker self etching into my mind as I continued to attempt to breathe evenly.

"Arraetta, you must calm down," Pa said, pulling me to face him, with a soft smile, "you are much too powerful to be scared off by such creatures as The Dark."

"But- but-"

"Arraetta, do you not remember the stories I used to tell you as a child?" He chuckled, coming to lean against the high brick wall, once again, making me look like I was but a child with my father, "you used to tell me how one day you would defeat The Dark and everyone will remember you as a hero."

"I'm no hero."

"Are you not?" he chimed and I looked at him, beginning to calm down, "not yet at least, but you have much to come in your life. For one, you are to be married to a prince who I have, no doubt, you shall save time and time again."

"Save from what?"

"Himself," Pa smiled, "just like your mother saved me so many times."

"Well, maybe I don't want to marry him," I lied, "he is so frustrating, he never tells me anything and he is keeping something from me - I know it."

"Do you know it, Arraetta?" he chuckled, "or, are you just seeing it from your own perspective?"

"He won't tell me anything," I moved to look up at him, "as soon as he knows I want to talk about The Dark or Rapidfire, he turns away from me, telling me that it's too soon."

Pa looked at me for a moment, "maybe he is right."

"Why are you on his side?" I asked him.

"I am not," he said, "but, you do need to slow down. It is no wonder you end up having such nightmares, your anger is causing your power to go into overdrive."

"That's the cause?" I frowned.

"One of them," he nodded, "I remember how it affected me, when I had first been gifted the power, and I did not have much time to learn to live with it."

"Sheika said that you asked for your power to be taken away."

Pa paused and then laughed heartily, "is that truly what they have been saying about me? No, Arraetta, I always had Divine Rapidfire, it was the only way I knew I could protect you."

"So, I also have Divine Rapidfire?"

"You truly believe it to be such a burden?" he chuckled, "my lavrae, you only have to learn to control it and you shall see it as more of a gift."

"How can I learn to control it when no one will help me?" I exasperated, "I feel so alone in this world and the one person, you would think, that could help me is just so… argh… frustrating."

"Seraiah shall come around soon, I am sure of it," Pa smiled gently.

"Do I have to… bond with him?" I blushed at the thought of how intimate it sounded, "they said a war will start."

"There must be a war to end what has come to pass. It shall be a war of all wars," Pa said with a slight chuckle, "you are very strong, Arraetta, you must use this time to allow yourself to learn more about your power, so that you are ready for when you must fight."

"Pa, is The Dark what we are fighting?"

"Yes," he nodded, "it must be destroyed, Arraetta."

"How?" I whispered.

"You shall know when the day is right," he placed his hand on my shoulder, "you must go now."

"Please, wait, just one more question."

He barked with laughter at my alarmed face.

"I can hold this for one more."

"How… how can I understand you?" I whispered, "you're speaking English."

"My child, we are not speaking English," Pa continued to laugh, obviously very amused, "we are in a realm where all languages are translated, but you, my lavrae, have been listening to me speak in our native language, Cre-estian, you just have not learnt to tap into the side of your memory that helps you remember it all."

"So, I'm not speaking English?" I whispered, taken aback.

He shook his head, "Arraetta, you must go."

"Will I see you again?" I breathed; my eyes full of hope.

"You shall, my child," he nodded.

Arraetta, a voice echoed across the space around us, as though we were in a hollow room.

"Lavrae, Arraetta."

"Pa!" I shouted as he floated back, the bridge seemingly getting wider.

Arraetta! A voice called once again.

I heard the fizzle of sounds echo in my ears, as though I had been placed under water, watching as the beautiful bridge crackled and, within a blink, my eyes were staring into Seraiah's worried ones. And as though I had not taken a breath for a long time, I gasped for air, reality kicking back in. My eyes flickered around, seeing that I was still standing in the hallway. A tissue was placed over my nose and my eyes connected back with Seraiah's. He was speaking to me yet, no matter what, I couldn't hear what he was saying, blinking to try to understand.

Shakily, I lifted my hand up to my cheeks, feeling how tight they were from, what I thought were, dried up tears but when I moved it back, I saw flecks of blood on my palm. Against Seraiah's protests,

I took a few weary steps past him over to the hallway mirror, not paying attention to anything behind me.

I stared at the girl before me; blood-soaked eyes, cheeks, and ears, all of which would look horrific to a normal person, but I was too dazed to make any reaction. A sharp crackle resounded in my ears, and I listened as the piercing sounds of the hallway shot back at me, within an instant, whilst everyone's shadows seemed to move in slow motion. Without control over my body, I fell towards the floor – a better resting place. And I was caught by Seraiah.

"I have got you," his voice was muffled as he lifted me up, my head lolling back to stare up at the ceiling.

A flash of the dark, ashen sky and I winced, turning my head away to see a pair of legs and the edges of a bed. Someone's hands pulled me onto my back, and I blinked up to see the face of Marie as she spoke over me to another. A cool, wet cloth swept across my face; the owner of the hand unknown as I couldn't seem to see clearly past it.

The face of my darker self fractured in my vision and I squealed, shutting my eyes to prevent it from attacking me again. Yet, as quick as it came, it went and I was back in the room, feeling my body being held down as I cried, trying to break free from it all. There was a sharp piercing in my wrist, and I tried to move my arm from the grasp, but to no avail as my breathing slowed and I succumbed to the darkness of slumber.

The sounds of life awakened me once more and I grumbled and blinked, coming to look up at the ceiling, of my bedroom, dazedly. Genie's face entered my view, with her looking down at me, sorrowfully, before sweeping another cloth across my face. I murmured and moved my arm up to stop her, and she tutted at me before stopping.

"I think you'll need to make me your personal nurse," she said lightly and I smiled as she sat back and looked down at me, "God, Arri, you had us so worried."

"I have the worst headache," I said, placing my hand on my warm forehead.

Genie answered, her voice hushed, "it's supposed to be me with the headaches, not you."

She was trying to make light of the situation, which I was thankful for, in these dark times, but they weren't making the headache go away.

"You never told me about those," I murmured.

"I… I didn't want to worry you," she whispered, "and, it's being resolved."

I nodded, not feeling like I could get her to elaborate any further in my state. I scanned the room, seeing we were both alone. Sunlight shone in through the window.

"What time is it?"

"It's about two," she said, standing up to go over to a makeshift wash bowl to clean her hands, "they had to put you to sleep."

"Nothing unusual there," I tutted, sitting up slowly. Genie rushed back over, urging me to take it as easy as possible. I placed my hand onto her cheek, "don't worry about me."

"How can I not?" she murmured as she placed pillows against my back, to soften the lean against the headboard, "I keep thinking you'll be fine and then something else happens."

"I didn't expect anything more to happen," I replied as she poured me a glass of water from a carafe and handed it over.

"I know," she smiled gently, "I'm not blaming you, I just wish there was a way for us to help you."

"I give you permission to go inside my head," I joked and she laughed.

"I think you had a lot of nightmares overnight, Seraiah was by your side for most of it."

I wasn't surprised I had nightmares overnight from what I'd seen the day before. I once thought I'd get used to them but, every time, I felt more fearful for what I saw because they were more realistic. I had seen myself in another form right in front of me, in the home that I had come to live in, as though it was real. Seeing myself outside my own eyes only made me wonder whether I was infected by The Dark; it would make sense with everything that was happening. The destruction, the chaos. Was I a danger to everyone? Was I the cause of war? What would happen if the war came to Earth? What would happen if The Dark came to Earth?

Would bonding with Seraiah be ultimately detrimental?

"Arri?" I looked at Genie's concerned face, "maybe I should let you rest."

"Sorry, I was just…" I trailed off as the door opened quietly. Seraiah walked in, looking exhausted, but he planted a smile of relief when he saw I was awake. The anger and annoyance I'd felt towards him disappeared as he came around to the other side of the bed and sat down, taking hold of my hand.

"Hey," he whispered, lifting his hand up to stroke my cheek lovingly, "I was very worried."

"I'll leave you both," Genie smiled. We both said goodbye to her as she left the room.

"How are you?" he asked.

"My head feels like it's on fire," I told him, moving my hand up to rub it, "but I'm glad I'm out of that."

"What happened?" he asked.

I looked at him, for a moment, and wondered whether I should give in and tell him or keep it to myself, much like how he was with me, but it was hard to keep things from him when he genuinely looked interested and curious.

"I don't really know," I told him, "I…"

"Hm?"

"I suppose it was a little similar to the hallucination I had the day at Sheika's," I explained, "I… I know you don't know about that. Seraiah, I know you don't wish to tell me a lot but is there more than one thing in The Dark?"

"More than one thing?"

"Yes, sometimes I see… sludge," I answered, "and, other times I see winged creatures."

"Ah, you are asking if it is a collective name?" he asked and I nodded, "yes, it is. I am unsure where it originated but it was coined The Dark after unnatural beasts were released from Mysc, the realm of nightmares. It was given many titles but eventually a collective name was given. Thus, The Dark was named. The sludge you speak of is called The Mire…"

Seraiah stopped as he noticed I was struggling to pay attention. The names were causing my head to throb and, although I was glad to get something new from Seraiah, it really wasn't the time. Mysc, a nightmare realm. The Mire.

"I am sorry," Seraiah whispered, stroking my arm gently, "you should rest."

"I swear you only wish to open up to me when I'm in a terrible state," I joked and he smiled softly at my humour.

"I… I am not trying to keep anything from you, Arraetta," he comforted, "I just wish that you would allow me the time to plan a full conversation, with you, over these little half ones that cause us to bicker."

I lay down into a more comfortable position as Seraiah removed the cushion that propped me up. I looked up at him dazedly through the fog of my headache, "I… I saw my father."

"Your father?" He raised his eyebrows as he swept some of my hair from my face.

"He… it's not the first time," I admitted.

"It was not a dream?" he asked.

"No," I whispered, "we spoke about things, we were on the bridge of Ryazark."

Seraiah looked emotional as I told him, as though it was all the confirmation he needed that Ryazark truly existed and was not just something he read in a storybook. He gently leant down and kissed my forehead before standing.

"I would like to hear more of your encounter," he said, "but, I do wish for you to get some rest."

"He confirmed about the war," I blurted. Seraiah froze for a moment before he solemnly nodded. I continued, "he, also, said I had to learn to control my power so that I may fight."

"What?" he frowned, "your father would not send you into the fight."

"I don't think I have a choice," I answered, "if you're going, so am I."

"No," he commanded softly, "I will not have my wife fight in this war."

I sat up, albeit a little too quickly, and tried not to wince at the pain in my head, "you can't control me."

"It is not about control, Arraetta," he calmed, "it is about keeping you safe."

"Don't you need my power to fight The Dark?" I huffed, "don't I have Divine Rapidfire after all?"

"Did your father confirm that?" Seraiah asked and I went quiet, realising I'd said a little too much more than I'd wanted to. I was hoping that Divine Rapidfire news would be something I could casually bring into a conversation, but it was out in the open already. My silence was all he needed, "then, this changes a lot of things. I need to speak to… to my father, please rest."

Before I could say anything more, he headed out of the room, and I grunted in annoyance as I lay back down properly.

Seraiah was so frustrating. He was angry and annoyed, one minute, and then he switched and was suddenly calm again. Maybe it was something he was taught on his journey to becoming the soon-to-be head of state, but it made me feel all sorts. *Balance,* I had to tell myself. It was all about *balance.*

I'm sure Seraiah would appreciate me to be less angry and stubborn, and feebler, sometimes. *Yes, Seraiah. I can do that absolutely, Seraiah.* But I couldn't be that person - I didn't want to be controlled, I wanted to be free to make my own decisions and, if fighting in the war was what would have to happen, especially if it was I who was the vessel of Divine Rapidfire, I would.

SEVENTEEN

I was back on my feet, within a couple of days, after plenty of bed rest that was imposed by everyone. To be honest, it was quite a nice relief to take some time out, after the crazy week I'd had with two episodes. But Seraiah spent less time with me, tiptoeing around the important subjects of the war by making it known he was only interested in discussing how I was, for the brief period of times that I did see him.

I knew that the sudden development of war on, our collective shoulders, had sparked something deep inside him, even if he was good at hiding that side of his personality, though I don't think it was anything more than fear. Seraiah always knew that, someday, he was going to have to go to war, to get his kingdom back, but I don't think he thought it would be confirmed as quick as it had done, especially as I had just appeared in his life, and I expected he hoped for some time of quietness where we could just *be*.

I knew that Seraiah would be adamant that I wouldn't fight; he would do everything he could to stop me, even if that meant locking me in a room with one hundred bolts on the door. I was Seraiah's everything. It wasn't something that hadn't occurred to me, but I knew I would always find a way to be standing with, or before, Seraiah on the battlefield.

Seraiah was beginning to make plans; with each day that passed, there were more important people turning up at the house and they would spend hours in one of the board rooms, devising strategies.

I knew that I had to spend time training my power, to become my strongest self and I was already making plans to get into good physical shape, once Iontine and the bonding ceremony were completed.

Then there was that. The bonding ceremony. Even with my strong feelings towards Seraiah, this felt like it was becoming an unwanted commitment – for both of us. I had been told that, a few days later, the rehearsals for our ceremony would take place which was making me even more nervous. Not only that, but everything had also been brought forward, with the celebrations for Iontine at the end of July, only a week away, and the bonding the first week of August.

I wanted nothing more than to be with Seraiah, but I also wanted to ask if we could just slow down a little bit, even if we could push the bonding back by a few weeks. I knew that my query would be shut down; the nuptials had to take place when the generator was at its strongest point. Whatever that meant.

With the celebrations having been brought forward, it meant that the village and, subsequently, the house was getting busier, with all the spare rooms being prepared, for the numerous guests that were to arrive, and every inch of the place was getting cleaned from top to bottom. I offered my services but they were dismissed, and I was given multiple options on what to do instead, including going out for a walk, having a nap, watching television, and reading a book. Yet, as much as those sounded like the greatest ways to spend time, I was bored of the same routine, especially without Seraiah. I also struggled to paint, I had no inspiration and grew uninterested in it quickly. In fact, I'd rarely painted in recent months, and I wondered whether it was becoming an old hobby.

Just like a cog in the machine that I was, I adjusted to my new routine.

"Your Royal Highness."

My eyes flicked up, from the book I was reading, to see Kadey and one of the newer maids, Elina, standing in front of me. I'd taken refuge in the stairwell, at the back of the house, tucked out of the way enough for the staff to move to and from without me disturbing them. I guessed that my whereabouts had been discovered by someone senior and I was about to be asked whether a room, in another part of the house, would be more comfortable.

"Hi," I smiled at them both, holding the page, with my finger, as I closed the book.

"Elina and I are here to inform you," Kadey smiled widely, "that you are being moved to the master suite."

"Master suite?" I blinked.

"Yes," she replied, "it will be the room that His Grace and you shall share once you are wed, but you have the luck of being in there first."

"What's wrong with my room?"

"It's a little small for both of you," Elina said and all three of us blushed at the implication. "and, I'm afraid that there are less rooms available for guests with the occupancy of yourself and Lady Genevieve."

"Is Genie getting moved as well?"

"No," Kadey smiled, "their second room has been emptied and, now, they both fully occupy one space instead of two."

"I see," I nodded, then stood up, "can you show me the master suite?"

Both beamed, seemingly excited to be the ones that could show me my new abode. They led me back up the stairs, down the wide east wing and around to the front of the house, before we crossed into the west wing, which housed the library and Tara's quarters. Towards the end of the corridor, we came to a door that I'd always thought led to one of the bedrooms, but instead it opened to another smaller space, which almost looked like an entrance hallway to a house.

To the right was a spiral staircase and we walked up until we were at the highest level of the house which, again, led to another long corridor, with a few peep-like windows on either side. Out of those windows, you could clearly see we were above both the ballroom and the library, yet the roofs were quite high, so, unless you were right at the back of the gardens with binoculars, no one would know this place was even here.

A hermit's paradise.

Kadey opened the door and we walked into, what I could only describe, as a modern almost apartment-like space, with a large window looking out to the front of the house and, what felt like, the view of the world with London's skyline in the foggy distance. If it wasn't raining, the view would be clear as day.

I followed Kadey and Elina into a huge bedroom suite. It was decorated with a white and gold colour scheme, with a large king-size velvet headed bed and a huge seating area, with cushions galore to the left. Sheets of glittery gold cloth adorned the high ceiling, suspended cleverly from ceiling trim to the centre, where a glorious glass chandelier was suspended. Like all other rooms in the house, a beautiful fireplace kept the pit of cushions warm. And, to the back of the room, was a door that led out to a balcony, which overlooked the back gardens to the view beyond.

The one thing, that stood out the most, was the artwork that hung pride of place above the fireplace. It was the painting from which Seraiah, and I had first experienced that feeling - that moment - together in the library. Though this version was not what I had last seen, it now had Seraiah's final touches, his own stroke of the brush so prominently telling the rest of the story. Whilst The Cre-este stood to one side of the handprint, on the other side was a similarly beautiful place that I knew to be Zika. I could see what the painting was saying now; both of us were from different places, different times, and different worlds but we had come together at that one point in time.

And, in this very room, Seraiah and I would soon spend the night, lying in each other's arms. Or, at least, I hoped it would be that way, with Seraiah remarking something funny to take the nervous tension away.

"Through here, we have your wardrobe," Kadey said and I turned to where she was standing at the door to another room, whilst Elina stood patiently by the main one, "and, you can access your en suite too."

"Thank you," I smiled, wandering over to take a look, "it's going to be quiet up here."

"I know you commented on wanting a bit of quiet yesterday," Kadey said and I laughed lightly in appreciation.

The walk-in wardrobe was impressive and was already full of clothes, shoes, and accessories that I'd never seen before; I knew they were preparing me to become a queen from the expense of it all. No longer would I be dressing in jeans and a t-shirt, in fact, I didn't see any in the wardrobe.

"It's a lot," I murmured as I took in the space, catching a glimpse of myself in the large floor to ceiling mirror.

"Lady Genevieve wanted us to make sure you had the best," Elina clapped her hands in excitement and I rolled my eyes; of course, this just had to be Genie.

We moved through to the biggest bathroom I think I'd ever stepped foot in. The one downstairs was big, but it was very much a guest's en suite, whereas this was a main bathroom, and even bigger than the one that I'd gone into on the night of the ball. It was made for a couple with almost double of everything, including the sink and shower. The way it had been decorated made it look as though it was a place abroad in a private villa, but it fit perfectly with the bedroom and the colour scheme. Honestly, no matter how much someone told me how much I deserved the life I had come to live, I still couldn't believe how different everything had become. And I'd be sharing all of this with Seraiah, even the smell of his shower gel, shampoo and himself would linger in the bathroom.

I looked over at the shower, immediately picturing Seraiah walking into it, whilst I was showering, both of us kissing intensely until he'd lift me up, holding me between the wet and cool shower wall and-

A clearing of a throat sounded behind me, and I spun to see that I was just feet away from the man himself, who was standing with his arms folded; his usual cocky look on his face. He knew full well that he'd caught me entranced by the thought of the two of us together.

"What are you thinking about, Arraetta?"

"Hello, Seraiah," I greeted as I moved over to the balcony door of the bathroom, opening it to feel the soft breeze of the cool air from outside, "I was thinking about how the place just isn't big enough for the both of us."

"Oh, really?" Seraiah raised his eyebrows, amused by my temperament. He started to circle the outer rim of the bathroom, moving away from me and so, to follow his movements, I started to do the same thing, keeping a comfortable distance between the both of us.

"Yes," I answered innocently.

"Actually, I was hoping you would not mind sharing a little earlier," he mused as he passed the balcony door and I moved through one end of the walk-in shower and out of the other, "it seems I am also being removed, from my quarters, to make room for guests."

"How about your...?" I quipped, the pace of my heart picking up as his feet began to move a little quicker, still both of us circling the other.

“Office? There is no bed,” he shrugged suggestively, “you should know that since you have been in there.”

“Have I?” I squeaked, wondering how he knew I’d been in there, and he chuckled.

“Oh, yes, do not think I did not know you visited my hideaway,” he answered.

“Well, how would you know?” I said to him.

Seraiah smirked, “well, you know I can sense your energy.”

“You weren’t even there that day,” I answered and then I gasped, covering my mouth as I realised I’d given away that I had, in fact, snooped.

“Oh, Arraetta,” he tutted, “I knew it. You are right, I did not detect your energy but, instead, saw that several things were out of place. Interesting how the key to my cabinet had gone missing and a few days later, on the day the generator blew, that exact book was on the floor, with the key.”

“You blew the generator!”

Seraiah barked with laughter, “trust me, I did not. I was not even anywhere near the library; do you not see I was trying to protect you from the wrath of the Zikan’s?”

“That sounds like a movie,” I teased.

“Arraetta.”

“Seraiah.”

We both came to a halt, at opposite ends of the bathroom, as we stared at each other, tempting the other give in but neither one of us succeeding. We were both strong characters so it would make sense that neither of us would back down in a fight… or a tease-off.

“Okay, Arraetta,” he nodded, “I shall let you off the hook this time. But only if you allow me to stay in this bed.”

We continued our charade.

“My bed is full.” I answered.

"Of?"

"Me," I pursed my lips to hide the smile, "I like to sleep like a starfish."

"No, you do not," he chuckled, running his finger across the edge of the sink, "you sleep like a cocoon."

"And, how do you know how I sleep?" I raised my eyebrows at him.

"Because sometimes... I watch you," he replied, eyes flicking to mine before he clicked his tongue, "I suppose, you do not find that strange."

"I just genuinely find you strange," I commented, lightly smacking into the glass frame with my back, as I backed into the shower. He was getting closer, his gentle strides quickening, "like it's strange you're just following after me now."

"Very strange," Seraiah murmured, his eyes intense, the connection between us beginning to grow with every accelerating heartbeat, "what were you thinking about when I walked in here?"

I shifted my eyes over to the shower wall behind him; the same thought of us together imprinted on my mind, then I made eye contact with Seraiah again, swallowing hard as I saw how aroused he was through his darkened look. He turned to look over towards the shower which I, standing just next to the door, took as an ample opportunity to escape the confined air of the room. As though I was running away from a predator, I darted out of the room, through to the bedroom and, very quickly, to the front door of the suite, attempting to pull it open until-

Bam.

The door was pinned shut by Seraiah's hand and his majestic physique hung over me, his front just inches from my back. His warm, heavy breath blew against my hair, whilst my heart pounded against the walls of my chest, beating faster as he moved his head down towards my exposed neck. The hand that held the door shut clenched a little as he quietly moved forward, so that his body was touching mine and, lower, I felt his hard cock trying to break free from the jeans he was wearing.

I swallowed again, filled with desire as I turned to face him, using the door as a leaning post as I perfectly angled my body towards him. I'm sure my own gaze was just as thirsty as Seraiah's; his eyes dipping to my lips, back to my eyes and then back to my lips, him leaning down just enough for them to be hovering over mine. The game of tease was becoming unfair, Seraiah held all the power in his hands, and I was just there to bend to it. And, no matter how hard I tried to win, I was powerless against him.

I swallowed, my mouth watering at the want and need to taste him, to savour the flavour of his tongue against mine. He moved closer, still not advancing to my lips, the centimetre difference between them feeling as if it were miles, even though we were so close to each other.

I let out a muted moan of wanting and, naturally, clamped my teeth down onto my inner lip at the thought.

"Oh, Arraetta, what you do to me," Seraiah murmured and then the centimetre distance, between our lips, was at zero as his struck mine, with a wanting passion, both of us releasing a moan as the sensations tingled our mouths. It was as though time slowed down and, for a split second, we lingered there until Seraiah deepened the kiss and our mouths began to move in a quicker motion, tongues battling. I slithered my hands up to clasp his beautiful golden locks, pulling our heads together as if there was still some distance between us, whilst Seraiah's hands moved around my waist until he effortlessly picked me up, my legs moving around his waist.

Seraiah began to move, neither of us seeming to pay attention, whilst we continued to smack our lips against each other's, but it was as though every wall and piece of furniture moved out of our way until he lowered me down onto the bed. One of my hands remained tightly gripping his hair, whilst my other moved around his back to grip his shirt as he gently rubbed himself against me. The friction of his jeans against my cotton skirt sent a ripple of pleasure, through my very being, and I moaned into his mouth.

Seraiah then broke the kiss, my hands immediately loosening from their grip, as he looked down at me with those desire filled eyes.

"You are so beautiful," he whispered in awe and kissed me again, this time moving my arms, so that they were above me, before he began to kiss down my cheek, followed by my neck. He tugged at my top, which was tucked into my skirt, and pulled it up revealing my belly, on which he slowly planted his lips, moving further south. I arched my back, clearly seeing in my mind what was about to happen as he pushed my skirt up, moving to take my inner thighs as his lips' next victim.

"Oh, Seraiah," I moaned, eyes rolling back as I prepared myself for the pleasure I so wanted to feel. I could feel his finger gently caress my white briefs before his nose took its place and he inhaled my scent, nuzzling against me. I was so close to begging him to just taste me; I wanted to feel his tongue against my sensitive skin, for him to tell me how good it was and for my body to writhe against his mouth.

"Oh my God, I did not want to walk in on this!" came a sudden voice.

Like a deer in headlights, Seraiah shot up, immediately, and I sat up, both of us looking over at Genie and Freddie, who were standing at the door. Whilst Genie had turned away from us, hands over her eyes, Freddie was seemingly enjoying the show, a cheeky smile on his face. Quickly, I covered myself as Seraiah straightened.

Genie turned back around slowly, peeking through her fingers to check it was safe to look properly.

"It's a good job we came in when we did, 'ey?" she barked, causing us all to laugh, though mine and Seraiah's laughter was a little awkward.

My lips tingled, from the passion we had both felt, and the taste of his lips remained in my mouth; my body wanting nothing more than to continue where we left off.

“Can’t you knock?” I asked, clearing my throat, before standing up, whilst trying to calm down the throbbing between my thighs, “or, must you always interrupt?”

“Actually, I believe that your precious other half asked us to meet here,” Genie raised her eyebrows, amusement clear in her voice, “I thought you’re supposed to be celibate.”

“We did not do anything further,” Seraiah said, clearing his throat, “but no doubt, if you both had not walked in, we would have made it through to the end.”

“Sheika would love that,” Freddie mused, then mimicked us, “oh, sorry, Sheika, we just so happened to have completed the bonding before it started.”

“It wouldn’t have gone that far,” I said seriously, “because I would’ve stopped Seraiah.”

“Really?” all of them echoed, raising their eyebrows in my direction, then laughed at each other’s matching reaction. Seraiah looked the most amused, knowing that I wouldn’t have been able to stop him, I craved him too much.

“Why are you here anyway?” I blinked at the two of them.

“Oh, because it’s time for us to do the dance,” Genie clapped her hands and spun around like an excited little girl.

“The dance?”

“*Our* dance,” Seraiah piped up.

“For the wedding?” I asked, “don’t we just dance awkwardly in a circle for like five minutes?”

“No!” Genie squeaked, “you must do a proper dance, Freddie said it’s tradition, so that’s exactly what we should do. Plus, you have the best teacher in the world… me!”

“I don’t have the energy to dance,” I grumbled, tucking in my t-shirt.

“But, you had the energy to almost shag,” Genie said bluntly. Freddie and Seraiah both chuckled.

"It was kissing!" I defended myself.

"Darling, your lips are up here," Genie motioned to hers, "and, unless Seraiah doesn't understand the female anatomy, the ones down there will not reply in the same way."

The boys continued to enjoy Genie's quick remarks. I was always a little floored by them.

"Right, come on," Genie said to us both, "let's go."

I groaned and went over to the bedroom mirror, straightening myself up. Before he left, Seraiah gave me a mischievous look, whilst Genie waited for me. I turned to look at her and she had a big smile on her face, knowing that she really held all the power right there and then over the situation.

"Don't give me that look," I whispered sharply.

"Was it good though?"

"It would've been better if you hadn't interrupted," I answered, walking towards her whilst pouting a little bit, "but, it's a good job like you said."

Both of us began to exit the room and Genie continued, "I won't interrupt you during the ceremony, I promise, and, really, we didn't even know that was what you two were doing."

"I felt like I wouldn't have stopped," I admitted, red faced, "I felt… on top of the world."

Genie linked her arm with mine, "well, you have an incredibly strong bond, Arri, so it's bound to feel like that. I think Seraiah looked much more shocked than you."

"Really?" I laughed lightly as we made our way downstairs, "it was… it was more than anything I've ever felt before."

"I thought you'd already kissed," Genie said and I looked at her, shocked. She smiled at me, "I suppose I expected you both to have anyway because of how close you've both become… God, you must've been in agony. I couldn't have waited this long to kiss Freddie."

"There have been several occasions," I told her, "where we've been in a similar situation. I think that the want for it just overcame us and neither of us could resist."

Freddie and Seraiah came to a stop at the end of the corridor, both watching us admiringly as we followed. Genie and I were two very lucky women to be in love. These two men were everything we could have ever dreamed of and I, sometimes, wondered how I'd stepped out of a somewhat standard life and walked into a fairy tale.

EIGHTEEN

In the ballroom, Seraiah played us a variety of classical music, from an old CD player, until we both decided on one that we loved. Then, Genie spent the next few hours teaching us a dance, as she had already expertly planned a dance for each song from the music selection.

Surprisingly, Seraiah had quite a strong opinion about certain things and managed to convince Genie to do a few different moves, that were somewhat easier, than what she had conjured up. Seraiah would whisper little flirtatious things, into my ear, from time to time, and I would throw them back, although mostly failing to match his quick wit.

One thing that was made certain, however, was the agreement that we wouldn't be left alone, without being chaperoned. Just in case what happened in the bedroom happened again before the bonding ceremony.

As I walked out of the entrance of the west wing, the next day, I stopped as Seraiah exited from the entrance to the east. We eyed each other for a small moment of time, almost as though this was the first time that we'd seen each other. Seraiah then straightened and nodded his head and I, jestingly, returned it with a curtsey as we both descended the steps to where the family portrait was hung.

"Seraiah," I greeted.

"Arraetta," he returned, moving his hand up to, affectionately, sweep some hair behind my ear. His eyes dipped down to look at my lips before he swallowed and then looked back to my eyes, clearing his throat, and stood back. I was a little saddened that he didn't move in for a kiss as I was desperate to feel his lips against mine, once more, but I wasn't entirely sure what the protocol was for publicly showing affection as royalty.

"Where are you going now?" he asked.

"I was going to find Genie. And you?"

"That is a shame," he pouted, "I would have hoped you had said that you were going to find me."

"Oh, so you were looking for me?"

He chuckled, "no, in fact, I was looking for Freddie, but I just know how obsessed you are with me."

I gasped. "Excuse me, but I believe it's you who is obsessed with me."

"I did not say I was not," he mused before he waved his arm, in the direction of the lower level. I smiled cheekily, leading the way for us both. Although we were being followed by Kadey and Elina, making a nice change from Alex and the other guards, they both kept a reasonable distance from us, which made our conversation a little more private.

At the bottom of the staircase, I turned to Seraiah and curtsied gently, to which he bowed in return, neither of us breaking eye contact.

"I suppose I will try this direction," I said.

"And, I shall try this one."

The house was still busy, and, in some ways, I was looking forward to it going back to the way it had been before the celebrations were upon us. At least it made it a little easier to flirt without knowing that someone was listening in. I'm sure that the gossip of the royal relationships and their scandals were big talking points throughout the Zikan's, and I was sure that, should anyone else other than Genie and Freddie have walked in on us, the day before, everyone would know about it.

Seraiah and I parted ways, and we began to walk around in our own directions. Depending on which corridor Seraiah decided to take, there was the possibility that I would bump back into him. I felt giddy, at the thought of it, and almost saw it as a race to get to the back of the house, picking up the pace as I flew past the usual dining room, down the corridor that led to a variety of rooms, including one of the sitting rooms, the stairs down to the kitchens and the baths, and all the way around to the back. Kadey and Elina didn't speed up, I think they knew what I was doing, and they would catch up either way, depending on if I'd bump into Seraiah.

Around the back end of the house, I walked past the staircase towards the ballroom door and stopped to see that Seraiah had also made it there, coming to a halt. As before, he bowed his head and I, trying to hide my smile, curtsied.

"That did not take you long," he commented, clearly amused, "you were down that corridor in a heartbeat."

"Or, maybe you walk incredibly slow."

"I stopped for a moment to speak with Terance," he stated, "but you obviously thought this to be a race."

"I did not," I stomped in jest, and he chuckled, moving closer to me.

"Then, why is your heart racing?" he asked, placing his hand onto my chest. The thumps of my heart were prominent. He leant down to my ear, "Arraetta, I should reprimand you for being such a terrible liar."

"I'm not lying," I whispered back as he moved to hover just above my face, in prime position to kiss me, "I'm just fast."

Seraiah chuckled, his eyes moving behind me to where I presumed Kadey and Elina were, then he looked back at me, with his mischievous look, whispering, "if these two were not here, what I would do to punish you for it."

"I'd like to see you try," I gleamed, moving myself away from him, "so, I shall continue my search for Genie."

I decided to try upstairs, but he caught my hand and pulled me back into him, holding me closely around my waist, "Arraetta, I have not done speaking with you yet."

"What is there to speak about?" I asked innocently and he tutted, shaking his head. I heard him talk to the girls, in Zikan, and, almost immediately after, they left, both disappearing around the corner. I laughed lightly, turning back to him.

"Seraiah, I thought we were supposed to be chaperoned at all times."

"I shall not be taking your clothes off here, Arraetta," he retorted and leant down so his lips were by my own, "but, I have wanted to kiss you since yesterday and I believe you have wanted the same."

"No," I replied jokingly and he murmured something, placing his lips onto mine.

I felt my body throb for him instantly, my hands moving up around his neck as he pulled me closer with his arm. We kissed passionately for a few moments until he broke away. I swallowed hard, licking my lower lip as his taste surfaced on my tongue and he indulged himself by staring deeply into my eyes.

"I do not think that was a wise idea."

I blushed as he pulled me in, so that we were holding each other. His *wise idea* was because of the pulse that was throbbing in his pants, which echoed my own, but I wanted us to do it again, especially in a more private setting, where the two of us could do so much more.

He squeezed me, "Arraetta, please do not continue those thoughts."

"It's your fault," I answered in a hoarse whisper and moved to break the hold. His eyes scanned the space around us but there was no sign of anyone who would've come to interrupt our moment of passion. I cleared my throat, "so, do you know where Freddie is?"

"Yes," he laughed, adjusting himself a little. I moved my eyes away which caused him to laugh even more, "Freddie and Genie are actually spending some time together."

"Time to... oh," I realised his exact meaning. Seraiah nodded to confirm.

He checked his watch, "I do hope he hurries up as I do have a meeting with him at four."

More meetings. More secrets.

"About what?" I frowned.

"Nothing you need to concern yourself with," he said, looking up the staircase. I glowered a little, angry that he wouldn't share whatever it was with me.

"I'm going to be your wife, Seraiah," I pointed out.

His gaze landed back on me, and he frowned, "yes, I am well aware of the fact."

"So, why can't you share with me about your meeting?"

He sighed, "because it is nothing-"

"-For me to concern myself with, yes, I heard you."

"Then why are you angry?" he asked, trying to keep calm.

"I'm not... it's just you've been secretive since I told you about my father."

Seraiah rubbed between his eyebrows and exhaled frustratedly, "Arraetta, you are the future queen-"

"-So, Seraiah, I should be in on those talks."

"No," he spat, shaking his head.

"So the meeting is about the war?" I said, probing. The sudden change of our conversation, from playful flirting to being serious, was noticeable by the tension in the air, and I couldn't help but get even more annoyed. He was dodging the conversation and wanted to keep me out of any talks that would involve me fighting.

"Arraetta, this meeting is none of your concern."

"You can't stop me from fighting, Seraiah."

"Arraetta," he bit through his teeth, but I continued.

"I-"

"Arraetta!" he half-shouted and stepped forward, "I could not care if you hold the power of one thousand suns, you are not involved with any talks because you are to be my wife and you will not ever... *ever* fight."

Intending for that to be the end the conversation, he began to walk back through to the front of the house, but I decided to follow him in haste, "Seraiah, my father-"

He growled and turned, stopping me in my path, "your father is dead, Arraetta. Whether he reaches out to you from Ryazark, or wherever he is right now, he would be stupid to send his only daughter - the only hope of keeping *our* bloodline alive - into a war against something as powerful as The Dark."

He started to walk away again but I went after him, "oh, so that's all I'm here for, huh? Just to continue *your* fucking bloodline."

"It is *our* bloodline, Arraetta!" Seraiah said, raising his voice, "*our* bloodline, you are the last remaining of your kind and I am the only royal blood of my own. It is our duty."

"Fuck duty, Seraiah! This is about us," I yelled, "you are constantly keeping things from me! What are you so afraid of, huh?" I pushed him for effect. "Tell me now! What are you so afraid of?"

"Arraetta," he glared, clenching his left fist.

"How can you even think about fighting The Dark, when you're so fucking scared to talk to me about the whole fucking thing?"

"Arraetta," he repeated, sharper as his breath became more shallow.

"Just grow up and speak to me for God's sake!" I shouted at him, "rather than keeping it all pent up-"

"-I do not owe you anything!" he bellowed, stepping forward as his body began to rise with the colours of his Rapidfire, "maybe if you were not such a spoilt brat, you would come to realise your place."

"My place!" I gasped, "what? A pawn in your grand game of fate."

Seraiah laughed, a different edge to his voice, "oh, Arraetta, you are a naive child. You do not know what you are coaxing right now."

"Maybe I want to see," I breathed, squaring up to him - my small form against his towering one. "It's about time you show me your true self!"

Within an instant, the warmth in the air evaporated and coldness lingered. Seraiah's eyes were no longer vibrant, but, instead, they were pits of endless darkness. "Is this what you want, Arraetta?"

His bellow shook through to my core. I felt the fear trickle down my spine as memories of the nightmares, of those exact eyes, appeared in my mind. Not just the nightmare at the altar, but also of myself just days prior. This was the epitome of all my fear - the endless darkness, endless nothingness. My body was already trembling, in response, but that didn't stop Seraiah's advances.

"I... I'm not scared of you," I stumbled.

His hand gripped the front of my shirt, and, within a heartbeat, I was pinned against the nearby wall, with a loud thud, causing a painting next to me to fall off. I winced, my heart racing fast.

"I can smell the fear on you," Seraiah growled, "it plagues you, lingering on your skin like a mark." He leant down to my ear, his voice a dark whisper. "My mark. I *own* you, Arraetta. I will devour you body and soul until you know nothing but my command."

"S-Seraiah," I whimpered as he pulled his head back; his black gaze cutting through me as sharp as a knife. Although this was Seraiah, it felt like it was something else entirely that had possessed him.

"Seraiah!" a yell murmured from near to the entrance hallway. I knew it was Jonah immediately; I could hear his feet hammering down towards us. Seraiah used his free hand in a swiping motion in Jonah's direction, not removing his eyes from mine.

I shook against him, eyes shifting momentarily to, where I could see, a cloud of black mist acting like a barrier, halting Jonah in his stead.

"Petulant boy," Seraiah murmured and his grip tightened as he moved to push me against the wall further, as if there was more room. I begged again; I could hear others joining in the hallway too.

Suddenly, the voice of my father echoed - *Arraetta, you are safe.* This wasn't a nightmare, this was real - Seraiah and I were standing in the hallway, no doubt surrounded by other concerned parties, and whatever had possessed Seraiah was right in front of me. My father's other words arose in my ears, whispering *you are much too powerful to be scared off by such creatures as The Dark.*

I snapped out of the feared trance, unsure whether minutes or seconds had passed. I knew that there was no way out, with someone rescuing me, so the only option was trying to get myself out of his grip.

Immediately, I shakily placed my hands onto Seraiah's face and pulled myself up to place my lips onto his.

Seraiah's grip instantly softened and, as my legs made their way to the floor, Seraiah balanced so that he could hold me there, as though I was about to drop a thousand feet. He had snapped out of his own hypnotic trance; I could tell as the coldness dissipated, within a second, and there was a gentle murmur against my lips. He gently allowed my feet to return to the ground as I slowly broke the kiss, both of us standing there.

"Arraetta," Seraiah murmured apologetically as I looked up into his chestnut eyes.

I didn't know what else to do, I could feel the anger bubble in my chest, but no words would leave my mouth. I could hear the commotion at both ends of the corridor; the guards were already on hand including The King.

I did the only thing I could think of doing. I slapped him. The sound resonated down the corridor and silence settled. I guessed it to be a mixture of shock that anyone would slap their future king and that it could easily anger him again. But it didn't. Seraiah took the slap, the look on his face as he turned his head away told me that he knew he deserved it.

"I... I don't deserve this," I whispered to him, pushing past him in an almost stumble.

"Arraetta," The King said to me with a concerned voice - the first thing he had ever said to me, but I didn't want to stay. I rushed past him, and the guards, hearing them talk with Seraiah immediately.

No one followed me as I ran up to the new suite I was given.

I found myself pacing there. First, I was fearful, unable to remove the image of Seraiah's dark eyes, from my thoughts, but then it rapidly changed to anger. I was a little angry at myself for coaxing it, but I was more angry that Seraiah would keep, that side of him, such a big secret. A secret because it wasn't something he could control.

And what would happen when we married? Would I have to tiptoe around him just in case that side of him came out once again? And, if we did follow duty - we did continue the bloodline - were our children going to be cursed with that?

I started to hyperventilate at the thought of how trapped I suddenly was. The room felt like it was closing in and I tried to steady myself against one of the bed posts.

Calm, Arri.

Anguish bubbled in my stomach. I took a deep, shaky breath as I tried not to think about the dark side of Seraiah but, everywhere I looked, I could see him. In the painting on the fireplace, against the bedroom door, on the bed sheets, in the entire house. Every good memory I had was rapidly being replaced by the image of Seraiah's darkness.

I had to leave, I needed space. I needed to breathe again.

I pushed myself into the wardrobe to try and find some normal clothes - anything that would resemble what I wore day-to-day before this all took place. Familiarity. Jeans, a t-shirt, anything. But there was nothing there.

My fear turned to rage. Everyone was controlling me, not just Seraiah, but all the guards, Tara, Freddie, Kadey, Elina, even Genie. All of them making plans for me, never allowing me to make up my own mind. How had I been so blind to not see that all along? Where had the old Arraetta disappeared to?

Immediately, I stormed out of the bedroom, down to the west wing and across towards the entrance hallway. My eyes saw as Genie rushed in; her own eyes wide when she saw I was storming down in her direction.

"Hey," she said apprehensively.

I could tell she had been sent to try and settle the situation.

"Where's my stuff?" I asked her sharply.

"What do you mean?" she asked, confused.

"My stuff - my jeans, my t-shirts, where are they all?" I shouted and she winced at my anger, eyes shifting down the corridor. I continued in a quieter, but still angered tone, "nothing is here, you have all taken everything from me. I'm fucking sick of this place, I'm sick to death of being controlled and don't you think, for one second, I'll be marrying that... that... argh... I'm done."

"Please, Arri," she begged as I began to storm further on. Genie quickly rushed to catch up and stand in front of me, "he didn't mean to."

"You're always on his side, Genie," I shook my head in disappointment, "all of you are. I don't have anyone anymore, just my own fucking stupid thoughts inside my fucking stupid head!"

I shoved past her and down into the entrance hallway, seeing Freddie and Seraiah both standing together with Jonah, Alex, Travis, and another two bodyguards, having a heated conversation in their native language. The King was nowhere to be seen once again. The front door was guarded by two doormen, as per usual.

Seraiah clocked me, his cheeks still lightly stained, with the dark veins that had appeared like a faded tattoo, and I glared at him, immediately, he pushed through the gathering and towards me as I came down the stairs.

"Arrae-"

"-Leave me alone, Seraiah!" I shouted at him, and he quietened. I could see the sadness in his eyes, the want for me to forgive him, but I needed to leave the claustrophobic place of the Zikan village and get back into normal civilization.

"Arri!" Genie said, bouncing down the steps after me.

I pushed past Seraiah and headed towards the door, where the two doormen moved to block the exit. I growled, "let me out! You can't keep me here!"

"Please, ma'am," Jonah said, stepping forward from his group.

The room was tense.

"My name is Arr-ae-et-ta," I spelt it out to him as I turned in his direction, "not *ma'am*, not *Your Grace*. Arraetta. I don't want to be here anymore. You can stick all this shit up your arse, I'm sick of being trapped and controlled by all of you. I'm absolutely fine at taking care of myself!"

My eyes scanned over to Seraiah seeing he was unsure what to do, the same doe-eyed look on his face, and I felt tears prickle my eyes, but I kept my front as strong as I could as I turned back to the door.

The tension in the air could be cut with a knife but my angered stance allowed for a little bit of change as there was slight agreement behind me. The two door guards stepped out of the way and one of them opened it.

"Is everything alright?" chimed Tara's voice from the top of the stairs. I didn't dare turn to face her, making my decision to leave without acknowledging her.

"Please, stop her," I heard Seraiah beg to someone but I wasn't acknowledging who it was to.

Outside, the warm air hit me, and I stormed across the driveway and down the street, still swallowing the tears.

I wondered a little about what interactions were happening inside, were they all horrified that I was fired up in such a way, ready to banish me for good or did they understand how I felt.

"Arri!" my name was yelled, once again, by Genie as I heard her shoes bounce down the pavement as she came running after me. I didn't turn to her but allowed her to catch up as I continued towards the crossroads that led into different directions of the complex, including the exit ahead. Genie took a deep breath as she came to walk next to me, "Arri, please just take a deep breath."

"What? Are you worried I'll have a panic attack?"

"No!" she matched my tone, "I just… I want you to just take a deep breath, for a moment, and pause. Let's chat about it."

"Chat about what, huh?" I spat back, coming to a halt as I faced her, "how much you just enjoy taking control of my life? Like he does!"

"Stop, Arri," she said sadly, "I am not trying to control you."

"I can't do anything by myself here," I told her, "I'm going to get a taxi and I'm going to leave."

"It's not safe for you to leave," Genie told me.

"How do you know, huh?"

"Because you have not even had your fucking blackout yet!" she retaliated, very loudly, and then winced at her own tone, quietening down, "can you imagine if you're out there and you have it? You need to be here with your people, with me."

"These aren't my people, Genie," I pointed out. My eyes scanned back to the house as I could see that some of the guards had come to be placed, in areas where I could be seen, whilst Alex remained on foot at a distance.

I huffed and looked at her, "look, they're everywhere. I can't have a moment of freedom without something shit happening. I… I thought me and Seraiah were good together and then he just goes and shows me that fucking side to him! He pinned me against the fucking wall, Genie, do you know how scary it was to see him like that? And I'm supposed to just marry him?"

"He loves you," Genie pointed out and I gasped at her, shaking my head in shock that she still chose to take his side.

"Good luck to you, Genie," I told her, pushing further on down towards the gate. The tears began to spill then, and they wouldn't stop, just like how it had been when I'd cried on the bench.

"Please, Arri!" Genie yelled, once again, her feet running after me, "I'm sorry, I'm sorry. I don't mean to; we're just trying to help."

I ignored her as I pointlessly wiped my eyes, moving further on. Genie soon found her way in front of me before she pulled me into an unwanted hug. I shrugged away and pushed her, causing her to stumble back some from the force.

"Why do you want to keep me locked up, Genie?"

"I don't," she started to whimper, "I just want to help you."

"I'm not getting help here," I replied, wiping my eyes as I tried to swallow the tears again but failed, "I don't even know what I'm doing. I'm so fucking lost, no one knows what's even going on and I've been told I'm supposed to marry a guy I don't even know."

"Why didn't you say anything?" Genie asked, "so many times you could've told me all this, but you never talk to me anymore, Arri. I watch you break apart, day by day, and you can't even tell me why."

"Because you'll tell Freddie, who will then tell Seraiah!"

"You're my best friend," she pointed out, "you are my number one, you always have been."

"It doesn't mean you won't tell him," I answered and cleared my throat before I continued on my journey, towards the gate. I listened as two cars came driving down the road, next to us, and I turned my head to see the same vehicles, we'd taken to the flat, speed past and come to a halt. A block.

I stopped and glowered as Jonah hopped out of the passenger side of the rear vehicle.

"You can't stop me from leaving," I told him.

"I am not, ma'am," he pointed out and then opened the door to the back of the car, "I am here to take you where you wish to go."

"I don't believe you," I told him.

"Genie, please get in the car," Jonah said to her.

Genie's feet scuffed, and I turned as she walked by me and over to the car, hopping in. I glowered more at Jonah before deciding to move forward past him but two other guards from the front car jumped out to stop me.

"Let me go," I stomped, seeing that there wasn't much option for me to get away.

"Here is the deal," Jonah said, stepping towards me, "you can get into this vehicle and I will take you wherever you wish to go. I could not care if you told me you wished to drive to Scotland, we shall drive there. You can take the time that you require to calm yourself in the car, away from the complex, and then we shall return here where you will come back and sort out the pending issue with His Royal Highness. Or you shall turn around and walk back up to the house and sort out the issue now. I shall not give you another option, you shall not leave without us."

"So, the only option I have is that I do have to come back?"

"I am giving you the option to leave," Jonah continued, "but it is at a compromise."

"Come on, Arri," Genie said, peering out of the car to me.

I stood there, my eyes switching down to the gates, that could be seen down the road from where I was standing, before looking at Jonah. I could tell that Jonah was good at his job and I wondered if he had been in a similar position to this before.

"I don't want to come back," I said.

"I am not giving you a choice on that matter," Jonah answered, "it is our duty to keep you safe, I cannot do my job if you are out there alone."

"This is not fair."

"Not everything is," he answered, "feel free to try and escape but, I can assure you, that you will not make it out of those gates without one of us with you."

He was giving me a compromise, but the compromise would always be that I would end up exactly where they wanted in the end. A matter of control. I didn't want to bend to it, I felt the ache to run, and wondered what it would be like as I skipped down to the gate and attempted to climb over. I could imagine Jonah restraining me without any issues and that the option to leave would never be granted again.

"I… I can't be with him like that, Jonah," I whispered, defeated.

Jonah sighed before walking towards me, "ma'am, do not discount Seraiah for what has taken place today. He is a good man; he is burdened by a power he has sought to control ever since it has tainted him. Come, let us go for a drive."

I nodded reluctantly and moved towards the vehicle, climbing in with the door closing behind. Even getting out for a short while would help me calm down a little, even if I was accompanied by others.

NINETEEN

I wasn't entirely sure where we were being driven to, but we soon ended up on a motorway, heading north from London. Everyone in the car was silent, with no music playing, just the soft hum of the roads outside. Jonah and Travis, who was driving, seemed relaxed, but I could feel that Genie was tense.

It had been a good twenty minutes since my tantrum ended and I could feel the embarrassment settling in as I realised how I'd been towards everyone. The anger that I had towards Seraiah was still there, but it wasn't directed at the way he'd thrown me against the wall, as though I was nothing more than a rag doll, but more because he didn't want to tell me anything when I asked him. Really, it was me who made him react like that because I'd asked him to show me.

"Is it okay to pull over at a service station?" Genie asked quietly to Jonah. He agreed and quietly spoke with Travis. The car fell silent for a bit longer, no sign of a service station ahead. Genie fidgeted a little as she chose what to say again. I could hear the cogs whirling in her head before she gently leant over and placed her hand onto my thigh.

She offered me a soft but apprehensive smile, "I still have your clothes. I asked them to keep them because I thought you might want them again at some point."

I nodded, "thanks."

"Plus, you're not Arri without your jeans and t-shirts," she joked and I smiled, the feeling of it strange as I felt my face crack from the tears that had dried up. Genie laughed lightly, fidgeting as though she was nervous, "sorry."

I looked back out of the window, sighing, "I just don't know what to do, Genie. I feel so trapped."

"Well… I think you could start by opening up to me," she answered, "like, it would be good to know what's going on inside your head… even just a little. And, well, as for Seraiah, he is just… you two are so similar. I think you think he's a really open person, but I know that he doesn't talk as much as you think he does… Unless it's about you, he could talk for days about you."

I blushed at the thought of it, looking over at her, "but, I don't know anything about him and then, the times I do get anything out of him, he closes off immediately."

"Like what?"

"Like he won't talk about Rapidfire, or The Dark," I told her, "he always says *there will come a time when we can both speak together* but why does that have to happen later? I don't understand why it can't be now."

"You just said you don't know anything about him," Genie said.

"I don't."

"But, you're not asking about him," she pointed out, "you're just asking about things that would affect you. What about all the important little questions? Like what's his favourite music? Or what novel did he love reading recently? Or, what's his bedtime routine?"

I looked at her as realisation washed over me. I had just been thinking about things I wanted to know because they affected me, but I rarely ever asked anything about him. He opened about the things he was passionate about, just like how he told me about the way Zika looked or how he loved the Wicker Windmill, but he closed off as soon as I mentioned The Dark or Rapidfire or the war. Was it deliberate? Did it trigger something within him?

"You see, that's where the issue is," she told me, then took hold of my hand, "I asked Freddie a really dopey question, when we first met."

"What was that?"

"I asked him if he could do one thing by the end of the year, what would that be," she giggled a little at the thought, the blush rising on her face as she remembered the moment.

"And, what was the answer?"

"He said marry me," she laughed louder and it caused me to laugh, shaking my head at the ridiculousness of it, "to be honest, I rolled my eyes a little at him but, now, we're engaged and maybe, you know, maybe we'll be married just like you and Seraiah."

Genie's kind temperament was calming and welcome.

"If you do not mind me saying, ma'am," Jonah chimed in, "Seraiah is very protective of you, I am aware he was angered in the corridor today, we can all feel it when there's a change in his tone. I am sure he does not wish for me to share this with you, but he begged for us to bring you back."

I was trying not to smile at it, instead, attempting to keep a straight face as I imagined Seraiah doing everything, he can to keep me.

"He is in love with you," Genie said, "he has said it so many times."

"To everyone but me," I rolled my eyes.

"For Seraiah, it has to be the right moment," Jonah added, "but, yes, Genie is correct. He is very much in love with you."

Following a trip to a service station, we made the decision to make the journey back to the house and attempt to patch things up. By the time we pulled into the bottom gates, we had been away for over two hours, which felt like enough time for things to have settled. I was a little worried that maybe Seraiah had thrown an even bigger spat because I'd left and a bunch of Zikan's were left for dead due to him allowing his power to control him. But everything seemed normal as we reached the first few houses.

We pulled into the driveway soon after and the concierge walked down, opening the car door immediately as it pulled to a stop. I felt a renewed sense of belonging, once I placed my feet down onto the gravel path, and just hoped that feeling was going to remain as Genie, and I moved to the entrance of the house.

Once inside, I saw that Seraiah was sitting solemnly in the middle of the stairs, but he, immediately, got to his feet when he noticed us, a look of relief on his face. He walked down, eyes on me before stopping and bowing.

"I'm going to find Freddie," Genie said, squeezing my hand before she walked away.

Seraiah and I watched after her before we both looked at each other, the blush of embarrassment rising on my face as I was unsure what to say more than, "sorry."

"Do not apologise," he told me, "come, let us go and eat, you must be hungry."

"A little," I admitted, although the chocolate, that we'd bought at the service station, filled some of a hole on the way back.

I hadn't realised Jonah had walked in behind me, until both him and Seraiah shared a quick interaction, before Seraiah waved his hand in the direction of the staircase.

"Thanks, Jonah," I said to him.

"Anytime, ma'am," he bowed gracefully before moving to speak to the doormen.

I looked at Seraiah as he gently smiled, waiting for me to lead.

Our journey took us to the library, both of us quiet whilst we walked there, and I was glad that Tara didn't appear, out of her nest, as I felt like I might have been scolded for my behaviour. Inside the library, on the coffee table, sat a selection of antipasti on wooden boards, alongside a bottle of red wine with two glasses.

Seraiah, immediately, ushered for me to take a seat whilst he picked up the wine and uncorked it. I wasn't much of a red wine drinker, but I decided that it was irrelevant, at that point, as it was the thought that counted.

"You deserve an explanation," he told me, pouring the wine into a glass before handing it to me. He poured the other, "there is much I wish to tell you and there is much you wish to know. I suppose I would like to start from the beginning."

I nodded as he came to sit next to me on the sofa. He gently tugged the coffee table forward enough, so that it was easier to reach the food, from the sofa, before he took one of my hands in his.

"My full name," he paused as I lit up, "is Seraiah Elias Johren Zika. I was born one hundred Zikan years ago and I am half Zikan, half Porton."

"Porton?"

"Yes, my mother is Porton," he replied, "it is another realm, our sister one, in fact. My mother's brother, my Uncle Jameia, is the King of Porto. Freddie is full-bred Porton and is my Auntie Merienne's son, she is my mother's sister."

"Do they know you're here?"

"Who knows?" he shrugged, "my father fell out with my uncle over a trading feud, a few years before the attack, and closed the borders. It was an ongoing dispute right up until we came here."

"Wait, but Freddie is here."

"Yes, however, he was able to travel to see his parents as he was appointed our international liaison," he explained, "it meant he usually visited Porto once, every few months, but he made the decision that he would remain in Zika, for a better quality of life. It isn't easy being under the thumb of Jameia."

"Is he that bad?"

"I would love to say that I hope you meet him one day but..." he chuckled.

"Well, things were good in Zika right?" I said, "so, what kind of things did you do when you were a kid?"

"Many things," he answered, "although some things were restricted as I was the Crown Prince and the only heir to the throne, so most things were done within the palace. I learnt about languages, history, music, art, science. They all fascinated me, especially art and science."

"What languages?" I asked.

"Many," he smiled, "Cre-estian, Porton, Zikan and Ancient Zikan. Latin."

"Latin? What about English?"

"No," he chuckled, rubbing the back of my hand with his thumb, "we had to use Latin to translate words into English, when we arrived, although it was quite difficult considering that no one had truly spoken Latin for centuries."

"Then, how did you know about Latin?"

"Well, there was a realm called Hamiean," he informed me, "it was the realm of knowledge and it is where the University of the Universe came to be placed. You may only visit that realm, if you have been invited. Many of our elders have spent time there and so they learnt about Earth, and its languages. However, Hamiean was another realm that was taken a hold of by The Dark and thus the world's knowledge now lies within their grasp. Time has since passed by quickly on Earth."

I nodded, somewhat understanding what he was saying, "why did you come to Earth though? Don't you think it's strange that I came here too? And, surely there are more of us here?"

"Slow down," he chuckled, taking some food and eating it before he smiled, "okay. Our ancestors told of a realm that was heavily protected, by an unknown source of energy, it was so protected that those who came to live in that realm would only be aware of their own existence. This was Earth. As a civilization, we had thousands of years of knowledge on travelling through portals as it is to do with energy waves and frequencies."

"So, you just built a portal to Earth?" I asked.

"Not quite, in fact the portal to Earth wasn't fully complete by the time the attack took place," he answered, "it had been tried and tested many times but it did not work. I am unsure entirely what happened that day, but I believe it has a whole lot to do with The Dark's energy and another's."

"Another's?"

Seraiah smiled, "the only person's energy that it could've been was yours."

"You say that but I've never seen you before," I told him.

"I know," he nodded, "but I promise you that I know, in my heart and my soul, that it was you. You were the one that pulled me out of there… from the grasp of The Dark."

"The grasp of The Dark?" I frowned.

"What you saw today," he cleared his throat, "I am imprinted with the stain of The Dark. I… I wanted to save everyone, but I was not strong enough. Do you remember me telling you of The Mire?" I nodded. "That is what tried to take me, that is what devoured my left forearm. It burnt, I-"

I grabbed his hands as I could hear the slight panic in his voice. He feared it, whatever had taken over him. "Seraiah."

"Sorry," he breathed, "I just should never have done that to you, it overtook my senses. I felt like I was watching through the eyes of another, which hasn't happened for a long time."

I could see Seraiah's apology was genuine.

"Thank you for telling me," I said to him, "you said that The Dark feeds off fear, right?" He nodded. "Maybe the cause of it overtaking you is because of that."

Seraiah smiled sadly, nodding, "yes, you are right. However, it is not as simple as just getting over the fear. It feeds on all my fears and that is not so easy to let go of, especially my biggest fear."

"Which is?"

Seraiah chuckled, coming to stroke my cheek softly, "losing you."

I smiled at him, the same feeling lingering in my stomach, even after the day that had happened. Sitting with Seraiah, alone, talking with one another, that was everything to me and I didn't want to lose that - lose him.

I decided to change the subject to make the conversation more light-hearted.

"So, do portals feel weird?"

"Feel weird?" he chuckled, sitting back, "no, it feels like stepping through a gentle breeze. One moment you are in one place and then the next you are somewhere else."

"I'd find that very weird."

Seraiah leant down and put some cheese and meat on a small slice of focaccia before holding it towards my mouth, coaxing me to eat. I suppose I hadn't even touched the food yet as I had been so enveloped in what Seraiah was telling me. I took it, laughing a little, chewing whilst covering my mouth.

"I suppose it would be a little strange," he said, making another bit of food for himself, "but I travelled through them from when I was very young so I am unaware of the feeling of it really. We had our own portal that would lead through from the centre of our home to the centre of the Porton palace, so we'd spend a lot of time between both."

I was about to take another sip of the wine but then Seraiah took the glass off me, immediately standing up with it, "I haven't finished with that."

"You do not like red wine," he stated, disappearing around the back. A few moments later, he came back with a clean glass and a bottle of white wine. I blushed as he placed the glass down so that he could uncork the new bottle.

"I would've drank it still, just slowly."

"You would be drinking for days," he said, pouring me a glass. He handed it over and I took it, thankful, as he placed the wine down and sat back down, "I believe tomorrow is supposed to be our wedding rehearsals, but I have asked them to postpone."

"What? No," I said to him, taking hold of his hand, "I'll be okay."

"I cannot force you into this, Arraetta," he told me, "I wish only for you to be comfortable with me and I will do everything to make it right."

"I did push you," I admitted.

"I should never have reacted the way I did," he answered, moving his hand up to stroke my face, "I have no excuse, I should always be open with you, and I will. I must make myself do so because it is going to, inevitably, be detrimental to us both, if I am not. Arraetta, I do... I have to tell you something but, before I do, you must know that I am not talking with Freddie about the war, we were talking about other things - about *us* - you and I. Things I cannot reveal because they are... Well, they are supposed to be a surprise."

"Oh," I whispered, a little ashamed about how I'd lashed out.

"And... there is a part of me," he continued, clearing his throat as though he had just become incredibly nervous, "a very big part of me that just wishes to protect you. I can only say it is because, well, Arraetta, I cannot live - nae -... I cannot *breathe* without you, it is as though when you walked into my life, all those weeks ago, everything fell into place and I could not understand how I ever lived without you... your presence, your being, your beauty, being around you is like breathing in the purest of air. It is not just a want but a need to be with you... It is a desire more than to physically entwine myself with you, it is a desire to open myself up to you, to be everything you have ever desired and wanted, to linger so often in your presence that, when we are apart, I long to be closer than ever to you... Arraetta, I wish to marry you not for the purposes of our fated destinies but for the purpose to love more than I have ever loved... to love you for an eternity and more. I love you, Arraetta."

My eyes welled up with tears, as he said those words to me, not one word said without looking at me in my eyes. I burst into tears, covering my face with my hands, and he shuffled forward a little to embrace me whilst I sobbed.

When I finished crying, Seraiah dried my eyes with a napkin that was on the side, and we lovingly stared at each other. I whispered, "I love you."

Seraiah smiled; his eyes watery too before he moved to kiss me. The kiss was wet and passionate, both of us tear-filled as our emotions were running so high. I was unsure how long we kissed for, but it didn't feel long enough by the time we'd broken apart. Seraiah cleared his throat and stood up, moving away from me to go around the corner.

He soon returned and I frowned as I watched him, wondering what he was up to. He soon sat back down, bringing his hand up to reveal a small box, made from pure gold. I didn't have to ask him what it was because, as soon as he opened it, there was a beautiful silver and gold carved ring with the Zikan lettering across it.

"I know we are already to be married," he said, "but, I do want to make this official."

"What does it say?" I whispered as he removed it from the box.

"It says aemre aer jove lamoure, it means Our Love is Forever

Bound," he replied and I looked deeply in his eyes, smiling.

Am-re i-er jo-ver la-mou-ruh, the words repeated in my head.

"That's so romantic," I squeaked, tearing up again, "I don't even think I deserve this."

"Oh, Arraetta, you deserve everything," he replied, stroking my damp cheek. He leant down, and kissed them both, before leaning back to place the ring onto the correct finger.

I looked down at it, playing with its beauty for a few moments before I looked back at him, "thank you."

I kissed him again but only for a short moment.

"Genie says I have to ask you some questions," I said to him.

Seraiah laughed, "have I not told you enough?"

"Nope," I told him, picking up my wine, "first... if you could do anything, by the end of this year, what would that be?"

TWENTY

By the time Sunday rolled around, Iontine was the only thing that was on everyone's minds. The whole house had been buzzing with the exciting conversations of their long-awaited celebration, to worship the Gods, and pray for more years of blessings and safe living on Earth.

From what I'd seen of the town from the window, they had transformed it top to bottom with yards of floral bunting and festoon lighting, whilst the residents had the opportunities to decorate their gardens. What was more, stalls were being set up outside homes and I guessed that it would come to open like a market town, in some ways, with food and gifts available for people to purchase.

I'd spent most of the previous few days keeping out of the way of everyone, having been told that I didn't need to get involved with the set up several times, even when I tried to insist. There seemed to be a widely known rule that royalty do not take part with helping, and that was why I never saw Seraiah, Tara or even The King get involved with anything.

Then again, I never did see The King and, sometimes, I wondered whether he even lived on the property at all.

It had been a few days since Seraiah and I had spent time alone in the library, in fact, we hadn't had the chance to be on our own with each other since. I'd been eager to hold his hand and share a secret kiss, but I guessed that wasn't going to happen until the bonding ceremony would take place.

On my way down to the gardens, on a small mission to find him, I had quite a spring in my step. The atmosphere was intoxicating in the house, and I was quite excited that I'd be taking part in my first Iontine, eager to offer my own prayer of worship to the Gods in hope that it would allow me to not have any more blackouts.

I was followed by Alex, as per usual, who kept up with my pace. I'd grown quite fond of him since he'd first come into my life and had gotten to know him relatively well, although he remained a reserved guy. He had become a constant companion, being with me most days, always staying at a distance enough to give me privacy but close enough in case I needed anything. Not that I ever did, of course.

I rushed down the grand hallway steps, greeting everyone individually that I came to pass and swung around to the corridor, that I'd had the confrontation with Seraiah in a few days prior.

"Your Royal Highness," a voice called, from back towards the grand hallway and I came to a sharp halt, turning as the old house butler, Terance, came forward, bowing gently, "I apologise for the interruption but His Majesty, The King, would like to speak with you."

"The... King?" I frowned.

There weren't many more words after that. An invitation to meet with The King was a big thing and he wasn't a man that had sought to speak to me much since I had arrived. I remembered the only full acknowledgement that I'd received from him was when he'd tried to stop me by calling my name in the corridor.

Surprisingly, Terance didn't take me back upstairs but escorted me out of the front door and to the right into, what I had come to believe, was named The Queen's Garden. It went quite far back, delicately aligned with hedges, soft flowers and, centred, a white domed pavilion with a few seats and a table in the middle.

There, sat at the table, was The King, with a paper in his hands, and refreshments for one in front of him. Two guards stood outside of the dome, neither of whom I recognised.

"Your Majesty," Terance greeted as we approached, "Her Royal Highness, as requested."

The King placed his paper down and stood up. I could feel the power radiating from him; this was a man that nobody would mess with, but I didn't fear him. He was my future father-in-law, after all.

I curtsied, and I saw a soft twitch on his lips as he studied me whilst I did, "Alex, you may be excused."

"Sir."

I watched as Alex bowed to us both and left, whilst the other guards and Terance remained. His Majesty spoke to Terance in Zikan and he left quickly following; I understood it to be a command. I looked at The King, once again, waiting for him to tell me what he wanted me to do, beginning to feel self-conscious under his gaze.

"Come, join me," he finally spoke, swaying his hand to one of the empty chairs across from him. I did so, looking at him as he took his own. I looked briefly at the newspaper, seeing it was one of Britain's biggest, "I do enjoy keeping up with the world of humans."

I looked at him as he spoke, trying to get more of an understanding of him. I guessed that he was very good at keeping his eye on everything around him; not because he was interested in a newspaper, but because he had seen that I had, immediately, shifted my eyes to the tabloid. I was sure he was very good at poker.

"Why?"

"Why ever not?" he raised his eyebrows, "we are creatures of this world, we must understand what is happening within it in order for ourselves to adapt."

The King's accent was the least noticeable out of everyone I had spoken to since my arrival. In fact, if anything, it would seem like he was an imposter with how RP-like he sounded in comparison.

"But, most of those newspapers are about politics."

"As are we," The King chuckled, "I am sure you have come to understand some things in your short time with us. Even our world is political. You are now a part of that world as a princess and soon, as a queen. Adapting is political."

"So, what you're saying is I've adapted wrong?" I replied sharply, my shoulders feeling tight.

Again, he laughed but it didn't stop the tension rising in my body. In fact, it made me feel even more on edge. Two maids appeared: one with two pots of tea and the other with fresh pastries. They cleared up His Majesty's earlier drinks and both left without another word.

"My staff have grown quite fond of you," he answered, although I couldn't tell whether it was to his own disdain or not. From my gut feeling, this wasn't a casual meeting between soon-to-be relatives, "I should suppose anyone would grow fond of someone who goes against the parameters of which we have come to live."

"I'm not sure I catch what you are saying," I said to him, although I could understand that change was most likely not something he enjoyed.

"You have not adapted incorrectly, Arraetta," he answered, "however, you have been brought into our world, not us into yours. Whilst I do admire a passionate spirit, I do not appreciate seeing my son going to the lengths he has for you to cooperate with us."

"And, what lengths are those exactly?" I replied, "I've done everything I can to adapt to this life. I've done everything I've been asked."

"Have you?" he raised his eyebrows, "or, have you simply grimaced every time you must do something. Let us take the other day, for example, in the corridor; you cannot take a simple no as an answer. You believe you are entitled to understand everything within our world just because you are now in it. Do you truly think we would inform you of our ways without trust? Do you think we do not know you are hiding something? The daughter of Ivan the Great does not even know who she is, what a blasphemous lie."

"I didn't know."

"No?" he snipped, sitting forward, "tell me, oh divine goddess, how do you know that we are supposed to embark on a journey into war? You informed Seraiah that you had spoken with your father, which would either make you a liar in order to manipulate my son into doing your bidding, or you are a messenger of the Gods. If you are a messenger of the Gods, then you will tell me, right here, something that would make us trust you."

"So, that's what all this is about?" I whispered, "you want me to somehow prove to you that my father contacted me so that you can trust me? How do you expect me to do that?"

"Make contact with him," he said to me, "prove to me that you can speak to him."

"I was unconscious every time," I replied to him, realising too late that I'd spilled some more information that I'd not told anyone.

"*Every time*," his gaze was penetrable. I wanted to not fear this man, I had said that I didn't, but he was fearsome, "there has been more than one incidence then? Interesting, Arraetta, how you kept that quiet from even my son."

"You don't trust me anyway," I said to him, standing up, "so, maybe I'm lying about that too."

"Sit down, Arraetta."

"Are you going to tie me to this chair?" I asked him sharply, "because I'm quite done listening to you."

I went to walk away but his next words stopped me, "I may not have the power to stop your bonding ceremony, but I do have the power to stop you from seeing my son subsequently. And it is my say whether you become queen or not."

"I have done nothing to earn your distaste," I spat back, turning to him, "I… I love Seraiah and he loves me; he wouldn't allow you to destroy what is between us just for your own benefit."

"No, but he would for that of our people," he answered, "Seraiah needs a strong and adaptable queen, someone who will support him in every decision that needs to be made and not bite back when they are told no. Therefore, I shall offer you a compromise, Arraetta. If you hold your tongue and become a good wife to my son, adhere to our ways without fault and listen, then I shall crown you myself."

"And, if I don't?"

"Then, you shall be sent away," he answered, "and, my son will have no choice but to take a second wife."

Jealousy stung. I hadn't met another woman that had their eyes on Seraiah but he was a beautiful man, so it wouldn't have been a surprise if there was. Maybe they'd been training someone up to the position whilst they waited to see who the Kindred Spirit would be.

"No," I said to him, "Seraiah is *mine*."

"Then, make it so," he answered, "you are excused."

I tried to fight the tears as they tickled my eyes, but they fell as I rushed away from the garden. What a sly, arrogant man. How did someone as kind and loving as Seraiah have a father like him? They were polar opposites.

The only place I could go, to hide away from everyone, was the bedroom but there would be too many eyes on my way, so I walked around towards the back part of the side garden which was set out in a maze of high hedges. My tears fell then as I walked through the little paths until I found a dead end, slumping down on the gravel, against the tall greenery.

That bastard had reduced me to tears. It was his plan the entire time to make me feel weak and I now had no choice but to do as he had said. What I couldn't comprehend was how he still hadn't accepted me, even though I had changed already. I didn't want to be an obedient wife, did Seraiah truly want that? Did Seraiah even know that his father had brought me in for a conversation that had ended so abhorrently?

Hiding away in the bushes was quite a blessing because I was able to clear my head. I guessed there wasn't much way out of what His Majesty had said to me unless I could get him to be on my side. Even that thought made me grimace; I could imagine the smug look on his face when he knew that he had tamed his daughter-in-law.

The bush behind me shook and I jumped, thinking something was about to pounce on me but then I homed in on the sound of two people kissing. The bush shook a little again and I wondered whether it was Freddie and Genie secretly smooching, until the two culprits broke apart and murmured to each other in Zikan.

Intrigued, I stood up, walked a little ahead to the bush opening, to my left and around towards the back of it. At least whoever it was could provide me some sort of amusement after my hellish meeting with The King.

I pretended to walk around a little too quickly and jolted back almost, immediately, as the two of them broke apart.

The two of them being none other than Jonah and Alex. I would have never guessed.

"Your highness," Jonah greeted as he stepped away from a swollen-lipped Alex, who Jonah seemed to have been dominating with his mouth. Alex looked flustered; he couldn't meet my eye as he tried to find something else to look at.

"Well, sorry to interrupt," I breathed, awkwardly. It all made sense now, especially when Alex had said that he would be punished for saying something nice about Jonah.

"No, ma'am," Alex immediately said, taking hold of my arm before he moved it back, almost instantly, as though touching me was dishonourable, "sorry. I... I thought you were with His Majesty."

"Oh, I was," I replied scornfully, "but, I was dismissed, so I decided to wander the gardens and-"

"-You have been crying," Jonah answered, stepping forward to me like a strangely overbearing mother. He pulled out his handkerchief, from his navy jacket pocket, and brought it to my eyes, wiping it, "I am sure Seraiah will not be happy to find out."

"He won't," I said to him, "I'm going to pretend the whole thing never happened." I took the handkerchief from him to take over. "Like I'll pretend I didn't see this, don't worry."

"It is no secret," he replied, looking lovingly at Alex for a second, who was still blushing from being caught, "well, apart from us being here and being caught together, it is maybe-"

"-Unprofessional," Alex cleared his throat, glaring at his beau, "I told you it was a bad idea."

The pair started bickering together in Zikan and I stood there, highly amused by the couple's change in demeanour. I could tell that the two of them had been together for quite a long while, just by their exchange, and I was a little annoyed with myself for not spotting it before.

Gently, I took a few steps back and moved away around the corner to leave them alone to their arguing, but it wasn't long before both men came after me, cornering me in the maze once more.

"What?" I asked them both, folding my arms.

"Just because you saw us, it does not change anything," Jonah said, stepping forward, as though he was threatening, but there was a glint of amusement in his eyes. It was at that point I noticed their stark height difference; Alex was much taller than Jonah, which made Jonah's dominating ways quite hilarious.

"Oh, you mean because you think I have one up on you," I said, eyeing them as they both nodded. I could see that the two of them kissing secretly, in the bushes together, whilst on duty, could be detrimental to their careers. Jonah was the head of security and Alex was my personal guard, both of which were positions that could be easily stripped if the two of them had been caught by anyone else - like His Majesty.

As much as I could use it as a prime opportunity to ask for more freedoms, I could just hear The King's words, in the back of my head, as he told me to be an obedient wife to Seraiah. I had to sit and bite my tongue until I was crowned, then I could speak with more free will because The King couldn't tell me what to do then. Unfortunately, that was at least six months away.

"You don't have to worry," I said to them, "I've made an agreement with The King that I'll be a good wife so I won't be using this, or anything else as an excuse to get out of anything."

Alex looked quite satisfied that I'd told them both that, but Jonah's brows furrowed, and I wondered what he was thinking about.

"If you'll excuse me," Jonah bowed and left immediately following, not giving his lover a second look.

Both Alex and I stood in silence, for a short moment, before I decided it was high time to leave the maze and move back into the main house. Alex, as per usual, followed me and so the day resumed. I took a few moments to clean up the dried tears, in the bathroom, before going back outside.

The summer breeze gently caressed my skin as I wandered out to the back gardens, of the house, seeing that the generator had been moved underneath a metal structure in the back right hand corner, of the middle gardens. It was surrounded by wreaths of flowers and a deluxe red carpet, and two distinct altars stood in front, as though it was part of a new museum exhibition. It glowed gently in the distance as the summer sun radiated onto it and, on the odd occasion, docile lines of electricity would spring out around it as it pulsated away.

All the magnificence of the bunting and flowers and streamers, made up of blues and golds and pinks and more, was captivating. I noticed that, in another tent, a bar of sorts was being set up and I chortled at the idea of how many drunk people there were going to be.

"Are you joining in the celebrations, Alex?" I asked him.

"A little, ma'am," he replied as he came to be in step with me, "although it shall only depend on what you do."

"You can't just live your life around me," I said to him.

"Can I not?" he chuckled, "are we not already doing that?"

I was reminded of The King's conversation and how he'd said the staff were fond of me but not necessarily for a good reason in his eyes.

I fell quiet as I walked down to the lake, and I could feel that my sudden coldness had confused Alex. He moved to being behind me once more; the conversation was over for us both. I had to be an obedient wife, not the one who was going to bring change to their world.

I cringed at the thought, but I couldn't stand the idea that his father would command him to marry another. I wanted to meet the other woman to understand what the competition would be.

"Alex," I said, suddenly turning to him, "is-"

I winced immediately, feeling a sharp ache in my forehead, and keeled over. Alex came to kneel in front of me, speaking, but I couldn't hear what he was saying as I tried to not fall unconscious from the pain. A deep, harrowing scream of chaos echoed around, piercing deep into my ears.

"Stop..." I breathed, hazily looking up past Alex towards the house, watching as several men were rushing towards The Queen's Garden, whilst a few others were running down to the generator.

I turned my head to see that the generator was no longer glowing and looking up it seemed like the shield was down. It made me feel weak, the same feeling I had felt when I was trying to control my power in the library.

Alex took hold of my face, finally, and I looked at him as he spoke to me, as though at a distance, "ma'am..."

"Seraiah," I breathed, looking back towards the corner that led to The Queen's Garden. I, immediately, stood and began to run up towards it, feeling an overwhelming need to find him. As I closed in, I could feel the coldness trickle down my spine, and I was reminded of when he held me against the wall.

Alex was hot on my heels, but he didn't stop me as we made it to the garden I'd been in with His Majesty. The dynamic was strange; there were several guards on their knees whilst soldiers, in black uniform, stood with assault rifles pointing down at them. Jonah, donning a bullet proof vest, and looking like he was part of the secret service, stood in the middle of the path that led to the pavilion. And, in the pavilion, was The King and Seraiah.

The dominance, that The King held over me, was eradicated when it came to the power that Seraiah held over him, as he pinned his father against one of the white metal pillars. Nothing else remained in the centre of the platform; the table, chairs and refreshments adorned the garden beside it.

The air was sour, cold, and unwelcoming whilst both men's Rapidfire was buzzing brightly. Unlike Seraiah's power, The King's was a vivid blue and the least powerful as Seraiah's dark Rapidfire seemed to be the one that overshadowed his father's.

I could hear Seraiah threatening him, whilst The King was biting back at him, and I was cursing myself again for not knowing their language. At least, I could have learnt something to understand exactly what was happening.

Seraiah pushed his father, further against the post, and I watched his father whimper just a little. Slight satisfaction rolled through me, but I wondered at what cost that feeling would have on the result of His Majesty's blackmailing.

Seraiah bellowed something, a dark edge to his voice, and I saw The King's eyes widen. Jonah followed with an order before he took to one knee, all the soldiers following suit, whilst no one else looked to make a move. Apart from me.

I stepped forward then, feeling a great need to intervene with what was happening, for some reason I couldn't understand. Alex's hand touched my shoulder, and I turned to him as he shook his head before he, too, knelt.

I moved onwards, listening as Seraiah continued his threatening words, until I came side-by-side with Jonah. Before I could say anything, The King's Rapidfire seemed to pulsate, and a strange hue of energy began to transmit from his body into Seraiah's. As though he was sucking his life force from him.

"What is he doing?" I whispered.

"He is declaring himself King," Jonah murmured, looking up to me. My eyes widened and I looked back at the two on the pavilion, wondering what that meant.

Did I have to bow too? I remember Seraiah telling me that I need never bow to him, but I felt strange being the only person standing up in the garden.

"Why?" I breathed.

"To protect you."

To protect me? I remembered then how Jonah had left very quickly and, I presumed, he'd gone to speak with Seraiah. But surely that was against the rules of their house, unless there was something else happening that I was unaware of. Looking at the difference between the guards and the soldiers made me wonder whether there was some form of division between the people in the house.

"Seraiah!"

Jonah mildly cursed under his breath as I looked in the direction of which Tara flew in from; a small crowd of staff covered the entrance to the garden and every one of them moved as she came through.

Her gaze landed to me, then to Jonah and, finally, moved to where her son and husband both were. Seraiah had not let up on his *declaring himself king* and I guessed it had something to do with the power that was seeping from his father's body into his own. Tara rushed on to the pavilion and over to the two men, her voice too low for anyone to hear.

Tara gently placed her hand onto Seraiah's shoulder, and he, immediately, looked at her. I noticed then the dark in his eyes, but it dwindled within an instant; his shoulders sagged and both men's Rapidfire's died at once.

Seraiah's grip on his father loosened and he let go of him, speaking with Tara briefly before he bowed and rushed off. Meanwhile, The King had seemed to be so weakened that his body sagged to the floor with a thud, and I knew he was barely conscious. Tara spoke to him sharply before she turned and descended the steps, shouting a command.

The command allowed for the guards, who were somewhat seized, to stand up and move to protect, and help, The King. The soldiers that had come to kneel were back on their feet and Tara stopped at Jonah as he rose and bowed.

Tara spoke with him briefly, barely acknowledging me, before she walked out of the gardens. Another sharp call came from her mouth and all the staff began to disperse, presuming to whisper about the events that had taken place.

Jonah turned to me before gripping my bicep, not too tightly, and he pulled me out of the gardens, towards the grounds at the back of the house. Alex followed, alongside Travis, who stood nearby, and two other soldiers I didn't recognise.

"What happened?" I asked, feeling a bit breathless and full of a headache, from the effects of the generator not working.

"He is still a prince," Jonah replied as we walked around to the back gardens. I wanted to go and find Seraiah, to see if he was okay but I knew that wasn't going to happen with Jonah and Alex around.

He was still The Prince. That meant The King was still in his position and that Seraiah's declaration of being king, however he was doing it, didn't work. Had Jonah told him what The King had said to me? Had it angered Seraiah so much that he only saw red?

TWENTY-ONE

After twenty minutes of being seated away from the house, at the bottom end of the garden, beside the lake, I was growing restless. I didn't want to be waiting around to find out about what had taken place and no one, not even Alex, was giving me any more information about it.

The space I'd come to sit in was a quiet alcove. It was surrounded by one large hedge with patches of summer flowers, two benches and one exit via a paved path. I had opted to stand as close to its entrance, as possible, so I could see up to the house, but I wasn't allowed to venture much further as the two gun-wielding guards took their places at the entrance, whilst Alex and Travis split themselves on either side of the enclosed garden.

Preparations were still very much in progress with not much having changed since the incident, apart from, I guessed, that staff were most likely whispering about what had occurred between the Crown Prince and The King. If I was a member of staff, and interested in gossip, I'd be very intrigued in hearing the tales of those I was serving.

I was no doubt part of the whisperings, however.

I wondered whether Freddie and Genie were far off from returning from their outing to see her parents. Genie had told me, the day before, that she was finally ready to speak to her mum about their relationship but wasn't going to disclose the engagement until a later date. I would have imagined that Seraiah, or Jonah, had phoned Freddie to tell him of the incident, especially since Freddie seemed to be Seraiah's right-hand man.

My head was still throbbing away, I was beginning to think about begging for a way for the generator to come back online just so I could feel at peace, within my body. I still had a lot of questions to ask about how it really worked, but it was the least important thing considering everything that had happened.

My gaze landed on Jonah as he came out of the house, followed by Seraiah who came to flank him as they began to walk towards the globe. Behind them were four soldiers, all walking in formation. Every eye that noticed them turned to watch; the ones closer to Seraiah bowing whilst others just were mesmerised.

Stepping a little further forward, I almost came out of the alcove, but the two soldiers moved to block the entrance, backs to me.

"He is bringing the generator back online, ma'am," Alex said, coming to stand just behind me. I could see in Seraiah's demeanour that things had calmed as he was smiling and joking, with Jonah, until they reached the large sphere, at the opposite corner of the garden.

Seraiah's body began to power up, immediately, and he stepped forward, placing his hand on the lifeless orb. The soldiers that were protecting him turned to face up towards the gardens, somewhat ready for anything to occur but I couldn't think what exactly would happen.

"Alex, why are there soldiers with him?"

"Protection," he replied, "there has been a shift in command."

"Is he now king?" I asked, watching Seraiah's Rapidfire seep, from his body, into the ball in an opposite effect to what he had done to The King. It began to power up again; I could feel the static from the electricity hum, even from my distance, and my eyes cast up as the shield began to appear like a wave of copper cloth. Once the dome had returned, the shield became invisible, whilst the generator buzzed in its dull colour, once more, and I felt revitalised, once again.

I looked as Seraiah stepped back from it, the power dissipating from his body as he turned and spoke something to Jonah. All the soldiers turned and bowed before dispersing and Seraiah's head turned in my direction. Both came to walk towards us, and I felt my heart flutter.

Before he could even get halfway to me, however, Seraiah's head turned up, towards the house, and I looked to see Freddie striding down towards him. Seraiah's attention was already turned from me and he, and Jonah, immediately, went up to Freddie before they all went onwards towards the palace.

I sighed, "since we can see I am-"

"-You are free to go, ma'am," Alex interjected and I guessed he'd received the signal from Jonah, through his radio. Before I could go, however, he gently placed his hand on my arm, clearing his throat, "if I may, ma'am, I believe you will find it wise not to liaise with His Majesty without speaking with His Royal Highness first."

So, everything had occurred because of the conversation that had taken place between The King and me. For something that seemed inadequate, it sure stirred and changed something within the palace. I had to find out as soon as I could and, I guessed, the only person who would tell me anything, if he even would, was Seraiah.

The two soldiers blocking the entrance turned and bowed to me, in sync, before making their way up to the palace.

"Are we going to war?" I suddenly asked Alex.

"We are already at war, ma'am."

Surprisingly, it was Travis who stepped up and I think it was the first time he'd properly said anything to me since my arrival, outside of *this way, ma'am* that I'd received a couple of times that he was with me.

Travis and Alex exchanged a few words before Travis nodded, bowed to me, and began to go up to the house.

"It's like you all speak in riddles," I said to Alex, folding my arms as I stood in the empty alcove.

"Ma'am, the most important thing is your safety," Alex answered, "that is our job, not yours and certainly not The King's."

"The King doesn't care about my safety," I pointed out.

"No, he does not," he agreed, a strange glower in his look, as he cast his eyes up towards the house, "that is why there has been a change in command."

Before I could continue onwards, with the conversation, and ask him what the hell he meant by the change, Genie's chirpy voice echoed down the garden, "guess who's back!"

She practically was skipping down towards us, and threw her arms around me, when she made it. "I didn't expect that we were going to come home to mayhem."

"Don't blame me," I held my hands up in surrender and she laughed, hooking her arm through mine as she pulled me away from Alex, who followed behind at a distance, "I need to find Seraiah."

"I think he's in a meeting," Genie told me, "I'm sure he'll come and find you later. For now, let's go and catch up."

Genie told me about how her parents reacted when they'd met the dreamboat that was Freddie. I knew that they'd love him as he was very charming and easy on the eyes, but I wondered what they'd think of him once they found out he was from another world. *If* they found out, of course.

Genie had ordered us both an afternoon tea whilst we sat in one of the sitting rooms so that we could be in a quiet space, without other ears. Even Alex was left outside the room.

Not once did the subject get brought back to the incidents that had occurred during the day and, although I was quite thankful for that, I also wanted to know whether Genie knew anything.

I found myself idly hanging about for the rest of the day, waiting for Seraiah to finally come and speak with me but that never happened, and I turned into bed around ten. Even then I couldn't sleep for hours as I tossed and turned at the need for answers. At two o'clock, I found myself sitting in a hot bath in an attempt to get myself to sleep but to no avail.

I dressed myself in comfortable clothes, around three, and decided to try and find him, opting for his study to be the best place, as that is where he had come to reside.

I snuck into the library, through to the door and tiptoed down, wondering whether he would be surprised for a visit, from me, since he hadn't taken me down there himself. I gently opened the door to a darkened room, apart from a soft lamp that illuminated in the cove that had previously had a sofa and, now, held a bed.

I heard soft breaths from the bed, and I knew it was Seraiah snoozing away. I was overstepping the boundaries by being in there, at such an early hour, but I felt like I had no other choice. I stepped closer to the bed, looking down at his soft face as his blonde curls splayed across the pillow.

Almost naturally, I went to move them so I could take a better look at him, at his most vulnerable. My heart pounded in my chest but, not from fear of being caught, more because of how intimate this was. Then, my wrist was grabbed, and I was thrown onto the other side of the bed, Seraiah on top, looking down at me with sleepy eyes.

"My, my," he chuckled, "this is a surprise."

I blushed, "you were asleep."

"I could feel you," he whispered, leaning down to kiss me, lingering dangerously close as he teased, "what brings you to my bed at this time?"

"I was worried about you," I murmured, "you didn't see me yesterday."

"I saw you," he replied, "from a distance, but you are always there, Arraetta."

"Is that not what you want?" I asked him, leaning up to seal the distance between our lips. The kiss deepened immediately, but it wasn't bruising and rough; just slow and passionate.

"I could get used to you being in my bed," he murmured when the kiss broke off and licked my lip a little, looking into his desire-filled eyes, "but, you are not here to please me."

"No."

"I would have hoped to catch you before breakfast anyway," he answered, sitting next to me on the bed. I sat up, noticing how he was in, nothing more than, his boxers and I turned my head away. He chuckled, "it is all yours."

"I know," I smiled, connecting eyes with him again, "maybe I just can't get used to it."

Tenderly, he moved his hand up to stroke my cheek before moving down to take a strand of my hair, twirling it in his fingers. "Get used to it, Arraetta."

I leant up and kissed him gently before moving back to my sitting position. I knew that Seraiah was mine and that I was his, but I couldn't get used to how beautiful a man he was, and how tender his gaze was when he looked my way.

"There is much you do not know about the palace," he said to me, still idly twirling the hair, "when we arrived on Earth, I was infected and it made me out of control. I remember a long period of time where I was drugged and strapped to a table whilst Sheika, and others, did everything they could to reduce the effects of The Dark. I was overcome with nightmares and that fear, as you know, fed the darkness that had reaped part of my soul.

"I did not know how much time had passed until it turned out I had been kept away from life on Earth for six months. I happened to figure out a way to escape and I got lost, in a brand-new world I did not understand. I found myself at a local village, around six miles away from here, where I was picked up by some officers who thought I was a spy because I could not speak a word of English. But The General found me, he had done quite well at learning the language and convinced them that I was mentally unwell."

"Mentally unwell?" I whispered, gobsmacked.

"Yes, and it worked," he told me, "I was brought back here, to the land of which my father had, somehow, purchased from a farm owner, where my people were living in tents whilst they tried to build a village. The largest tent belonged to my parents, and I was escorted there, fearful that I was bound to be strapped to a table for evermore.

"However, once in the tent, my mother engulfed me in a hug and she cried against me, telling me that she had nothing to do with the decision that was made."

"It was your father."

"Yes," he nodded, "it was my father. You see, something had changed during the crossing. My father despised me for what I had become because it was what had destroyed his homeland. He hated not just me, but anything infected by The Dark. He told me I was a monster and that he would not allow me to rule my people until I had found a way to *control* it.

"Rather than sentencing me to being a science experiment, he made me the scientist. He knew that it had interested me back in Zika, but this was not for hobby purposes. I had to spend six days a week working on three things. The first, I had to find a way for our people to survive on Earth, without them getting sick with the energy levels; the second, I had to learn to control my Rapidfire and the third, I had to figure out how to open a portal back to our world."

"How long did it take you?"

"Well, science was new to the world here," he replied, "so finding the things I needed was more difficult because I was not allowed to scour the land for them. That was part of my imprisonment; I could only send others out for materials I needed and that would take a long period of time. In the end, it took me ten years to successfully create the generator and shield, which helped with our energy. All the while, I trained my Rapidfire with Freddie, which was the only recreational time I had. Anytime that I flared, my father's men would sedate me."

I remembered the garden incident and wondered whether he'd been sedated following because he seemed fine a little while later.

"I do not get sedated anymore," he said, as though reading my thoughts. He sat back and spread his legs out next to me, "no, that stopped around twenty years into our being here. I decreed that my sentence was ineffective and that I would do everything for my people, no matter whether I was kept under lock and key. I remember reminding him that I was his son, and the future king. He declared *you are no son of mine, and no kingdom would want a king like you.*

"I flipped. My anger raged and I found myself pinning my father on the ground, whilst I had changed into the thing that he hated the most. The monster he *feared* the most. I saw it in his eyes; I felt it deep within his soul. My father did not just hate me, he feared what his son had become, and he could not see passed it. His soul was burdened with grief for the loss of me, but I was not dead. He repeated with a voice that was strong even as he trembled. '*you are no son of mine*.'"

"Did he lock you up again?" I asked.

"No," he replied, "I was not sedated by his men either, they did not get the chance as my mother stormed into the tent and declared a truce. As well as my mother, Freddie, Jonah, Dixon and several others, you will come to recognise, stood with her. My father's men outnumbered them but there were enough people to enact a treaty.

You see, under our laws, a treaty must have seven people ready to sign a declaration of peace."

I could feel how proud the story made me; that all these people had come to Seraiah's aid because they knew he was being punished, even when it wasn't his fault what had happened to him.

"Not only that," he continued, "but, little did I know that, many of the folk had come to my own aid also. My mother produced a piece of paper - a letter - which had many signatures on it asking for the pardon of The Prince."

"I love your people," I grinned, clapping my hands together like an excited child.

He chuckled, "they are your people too. Although, I will admit that I believe many of them, initially, signed more out of fear."

"What did the pardon say?"

"It was a simple letter which talked about negotiations," he answered, "so, my father's council and my own, new, council stood in the dining area of the house, which now is the grand hallway. We argued and agreed for hours, negotiating every little detail. My father did not want to declare me king, that he would not want to see me crowned but his council reminded him that it was a rite of passage. The final agreement made was that I would only become king once my fated Kindred Spirit would arrive."

"So, you declared yourself king yesterday."

"Yes," he nodded, "but my mother reminded me of a promise I made, which was that I would have a traditional coronation in which I am declared king, in front of my people, and that I would not seek to declare myself king prior."

"And, what does it mean for you to *declare yourself king*?" I wondered.

"It means that I would render my father powerless."

It was all he needed to say because I understood from what I saw that he was almost sucking his father's power from him. But Rapidfire was our life force so how would his father survive? Would he leave just enough left that his father would linger, or would he kill him?

"I am tired," Seraiah said suddenly, pulling the duvet from underneath him, so that he could slip under. He held his arms out to me and I smiled, knowing how nice it would be just to lie in his arms and fall asleep. But I couldn't because I wasn't allowed.

"I'll leave you to sleep."

"Do not leave me," he begged like a child, "I wish to hold my wife."

"I'm not your wife yet," I whispered, moving off the bed, "I also hope you don't plan to render me powerless."

"Oh, Princess," he chuckled, sitting up to watch me, "I definitely plan to."

I bit my lip, the urge to climb into bed with him and let him do that to me was overwhelming but I couldn't allow it. I walked to the door and opened it, looking back at him as he watched me in the dark, "thank you for telling me."

"I promised I would."

As I wandered through the library, I wondered what Seraiah's mother did in all the time that his father had been punishing him. Why had it taken her so long to come to her son's rescue? Maybe she didn't have many rights as a queen, maybe they were stuck in their traditional ways where the man was king and everyone else was beneath him. I hoped it wasn't the case, however, as that wasn't the kind of queen I wanted to be.

Kadey and Elina woke me up a few hours later and I felt groggy from the lack of sleep. It was the first day of Iontine and the two maids helped me get ready to be as presentable, as possible, for the opening ceremony.

Both were very excited for the event but all I kept thinking about was how much I was going to notice the cracks, in the foundation of the palace, since Seraiah had told me more about it. I wondered how it would affect things going forward and Alex's words came back to me, *there's been a shift in command.* I didn't get around to asking Seraiah about that; it seemed that he wasn't king, but something had changed.

If there was a split in the household, did that mean that half the staff worked for His Majesty and half worked for Seraiah? Or did everyone work equally for them, apart from the two councils. It would mean that decisions, within the palace, had to be made between both parties, which would've included allowing me to stay with them.

"Are you okay, ma'am?" Elina asked as she gently combed my hair. I must've been quietly staring off into space as I allowed my thoughts to divulge themselves.

"Yes, thank you," I smiled kindly to her, picking up a couple of the glass hair grips that were laid out, ready to be placed into my hair. I twisted them in my fingers idly, for a few moments, before I looked at her again, "who do you work for, Elina?"

Kadey froze from her duties of steaming a blue summer dress, in the back corner of the room, whilst Elina tensed behind me, and I wondered whether this was a conversation that wasn't meant to be with them.

Elina swallowed, "well, it is not so simple."

"Seraiah told me that there's a split in the staff," I went on to explain, looking from Elina to Kadey. It wasn't quite what he had said. In fact, he hadn't mentioned that there was a split in the staff, he had just told me that a lot of people had signed a letter of pardon. But I noticed the split following the incident.

"When have you seen His Grace?" Kadey asked, turning to me, "I was unaware that you had met with him."

Ah, that was something I didn't really have an answer for. Except, of course, that I'd tiptoed out of my room, only a few hours before, to go and see him whilst the staff slept.

"I have my ways," I answered, in hopes that the conversation would move swiftly back.

"We work for Her Majesty," Kadey then replied, after a few intense seconds, whilst she figured out in her head how Seraiah and I had met. Or I guessed that was what she was doing, "the palace staff work directly for her, and she gives her orders to Mr and Mrs Finch, who are, in a sense, our bosses."

Mr Finch was Terance and was Mrs Finch's husband. Terance, I had seen liaise with both Seraiah and His Majesty, on occasions, around the house and I knew that Seraiah was fond of the old man, whilst I had only seen Terance speak with The King once and that was the day prior, before the incident had occurred.

Tara oversaw the staff, which made sense. She was essentially Switzerland, or neutral ground, when it came to the two men and so I wondered what else she had control of.

"So, does everyone work for Tara?" I asked her.

"Not everyone," Elina admitted, chewing over her next words as she took one of the grips, from my hand, to place some hair back from my face, "I am unsure what His Highness has informed you, and we could get in a lot of trouble for talking about things that are not so widely spoken about these days, but you should know that His Majesty and His Royal Highness are both king's here."

"Elina!" Kadey chided whilst steaming the dress.

"Sorry," Elina replied in a quiet voice.

The room fell quiet, for a few moments, as I waited for one of them to elaborate a little more if they would. I wanted to understand Elina's meaning more but it could mean that she loses her job, and I didn't want that.

"His Grace is not a king," Kadey finally said, turning the steamer off, "not yet. It is not official until he is crowned, that is the way it is. However, he has an equal amount of power to The King and, thus, all decisions are made between The King, His Grace and the two councils."

"The two councils…" I coaxed.

"Ma'am, if Her Majesty finds-"

"-There are three of us here, Kadey," I answered, trying not to sound too frustrated as I turned to her, "I am sure neither of us will be telling anyone."

"If I may be so bold, Your Highness," Elina replied, stepping away a little, "you… you have a small habit of spilling things when you are frustrated."

I looked at her a little shocked at how bold she was, but even Kadey's expression was agreeing with Elina. She was right, I supposed. I had a habit of telling others things, mainly Seraiah, when I was angry.

"And, also, you may drink today," Kadey added, "which may mean you speak outwardly without meaning to. It is not that we don't trust you, ma'am, it is that it is important, until you are queen, for these conversations to remain between yourself and His Royal Highness."

In other words, *we do not wish to speak to you until the conversation has been had with The Prince*. That's what she was saying, and I couldn't do anything more than nod, allowing things to resume as they got me ready, without another word. My only issue was that I had to somehow bring up the two councils, without it being obvious that I'd had a conversation with the girls and that would be difficult, especially since I didn't know when I'd next be alone with Seraiah.

I'd have to sneak into his room again.

Once I was ready, I was escorted down to the west wing, where I was met by Alex and Travis, and we headed towards the grand hallway. The door to the library opened, on our way down, and I watched as Seraiah and Freddie both exited.

Seraiah looked over and smiled before both men bowed to me.

"Where's Genie?" I asked Freddie.

"She is busy helping with some final preparations," Freddie replied, "but, she shall join us for breakfast and will be around before the opening ceremony."

Seraiah placed his arm out, for me to take, and I hooked my hand onto it as the entourage made its way onwards. I wondered whether he'd mention about the night before, but we remained quiet as Freddie moved into step behind us with the other two men.

I couldn't help but look at the staff members, as we worked our way down to the breakfast room, wondering which side everyone truly was playing on. I knew Seraiah to be a kind person but I guessed that the dark side of him scared many, and so they may still come to resent him. For His Majesty, however, all he really had was being a ruler and I presumed he was a good one - even if he was arrogant and callous towards me.

Genie joined us for breakfast. Conversation was light, mainly about the celebrations which were to come, of which were going to be heavy from the sounds of it. An opening ceremony followed by five days' worth of worshipping, dancing, drinking and festivities. Everyone, including staff, were entitled to be part of the festival.

"You're quiet, Arri," Genie poked as we exited the room together, "you okay?"

"Just tired," I smiled gently.

"Maybe you should take a nap," Seraiah suggested as we stood as a four together. I pointed to my hair and, dramatically, to my clothing in answer and he smiled, knowing exactly what I meant. Plus, I didn't think that Elina or Kadey wanted to spend time alone with me, just in case I decided to ask them more questions.

"How about a walk?" Freddie asked us, "we could walk the streets of the town together and be back in time for twelve o'clock."

Freddie's idea was a good one and it meant that I could finally see the town a little more.

Guards - no, *soldiers* - were assembled quickly and I wondered whether there was the possibility that someone might attack Seraiah, or even me, whilst we walked together. It could be possible if someone didn't want a man infected by The Dark to be their ruler.

"What's with the soldiers?" I whispered to Seraiah as we began our walk.

Two soldiers walked ahead of us, two walked at a distance behind, whilst Alex and Travis were on our tail much closer. Freddie and Genie were ahead of us, chatting away as though they had never spoken to each other before.

"Protection," he answered, "they are part of our guard."

"You never had this many before."

"I have never had to worry about my father as much as before," he said and I looked at him as he cast his eyes ahead, thoughts flickering in his mind. He swallowed and looked down at me, offering a small smile, "I will do whatever I have to in order to keep you safe."

"Your father isn't going to kill me," I whispered.

"You do not know what my father is capable of," he growled lowly and I wondered whether the intensity of the glare, in his eyes, would burn a hole wherever it was directed, "he would not kill you but there is, no doubt, he will take you from me when he finds the right moment."

"You're talking about the deal."

He stopped and turned to me, "was it a deal or a command?"

"He seemed to want what was best for you..."

"Best for me?" he laughed humourlessly, shaking his head, "he would not know what was best for me if it stared him in the face. In fact, you were right in front of him the entire time. Do you not understand, Arraetta, that if he could find a way to control me anymore, he would?

My father is not the same man that I once loved, he is but a shell of it."

"Sorry."

"Do not apologise," he replied, keeping his voice quiet, "it is not your fault that that arrogant man backed you into a corner. I just wish I had made him cry like he made you."

"I only told Jonah that I-"

He interrupted, "it was not Jonah who told me. It was one of the guards, although Jonah came to me just in time, with confirmation that he had seen your cheeks stained with tears and it was enough to throw me over. I cannot lose to a man who seeks to ruin the only thing worth living for, Arraetta."

The only thing worth living for, in his eyes, was me. But there was so much more worth than that, including an abundance of friends who supported him. Or at least I hoped they were his friends. I looked down to see that Freddie and Genie had stopped, a little further away, neither of them looking at us, whilst the other guards around us waited patiently for us to move on.

"They are here for us," Seraiah said and I looked back at him as he offered me a soft smile, "they move for us, and with us, we are the command, Arraetta. You move, they move, it is how it is."

"I guessed," I laughed gently, "Alex doesn't ever leave me alone."

"Apart from at night time," he replied, moving down to whisper in my ear, "when only the cameras know of your movements and no one can stop you."

"It's a shame the cameras are there," I provoked, placing a gentle kiss on his cheek before moving onwards after Freddie and Genie. Seraiah fell into step quickly, taking hold of my hand but he didn't say anything further as we caught up to the other two.

We spent an hour walking around, greeting various people, around the estate, whilst taking a full tour of the place until we made it back to the house. Tara stood waiting for us in the grand hallway, dressed in the most beautiful floral summer dress that stuck to her light curves and ended at her knees.

Seraiah greeted his mother affectionately whilst Freddie and Genie appropriately bowed to her. Tara looked at me as she spoke with Seraiah in their native language, and I wondered whether what she was saying was positive or negative. I guessed by the soft smile on her lips and her move past her son towards me meant it was positive.

"You look radiant," she complimented, "I hope you come to enjoy the celebrations this week, it is very exciting that you have come to join us on your first Iontine." She looked at Genie. "And, you as well, of course, Genie."

Genie smiled and curtsied, "thank you, ma'am."

"If you will excuse me, I must go and meet my husband," she said with a little hint of disdain in her voice. All of us watched, after her, as she went around to the central corridor towards the gardens.

"Let us go," Seraiah said, and I looked at him before he held out his arm again, "it is time to enjoy our celebrations."

TWENTY-TWO

The entire garden was alive with numerous attendees, dressed in their finest summer party clothing. Seraiah and I walked across an empty area of the floor to a long-stage, which had four seats upon it; one of which was a throne I hadn't seen before. On that throne, His Majesty sat carelessly, whilst Tara took the chair next to him.

"Father," Seraiah bowed to him, before he pulled me to the spare seats, with Seraiah taking the one that was next to The King, "is the throne necessary?"

"After your incident yesterday, I must remind everyone, including you, who is still king here," The King spat quietly at him. I was surprised the exchange was in English, but I guessed it was so that I understood too.

I didn't look at the two of them in case I sparked a further feud. Instead, I looked out at the large crowd surrounding the empty space, all waiting patiently for what was to come. I could feel the excited atmosphere amongst everyone, whispering away in their groups. I wondered, once again, who would be prepared to take down Seraiah, and who would protect him.

The King stood, speaking to everyone naturally in their language without once bringing it back to English. It was fair enough, I suppose, I was a foreigner in their world. I had wondered whether asking Seraiah to translate would be a good idea but, when I looked at him, I could tell that he was idly listening whilst scanning the crowd.

It was then I noticed he would pause, every now and again, and I followed his eyeline a little, seeing there were quite a few soldiers amongst the crowd, blending in well. The King bellowed something, before he sat down, and the crowd parted as a group of young dancers came forward, taking their places.

Genie stepped forward into the middle of the dancers and I couldn't help the smile on my face as she professionally looked at us all. She curtsied and, when she rose, her eyes landed on me, sending me a small wink. She turned to the crowd and called, "I present to you, the Dance of the Goddess."

With that, Genie moved off the dance floor and some music began to play. The dancers, in formation, began to sway and move together until they came to be in a circle formation, their bodies in sync. It was as though they were dancing around a fire. Next more dancers came in, swaying until they broke apart and fell to the ground.

A woman moved forward, from the middle of the crowd, in a soft lace dress and a crown of flowers that sat on her head. She came to stand in the middle, moved her arms out to the side and closed her eyes, swaying gently, back and forth, until those surrounding her began to rise once more. No words left her mouth, but that wasn't needed, the story was told in her motions.

A story of how a desolate land, ravaged with untamed beasts, was saved from destruction when a young goddess came to save them.

"Do you understand?" Seraiah murmured, leaning towards me and I nodded, mesmerised by the scene in front of us. Several men, representing a gigantic beast, came into the circle and the goddess fought it with all her might, using her arms to represent power. They fought together in rhythm, their dance portraying the wins and losses between them until she had slain the beast. The men fell.

Silence lingered as the goddess rose once more, eyes closed, until a large man stepped through the crowd, burdened by something. The goddess turned to face him as he fell to his knees, in front of her, begging her for help. He stood and the dancers, which were lying on the floor, rose once more, beginning to dance again as he explained to her, using movement, what he needed help with.

It was then that I understood who this was. It was a representation of my pa. I sat up a little straighter, swallowing tears that had subconsciously gathered themselves in my throat as I watched him. The ensemble fell to the floor again and the goddess moved forward, blessing him before she fell.

The man, or Ivan, tried to control his new power as he trained it, failing several times until the beast rose once more. I remembered how Pa had told me that he struggled to take hold of the power within him, and this was what was being portrayed. The brawny dancer fought against its enemy, Roxecluf, until it symbolised that the being was locked away somewhere.

Ivan fell to his knees, body moving dramatically to show how heavy his breath had become until four beings strode forward. Mirroring the goddess that had come to be in a similar position before meeting him. He stood and turned to them, before kneeling to one knee.

The next part showed the decision of which Ivan could make. The goddess from earlier, the one who had sacrificed herself, stepped forward and I wondered whether she was representing my ma as a secondary character, or whether my ma was the goddess. And, as per the tale that was told, Ivan decided to marry the goddess and split his gift between the four realms.

The troupe of dancers came to stand and bowed to us all before turning to the crowd, who had erupted with applause, upon them finishing. Genie stepped forward and bowed and I felt so proud that my best friend had choreographed such a beautiful piece of work. The four of us on the stage clapped and I toiled with the thoughts of the meaning behind the dance and the beauty of it.

A few musicians stepped up into the empty space as the troupe disappeared before they began to play some music on a variety of instruments. And, so the opening ceremony continued with a few other performances until His Majesty declared Iontine officially open, according to the words of Seraiah.

"Let us eat," Seraiah said, standing up to his feet, before he offered his hand to me.

The King made a comment and Seraiah chided back to him before pulling me away, from the stage, and I wondered what had been said.

Hours later, the festival was in full swing, and I was a little merry from drinking wine and eating too much food. Genie and I were sitting together near the lake, talking about the meaning behind the dance, and waited for the return of Seraiah and Freddie, who both had disappeared to retrieve something.

"Are you going to worship?" I asked her, looking at the crowd that had gathered around the globe, giving offerings.

"I might," she shrugged, sipping her wine, "I can't speak Zikan very well though, so I don't think I'd be able to coherently speak with them."

"They would understand you," I pointed out, "I'm sure they're not limited to one language."

In fact, as Pa had said, all languages translated in Ryazark.

"Isanhowad!" Seraiah declared, from a little further away from us, and we both looked as the two boys returned, a small bag of something in their hands. Seraiah threw the bag down to the floor next us before he sat opposite me, joined by Freddie.

I picked up the bag, of what looked like weed, and I laughed in shock. "No."

"Yes," Seraiah replied. He was quite drunk.

"No," I repeated, looking at Genie, who was chewing over the thoughts of taking it. I remember Genie and I always joked that we would try weed one day, but I was always worried about the effects it would have and that my four-yearly experience of the blackout would occur sooner because of it.

"It is not weed," Freddie pointed out, snatching it from our hands, "it is Isanhowad. I think you will like it; everything will be blissful."

"Blissful," I repeated, "and what is wrong with how we are now?"

"You do not need to take it, my love," Seraiah said, holding his hand out to Freddie, as Freddie scooped a small amount of it into his hands, "but, it would make this evening so much more fun."

Seraiah shoved the mix into his mouth, and I cringed as he easily chewed and swallowed it before taking a swig of his drink. Genie took a portion from Freddie, looking at it, like it was a science experiment, before gingerly chewing on a small bit of it.

"Oh, it tastes good actually."

"Feels good too," Seraiah chuckled, eyes landing on me, "come join us on the freeing side of life, Arraetta."

Freddie was already holding my portion out to me, whilst Genie ate the rest of hers. I slowly took it from him, looking at it as Freddie knocked his head back and shovelled the rest into his mouth, as though finishing a packet of crisps.

A few moments later, Genie giggled whilst Freddie and Seraiah shared a grin, all already high as a kite. "Come on, Arri."

I looked at her, before rolling my eyes and throwing the mixture into my mouth, idly chewing it before I swallowed. At first, nothing happened until everywhere seemed to get brighter and more illuminated. Bliss settled in my body, and I felt like I'd never been so free before.

"Let us dance!" Seraiah shouted and, before I knew it, the four of us were on the lively dance floor amongst others. I'm not sure how long we danced for, but I could feel sweat beading my forehead, after a while, and needed to get myself a drink. I stumbled towards the temporary bar.

"Water," I whispered, then giggled.

"Of course, ma'am," the bartender replied, moving to sort it out and I turned to scan the busy tent, full of drunk patrons.

A little girl's laugh sounded, from the entrance of the tent, and I looked over at her, seeing her peer at me, with pure content on her face. She looked familiar but I couldn't pinpoint where I knew her from. She waved frantically at me to come to her, and I smiled, heading to follow her out of the tent, back into the basking sunlight. Everything was glowing, moving in and out of focus like a magical fairy realm, and it made me laugh with glee.

The girl's giggle sounded again, to my right, and I looked as she waved me down towards the generator. The globe pulsated ferociously; it was beautiful. One foot after the other, I walked down towards it until I stood mere feet away from it. I could see how the energy buzzed around it like electrical currents in formation.

"Touch it," a whisper sounded from my side and I looked down as the little girl stood there, once again. She looked up at me with a cheeky smile on her face, "go on."

"Who are you?" I asked her.

"I'm you, silly," she giggled and that's when I noticed all the similarities, as though they had been masked by something. This was the version of me that I'd seen in The Cre-este, running around with her friend. She laughed and danced around me in a circle, whilst holding the ends of her white and pink summer dress.

"Princess, where are you?" I looked to my right, but no one was around.

"Oops, I have to go," she squealed, from behind me, and, when I turned, she was no longer there. I laughed gently to myself before turning to the globe once more.

"Your Royal Highness."

I looked as Jonah came to stand next to me, looking a little concerned.

"Jonah," I breathed and threw myself at him, in a very clinging hug. He braced for a fall just in time and managed to keep us upright, "where's your lover? Are you not kissing him now?"

"Ma'am," Jonah said sternly, coming to hold me at arm's length, "let us get you some water."

I gasped dramatically, "oh, I asked for some but then the little girl came and so I found myself down here."

"Little girl?" he frowned, eyeing the area before he shouted something in his native language to someone. I moved out of his grasp and turned back to the ball, blinking as its brightness seemed to only grow. "Your Highness, no!"

I hadn't realised I'd even walked forward to it, nor that I was curiously reaching out, until my hand touched the surface and an intense white flash washed over the surroundings.

Silence.

I blinked and adjusted my eyes as I came to be in a pure white room.

"Hello?" I shouted, taking in my surroundings of nothingness. Was I dead? I swore these things only happened when someone was about to pass on from the world. Maybe touching the ball of electricity fried me to the core, but was it dangerous?

Arraetta.

I turned in the direction of the voice, still met with the same blank space.

Arraetta, the voice called again from the same direction.

I started to walk forward, glad that I was surrounded by light, not darkness.

"Hello?" I called, hoping to finally see someone, but it was a long walk until I found anything, coming across a door. The effects of the drug were wearing off quickly, although maybe this was part of it.

As I approached the door, it swung open by itself, showing only a space of complete darkness. I halted, feeling fear creep up my spine as I looked at it.

Arraetta, the same ghostly voice called from within, but it didn't entice me anymore. I turned and began to run back towards the way I came from, looking for another way out, but I only came up to the same door, its exit wide open for me.

Arraetta, do not be afraid.

"Let me out!" I shouted, looking around for an exit, before whispering to myself, "this is only a dream, I can control it."

Can you? They replied. *All I see is that you are fearful of the unknown, it is that fear that controls you.*

"I'm not scared of the unknown," I whispered, eyeing the dark space through the door and swallowed the bile that had risen in my throat, "the unknown is inevitable."

Then, what is it you fear?

I paused, looking directly at it before straightening my shoulders.

Darkness, Arraetta?

"No," I stumbled, stepping back a little, "no, not quite."

Your heart is racing. The only way to overcome your fear is by facing it head on. Step into the darkness, for only then can you truly see the light.

"I can't face it alone," I breathed, clenching my sweaty palms.

You must face your fear to truly control your power.

"Who are you?" I shouted and the sound echoed around, as though I was in a tunnel.

Come in and I will show you.

Step by step, I moved forward, bracing for something to jump out at me until I was inside the room of darkness. Before I could even turn back to the white space, the door slammed behind me, and my sight was engulfed in darkness.

This way.

The voice called ahead of me, and I shuffled onwards, worried that I'd end up standing on something or tripping over. Until I was satisfied that nothing was there, I allowed my feet to keep moving.

My confidence grew as I came accustomed to the darkness, the worries having disappeared until something swept passed my face. I squealed and flinched, dipping down to the ground to hide myself from it.

"What was that?" I whispered, bracing myself for something else. I gently rose to my feet and called, "hello?"

"Hello," the same voice echoed, right in my ear, and I spun in its direction; the room was still shrouded. I couldn't feel a presence, but my body was on high alert, waiting for something else to come.

"Where are you?"

Here, they called from across the space; no longer close to me.

"Or here," their voice whispered into my ear and I turned in their direction, immediately reaching out to fight them. The voice chuckled, "that's the spirit."

"Show me who you are!"

"You can already see, Arraetta," they laughed, not too far behind me this time, "all you have to do is tune into the light."

"Tune into the light?" I breathed.

"Yes," they answered against my ear and, this time, I didn't flinch or turn to them, "you are the embodiment of luminescence."

"How?" I breathed.

"Feel it within yourself," they said, now in front of me, "dig deep into your soul and breathe the power through your veins."

I closed my eyes, not that it made much of a difference from being open and began to take deep breaths. I wondered whether this was somewhat like Rakatan, allowing myself to feel it, but nothing happened.

"It's not working," I sighed exasperatedly.

Not far to my right, they spoke, "the power that lies within you is your life force, your energy, hone into that. Be one with it."

Shutting my eyes again, I did my best to latch onto the power that lay partially dormant within my veins, but it was to no avail.

"You are thinking too much," the voice chided, suddenly in front of me, "this should be as natural and easy as breathing."

The voice silenced again, and I turned the switch of my thoughts off to allow me to concentrate. For a long while, there was nothing but then I found a subconscious murmur, in the distant parts of my mind. It brought me back to the present, as though I'd fallen into a lulling sleep, and I whispered, "I can do this."

The voice didn't answer but I didn't need them to. Instead, I homed in on the power, in my body, and pushed it through me. It felt like the early stages of pins and needles, at first, but then it became smooth, and the feeling was like nothing I'd ever felt before. It felt silky, elating, and *powerful.* The light shone through my closed lids, and I, immediately, opened them to see how my body was lit up like a golden lightbulb.

"I did it!" I squealed, looking around for the voice but, instead, I stared into a mirror of myself, in a room surrounded by them.

My lips of my mirrored-self twitched, and she stepped forward, the boundaries of the glass remaining between us, "well done."

"You're me," I said to her.

Or she was similar to me. A little bit older, eyes worn from lack of sleep, scars covering her face and her hair just below ear length. She was dressed in military-like black clothing, and I understood that she was battle-worn.

"Arraetta, you must promise me something," she said to me, her tone changing to being serious, "many things are going to happen but you must always remember who you are, even in the darkest and toughest of times. You are Arraetta, Princess of The Cre-este, Goddess of Divine Rapidfire. You must keep that protected, within yourself, to get you to where you need to be."

"What do you mean?" I whispered.

"Things are going to take place," she replied, "everything will change. I cannot tell you more than that, it is against the laws of the universe for me to do that."

"Please, you have to tell me something," I answered, desperately.

For one minor moment, she was thoughtful until she looked at me, "you are the key to destroying the darkness that has shrouded Seraiah; you must free him from his pain, you must save him from himself."

"How?" I asked.

"Not now, I cannot tell you now," she said and took a step backward, "I am being called, I must go."

"Please!" I begged her, reaching out to the mirror, "tell me how!"

My hands landed on the mirror and it all but shattered around me like a bomb. I winced, waiting for the sharp edges to cut my face but it didn't happen. Instead, my eyes opened, and I looked directly up at Seraiah, who was leaning over me with a very worried expression on his partially sweaty face.

"Arraetta," he whispered, relieved. His head dipped as he took a deep breath, and I noticed how the sky above was darkening as it was prior to wherever I'd been. It must've only been minutes even though it felt like hours.

"Is she okay?" Genie came and knelt by me, a glass of water in her hand.

I grimaced as I sat up, placing a hand on my achy forehead. I was still next to the globe, but it was no longer buzzing in its dull colour, instead, it was vibrantly dancing a flaxen colour.

"What happened?" I grumbled; my voice sounded hoarse.

"Jonah said you touched the globe," Genie explained, pointing at it, "then you sort of just lit up and collapsed. Two minutes later, you're awake again."

"I'm fine," I said to her and then looked at Seraiah, who was sitting back on his arse, one hand through his dishevelled, sweaty hair and the other draped over his knee.

The voice of the mirrored version of me, presuming myself from the future, echoed in my head as I looked at him. *You are the key to destroying the darkness that has shrouded Seraiah.*

But how was I going to do that? How was I going to destroy the darkness? Was it through my power, or maybe it was through our bond? I had only wished she'd stayed longer and told me something more.

Strong Zikan words were being spoken behind us, and I turned to see that an older man, of whom I didn't recognise, was arguing with Jonah and Freddie. Soldiers and guards were in the vicinity, both on guard to do something in case of an attack.

Seraiah growled under his breath and threw himself to his feet, storming towards the men, to join in with the angered tones. Seraiah, Freddie, and Jonah looked like three school kids trying to show their strength against the brute.

"Here," Genie said, bringing my attention to her. She handed me the water and I drank it, gladly, seeing that she was very sober.

"When did the drugs wear off?"

"When you collapsed," she answered, then a tiny giggle left her throat and I bit my lip, attempting to stop myself from joining in with her, "most of it."

I pulled myself up to my feet and she followed, keeping a hand on me in case I wobbled but, apart from the headache, I felt fine. I looked up past the men arguing to see that the party was still in motion, although there were a lot of people curiously looking down towards us.

"Arraetta, are you alright?" Seraiah asked, looking at me with his hand pointed out. I nodded and he turned back to the man, continuing in English, "see, there is nothing to warrant any form of arrest."

Arrest? What did he mean by that? Were they looking to arrest me for touching the globe? I suppose something so sacred as that would be punishable in some way.

"You forget your father is still king, boy," the older man grunted, glaring at Seraiah as though he was a little child.

"And, you forget your place, *sir*!" Seraiah chided back, stepping up towards him, "unless you would like me to remind you of it."

"You do not scare me, Seraiah," the man replied in the same tone, "I have had enough preparation taming beasts in my time, I do not mind taming another."

Seraiah moved to pounce at the man whilst Jonah and Freddie pulled him back. Seraiah spoke with him angrily in Zikan again, before yanking himself out of the grip of the two men, stalking down towards me. Jonah spoke then to the man, in a similar tone, and it seemed enough to get the man to back off with his guards. The soldiers remained.

"You should have just let me kill him," Seraiah growled at Freddie and Jonah.

"And, what good would that be?" Freddie replied, looking upwards at the man who had left us, "the treaty would be broken, and we would not have a leg to stand on." He turned to the group of us. "You must cut the head off the snake first, Seraiah."

"I had the opportunity yesterday," Seraiah bit back, "but my mother..."

The men silently agreed, with a nod of the head, before Jonah eyed me, "are you well, ma'am?"

I blushed in embarrassment, remembering that Jonah was the one who had tried to stop me from touching the ball, "who was that anyway?"

"The General," all three men replied, disdainfully, and then equally chuckled at their reply. The first time that I'd heard of 'The General' was, earlier that morning, when Seraiah had told me he was the one who had hunted Seraiah down many years ago.

"I've never seen him before," I replied.

"My father's wing of the house is usually where he is," Seraiah informed me.

"I hope you may explain what happened when you collapsed," Freddie then spoke up, nodding his head towards the vibrant ball of energy, "because, after your Rapidfire fired up, the colour suddenly changed."

"More than changed," Seraiah chuckled, "I suddenly felt like my energy had been sated."

"Agreed," Freddie nodded in reply.

I thought about my meeting with myself, how I'd started in a bright room and been forced to face the darkness. How I was told to home in on my energy and bring my power alive, and then there was the conversation we had.

In the franticness of waking up from it, I didn't exactly know what I could tell them because I hadn't come to terms with what had happened. I wasn't even sure if the whole thing was real, apart from I felt a lot more energetic, and the ball of electricity was buzzing away brighter than it had ever been.

"To be honest, I was very high," I smiled cheekily to them and even they returned it.

"Where did you get Isanhowad from?" Jonah piped up, "if I had known, I would not have allowed you to have it."

"That is why we would not tell you, Jonah," Seraiah patted his shoulder, "it is for recreational purposes only, and a little fun when it comes to events like this."

"Until it causes your wife to put herself in danger," Jonah said, a little sternly, and Seraiah winced.

"Can we go and enjoy the rest of the party now?" Genie grumbled, swinging herself on Freddie's arm.

"No more Isanhowad," Jonah told us all.

After a few more words, it was decided that I would go back to my quarters to get changed, Genie following, and that we would all meet later for some food. We weren't the only ones going. On top of my two maids, we were also flanked by Alex, Travis and four other soldiers and the feeling of the change that had taken place was heavy.

Alex was right, there had been a change in command. It wasn't just down to the incident that had occurred the day before or the heavy number of soldiers at play but even The General's appearance solidified it. At a time where I was supposed to be joyous about becoming part of the world, and being married, I felt the cogs of fear turning in my mind one by one.

TWENTY-THREE

The rest of Iontine flew by quickly. Since my run-in with my future self, I didn't have any more occurrences of hallucinations or blackouts, and I returned to having dreamless sleep again which was a blessing. I decided that I would enjoy myself, as much as possible, even though I felt the eyes of many upon me, including His Majesty and The General, who lingered around a lot, seemingly waiting for a time to strike.

I knew that best thing was just not to *fuck up* anything further in the house, so I drank as much as I could handle, ate food, and socialised with lots of people. Most of the chatter, I had, was about the upcoming nuptials, which were taking place on the Tuesday of the following week, and how excited they were that their Crown Prince was in love with such a *beautiful* woman. I had to scoff a little to myself for that.

Towards the end of the week, several wedding gowns were delivered to my quarters, and I managed to pick one that I loved, with the help of Genie, Kadey, and Elina. Then, the festival was over, and things resumed in the house, although preparation was busy for the ceremony.

I felt a higher presence of soldiers than guards, across the house, noticing a few of the guards that worked for His Majesty, or even

The General, had changed uniforms. I had a feeling that as soon as the wedding was upon us, Seraiah would call for the coronation to take place and things would move quickly. If either of us weren't separated, or dead, beforehand.

Unfortunately, I was unable to see Seraiah once Iontine had finished. He was moved out of the palace to reside in one of the houses, on the estate. I was unsure whether it was because he truly wasn't supposed to see me, or whether the change of things in the house meant that more plans had to be made.

I'd guessed it was more of a ceremonial thing, however, as I was sure I would've been moved out of the house for my own safety as well. For most of the days, I spent time between my bedroom, the library and guarded in the garden. Genie was in and out a lot, between juggling her relationship with Freddie to organising wedding related things.

And even though I was getting married, and I should've been the happiest person in the world because of it, I felt like it was just another standard event that I was attending. I wondered, when things were less heated and everything calmed down, whether we would marry again in a more intimate setting.

And, if time couldn't go quick enough, it was my wedding day and I sat on the bed, in the room that I'd been sleeping in solo, watching my two maids rush about to make sure everything was perfect.

First, I was bathed by them both, a routine that I'd gotten used to, over the previous few weeks, before I went through to get ready. I was delighted that my breakfast was already there, and I saw that Genie, who had since arrived, was also munching away at some food too. Elina began to rub products into my hair and diffused it dry, whilst I ate.

We decided on a hairstyle where my locks would remain down but pulled back from my face. Kadey worked on my makeup, making it natural and then we put my dress on. I suppose in some ways it was a similar style, yet less wide, to the dress I'd worn at the ball. It flowed down to my feet with a slight train. It was white, of course, with flowers embroidered in sections. There were soft sleeves that started from my bicep, as though I was holding the dress up with my arms.

"You look stunning," a new voice added and we turned to the door to see Tara standing there, already dressed in the family colours. Everyone greeted her, accordingly, and she looked at me.

To be honest, I was quite surprised as I was still unsure what Tara thought of me since the only time, we'd truly had a full conversation was when she told me of the *myth*, which was my actual past, and everything had become quite chaotic since.

"I hope you do not mind my intrusion," she smiled, "I have brought you a gift."

She stepped into the room and one of her maids followed her in with a necklace box, which she handed to Tara. Tara then opened it and presented it to me. Inside, there was a beautiful crystal necklace and earring set that was entwined with gold; it looked incredibly expensive.

"This was my own when I got married," she said and I looked up at her, taken aback, grateful for her gift, "and, I want you to have it as I would have gifted it to my own daughter, should I have ever had one."

She handed the box back to her maid, still open, and removed the necklace before nodding for me to turn around, so she could come behind to place it around my neck. Through the mirror, I looked at Genie who was proudly watching, tears filling her eyes. Once the necklace was on, Tara offered me the earrings, one by one.

"Oh," Tara gasped a little and turned to her maid, immediately, speaking to her in Zikan. Whatever she said even caused Kadey and Elina to gasp a little. I found it interesting the way that Tara interacted with her servants as queen, everything moved and worked to her command, and I knew that this would be the same with me, when I was crowned.

Tara looked at me through the mirror with pride before she moved to stand in front, "now, Arraetta, I want to say that I am absolutely delighted to welcome such a beautiful and courageous young woman to our family. I know that you have had to adapt very quickly, and I am aware that the situation, within this house, is less than ideal. It is unfortunate to see my husband and my son at war with one another, but it is something that I have grown very accustomed to over the last fifty years, and so shall you."

I smiled politely at her, a little unsure whether it was something I could become accustomed to, "thanks, Tara, I didn't want to cause any trouble."

"You never caused any trouble," she smiled, sadly, "my husband… I love him but he is a changed man. It is no excuse, of course, but I hope that someday the feud that has come between them is resolved."

I think her hope was different to my own. Mine would be removing The King from power completely and exiling him, although I believe that idea had only crossed my mind, following the previous few days.

Tara's maid soon hurried in, a little out of breath, with another box in her hand and we all turned as Tara walked over and opened it to reveal the most beautiful crystal tiara.

"This is a gift to you," Tara said, nodding for me to join her and she held it up for me to take, "it has been specially crafted for you and may be a little heavy, although, they did their best to make it as light as possible."

I slowly placed the semi-heavy tiara onto my head, wincing as I pulled a little hair out of place. Elina and Kadey jumped up to perfect it and I'm glad they were there, otherwise it probably would've fallen off. Once it was in the right place, and pinned in, I looked at Her

Majesty, who smiled and then said her goodbyes.

"How long have we got?" I asked my maids.

"About an hour," Genie replied, "which means that I need to get ready, so I shall do that, being your maid of honour."

"I don't have a maid of honour, do I?" I laughed as she dashed out of the room.

"You do now!" she shouted.

"Should I get you something to eat, ma'am?" Elina asked, "my mother told me she was hungry on her wedding day."

"Something small and not messy would be great," I smiled, and she curtsied before leaving the room. Kadey tidied up a little and then left, to make sure some things were sorted. I stared at myself again in the mirror, at the woman that I'd become over the last couple of months, and saw how much I'd changed from Arraetta the delivery pizza girl to Arraetta the Princess. How I used to dress in casual clothes and was, suddenly, wearing gowns and dresses, whilst enhancing my beauty with expensive makeup and nice hair dos. How I was single and living a normal everyday life to meeting my one true love, who I just so happened to be destined to be with.

Through the mirror, my eyes landed on the bed, that was perfectly made, and I started to think about how the wedding night between Seraiah and I would take place. There was no way, after every moment that had occurred, that we would not be making love, with one another. After the time in the baths, we'd had little time to rekindle that lustful feeling, with each other, but the kisses, and the incident in the bedroom, made me know that we would bind our bodies together.

Genie arrived around ten minutes before we had to leave, wearing a long midnight blue chiffon dress. She was stunning. In her hands, she held a long box and walked over to the bed, where she placed it down, "this is the final piece of your outfit."

I walked over as she opened it up, revealing one of the blue sashes, that the royals always wore, and pulled it out. She placed it over my dress, careful to not touch the tiara.

A shuffle behind us and we turned as Kadey appeared with a smile, "they are ready for you."

"Is Seraiah there?" I asked nervously.

"Of course, ma'am."

I led us all down to the west wing, where Kadey scooped up my train and, carefully, placed it down on the floor. Genie came forward and linked arms with me whilst Elina joined Kadey, at the back, before all of us moved down together.

"Seraiah was a bucket of nerves this morning," Genie said, "I just so happened to catch him, as I ran into the room, I think he was worried you wouldn't show."

"I have to show."

"Do you really *have* to?" She raised her eyebrows and I laughed lightly.

There weren't too many people, in the grand hallway, as we descended the stairs and went through the tunnelled corridor. I stopped suddenly and Genie looked at me wide eyed, as if expecting me to say 'No, I can't do this', but, instead, I asked, "Do I look okay?"

"Oh, Arri," She frowned with humour, "you look so beautiful, he is going to be blown away by you."

I nodded, swallowing the nerves that were rising in my throat, "how did we even get here?"

"You almost didn't," she took my hands into hers once again, "you almost ended up working a pizza shift."

I laughed, the tears that had formed disappearing.

She whispered, "ready?"

I nodded, "yes."

We walked to the door, where I could see the crowd of people outside, sitting and waiting for me, but I couldn't see over them to spot Seraiah. Genie moved to stand at the back, picking up the train of the dress, and thanked the girls. I took a deep breath and started to walk out into the warm summer day; the sound of a piano gently beginning to play the song that Seraiah and I had danced to but a few months earlier. Everyone began to rise and turned in awe as I made my way down.

Confidently, I offered a few gentle greetings, coming down to where the garden sloped and, finally, I saw the back of Seraiah's head. Freddie was looking up, beaming from ear to ear, and he turned to whisper to Seraiah.

Seraiah turned around and our eyes met, both looking at each other in admiration. He looked so handsome, wearing a white and blue outfit, that one could only imagine on a prince, beautifully crafted and entwined with gold patterns all the way up it. And, across him the signature blue sash.

My eyes welled up and so did his, with everyone else around us seeming to disappear; both Seraiah and I being the only ones there. As I reached him, he smiled before bowing gently and I curtsied deeply, feeling Genie place the train down behind before she moved away. At that moment, it was as though no one else existed.

He stepped forward and whispered into my ear, "you are so beautiful."

The wedding officiant, an elder named Marcus, stood next to us both, facing out towards the crowd. He was dressed in a long white kaftan robe, which entwined the usual golds around the rim, and he embodied the type of person that would be in a large church. On the left-hand side of his cloaked chest was a small lapel microphone. He gently cleared his throat, and we resumed our positions, next to one another, as the music stopped playing. At first, Marcus spoke in Zikan to the gathering, and I assumed it was to ask them all to take a seat because everyone did so.

I cast my eyes a little across the crowd then, seeing a lot of faces that I'd met just the week before at Iontine. In the front row, Tara sat next to a few women I didn't recognise. There was no sign anywhere of His Majesty, or The General. In fact, even most of the guards were dressed-down soldiers, which made me wonder whether there was anyone from The King's side of the 'war' taking part in the ceremony.

Strangely, I felt a little sad for Seraiah that his father hadn't come to see him wed.

It was on the left-hand side of the aisle that I saw Sheika sitting with a woman, who was rumoured to become the next Shaman, once she either dies or passes it on. Her protege. I hadn't had too much time to chat with Sheika during Iontine, nor had I seen her since the day she told me of the bond and the Rapidfire. She offered me a polite smile, noticing I'd looked at her, and I looked back at Seraiah, who seemed to have done the same.

"Today is a wondrous day," Elder Marcus spoke, his voice echoing, through speakers that were decorated casually around the place, "we come together to not only witness the matrimony of our beloved Crown Prince and Princess but we also witness the bonding of the souls of Kindred Spirits. This ceremony is special and only those who bear witness to this today, on this Earth, shall know that this has taken place. Two months ago, the two that stand before us, His Royal Highness Seraiah, Prince of Zika, and Her Royal Highness Arraetta, Princess of The Cre-este took to the floor to dance to the very same song, that you have just heard, and now they stand before us, willing and ready to be together in this life and the next.

"The process of the binding of souls is much different to that of an ordinary marriage. Today, you shall all witness something that many of you will never have seen before, so please be aware that anyone caught with their video phones or cameras, during this process, shall be removed from the ceremony."

Instinctively, I looked up at the crowd, seeing a few people placing their phones away before I looked at Seraiah, who seemed amused.

"We are gathered here today," Elder Marcus announced, "to ask the Highest Gods to bear witness, and bless, this ceremonial bond with the greatest love and light, and let this bond know of no bounds of which it should ever falter below. We ask The Universe to support the two before us, The Kindred Spirits, as they become one - Kindred - and to protect them, as if they were its own children. A bond that should never waver, or die, and one that cannot be explained except by the Gods."

I looked at Seraiah again, remembering those same words, when we touched hands and experienced that ethereal moment together in the library.

"I ask the two before us," he continued, "to take each other's forearms as though swearing a pledge to one another." We did so, twisting our arms in a soft grip; my right arm above his elbow, his left underneath mine. "And, to speak truthfully and without hesitation. As we are not only binding souls, but also the lives of two beings, it is customary for us to start with the highest ranking. Her Royal Highness shall repeat after me."

I was attempting to hold the smirk in as Seraiah knew exactly who he was going to turn say.

"I, Arraetta, Princess of The Cre-este, Goddess of Divine Rapid-fire…"

"I, Arraetta, Princess of The Cre-este, Goddess of Divine Rapid-fire…"

"…understand wholly and undeniably…"

I repeated each of the words.

"…that Seraiah, Prince of Zika…"

I repeated, not taking my eyes from Seraiah's once.

"…is my one and true Kindred Spirit…"

I felt a strange sensation tingling in my body as I spoke the words.

"And that I, Arraetta, Princess of The Cre-este, Goddess of Divine Rapidfire..."

"...do swear and honour that bond by binding my soul..."

Another tingle...

"...to Seraiah, Prince of Zika..."

"...and allow The Highest Gods and The Universe to protect and honour this binding..."

I spoke the words, more tingles flaring up my arm, and I could see my veins begin to come alive from the power of my Rapidfire. However, no matter how captivating it was to others, we both knew that we could not break eye contact, during this part of our bonding, no matter what.

"...and so it shall be." Elder Marcus finished.

"...and so it shall be."

Members of the crowd were amazed by what they were seeing and, as I finished up the words, my grip tightened and Seraiah grunted a little, feeling the invisible force of it.

"We resume!" Elder Marcus bellowed; everyone quieted down. "I, Seraiah, Prince of Zika understand wholly and undeniably..."

Seraiah began to repeat Elder Marcus' words and I felt the force of something come from him; watching as the golden hue from my own Rapidfire was enveloped by a darker, vibrant blue. This only grew as Seraiah looked directly into my eyes.

"... and so it shall be," Seraiah finished and his grip on my arm tightened. Our hold was unnatural as we both looked down, seeing rings of energy begin to form in the air above our arms, dancing around together as they bound around us. On our skin, the veins that were not glowing from our Rapidfire began to tattoo themselves on our skin, from the back of our hands up to where our arms connected; creating some form of strange archaic design, that glowed blue and gold. The rings above stopped turning, once the symbols had finished forming, and our forearms squeezed tightly together, as though someone was pulling a string around them. Loops of additional marks began to appear around sections of our arms, including our ring fingers, before they stopped.

"Your eyes," Seraiah whispered and I peeked up, seeing the edge of his brown irises tinted with gold.

"Your eyes," I whispered back to him, mesmerised by them. I reached my hand up to his face, smiling, before my ears became attuned to the cheering, from the crowd. Seraiah and I both laughed as we pressed our foreheads against the other's, continuing to stare into each other's eyes, "I feel so..."

"Alive," he breathed and I beamed, laughing more.

Elder Marcus called everyone to be quiet and Seraiah and I leaned away from each other, coming to hold the hand of both tattooed wrists.

"I understand that His Royal Highness has prepared some words that he wishes to convey to Her Royal Highness."

I blushed as Seraiah looked at me, no nerves, just pure love, and admiration, "Arraetta, I am truly, and wholeheartedly, in love with you; it feels like so long ago since I met you on the night of my birthday and before then, truthfully, I had lost hope with the life that I was living. I was told by Gods, in a dream, that, one day, I would meet my Kindred Spirit and I have lived a lifetime wondering who that would be and then I met you. Beautiful, perfect, sometimes a little bit bothersome, you light up every part of any room you enter, leaving no time to catch one's breath. Arraetta, I long to hold and cherish you, with each passing day, and cannot bear to spend any moment apart. I cannot wait to spend my life with you, by my side, as my wife and my queen. I promise that I shall always love and protect you with every fibre of my being and my soul. Lavoure, Arraetta."

Tears sprouted in my eyes and we both kissed briefly before turning to the crowd, who were standing and clapping in celebration. I looked up towards the top of the garden where I caught a glimpse of The King before he turned and walked away.

I knew that Seraiah caught it too as he squeezed my hand and, when I looked at him, he offered me a soft smile that told me that I didn't need to worry. After all, Seraiah would soon be the king and his father would not hold any power over him again.

TWENTY-FOUR

The day flew by in a heartbeat. Seraiah and I celebrated with everyone, of importance to him, drinking and eating to our hearts content. Even Jonah seemed relaxed, although I didn't see him drink anything and I could tell that he was constantly preparing for someone to come and destroy the celebrations.

Genie and I found ourselves dancing together, for quite a long period of time, joining in with locals in their choreographed dances, whilst both Seraiah and I were still to do our official dance, which was to take place a little later in the evening. Genie dragged me off the dance floor, at some point, and over to the bar where we both drank water as if we'd never had a drop in our lives.

"I am so sweaty," she giggled, pulling at the under sleeves of her dress.

I agreed, sweeping my eyes around the tent. I couldn't see any sight of Seraiah, nor could I see any of the men, that had been sitting around one of the tables, not too long beforehand. I frowned, searching a little bit further until I eyed Alex, making his way up towards the house, in a bit of a hurry. Something was wrong.

I followed suit, rushing out of the tent in my white dress, but was stopped when Travis blocked my way, "ma'am."

"Let me pass, Travis," I told him sharply.

"I have been asked to keep you here," he replied, maintaining his guarding stance.

"What has happened?" I asked him, but he didn't answer, so I pushed, "it's my wedding day, Travis. I deserve to know."

He sighed, "His Royal Highness is speaking with His Majesty in the corridor."

"Oh for fuck's sake," I swore and decided to try my luck, by pushing past him, but he only stepped in the way. I growled, "if you do not let me pass, I will make sure that you are out of a job as soon as I am queen."

Travis' eyes caught mine and I glared at him, not giving in. He gently nodded and it was enough to let me rush onwards. The interaction, luckily, hadn't caused any guests to listen, but I wondered if they would have thought I was being a little premature in my bossy ways.

Genie was on my tail, instantly, keeping quiet. We rushed into the house, and I could hear the heated reaction coming from the grand hallway, all the way down through the corridor. She tugged me to go via the upstairs way, to get closer, and we did as quietly as possible.

Once we arrived, we stood as near to the staircase of the entrance as we could, although I couldn't understand what they were saying, apart from the odd mention of my name. It was getting heated, and I wondered how close Seraiah was to flaring up.

"The King is angry," Genie pointed out quietly, "I don't understand a lot, but he mentioned you and, I think, he is saying something about the relationship being... I translated it and he said, 'childish'."

"Childish," I whispered, looking at her, "are you sure that's right?"

"Yes, Freddie used the term to describe Seraiah," she gently laughed, then cleared her throat, "obviously, this isn't funny. And Seraiah is now defending you, he called you his wife and-"

"-Forget it," I whispered and moved down to the steps, looking down on the interaction. To the left, with their backs to me, was Seraiah, Freddie, Jonah, and a few others, and opposite them was The King and The General. Not only that, Tara and Sheika were in the corridor almost like mediators. All surrounded by guards from both The King and Seraiah's side.

Those on the right noticed my arrival but it was The King's glower that caused everyone to look up at me.

"If you have something to say to me, *sir*," I called from my position, which seemed to give me a little bit of power, "you may say it to my face."

"How dare you address The King in such a way!" The General spat, coming towards the stairs but stopping as Jonah aimed a gun in his direction.

"One more move, General," he snapped.

The General barked a laugh and turned to Jonah, "my son, how mighty you have become."

I was taken aback by the sudden bit of information, but I could immediately see the resemblance between them once he had.

"This is getting out of hand!" Tara snapped, "this is our son's wedding day, Charles."

"He is no son of mine!" The King replied, in the same tone.

"So I have been reminded, Father!" Seraiah growled, stepping forward, "might I remind you that you are only king because Mother made me vow I would not take the throne."

"You are not worthy of the throne!" The King snapped back, "and neither is that piece of filth you now call your wife."

Seraiah snapped, in an instant, and pounced on his father; Rapidfire flaring. He smacked his father, around the face, whilst everyone else was unsure what to do, even the guards weren't sure who to defend. Jonah still had the gun pointed, at his own father, whilst Freddie stood back and let Seraiah give his The King a few bludgeons.

"Stop this!" Tara screamed and it was enough for Freddie to move in, pulling Seraiah off his stricken father, who grunted on the floor.

"You speak of my wife in such a way again," Seraiah spat, "and I shall have no reason to spare your life. Your days as king are numbered and, when I am king, I shall exile you to suffer your final days in the human world!"

The King rose to his feet, his side man, The General, returning to stand by him before he looked up at me, bitter coldness in his look.

"Your Majesty, you are a shame to your son," I said, finally making my way down the steps towards them, "how can you treat him like he has brought your life so much pain when he has done nothing but work hard for his people."

"You are an ignorant child," The King spat back, "how can you truly know everything when you have been here, consciously, for merely six weeks?"

"I may not know everything," I told him, coming to stop half way down the stairs, "but I know that Seraiah is a good man and, whether he is infected by The Dark or not, he is still the same person you loved."

The King snorted, "You are naive, Arraetta, it is a shame that you were not brought up in your own world as, you would have learnt, that the world of royalty is nothing like what you read in your fairy tales. My son died in battle. This... *thing* may look like him, but he is not Seraiah. You will come to learn that very soon; I have no doubt." He looked at Seraiah. "One wrong move and he will no doubt be casting dark shadows, in your mind, until you are but a shell of yourself."

Seraiah grew aggravated instantly and I saw the darkness overtake him like a wave, pushing Freddie off him. He lunged again for his father, but The General jumped in front of The King to protect him. Everything from there happened so quickly as Seraiah was on top of

The General, before he was soon underneath him as the older man's strengths kicked in. The man, weightier and stronger than Seraiah, chided something as he went to grab something from the back of his pants.

Bang.

Everyone in the room froze as blood splattered across the hallway, silencing the entire house. The General was dead. Red oozed from a bullet wound in his head and Seraiah pushed him off in a heap, scooting back out of breath.

The King was astonished, and I could see he was trembling, but it was the owner of the gun that stood a little more perplexed. Jonah's head turned in the direction to where Travis was standing, the gun in his hand.

"Travis," Jonah whispered and I couldn't tell if he was upset about the sudden death of his father or that he hadn't been the one to pull the gun.

The King looked down at his dead companion before looking back at Travis, "this is treason."

Travis regained his posture, looking at The King, with such deep hatred, before his eyes rested on Seraiah, then up to me. "Long live the Goddess of the Light, may the darkness be forever destroyed by your divine power."

Seraiah's voice called *no!* but it was too late as Travis, eyes still on me, lifted the gun to his chin and pulled the trigger. My whole body froze as he sank to the floor; chaos seemed to ensue around me. Guards pulled forward to move The King out of the way, to his quarters, whilst soldiers were trying to sort out the mess.

At some point, I was moved away to one of the lounges, in the west wing, the party well and truly over for my wedding day. Time passed, the day turned to night and no thoughts really came into my head, apart from that same phrase that Travis had said before he'd killed himself.

"Arri," Genie said, kneeling into my view and I blinked, looking at her, "drink this."

I took the water from her and drank it quickly before I felt the floodgates open. I cried for a while and it wasn't because of Travis' death, I didn't really know him, it was because he had stared at me and said those words before he pulled the trigger, without losing eye contact.

A knock sounded on the door, after a while, and I looked up as Sheika came in; she offered me a soft smile, "I am aware of the events that have taken place, this evening, but I am afraid we must complete the bonding. I shall give you a few minutes and then come to your suite."

I wasn't sure if I was in the mood to be finishing the bond with Seraiah. So much had taken place and the last thing I wanted was to be lying in a bed with him, after we'd both witnessed two people die.

"Arri," Genie said, taking my hands as she continued to sit before me, "don't keep thinking about what happened. This is your special day."

"Maybe if I hadn't appeared they'd both still be alive," I replied, feeling tears creep up in my eyes, "it's my fault."

"It's not your fault," she answered, "you didn't know that was going to happen and you sure didn't put that gun into Travis' hands. He was only trying to protect Seraiah."

"But, then he killed himself."

"He would've been killed anyway," she replied, moving to sit next to me.

"Even if he was protecting Seraiah?"

"Travis worked under Jonah," she explained, "and he wasn't given any orders, so he would've been found guilty and sentenced to death. They have different laws here, especially when it comes to those on the council."

Everyday there was something new that I had to learn about. It was as though I was a thousand miles behind everyone, and I didn't know how I was ever going to catch up at the pace everything was going at.

"Come on," Genie said, standing up, "now isn't the time to be sitting here pitying the dead, Arri. You are going to spend the night with Seraiah now, it's what you wanted."

It *was* what I wanted, yes. I wanted to spend hours draped in Seraiah's arms, feeling his lips on my skin, and disappearing from the harshness of the reality that had just taken place, but my thoughts were all over the place and I wasn't sure I could shut off from Travis' piercing gaze that had burnt itself into my mind.

I allowed Genie to pull me to my feet and guide me out of the room, seeing that the hallway was scattered with The Prince's guards, back to wielding large guns once more. There was a possibility, after the events that had taken place, that The King would attempt to stop the bonding from happening.

At the bottom door, we met with Kadey and Elina who curtsied to me. Genie said her goodbyes to me before the two maids took me up to the room. My heart pounded in my chest with each step.

Walking into the room, the first person I saw was Sheika, who sat in the middle of the room humming some ancient chant, alongside her protege; neither of whom acknowledged my arrival. Although the door to the bathroom was shut, a gentle splash of water could be heard. There was an additional futon at the front of my bed, and I was coaxed to sit down on it to wait; my eyes flickering around at the activity in the room. Wine, water, and cake were delivered and placed onto the table, whilst Elina gently began to remove my tiara and hair pins. Kadey was making sure things were perfectly neat, in the room, whilst she liaised with another man who I didn't recognise. It was strange because the room was huge but, with all the people in it, it felt small.

I started to wonder whether all the people were going to stay in there, whilst the act happened, and my entire body tensed at the thought. The idea that someone would watch something as intimate as our bonding was both overwhelming and nauseating. I let my eyes roam, looking at each person, making up ideas of what they would be thinking, if they did watch, and a shiver tickled my spine. Instead of overthinking it further, I forced myself to decide that they were just there to prepare us and wouldn't stay for the bonding, that they would know, in themselves, that it had taken place and didn't need a visual show of it.

The door opened from the bathroom and Seraiah walked in, wearing a long white nightgown, that looked incredibly fitting for him. I noticed his knuckles had been treated, although some cuts remained, from when he punched his father. He nodded gently to me but didn't say anything as Kadey and Elina took me into the bathroom in his place, shutting the doors behind us.

"This is all strange," I admitted, leaning down to massage my feet, "is everyone going to watch?"

Elina let out a laugh then, immediately, bit her lip. Her reaction made both Kadey and I chuckle quietly.

"No one will be in here apart from the both of you," Kadey replied.

I sighed gratefully, whispering, "I was worried, just in case someone wanted to be on standby because of today."

"Try not to think of today," Kadey said gently with a soft smile, "at this moment, there is only His Royal Highness and you; you mustn't worry about it."

"Plus, there are a lot of guards downstairs," Elina added.

Although Elina was right, I wasn't sure if it made me feel any less on edge. Then again, how did Seraiah feel? Maybe this was a burden to him because he'd just seen someone kill themself, especially whilst, somehow, claiming allegiance to me. Travis was a man that I knew Seraiah liked, or at least I got the feeling he did anyway.

It didn't feel like I was in the bath long enough, most of it was spent with one of them removing excess makeup from my face, whilst the other spent time sorting my hair out. Then, I was dried and dressed before I was escorted back out. My eyes stayed on Seraiah's back as he faced towards the prayer circle until I was encouraged to sit next to him. Neither of us looked, or touched, each other as the chants were ended.

Sheika stood up, speaking to us both in Zikan, which I only wished I understood, before she bowed deeply and left. Everyone else followed in her stead and, just like that, we were both alone together, as though we were strangers trying to come up with conversation, for the first time. I wondered whether we should talk about what had occurred earlier, but I had a feeling that it wasn't the right time to bring it up.

Instead, Seraiah took hold of my hand gently, stroking the skin and I found myself nervous about being alone with him.

I gazed up instead, eyes immediately landing on the bottles of wine. I hopped up, removing my hand from the warmth of Seraiah's own, before walking over to it. I heard a little chuckle from him, presumably amused by my being drawn to it. I picked up the white and waved it in his direction, as if it was a trophy.

"Wine?" I squeaked, heart beating madly in my chest. Seraiah watched, for a moment, before he stood and walked towards me. At first, I thought he was going to pull me in for a kiss but, instead, he removed the bottle from my hand and picked up the bottle opener.

"Allow me," he said, uncorking the wine and then he picked up a glass, pouring it in. I caught his eye briefly before averting my gaze.

"You need not fear me, Arraetta."

"I don't!" I chimed loudly and cleared my throat, "I just... should we talk about what happened?"

Seraiah sighed gently, handing me the glass of wine, "do not worry about those things, Arraetta."

"But, he killed himself," I whispered, meeting his eyes, "after killing The General and we're here now pretending like it didn't happen."

"I have not once pretended like it did not happen," he replied softly, pouring his own, "I am sad for the loss of my friend, and I shall mourn him, but I am now standing in a room with my wife and she is my only priority."

"You're not sad for The General?" I asked, although it was a stupid question as the answer was obvious.

He shook his head, "good riddance to the bastard. I would not be sad about a man that could not accept his own son for his choice of lover." Alex. "He used to beat Jonah into submission, did you know that? We were much younger, back in Zika, but I saved Jonah once and Jonah pledged that he would serve me in whatever capacity I would prefer."

"So, you offered him the role of your commander."

"Of such," he nodded, "he would be my commander when I would become king but then things changed once the treaty was signed and he has been in the position ever since. For Travis, he was a good man but knew that he would not win in a lawsuit against my father, who still remains king. He killed himself because he knew he would face death in his sentence anyway."

"Then, we should toast to Travis," I said, holding my glass up.

"We should toast to you," he answered, smiling proudly, "to the woman who stood up to my father, my beautiful, courageous wife. The Goddess of the Light."

He tapped my glass, but I turned away, moving towards the balcony doors. I couldn't tell if Seraiah was mocking Travis or whether he understood the words that Travis had said, believing them to be true too. The name swirled in my head; I couldn't tell if it was another version of Goddess of Divine Rapidfire or simply something new.

Outside, I placed my glass onto the thick ledge, moving to hold the black balustrade and looked at the view of the dark evening. I took a deep breath, listening to the bristle of the winds against the trees. The wooden slats below my feet vibrated gently as Seraiah came to stand behind me, and he placed a hand gently on my waist, his breath steady against my hair. The breeze blew my hair gently to the left, revealing part of my neck and shoulder, which gave him enough time to place his wet lips onto them.

That time, I didn't move away as the tingle was soothing and my heart calmed. He came to press his body against mine. My grip tightened a little as his arm slithered its way around my waist and he kissed me again; a soft moan in want left my mouth as I melted back into him. All the nervous thoughts washed away, in an instant, and I slowly turned around to face him, staring up into those loving auburn and gold rimmed eyes. I swallowed as my gaze lowered to look at his lips, then back to his eyes. Then he leant down, teasing his lips against mine, lingering there. I shut my eyes as I moved to close the gap, between us, but Seraiah's head moved away. He looked at my own, filled with desire, before he crashed his lips against mine.

Seraiah lifted me as though I was nothing but a feather, carrying me through to the bed where he gently laid me down, making sure to bring most of my gown to above my bottom. I lay almost naked in front of him as he towered over me, staring down, admiring me for all I was.

"God, you are so beautiful," he whispered, moving his hands to split my legs, "I have wanted to do this for so long."

"We were interrupted last time," I breathed, my voice quivering as my body braced itself.

"We shall never again," he murmured.

TWENTY-FIVE

Sex. A need that my body craved excessively; my every thought overpowered by its devilish touch. Seraiah's body against mine, both of us grinding and thrusting, lavishing in the emotion, his pleasured echoes singing with mine. Not once either of us wanting to give up control but both of us lost it to the other either way. Hours of sweat and bliss and constant movement across the bed, in the bathroom and even against the damp balcony; our cries disappearing into the gentle winds. To any human, going this long would be unnatural but both Seraiah and I, fuelled by the energy of our bond and our Rapidfire, would not give up being together as one.

The only people we laid eyes on were Arion, Seraiah's servant, and Elina, both of whom would deliver food every now and again when we called for it, neither saying anything but a minor greeting and neither ever coming together. Light rain fell during the day, but we kept the windows and balcony doors latched open, so that the air in the room was fresh. Both of us would replenish our energy with a nap, Seraiah always being the one to wake first, gliding his soft fingers against my damp and exhausted body, whilst watching me intently until I'd wake. And, then I'd wonder what he'd be thinking about as I stared up at him lovingly, not saying a word before both of us would start kissing again.

The second day of our nesting passed in a heartbeat but neither of us were keeping track of time, and it allowed us to whisper tales of our lives to each other. Seraiah's was much more exciting and daring than my own. He would graze his finger over my areola and the vibrations of it would make my body murmur some. Sometimes, he would run his finger, from my forehead to my lower belly, before it would glide a little further down and I'd whimper oh so quietly, trying to concentrate on what he was saying. By the end of that second day, Seraiah knew what pleased me the most, even if we were still discovering each other's bodies, and he would tease me, stirring me in ways I didn't know was even possible. He dominated me with every stroke, every thrust, every touch, and he knew that I would weaken under him. He knew that, if there was a fight to be won for control, it was he who would win no matter how hard I tried otherwise.

No matter how much I would push to dominate him, to attempt to get my body and my temptress ways to overpower him, it would not work. His body sang to my rhythm, but it was his words that would make mine crumble before him. Even when I rocked my body against him, sitting tall, his hands would grasp my hips and he would plunge into me, and I'd collapse under the pressure of it. It didn't matter that my flirtatious and teasing scripture would pull him back in, for his words would devour my own in a heartbeat.

Both of us fell asleep sometime in the early hours of the following morning, I continued my nurtured cocooning whilst Seraiah would hold me tightly. At first, I had guessed I would have a perfect night's sleep because I was tired from all the strenuous exercise but, after the first night, I concluded it was because I felt safe in the arms of my lover.

Seraiah was playing with a lock of my hair as I half-snoozed, "Can I have this?"

"In case I die?" I joked, reaching to touch the section of hair. He tutted, not enjoying my bad sense of humour, "why?"

"Because I wish to keep it," he repeated, shrugging.

A little perplexed, I looked at him before nodding, then shuffled out of the sheets and walked over to the dresser, looking for a pair of scissors. I could feel Seraiah's gaze burning into my naked form, as I rooted around, and, eventually, found some amongst a few sewing materials. He murmured something to himself and shuffled a little.

"If only I could draw you like that right now."

I blushed and peered around at him, showing him the strand of hair, I was holding, "this much?"

He nodded and then smiled innocently, "can I take a picture of you?"

"No!" I squealed, dropping the section of my hair as I covered myself.

"Why?" Seraiah chuckled.

"Because it may end up on the internet," I answered like a child, red faced. Seraiah burst into laughter, stopped as he watched for my reaction, then laughed some more.

"It's not funny!" I stomped, lightly, "why would you want a picture?"

"Maybe so that I can draw you later." He shrugged, still humoured, "Arraetta, I do not mean to have myself off to it, I mean to delete it once I have finished the painting."

"And... and where would you put the finished piece?"

"In my office," he said and I could tell that he was serious.

"Well... fine," I agreed, "but... it would be unnatural as, now, I will need to find a position to be in."

"Just relax," he said, trying to calm me, "turn to the mirror and resume what you were doing."

Heart beating in my chest, I turned to the mirror and tried to be natural, my eyes moving over to see him take the picture, before he moved for a better angle and took one once again. I cut the strand off and then stood up quickly, turning to him, "is this long enough?"

He nodded, barely looking at the images on his phone, before he shuffled himself to the edge of the bed and allowed his feet to touch the floor. He held his hands out, coaxing me towards him, and so I placed the scissors down, on the side, and moved back to the bed. I handed him the lock and he took it from me, with his other hand coming around to caress the cheeks of my bare bottom, "I love you, Arraetta. My wife."

"Maybe I should take a picture of you," I teased, poking his nose and he chuckled, leaning down to place a soft kiss on my stomach before he cheekily looked back up at me.

"I cannot believe how perfect you are; there is no one more perfect than you in this entire universe."

A distant rumble in the sky caused us to pause, both of us looking outside as the skies began to darken and the soft taps of rain fell against the glass. Seraiah stood up and walked over to the open window, shutting it to prevent any water splashing in.

"Hey, look at this," he said, waving me over. I walked over, seeing how the lightning was crackling heavily at a close distance, the thunder rippling just afterwards.

"Have you never seen lightning before?" I jested, moving to cuddle him.

Before he could make a comment, the thunder crackled closer, and I jumped a little. He laughed, "do not tell me you are scared of a little thunder."

I tutted, moving back over towards the bed, "not scared, it just made me jump. There's a difference."

Seraiah turned, in all his glory, and waltzed back to the bed, the lightning rippling delightfully behind him as he came to climb over me. He mimicked, "there's a difference."

My heart leapt in delight as our lips crashed together, the passionate kissing beginning, once again. Not long after, we were back in our same routine of Seraiah mercilessly taking me as his prisoner.

The heavy storm took London as its hostage, ricocheting its beats against the skies and lighting them up, in a spectacle of flaxen colours. It would gently jolt me, from my slumber, as I napped in the arms of Seraiah. Another few hours had passed, since Seraiah had asked for a piece of my hair, both of us exhausted from our constant battling with each other's bodies.

I opened my eyes and looked out at the dark skies; it felt like winter had already come, not because it was particularly cold but because it was so gloomy, outside the window. I quite liked seeing the rain splatter against the glass, whilst the whistle of a breeze tried to break through the cracks of the panes, unsuccessfully. It was so sombre that I wondered whether we should've opted to put the fire on, but the room remained at a warm temperature, whilst Seraiah's body provided extra heat; his heavy breath against my hair - asleep. No surprise, of course.

I watched the clouds for a longer period, no longer sleepy enough to be tempted for a longer nap but too comfortable to make a move out of bed. Not that I wanted to go anywhere, being in Seraiah's arms was the greatest thing because I felt the safest and happiest there. No one outside the four walls of the room existed, it was just the two of us.

At some point, the clouds began to clear, and the storm settled some - still producing a loud crackle of thunder and intermittent flashes, from the other side of the house, further in the distance. I watched as the black skies softly turned to grey, the rain coming to a stop, and everything settled.

Behind me, Seraiah grumbled, and his arm tightened, around my waist, as he spooned me; his breath becoming steady again as he continued to snooze. I brought his intricately tattooed arm towards my face, without waking him, so I could study the patterns on it. Both of our arms looked quite similar to one another, except there were a few symbols which were different. Seraiah's were much more hard-lined, whilst mine were soft, which made me wonder whether it was a feminine versus masculine meaning, or whether it was because our Rapidfire was different.

"Are you attempting to dissect it?" Seraiah's voice murmured behind me, and I smiled. Seraiah shuffled closer, as if there was any space, and gently began to plant kisses on my shoulder blade, "any luck?"

"None," I whispered, allowing myself to move as his hand slithered its way around my body. I pined for him again.

"Arraetta," he said lowly, "I do not think I can let you leave this bed."

"Maybe I don't want to," I answered, rolling myself so that I could face him as his hand went further down, "maybe I want to stay here forever."

"Mm, I am glad you said that," Seraiah whispered, his lips moving down to take my nipple into his mouth. I murmured in pleasure as my body arched into him, watching as he moved further down.

We both were startled when another huge clatter of thunder sounded, above the house, and we muttered a laugh. Then, there was another one, immediately, afterwards and we both froze in our positions with Seraiah soon sitting up. I looked out of the window as the rain had stopped but there were strange flashes penetrating across the shield.

"Stay here, my love," Seraiah told me, as he slipped out of the bed, putting on a pair of shorts before he walked to the balcony door. My heart thumped in my chest, for some reason I felt like something bad was happening and Seraiah's pace put me on edge. He unlocked the balcony door and, barefoot, stepped out on the dampness outside, looking up. His face changed from being worried to being in awe, before he looked at me, "come and see this."

I slowly scooted off the bed, nervous, and went over in his direction, grabbing a robe and throwing it on.

"I'm going to get my feet wet," I stated, stepping out onto the cold ground. Seraiah spun me to look up above and I was astounded by what I saw.

High up in the sky, the clouds were rippling, with soft lightning, and swirling in a circle in a strange orange and red colour. The clouds were stretching from above us across towards London, although I couldn't see where they ended as the house blocked that view.

"What does it mean?" I asked him.

"I do not know," he answered, "I am sure the storm has caused it."

I nodded, hugging my robe into myself so that I wouldn't be cold. The clouds rippled with tremendous thunder again and we both jolted from it, listening as it echoed away from us across the spectre.

"Come, let us go inside," Seraiah said and I agreed, both of us drying our cold, damp feet on the carpet, "where are you going?"

"I'm going for a bath," I informed him, as I went to the bathroom door.

"You know I shall be in there with you," he told me and I shrugged, slowly pulling the door closed, whilst peeking at him as I disappeared into the room. Seraiah laughed at my childish ways, but didn't follow me, as I went to run the water. The skies out the back had cleared up some but remained grey.

I soaked for a long while, thoughts of the last couple of days, with Seraiah, mixed with what had taken place over the few weeks beforehand.

There was a loud rumble, outside again, that shook the house and caused a few things to fall onto the floor. I jumped in fright, heart pounding in my chest - something was not right. Not only that, but I also hadn't heard from Seraiah in a while, and it all seemed awfully quiet.

"Seraiah?" I called.

No answer.

I got out of the bath, threw on a towel robe, and made my way back into the bedroom to see that it was empty with the door out of the room open. But it was strange flashes outside my front window that had my full attention and, slowly, I walked over. Outside, I saw that the shield was buzzing as though something was trying to break through it.

I guessed Seraiah was already downstairs, considering he wasn't in the room, so I quickly dried, threw on some casual clothes and shoes, and rushed to find him. It was strange being down there, after it had been a few days since I had, especially because the atmosphere was unnerving. I heard a commotion in the grand hallway and scurried down, seeing Seraiah talking with Freddie, Jonah, and some other guards - all of them looking outside, talking in their native language.

The events of my wedding day seemed to no longer exist, with not a drop of blood or violence evident in the space.

I stood at the top of the stairs, looking down, guessing that the static on the shield was making them worry. Walking down a couple of steps, Jonah's head popped up in my direction and he immediately bowed, jolting others to look over at me. Seraiah broke away from the group and ran up the stairs, wearing nothing more than a pair of pyjama bottoms and a robe.

"Hey," he greeted, kissing my cheek gently, "I did not mean to leave you."

"What's happening to the shield?" I asked, eyeing the door.

"Do not worry," he informed me, "we are dealing with it, go back to bed."

"No," I told him, "I've been in there long enough."

"Long enough?" he piped as I walked past him. He, immediately, followed and pulled me to a stop, murmuring, "my love, you said you would stay there forever."

"But, now I'm up," I smiled gently.

Seraiah grumbled as I descended the stairs, immediately greeted, formally, by everyone at the door. I was shocked that Freddie didn't even throw any banter in my direction, but it was no surprise when I looked out of the front door to see the shield going haywire.

"Your Highness, please stay back," Jonah said, moving to guard the door a little as if I was about to run out there.

"What's happening?" I asked him. I could see there were a lot of guards, on the ground outside, preparing as though something was about to come down and attack us from above. There were plenty of residents, as well, out of their homes trying to see what was happening.

I felt Seraiah's arm slither around my waist as he pulled me gently away, from the door, and I grumbled, "I can walk on my own."

"Please go back to bed," Seraiah begged into my hair.

"I think everyone should return to their quarters," announced Tara's voice from the top of the stairs and we all turned as she walked down. A variety of greetings were flung her way as her eyes landed on me before she looked at Seraiah, "I am sure that you both do not need to worry about this."

Seraiah nodded and pulled me back up towards the bedroom.

Something really wasn't right; I could feel it in the pit of my stomach. I wondered whether Seraiah was worried about it, but I couldn't make out whether the look on his face was him thinking about what was happening, or just determination to get me back to bed.

"Aren't you worried?"

"It shall be fine," he told me, though I wasn't so convinced.

"But, what if it isn't?" I whispered. Seraiah pulled me to a stop so that I would be facing him.

"What are you so afraid of, Arraetta?" he asked, with all seriousness on his face.

"I'm fearful that… you're going to be locking me up in that bedroom for the rest of my life," I joked and he smiled.

"You may tell me anything, my love," Seraiah said.

"I know but do you really deserve to know?" I smiled cheekily, waiting for him to embrace me again but the house shuddered heavily, causing both of us to tumble to the floor.

"The generator," Seraiah cursed, standing up. Footsteps sounded down the corridor and we both looked as Jonah came pelting down, followed by Freddie and Alex. The exchange between Seraiah and the three of them was short and quick, no room for any sort of interjection, before Jonah nodded and looked at me.

"Let's go," he said, holding a hand out for me.

I frowned but took it, allowing him to bring me to my feet.

"Listen to Jonah," Seraiah commanded gently as I looked at him. He briefly kissed my lips before moving his head to motion for Freddie and Alex. Jonah, however, placed his hand to my lower back and pushed me in the direction of the grand hallway.

"What's happening?" I asked him, doing my best to look behind as the men went into the library.

Ignoring me, Jonah led me to the grand hallway and down the stairs, making sure that I wouldn't trip, as he guided, before he ushered me down to the left and around the corridor, to where the steps lead down to the staff area.

I'd never been down to that part of the house, but I saw it was, essentially, an underground corridor with several rooms peeling off to bedrooms, the kitchen, a lounge area and more - all doors were wide open. Staff were rushing down the corridor in the direction that Jonah ushered me in.

"Where are we going?" I asked him.

The house rumbled again but Jonah caught me, moving to grip my wrist as he pulled me onwards. It didn't hurt but it was strong enough for me to know that he would do anything to stop me from running. To protect me. But, from what?

"Jonah, why are you ignoring me?"

"Ma'am, please."

It was a desperate plea that I'd never heard before. The corridor we walked down ended with another door, that led down a concrete staircase, with staff members moving quickly. The place almost resembled a sewer, but without the rotten smell, just a damp one that lingered heavily. My heart thudded as I watched for the possibility of rats but there was nothing but the quiet echoes of whispers.

At the end there were two doors, one a little further ahead and one to the right. I saw that most of the staff had gone through the one at the end, but Jonah stopped to the one at the right, removing his hand from mine. He removed some keys from his pocket, and I suddenly panicked, stepping back.

"Ma'am," he paused as the key went into the lock. I eyed the door, wondering whether running would be a good idea, but my wrist was taken soon following and he pulled me forward down another corridor, leaving the door open.

"You know, if you wanted to kill me…" I joked humourlessly, the fear creeping up.

"I would never want to kill you," he answered truthfully, then he let go of my wrist as he turned to me, "it is my duty to protect you and that is what I'm doing."

"By taking me down creepy corridors?"

"A short cut."

I frowned as he nodded his head to follow him. A few moments later, the Earth above rumbled, and I tumbled against the wall, grimacing as I lightly hit my head against it. Jonah's concern turned to urgency, and he ushered me onwards, continuing down the dimly lit corridor.

Eventually, another door appeared and he walked to it, unlocking it as well.

Jonah swung it open and when I saw concrete steps, leading back up, I breathed a sigh of relief, thanking the Gods that I would see daylight once again. Jonah led me until we were faced with another door - this one not locked.

The door opened to, what looked like, a royal dressing room parlour. In several encasing, there were magnificent royal gowns, on headless mannequins, from the royal cape to a dress that I guessed to be a coronation dress, of sorts. In the middle, three glass cases stood, each with different crowns - one for each of the royals. All of them were made of the most beautiful jewels; the one to the left made primarily of amethysts, the middle crown made of blood diamonds and the one to the right of emeralds. All unique but the middle one was the largest of them all.

Red drapes hung heavily from ceiling to floor, around the walls, whilst a silver and gold chaise was tucked against the right one.

Jonah pushed through to the back, pulling back a curtain to reveal another door, as he played around with the handle and lock, before turning back to me.

"Is it time to play dress up?" I joked.

"You're to stay here," he informed me, wandering back towards the door we walked into, "until it's over."

"What's over?" I frowned.

"There's a high surge of energy right now," he answered and was about to slip out but I jumped in quickly.

"I'm sorry about Travis."

He nodded and bowed, "may the darkness be forever destroyed by your light."

With that, he shut and locked the door. I blinked and attempted to go and open it, but there was no luck.

The glass casings let off a strange sound, like a finger against a glass of water, as the Earth quaked above the room, but everything remained static. I wandered over to the crown, in the middle, placing my hand onto the casing before slowly removing it. I hadn't anticipated it to be so easily removed, expecting much more security, on such exquisite items. Then again, I didn't even know the room existed until five minutes ago.

I placed the glass on the floor and picked up the heavy crown, wandering over to a mirror as I came to place it on my head.

"Oh, hello," I said to myself in a mock-posh voice, "I am Arraetta, Queen of Zika. How do you do?"

I laughed at myself, then pulled it off to look at it closer. It was beautiful, made of some sort of gold, with intricate detailing in the metal work, which counterbalanced the blood diamonds.

Another shake above and I toppled over, the crown breaking as it flew across the floor to the other side. Before I could go and try to mend it, the lights in the room fizzed and the place plunged into darkness.

Silence.

I had had so many dreams where I had been trapped in complete darkness, hearing things around me, and I suddenly felt the reality of it hit me. My heart thudded in my chest as I slowly breathed in and out.

"You're not scared," I told myself, remembering my run-in with my future self, "you are Arraetta, Princess of Zika, a goddess, you cannot be scared."

A rumble.

I screamed. I clamoured to my feet, moving slowly with my arms reached out as I attempted to find my way to the chaise - at least it would be comfortable to lie on in the dark.

My hand touched the glass, of one of the casings, as I shuffled around and I used it to continue the movement, reaching blindly for the chaise as I pushed myself in its direction. Another rumble, this one shook the room wildly and I fell backward, unprepared, knocking my head on the casing.

Darkness.

TWENTY-SIX

As my eyes opened, I looked up at a great hole that broke through the Earth above, revealing the darkened skies. Weightless, I stood to my feet and used the glass casing to lift myself out, climbing and climbing until, finally, my hand broke onto damp grass. I used all the strength in my body to get onto my feet, looking from the bottom of the garden, up at the large palace.

I ran up to the house and into the back entrance, making my way through to the grand hallway.

"Seraiah?" I shouted.

There wasn't a soul in sight and a sharp whistle of a breeze echoed, through the centre corridor, from the front of the house, making me shiver. Wearily, I moved forward, heart pounding rapidly in my chest. Halfway up, my foot crunched on something, and I looked down to see the remnants of a bone there. I gasped, shakily lifting my head as I saw debris of blood, bone and skin lining the floor, as bodies lay heavily one by one in front of me.

"Arraetta!"

I jolted and spun around to Seraiah's voice, not seeing anyone there, except more bodies that I'd somehow idly walked over. The ghost of a touch, on my shoulder, caused me to turn again and I was suddenly at the top of the hallway, in the grand entrance.

The glass chandelier was shattered across the floor, next to a pile of faceless bodies; more body parts, blood and dirt strewn around also. The paintings from the walls were shattered; the room was a carcass of war. A grunt sounded, from the top centre of the body pile, and I looked up as I saw the familiar figure of a man, struggling against the weight of, what can only be described as, a large spear, shrouded in black matter.

"H-Help, p-please," The King struggled and I rushed forward, climbing the body pile to get to him, clawing my way up, but it only seemed to get bigger as I did. He continued to splutter at the top.

I accidentally grabbed hold of a bone, that stuck out from the heap, and squealed, moving my hand back. It was caked in blood.

I tried to ignore it, about to continue my mission to get to The King, but I stuttered to a halt as a hand grabbed me, through the middle of the bodies, and pulled me in. I screamed for freedom, fearing what was to come as I was enveloped by the corpses.

"Arraetta."

The soft face of Seraiah was in front of me. He rolled me over and brought his lips down to mine, both of us kissing deeply. Gentle, cold drops of fluid began to leak onto my cheeks, and I pulled away, looking up into void filled eyes, dripping with blood.

I gasped and tried to pull away, but I was stuck. He darkly chuckled, "look at what we have created, my queen."

Around me, the heads of the corpses began to turn, until all their eyes were watching us - some were just skulls.

"Seraiah," I begged.

"Come with me, Arraetta," he said, in a sickly sweet voice, that opposed the look in his eyes. His hand automatically pulled me until we were no longer in the pile of bones but, instead, somehow floating above them, looking down at his father, who spewed black blood as his skin melted away around the spear, that pierced his throat.

"It is beautiful, is it not?" Seraiah laughed, "my father is dead, long live me, The King, and you, The Queen. We shall rule forever-"

"This is not real!" I screamed, pulling away from him and felt the momentum of the drop and I braced myself as I fell from where we were floating to the floor, with a thud.

I took a deep, shaky breath as I opened my eyes and adjusted my sight to a sharp light above me. I grunted and stood up, placing my hand onto my head, where I'd hit it and looked around at the ornament room, I had fallen unconscious in. The glass casing, holding the outfits, was smashed and the outfits strewn across the floor, whilst the two remaining casings, with the crowns, remained intact.

My eyes moved to land on the shattered crown on the floor and I swallowed, somehow understanding what had happened.

The King was dead.

I heard a key in the lock and looked as the door flew open, and Genie stood there, out of breath, still in her pyjamas.

"Arri," she said and then she started to cry.

I shakily stood up and moved over to her, engulfing her in a hug. She didn't stop crying as she spoke to me, "we need your help, it's a disaster, they're everywhere."

"Who?"

"The… the creatures," she whispered, and I worried that I was still in the same dream, but she continued, "The King is dead, he was shattered by this… by this…"

"Spear."

She frowned, drying up her fearful tears, "what? How did you-?"

"I… a dream," I told her and then she frowned, moving her hand up to the side of my head.

"You're bleeding."

"I hit my head," I told her, moving to push past her, "I'm okay but I need to know what is happening."

"The sky started to split," she said shakily, "then, these strange creatures came down…"

Genie continued speaking but her words started to drone out as my hallucinations came to mind. The ashen skies, the fracture, the creatures, the flaxen lightning. If what she was telling me was true, they weren't hallucinations, but I had seen the future.

"Arri?"

I looked at her as we both came to a stop at the door that led back into the servant's corridor, "yes?"

"I can't go with you any further," she told me, "I'm… I'm pregnant."

I gasped, overwhelmed with emotion as she told me and she teared up again, smiling softly. I pulled her into a tight hug, "I'm happy for you, Genie."

"Yes, well, it will be no good if we're all dead," she answered with a sad smile, "I… I've been trying to protect you all my life, Arri, but I have something new I need to protect. I had to find you because I know you're the only one who can save us."

"How do you know?" I frowned, the corridor abruptly shaking as something hit the Earth above us.

"Because you're Arraetta," she laughed softly, "and, Sheika said you are the one who will fulfil the prophecy, that you were the one who would save us all. And, the boys have been unsuccessful so far quashing this, so this must be your moment."

I looked at her and then nodded, the nods becoming more certain, and rapid, as I thought about it all. If Sheika was saying that I was the one to save us, then it must be true. I only wished I knew what I needed to do. I had to find her urgently.

"Did she say what the prophecy states?" I asked her.

Genie shook her head, "no."

"I have to go and find Sheika," I said to her, hugging her tightly, "I love you, Genie."

"Please don't die, Arri," she answered and I smiled sadly.

"I can't promise that."

She paused before nodding. "I know."

"You should go to the crown room," I told her, "it's safe there."

"I love you, Arri," she teared and we both engulfed each other in one final long hug before gently we moved away from each other, parting ways.

I took a deep breath, readied my shoulders, and put on a brave face rushing onwards, ready to face what was to come. Every step I took was careful; careful to not make too much sound and to protect myself. At the top of the staircase, I could see the devastation, immediately, as pictures that adorned the walls were broken, glass lounging lazily on the floor, whilst splatters of blood and debris were everywhere.

I could hear the shouts of voices and see flashes of light as the powers of Rapidfire were desperately fired, reflecting down into the hallway. As I moved to the front entrance, I braced for a huge pile of bodies but, instead, only saw a scattering of corpses and, centred, the dead king.

He looked even more spine chilling, as the bones of his corpse were vivid in the light, whilst his skin continuously sizzled off him, dripping like drops of water onto the floor. Even though I had a lot of hatred for the man, I couldn't imagine the pain he would've been in as it slowly killed him. The chandelier had fallen on top of him, as the ceiling of the house had collapsed in, causing piercings of glass to glitter against his melting skin.

And, above him, the ceiling of the house had caved, open to the elements of the ashen sky above. The only thing that seemed to remain was the corner of the mural that showed the Rapidfire being used by two people; the blue was Seraiah's, but I wasn't sure who the green one belonged to.

The portrait of the three royals was hanging by a thread; The King's face burnt as though the universe was trying to make it more obvious that he was dead. Like the crown, the dream, and his unfortunate demise.

I heard an Earth-shattering roar and flinched as a winged creature flew over the top of the house; blue and green Rapidfire firing in its direction. I remembered how I'd tried to confront a similar creature with my ma before she was killed.

I could hear voices yelling outside and knew one to be Seraiah's. He was giving orders, of some sorts, and others were shouting too. I heard loud gunfire and hid against the wall next to the entrance door, which was hanging heavily off one hinge.

I came to understand the counting of numbers when they were ready to fire again. The beast, seemingly having flown in the other direction, mustn't have been the only thing they were fighting. The gunfire must've hit its target because it made a strange squeaking noise, like a hyena laughing in a way.

Gently, I pushed myself forward, moving to the front door and peered out, seeing fifty or so soldiers scattered across the front of the house, most of them using decimated cars, walls, and hedges as shields. In the sky, the other creatures, small with wings and a long dragon-like tail, flew around, whilst large rat-like ones were feasting on dead bodies.

The front gates to the house were wide open and the area was lit by houses and cars that were up in flames, which meant I was able to see as far as my eyes could, at the devastation of the estate. It was like a post-apocalyptic world. High up in the sky, I could see the fissure settled not too far away from the other end of the estate.

"Arraetta?" I jumped and looked across at Seraiah, to the right side of the garden, as he bolted towards me. I hadn't realised I'd stepped fully out, into the spectacle of the front of the house, but it had blown my indiscreet cover.

Jonah's voice came from the left, but I didn't have enough time to see him as Seraiah made it to and pushed me into the house, around the door and against the wall. I was going to say something, but his hand went over my mouth, pushing himself against me as the winged demon roared, over the top of the house, doing its best to find its prey.

"Blind, not deaf," Seraiah whispered. In other words, I had to be silent otherwise that creature would kill me. That's why ma died because I couldn't be quiet at my young age. He removed his hand, from my mouth, continuing the hushed conversation, "what the hell are you doing here? You are... you are bleeding, why are you bleeding?"

"Hit my head," I answered quietly, moving to look over at his father's corpse before looking back at Seraiah, whose eyes were oddly sorrowful.

"He sacrificed himself for me," Seraiah said, looking over his shoulder at the dead man before he looked back, "he jumped in front of the spear as it came towards me. After all the years of hate, it all culminated in him being killed by the thing that he feared the most."

During the time I was knocked out, it made it seem that Seraiah had killed him, but I guessed my mind was playing tricks on me again. Seeing Seraiah in that moment, I knew that, no matter how much pain his father had caused him, he loved his father, and his father loved him. The King sacrificing himself for him showed that.

"I'm sorry, Seraiah," I said to him.

Seraiah stroked my cheek and leaned his head to my forehead, "you are the only thing worth living for, Arraetta, I would never have changed anything that has occurred, between my father and I, because it led to us."

"There won't be much of us left at this rate," I whispered, "I need to fight."

"No," he answered, looking away from me, "no, you… you need to go back there."

"No," I replied, moving my hand to his chin, to bring his head to look at me, "you know I can help you."

"I need you safe."

"I am safe," I said and softly kissed him, breaking apart as gunfire shattered outside the house before a voice yelled, something like 'clear'.

"I am king now," Seraiah said as he brought his hand up to stroke my cheek, stopping himself abruptly, "I am king and…"

"Don't tell me I do as you command," I whispered, searching his eyes, "you cannot change what needs to be done."

"I promised to protect you, always."

"And, you will," I told him, "I-"

He cut me off by kissing me and, at first, I thought that he was just after a bit of tenderness, but the creature roared overhead again, which meant he was trying to silence me. I leant into it though, needing to feel his lips against mine because, I very well knew, it could be the last time.

We broke the kiss, breathless and he looked at me, "Arraetta, I need to know if you can use your power."

"A little," I replied honestly, although it wasn't the right time to go into the finer details of my encounter with another version of myself.

"There is not much power here," he said to me, "the electrics have tripped, the shield is down and the generator was destroyed but I have enough power to share with you."

"What? No, that's absurd," I replied.

He shook his head, "when my father died, I took his power. It strengthens me but it is of no use if I do not have Divine Rapidfire. I give you my strength, Arraetta, I give you this power to use to protect yourself."

His body vibrated alive, with his midnight blue power, as he pushed it from his body into my own; just like he had done the first time he'd shown me by the lake.

"Hone into it, allow my power to become one with yours," he said, connecting eyes with me, "feed from me."

I did so, taking hold of it mentally, as though it was a cord of energy, and allowing my own power to utilise its strength. My body powered up; my veins beaming alive as they glowed in the darkened room, we stood within. Seraiah removed his hand and the invisible cord, though fragile, remained between us as our powers radiated off one another.

He smiled proudly, admiring me, "beautiful."

I laughed gently, "now, isn't the time for compliments."

"If only we were alone right now..." he tried to make the joke but it fell a little flat as the sadness settled instead. This wasn't a goodbye, we didn't even know what was going to happen, but I knew that, somehow, from my dreams, the fissure had to close. "I-"

Seraiah cut himself short, as a loud thud sounded above us, and we both looked up as the winged creature decided to perch itself on the side of the roof, searching with its nose and ears for us. Seeing it so close made me tremble a little, it had black and silver scales across its long body and pointed wings that made it look fearsome. If we were inside a realm of pure darkness, the only thing that would be able to be seen was its piercing yellow eyes that had an odd glow in them.

The creature threw its head back and roared with all its might, declaring its presence, and it was enough to make me gasp as the sound rippled through my body. And, like The Fates cutting the cord of life, my power turned off instantly, whilst Seraiah's remained.

The sound of my gasp was enough for it to find us, and its eyes landed in our direction.

"Fuck," Seraiah murmured. He instantly threw his Rapidfire in its direction; the lightning sparking from his hands before it hit the creature in its head. It only caused the creature to anger as it reared its head, sucking in air as its mouth came to life with strange black matter.

"Seraiah," I whispered but he ignored me, only doing what he thought would be best, at that moment. Mimicking what had happened the night my ma had died, Seraiah grabbed my hand and threw me around the side of the door until I was, on my arse, on the gravel outside. The door shut with a slam.

I was too fearful for Seraiah dying to notice the grazes on my hands, that occurred from my landing, but I knew they were there as it stung a little. Instantly, I stood and pushed myself towards the door to go and help him, but an arm trapped me from behind and pulled me away.

"No, no, let me go!" I shouted, soon muted as a hand was thrown over my mouth too. I heard a yelp of pain, from inside the house, and a shudder trickled down my spine as I knew it to be Seraiah's. Then, the door fell off its hinges, revealing the decimated insides of the grand hallway, with no sign of him.

Tears were already falling, from the heartache I felt, and they didn't stop as my assailant placed me behind one of the front garden bushes before he knelt in front of me. It was Alex.

"Ma'am," Alex said, trying to get my attention, "ma'am, please listen to me."

"Seraiah," I cried, burying my face in my knees. If I hadn't made such a timely appearance, Seraiah would still be alive.

But he was dead.

I felt a pair of hands on my face, and I was coaxed to look up from my crying position into the eyes of Jonah, with Alex having moved next to him. "Do not give up hope, Seraiah is much stronger than you think."

I nodded slowly, trying to calm myself as the battle around us continued. He was right, Seraiah could be alive.

"I do not know how you escaped," Jonah said seriously, taking a gun out of his back pocket, "but, you will need to protect yourself now."

He handed me the gun and I stared at the metal object in my hand, wondering about how I was supposed to use something like that against such a beast.

All of us winced as three fighter jets flew overhead and watched as they headed towards the fissure. Each of them fired a bomb that went towards it, but, as though there was a barrier that was protecting it, the bombs ricocheted and exploded, immediately, without causing any damage.

"Human weapons will not work," Alex said, tutting as though it was just child's play.

"But, hopefully it deflects them from coming here," Jonah replied, taking hold of Alex's hand softly, "that is the last thing we need."

"Is there more than one of the winged creatures?" I asked Jonah.

"There are several," he informed me, "this is going to be a global catastrophe, if we do nothing about it, but we are exhausted; we lack adequate weapons and we have no portal out of here."

"Jonah, we cannot escape this one," Alex pointed out, "you are not your father, you do not outrun problems, you fight them head on."

"I know," Jonah whispered, looking at his lover, "I just do not want to lose you."

"We will all be dead, if we do not make a plan," Alex answered, softly kissing Jonah to calm him.

"You may be better at my job," Jonah joked softly, stroking Alex's cheek. The moment was needed, and I was glad to see them interact in such a way together, only wishing I'd done so more over the last few months of knowing them. Jonah's eyes landed on me, "We need to create a strategy."

I looked between them and nodded, gripping the gun as I sat into a better position, "I have one, don't ask me how I know this, but I need to get to Sheika's."

"Okay, and your plan from there?" Jonah asked, "I can get you there, I can get you anywhere, but I need to know the end goal."

"The end goal is to close the fissure," I told him, "I think I know how but I need confirmation from her first; she said there's a prophecy."

"Shaman's and prophecies," Alex chuckled, with a childish eye roll.

"Okay, I have a plan," Jonah said, calculating in his head before he spoke to Alex, who moved away from us to speak with another soldier. Like Chinese whispers, the message found its way from our end through to the other, where I saw Freddie pop his head over the bush. He looked at Jonah at first, then to me, before he nodded.

"Freddie will stay here with half the troops," Jonah said, "the rest will follow us. I will lead, we will protect you and we will get you to where you need to go. The most important thing is silence. If that creature flies, we drop and we are silent. That gun will kill the smaller creatures, there are more further down. You must always keep alert."

"I understand," I said to him.

"You are also in barely anything more than your pyjamas," he commented, "that is not enough to protect you."

Jonah began to take off his bulletproof vest, but I put my hand on him, "no, you need that. I'll stay behind you."

He stopped and then nodded, "repeat what I said about the silence."

"We stop and drop, when the creature flies," I replied and he nodded, satisfied.

"With me," he whispered and stood, pulling us through to the gates, past the line of men that were ready to come with us. He stopped and turned to me, "these are your signals. You always watch out for them from me, you listen at all times."

"I get the gist," I almost rolled my eyes but then he began to show me the signals.

"You," he pointed, "me." He demonstrated each one. "Follow. Freeze. Enemy. I understand."

When he did, *I understand,* I copied the signal in the 'okay' sign and he nodded. Jonah was good at his job; I wonder whether he'd trained in an army from how good he was.

Silently, he waved the follow sign and we all started walking down. The parade of us looked ridiculous but it was soon broken up as Jonah sent an unknown signal and the soldiers dispersed around us, finding spots that kept eyes on us and the skies. The only people who remained in our moving group were Alex, another three guards, Jonah, and me.

"Is this a bad time to say I've never shot a gun?" I whispered as quietly as possible, looking at the small machine in my hand.

The winged creature roared from within the building, and I turned sharply, all of us seeing as it rose towards the sky. I worried that it was me who had caused it to come out of its hiding spot, but it seemed to fly in the opposite direction.

"Go," Jonah whispered, pulling me to continue walking.

I saw the creatures ahead of us on the ground, enjoying their feast of decimated corpses. One of the guards shot at the first one and it, immediately, disintegrated. I could imagine if it was a standard target, on a day of practice, they might've cheered, but the gun shot echoed in the silence and the only other sound was the faint shuffling of feet. Then, another gunshot. Then, silence.

A constant rhythm.

I turned my thoughts to what was about to come. We were moving closer to the fissure, and I had to figure out how we could close it. There had to be some way for me to use the Divine Rapidfire - to destroy it from its interior. My main issue was that I wasn't trained in using my power and I was wary that the borrowed power, from Seraiah, alongside what I learnt from my future self, wouldn't be a force powerful enough.

I stared up at the fissure, watching it as, every now and again, creatures would be released.

The roar returned and everyone knew immediately to duck and remain silent. I heard a spine-chilling scream down the road and my eyes zoned in on a man, who was moving back on his hands. I prayed for his silence, but his fear was too powerful. The winged demon flew over us and down to the man, landing heavily and I watched as the creature bellowed over the top, sucking some sort of life force out of him before it craned its neck and released into the ether. The body dropped.

"What is it doing?" I found myself asking quietly.

"The more life force it consumes, the more powerful it will become," Jonah replied just as hushed and then nodded up to where the figures hung in the sky, "this is something we never understood."

"It looks like it's trying to create a place from a nightmare," I commented. I knew that because I had been in those nightmares.

"Mysc," he answered. Mysc - the realm of nightmares. The place Seraiah had told me about whilst we were sitting in the library. Jonah stood, motioning us all to continue as the beast left the ground again. "It could make sense that it is trying to recreate its home realm, which is what it did with Zika."

"That creature was in Zika?"

"And, most likely there is a whole family of them swarming now," he commented with a nod and I grimaced at the thought of it.

Gunshot. Silence. Gunshot. Silence.

My eyes cast back up to the fissure, watching as creatures dropped one after the other. Then, the realisation hit me.

"Stop your firing!" I shouted and then bit my lip, worried I'd stirred the creature back again. Jonah raised his eyebrows at me. Then I whispered, "every time you kill one, another drops down."

Jonah looked at the fissure, then towards a creature feasting on the dead man, that had his soul sucked away. "Shoot that."

One of the men fired and Jonah watched the fissure. Surely enough, it dropped from the sky, being caught by one of the miniature winged creatures, that seemed to fly it down to the Earth before floating back up.

"Fuck," Jonah cursed, "we are wasting bullets."

Jonah immediately turned his exchange to Zikan, speaking to the soldiers who seemed to agree something with him before he beckoned us to continue. He quietly spoke, "Alex is in charge of shooting the creatures, that way we're wasting less ammo. Whether they keep sending them down or not, it is our job to get you to where you need to go."

I understood and didn't question it. We stepped past the partially-eaten man and I tried not to feel nauseous looking at his dead corpse, instead I just felt remorse for him. The same for everyone else who lay dead down the road, some who were just bone, which meant that the creature could eat the corpses rapidly.

The atmosphere was heavy, and I could hear some emotion from some of the guards, even though they tried to remain as professional as they could. These people were family and friends to them, some of them I'd met at my wedding. Tears caught in my throat as I came to a stop, looking down at the body of a little child, toy in hand but only the skeletal remains were there.

"Come on," Jonah coaxed softly, pulling me onwards. I could hear what he wanted to say next, it was only going to get worse. And it did. I wondered how many people were safe, inside their homes, hiding in basements like I had, like Genie was.

Soon, we arrived at the path that led up to Sheika's home but, as we ascended, the air felt colder, and I knew something bad had happened. Jonah put his arm out in front of me as we arrived, moving to go ahead of me to the ajar door. It was then that I caught onto the gentle hums and sobbing that came from inside the house.

"Zela," Jonah whispered to himself, as we entered the house, and we moved through to the living room, where Sheika lay dead in front of lit candles. Next to her, the woman I'd seen several times with Sheika, her protege, was making the varied noises.

"Zela?" Jonah repeated, stepping a little forward but he stopped as she stood and turned abruptly like something had possessed her. Zela's green eyes pierced into mine and I took a step forward towards her.

"Arraetta," she began in a monotone voice, "Princess of The Cre-este, Goddess of Divine Rapidfire, it is time for you to fulfil the prophecy. The Gods have spoken. Only your power can destroy that which has shrouded this world in darkness, only you shall rise and rise you shall and only you shall walk the path of insurgence alone."

I swallowed, "what do I need to do?"

"Call to the dark for only then can you truly use the divine power of the light," Zela finished, and then stumbled a little, no longer possessed by the teller, before she began to cry once more. Turning around to fall to her knees, robotically. Repeatedly, she murmured the name of her master.

I knew I wouldn't get any more out of her, so I walked out of the house, taking a deep breath. Jonah followed, the other men waiting on high alert. From Sheika's house, I could see the town below and took it in - the decimation of such a beautiful place, a place that had become my home. A place I had met Seraiah, fallen in love and married him, a place I'd become a princess and a queen.

TWENTY-SEVEN

The beast roared again, flying over the town in search of more prey. Everyone ducked, everyone but me as I watched it. It disappeared behind a house, and I tilted my head up to see the figure appear in the sky. The beast flew up again and fled once more. Perhaps its breaks were to savour energy, or perhaps it was feeding something at the back of the palace.

I played Zela's words in my head repeatedly, looking up at the fissure for a while.

Call to the dark for only then can you truly use the true power of the light.

Call to the dark for only then can you truly use the true power of the light.

Call to the dark for only then can you truly use the true power of the light.

I had to face the dark to save them. The only way I could get myself anywhere near close enough to the fissure was to…

"Jonah," I said to him, still gazing upwards.

All the men rose as he did, waiting for more orders.

"No," he said, shaking his head, "Seraiah will never forgive me."

Alex stepped forward, placing a gentle hand on Jonah's arm to tell him that I was right, that the only way to win would be to sacrifice myself. Jonah looked at Alex, then back at me before he nodded, "and, how do you know the plan is going to work?"

"I don't," I breathed, "but, the Gods be damned if I die, any other way, because the prophecy has to be fulfilled some way."

Jonah nodded, then instructed his men before we went back down towards the road. I felt my heart thump in my chest, I was walking towards my own demise - I was sacrificing myself to save the greater good. Yet, I didn't think I was supposed to die. I thought that I'd spend forever with Seraiah so that's what pushed me on. When I became an ornament in the sky, I had to push through any pain, any suffering, any longing and bring out my power as much as I could.

"Your best to do this at the crossroads that leads down to the town's gate," Jonah told me quietly as we continued our rhythmic shuffle. I could see why - it was the most open space since the trees, that once lined the road, were fallen or on fire.

"Promise me that you'll make sure that Seraiah, Freddie and Genie are okay," I said to him and he looked at me with a soft smile. We didn't say anymore as we closed in on the crossroads, Alex would fire his pistol, every now and again, not helping the fear of the situation. And, to make matters worse, those outside of the Zikan estate were still attempting to bomb the fissure.

I had to be brave. I had to be ready for the sacrifice.

I was a Goddess.

"We shall leave you here," Jonah said, when we were not so far from the crossroads. He had to protect his men and let me walk on alone.

I turned to him, "thank you, Jonah."

Jonah called his men to halt as I continued onwards. The walk to my demise wasn't long enough and I didn't have much time to collect my thoughts, when I got there, as the roar of the beast belted from behind the palace again.

Taking a deep breath, I slowly turned in its direction, straightening up. At first, my eyes landed where Jonah and the guards were, guns at the ready in their crouched positions. Then, my eyes swept upwards, to the palace, as the creature flew over. Without noise it wouldn't know where to find me.

Slowly, I lifted the gun up and pointed it towards the sky. At the prime moment, I opened my mouth and shouted, "come and get me you bastard!"

The gun fired in the echo of the gentle laughter, from the guards, and the creature roared, coming towards me, without a moment's hesitation. I fired the gun again, so that it wouldn't get distracted by much else.

Suddenly, the fear disappeared, and I threw the gun, arms wide open as I embraced my fate, not closing my eyes as I stared straight into the yellow eyes that closed in.

But before the sacrifice could be made, a dark blue spear of lightning jolted upwards from the house and rocketed against the creature's body. In the distance, I saw Seraiah was standing in the gateway, both of us looking as though we had blocked the enemy in. Distracted, the creature reared and flew back to the house.

I had no time to be grateful that my lover was alive because I knew I had to go ahead with my sacrifice no matter what.

"No!" I shouted. "Shoot it!"

Jonah and all the guards immediately fired their guns. It was a clamour of sounds that shattered the quiet air but was enough to bring the dragon back towards us.

Seraiah was relentless with his power, doing everything to stop it from coming in my direction, and he moved closer as he did, looking like a little piece on a chessboard. He was doing everything to prevent me from making the sacrifice, that I needed to make, but it would just end in more bloodshed if I didn't.

I turned in the direction of the gun I'd tossed and went for it, picking it up once more, but the noise from my own pistol wasn't going to be any louder than the ones the men were firing. From the top of the hill, the guards were also shooting, providing some sort of protection for Seraiah as he made his way down the road.

I saw green Rapidfire sprout from the palace, and I could see that Freddie was doing his best to attempt a distraction. The creature, confused and disgruntled, flew higher up into the sky, until it was unreachable, and disappeared back to behind the palace.

"Fuck!" I shouted as the silence settled again. Seraiah, bruised and bloodied, stormed down with anger on his face - more than I had ever seen. His eyes were pure black, telling me that the darkness had overtaken him.

He looked at Jonah, "what the fuck were you thinking?"

I stormed forward to meet them, "Seraiah, why did you stop me?"

"You think that sacrificing yourself is the fucking answer?" he shouted as he arrived at me. He was so angry I thought he may slap me, but, instead, he wrapped his arms around me, his heart racing heavily in his chest. It was a surprise considering the state he was in. He murmured, "I cannot lose you, Arraetta."

"You don't know what I was doing," I told him as we came to be at arm's length of each other.

"You were going to let it devour you," he said to me, "but, you cannot do that. You will not survive, no one survives that. Your soul will shatter. That is what it will do to you." He turned to Jonah. "So, your plan was to let her sacrifice herself?"

"I did as Zela told me," I replied.

"And, what did she say?" he asked, "repeat the words and, maybe, we could actually work together to figure out what exactly they mean."

"She said, *Call to the dark for only then can you truly use the true power of the light.*"

Seraiah blinked, listening to the words as he repeated them, in his head, and then he stood back. Before he could speak, I said, "she also said something like… the Gods have spoken. Only my power can destroy the dark, only I can rise, which I shall and walk the path of insurgence alone."

Seraiah looked up at the fissure above and I turned to do the same, looking into the void that seemed to hold nothing inside it.

"Okay, well, your deepest fear is not dying," Seraiah said to me, "it is facing the dark. Not The Dark, not the creatures, but the nightmare itself. The fear of being alone in the dark. Home in on that."

I bit my lip and looked at him, nodding. He was right, being in complete, silent darkness was terrifying. It was terrifying to think of being alone inside it, without anyone else with me.

Seraiah backed off then, stepping back one after the other before he said, "feel the power of that. Be the Queen of Darkness, overcome it."

Feel the power of the darkness. I stepped back and closed my eyes, beginning to think about all the scenarios where I'd ended up alone in the darkness, the house in my hallucination, every time my eyes were closed to avoid the void-filled eyes of my doppelganger. I was always running away from it, never facing the fear of it. I felt a pull against the motions of the void above, watching it my mind as it pulsated back and forth, opening and closing.

I felt a buzzing in my arms and a rocketing of gasps from the guards, but I didn't let myself stop picturing the fissure in the sky. Eventually, the fear dissipated, and I felt at one with it, the controller of it.

This was true power.

I was breathing gently, allowing my body to relax. I opened my eyes and saw how the sharp hue of my body bounced against glass, that was scattered across the ground, and in the irises of those who stood to watch. My eyes landed on Seraiah who, though shocked, grew a semi-smug smile on his face. Smug because he was proud.

A crackle above and my head darted up to look as flaxen lightning pierced through the dark clouds, surrounding the crack. As though it was some sort of creature itself, it began to wail a cry of pain and I could feel as if it was trying to force me out of its control.

But I remained in it.

I was Arraetta, Goddess of Divine Rapidfire.

The winged creature flew up again, ready to fight a battle that it wasn't aware it was going to face. A battle to save its new home from those who already owned it.

"Control it, Arraetta," Seraiah said and I watched as his own power lit up across his body, "let us end this… together."

I nodded as it came towards us. Seraiah gave an order to Jonah and Jonah echoed something similar to all the men, before they began to disperse around the houses, ready to fire at will.

"Let's end this fucker," I said sharply and Seraiah chuckled as I came to stand next to him.

"Now, now, Arraetta," he commented darkly, his eyes strangely looking beautiful when he honed into his power, "if you come to talk like that, I will have no excuse but to lock you in the bedroom."

All the fear that I'd had was no longer there, instead his new aura made me feel stronger and proud to be one with him.

The creature flew down at us, roaring, and I could tell that it could finally see us. I don't think it was necessarily smell and sound, it was the atmosphere that we gave off. It darted in our direction but both of us prepared ourselves.

"You can have the honours," he chuckled.

I smiled and let the power leave my body, firing a piercing bolt, from my hands, which shattered the creature's body in half, flying over us until it crashed onto the hard ground. I could hear a small cheer that the creature had been defeated, all of us looking at the beast as its skin instantly melted from its bones; I couldn't believe how easy it was.

Unfortunately, however, the fissure was still open and, as I looked up, I felt my power, instantly, evaporate as the void pushed me out of it. I grunted and fell to my knees, knocking Seraiah's confidence as he knelt with me.

"It's not over," I said to him. We both looked up as a spine-tingling roar echoed and another creature crawled out. If we were worried about the winged creature before, it was nothing in comparison to this one. It was bigger than anything I had seen, almost the same size as the palace as it landed perfectly on its wings and scouted the land for its prey. For us.

"Fuck," Seraiah said, stepping back, "shit."

"How many people with Rapidfire does it take to kill a fucking dragon?" Freddie's voice commented, from behind, and I turned to see blood and cuts all over him. He was worse than Seraiah but was holding himself up fine.

"I've read enough fairy tales to know that's not a dragon," I commented, looking back up as it flew around in circles. This creature was no dragon. It may have wings and a tail similar, but it also had three heads that, somewhat, resembled the mythical Hydra, whilst its body pulsated, with a strange flaxen light that throbbed on and off as it breathed.

"How do we kill it?" Freddie asked, looking up at it.

"We can always go back to my first plan," I commented.

"No," Seraiah, Freddie and Jonah stated, immediately, and I held my hands up.

"Well, we're currently standing here waiting for it to eat us," I shrugged, "and, that fissure needs closing."

It was strange, all of us standing around like a bunch of housewives, waiting for the kids to come home, looking up between the creature that had yet to come down, and take us for its meal, and the black void.

"I have a plan," Seraiah said with finality, "I trust you not to let my wife attempt to commit suicide this time, Jonah." Jonah nodded awkwardly. "Arraetta, you need to find a spot, out of sight, where you can hone your power back into the fissure, be one with it, whatever you did before. Freddie and I will distract the dragon... creature. Once it is closed, it will be easier for us to rip it apart, without worrying about another coming through."

"Do not forget me," we jumped and looked as Tara stood there, in full war-like garments as though she was the commanding officer. If she felt any pain from The King's death, it wasn't obvious beneath the shroud of anger.

"Mother," Seraiah sagged his shoulders and I could see that a weight had just left him. If he could, I guessed he would cry and hold her, but he kept strong as he swallowed and nodded his head at her, "then, you should be with us. Three lots of Rapidfire against this thing should distract it enough. Jonah, I need two men, per each of us, who can help protect in case. I entrust you to protect Arraetta."

I had no say in the plan, but it was a good one. I couldn't deny it.

"Arri, tell me Genie is okay," Freddie suddenly said and I looked at his worried face.

"She got me out of that room," I informed him, "and she said she had to stay... for the baby."

Freddie slowly smiled and nodded, "good, she is safe."

"Baby?" Tara gasped, the only other that didn't seem to know about Genie's pregnancy. Each of us shared a smile; Genie and Freddie's baby was a hope, in a desolate and dark time. And it's what we all needed.

The beast roared and there wasn't any more time for talking about it. Each of us split off, with Seraiah and I not having much more, of a moment, than a quick hug and a kiss before we shuffled away. Neither of us made promises to each other to survive because we didn't know if any of us would. There was just hope.

Jonah and I, alongside Alex and two other men, wandered up the road until Jonah coaxed us into the backyard of a house. "Is this yours?"

"Yes," he informed me, glad that it was still intact. Jonah opened the backdoor and we walked into the living room, getting a strange whiff of both the smell of Jonah and Alex. I suppose I wasn't surprised that they lived there together, nor was I surprised to see all the photos on the shelves.

They both looked like a happy couple, and I even saw some images of Seraiah and Freddie with them. Happier times had been, memories that would forever be treasured. Tears tickled my eyes as I picked up one of them.

They were in Zika, which made me a little surprised that they had cameras, but, then again, it wouldn't be a surprise if such inventions had been created elsewhere. The image was of Seraiah, Freddie, Jonah, Alex, and a couple of other guys, in some sort of sportswear, with mud decorating their smiling faces.

"War cry," Alex said, coming to stand next to me, "it was an old game we used to play, splitting into two teams and we would go head to head in a field of mud, trying to outsmart each other." He chuckled. "This was our team. The two guys, next to us, were our friends Andrieu and Marash, they died in the attack."

"Good men too," Jonah added, coming to join us, "although Andrieu would be doing his best to get into your knickers."

I laughed, placing the frame down and turned to the two men, "and, not your pants?"

"That would be Marash," Alex smiled, before he, sadly, turned his head. Jonah placed his arm around Alex and pulled him in for a hug, murmuring to him in Zikan, which made Alex laugh.

At that moment, I didn't care that I didn't understand because I knew that it was intimate and loving.

"Well, we were right on one thing," Jonah said to me, "you bested The Prince. Or, The King should we say."

I grinned but my smile was cut short when I heard the wail of the beast near to us.

"We need to go," I said, "I think I need to be outside just in case, you know, I blow up your home or something."

Both men chuckled and nodded, and we moved outside, where the other two men remained on high alert. Jonah and Alex found places nearby, in the picket-fenced garden, where they could protect me.

I closed my eyes and pulled myself into the fissure, allowing the darkness to creep in and the numbness to overtake my senses. The dark wasn't my foe, it was not even my friend, I was its master, and it would fear me. It would fear my power and obey me.

Once again, I was stuck in as I took grasp of it, another wail overtaking, but I allowed the noise of it to bring me peace. I wasn't sure what was happening with Seraiah, Freddie, and Tara but I knew that they, no matter what, would play their part. We were like an orchestra, one wrong note and everything would fall apart.

I heard the roar of the *dragon,* as Seraiah and Freddie had so named it, noting that it was close. It roared again, this time in pain and its direction had turned. It was doing its best to come towards me, where it could destroy the thing that sought to destroy it, but I understood that, every time it attempted, it reared back towards the attackers - back towards Seraiah and Freddie and Tara. Alongside that, there was also gunfire which helped me understand where the creature was.

I continued to feel for the weaknesses of the fissure, imagining that it was beginning to seal slowly as I pushed my Rapidfire through it.

"It is working," Jonah's voice noted and, slowly, I opened my eyes, still seeing the fissure in the corners of my eyes, pulsating constantly as part of my vision. My head tilted up, in its direction, until I could see the pulse of it and watched as it resealed.

The dragon roared again; it was too close. The men near me started firing and I saw Jonah, in my peripheral, run out. Alex yelled to him, which caused my head to turn as Jonah bolted in front of me, firing his gun. The dragon had been aiming for me but the claws of it grabbed at Jonah's body and wiped him from the garden.

Alex called for his lover, but it was too late as we watched Jonah's body crunch, in the claws of the creature, dropping him from quite a height near to the corpse of the original dragon below.

The fissure burst open again as I let go of control, body shaking. The men were still shooting whilst I stood there, my friend dead in my place. I started to cry, and I could hear the dragon flying back towards the house, hearing several more deaths occur.

In that moment, the memories of Jonah flooded in, and I couldn't help but feel the pain of loss for the man, who had done everything to help and protect me. How I'd been so blind at the start to think he was an arsehole, to learning about his relationship, to him convincing me to go back to Seraiah and so much more. He was one of Seraiah's closest friends, Alex's lifelong lover and one of my protectors.

I looked at Alex who was on his knees, defeated, staring in the direction that Jonah's body had fallen in and he cried for him. I swallowed my own tears, and I knew, at that moment, that I couldn't let his sacrifice be in vain.

I picked up Jonah's assault rifle and started to walk away, out of the garden, at a sorrowful pace, wiping my eyes as much as I could as the tears fell. I wandered back towards the crossroads, the image of the men in the photo, burning in my mind, and I thought about how their happiness was wasted. I played the scenario of Seraiah coming to save me at the right time but now Jonah was dead - and, no doubt, many others.

I looked up at the fissure. The only way to destroy it was to go up.

My original plan was the only one left. I looked up towards the palace where the green, blue, and red Rapidfire would sprout, at separate times, as they attempted to subdue the creature. I could see their power weakening. The battle was becoming exhausting.

"I love you, Seraiah," I whispered. I held the abnormally large gun up again, with both hands, and fired it. The creature reared its head but, as Seraiah's blue Rapidfire rose again, I countered it with more gun shots until I had the creature's full attention.

I aimed the gun at it, fired once more, hitting it as it continued closer.

Below it, up the road, I saw Seraiah come out from his spot and he started to run in my direction. He was going to attempt to stop me but there would be no time. I watched as Freddie came out too, both at a distance running towards me. Firing their Rapidfire as much as they could but missing as the dragon sped in my direction.

"Come and get me!" I shouted at it and threw the gun, letting myself be swept up in the dragon's claws, loudly roaring with anger and sorrow. The grip was tight, I could feel one of its nails pierce the skin on my back, not tight enough to shatter bones, and the pain overwhelmed me, instantly. It was useless to fight against the beast but, even in anguish, I had to destroy it.

It wasn't until then that, I realised that, it wasn't the creature's desire to kill me but, instead, take me away for whatever reason it had. Heading back upwards into the fissure.

"Arraetta!" I heard Seraiah's voice pierce through the air, but I couldn't see him as we disappeared up into the sky; my head looking up at the creature's pulsating stomach.

"Rapidfire," I murmured. Then, I closed my eyes, allowing myself to feel the Rapidfire, within the dragon, breathing as gently as I could against the pain that was growing in my back. My body lit up and the dragon wailed, the grip loosening, but not enough for me to fall, and we made it through the clouds of the fissure.

"This ends now!" I screamed, letting my power flow, from my body, and shatter the surrounding darkness. The dragon roared in pain as it too exploded with the power of the light, from the Rapidfire, finally dropping me. I saw the fissure closing as I fell towards my death, the town miles below me still in view, but too far away for me to make it through before the darkness enclosed around me.

I felt the pain in my back throb, and I grimaced, fighting the pull to death as I fell in endless darkness, my body flashing on and off, like a flash light, as it fought to keep me alive.

Then, there was nothing.

Until there was life. I gasped loudly as I shot up. For a moment, I couldn't tell where I was, until I realised, I was in the bedroom I'd spent many years in, at the block of flats. My heart raced wildly as I looked around, taking in the space. It was all the same, as though everything that had occurred had been a dream.

I got off my bed, shakily, and tiptoed to the window, opening the curtains to peer up at a normal sunny sky, the sounds of the world outside humming gently.

I turned and walked to my door and peered down the hallway, "hello?"

I heard a racket from Genie's room, and I braced myself in fear of what was about to run out, but it was just Genie, popping her messy bedhead out and looking around, "did you hear something?"

"Genie, I..." I whispered, tearing up, instantly, as I went to engulf my best friend in a hug, unsure how to comprehend the situation.

"Are you okay?" she laughed as I held her at arm's length.

"Where's Freddie?" I swallowed, looking around, "and, and Seraiah, are they all alive?"

"Seraiah?" she frowned, "did I tell you about him? Now, you two are bound to be in bed together tonight!"

I stuttered, taking a few steps back as I rushed to look around, walking into the living room. Genie followed me; I presumed looking quite concerned.

"What's going on?" she asked, "did you have an episode?"

"I… what day is it?"

"Saturday," she said, as she lingered at the door, "I hope you're not trying to get out of going, again, because I won't have it. You will go to the ball!"

"To the ball," I whispered.

"Yes, I've booked us in to get our hair and makeup done," she squealed excitedly, "right, I'm going for a shower."

She skipped off and I looked over at her before turning to look into the mirror. There wasn't anyone there, I didn't exist in the reflection, in front of me, as though I was a ghost. I shakily brought my hands to my face, wondering whether I really did exist.

I began to hyperventilate. Where was I? Why was I suddenly back at the start of it all? Where was Seraiah and why did he not exist yet? Had I dreamt it all?

The soft breath of another and I felt a dark, spine-tingling presence behind me. Slowly, I turned around, prepared to face another version of me, again, but, instead, I looked at a strangely familiar man, who lingered in the kitchen. He was tall and thin, with soft white skin, a black beard and a cloak that, almost, resembled the Grim Reaper. But this was not the bringer of death. I swallowed.

"Hello, Arraetta," he chimed darkly, stepping forward some before he waved his arm and the entirety of the room dissolved into a black rock formation, floating in endless ashen clouds, "welcome to Nowhere."

EPILOGUE

Seraiah

Arraetta was gone. I watched as the beast took her and I couldn't do anything about it. My body had grown weak, from the exhaustion of battle, but it didn't stop me overpowering in grief as I roared for her; my Rapidfire rupturing the skies above. Then, it was gone. Like her, like the fissure and the three-headed dragon. All that was left was the complete devastation in its wake - the deaths, the destruction and Arraetta's sacrifice.

Freddie knelt next to me, hand on my shoulder as I desperately looked up at the skies for her, seeking a shooting star of lightning, that may just give us enough hope of her survival, but nothing.

I heard the footsteps of those, who were left, clamouring out of places they'd been hiding - guards, children, men, and women. What was left of us. Over two thirds of our population wiped out, in the space of a few hours. They came forth to surround us, wails of cries and soft sobs could be heard from the crowd, and I swallowed.

Freddie stood up and shouted to them all, "all hail The King."

All hail The King should have been all hail The Queen. It wasn't right that he shouted it, but everyone repeated it, coming to bow down to me, whilst I remained in a knelt position. Freddie patted my shoulder and helped me rise to my feet as I looked around at everyone.

I saw that my mother had also bowed down - she was no longer queen, that position had automatically shifted to Arraetta, and she was gone.

I looked for Jonah, but he was nowhere in sight, confirming that I had seen the creature carry someone off. He must've done his best to try and protect her because she wouldn't have chosen to face the creature without a reason. The reason being that all else was lost.

I knew I had to give my people hope, in that moment, things would change whether Arraetta was there or not. Everyone knew that this was the beginning of a new time. The beginning of the end.

I called to them loudly, "today, we have lost many to a familiar foe that we faced back in Zika. We have only survived because of the sacrifice that was made by my wife, Arraetta, your queen."

"Arraetta isn't dead!" Zela's voice echoed, across the crowd, and everyone looked in her direction as she pushed through towards us. The crowd parted ways for our new shaman and she looked at me, "Your Majesty, Arraetta has but sacrificed herself to save this realm, but she is not dead. The prophecy does not end here, she shall come back to us. You must have hope."

"I do," I said to her, swallowing, "but, I cannot sit around idly waiting, for her to return, if we are to get back to our home. I must find a way to open a portal."

"A portal will open," she called out, "the Gods have spoken, it is now the right time to build one, with the materials we have access to. Use the power that both you and Arraetta share, take us home."

I felt the hope of my people in the air, and I swallowed. I understood a lot about Rapidfire, but I didn't know anything about the Rapidfire in the bond, between Arraetta and myself, because it was too new. Zela knew I could make a portal, so did a lot of those higher up in the Zikan community.

"The bones of the dragon," I said, looking to Ryin, one of the on-site scientists, "we can use that to create the shape, I'll work on the rest."

"Sir," Ryin nodded, speaking to a couple of others, who began to move towards that end of the complex. I looked at Freddie and he nodded. There was a strange understanding between Freddie and I, never needing to say too much because we knew what needed to be done.

"Alex," Freddie said to our long-time friend, who stood with tear-stained cheeks. I felt the loss of Jonah, greatly, and he and Alex had been together for as long as I had known the two of them. "You are now the commanding officer, it is your duty to make this place safe again. Elliot." Elliot, one of our older men who worked as a journalist in the city, stood upright. "I need a report on the damage, further out. I want to know what they are saying and whether any investigations are being brought up to this estate. Mare." Mare looked as professional as she always did. "Find us a new home. For now, let's get the shield back up, I'd like to breathe a little." He spoke to the crowd. "Bury the dead, let us build a memorial for them."

The crowd began to disperse, leaving very few people standing around. Zela, my mother, Freddie, Kadey, Elina, and a couple of others remained.

"Freddie!"

We all turned as Genie came bolting down the road, straight into Freddie's arms. I felt more sadness watching them, but it was a strange reminder of what we still had. Genie stood back, swallowing tears, and looked at me, her natural tongue coming out, "she'll be okay. I know she's going to be fine, and we'll be ready for her when she comes back."

I swallowed, nodding my head slowly. Yes, I knew she was alive - I felt it deep in my soul - but I ached for her. I loved Arraetta, she was the shining light when all else was dark. And, when she was ready, I would be waiting for her return.

Arraetta and Seraiah will return

in

About The Author

This is Charlotte Bedgood's debut novel.

Nicole Pott, who writes under the pseudonym Charlotte Bedgood, is a Bafta long listed filmmaker, who began her passion for writing at the early age of ten years old. She wrote novels on Wattpad for most of her teenage years before taking a ten-year hiatus in writing novels to pursue her career as a director.

She has a huge passion for reading and enjoys a lot of new adult fantasy fiction, whilst balancing her passion for watching Korean and Thai dramas, walking, and listening to music.

9 781399 947060

Printed by BoD™in Norderstedt, Germany